Rachel Cade

CHARLES MERCER

Rachel Cade

G. P. Putnam's Sons   New York

© 1956 by Charles Mercer

TO ALMA

with love

For it is a day of trouble, and of treading down, and of perplexity by the Lord GOD of hosts in the valley of vision, breaking down the walls, and of crying to the mountains.

ISAIAH 22:5

The Ruwenzori is a mountain range rising to 16,798 feet near the equator in Central Africa. Its highest peaks are covered by glaciers and snows, but few people have seen them, for they are wrapped almost constantly in clouds. For centuries the Ruwenzori, which means the Rain Maker in Swahili, has stirred the imaginations of Africans. As long ago as the second century Ptolemy, the Alexandrian, placed the mountains quite accurately on his map of the continent. He called them the Mountains of the Moon, and by that name they are best known to this day.

There is, or there was until recently, a legend that God dwells among the summits of the Mountains of the Moon. For Africans generally believe in the existence of God, a Supreme Being, the creator and dispenser of all things. But they do not worship Him until goaded to it by white peoples, preferring to leave Him alone and not draw His attention to themselves for fear of angering Him.

Once, many years ago, the legend recounts, a few white men came to climb the Mountains of the Moon. But they failed, and in their failure one of the young men of a village near the foot of the mountains lost his life. Disgruntled, the white men went away west across the plain and into the forests and never again were seen in that place.

Then the medicine men cast a strong curse. They told the people it was the most powerful thahu ever cast. This is the thahu: If any white ever tried to climb to the highest peaks from this place in the western shadows of the Mountains of the Moon, his body would be racked by pain and his soul doomed to eternal suffering.

At the time our story begins, no one had climbed to the highest peaks from this place. The name of the place is Dibela. When the American, Rachel Cade, went there, she had not heard the legend.

Part One

I

MUSINGA, who had taken the title of Doctor, told Kulu to stop the car on the last rise.

"Stop here?" asked Kulu without stopping. "Or shall I stop up there?"

Musinga did not answer him. He touched two more notes on his likembe. It was a fine likembe, the finest in the country, for he had fashioned it himself from the ribs of a broken umbrella belonging to Dr. Bickel. Today, jouncing over the rough road from Dibela to Rugeri on the back seat of Dr. Bickel's old Ford, he had stroked some of his finest music from it, music so sweet and haunting that even Kulu had listened and nodded approvingly. Now, pressing the small instrument against his cheek, he touched the high note again and again, thrumming it ever higher until his spirit soared ecstatically into the pale blue sky.

Kulu jammed the brake and Musinga was flung forward.

"Fool," Musinga said as he climbed from the car. "Careless, stupid fool. I've worked so hard to teach you to drive and you cannot learn."

Kulu said nothing. He never had discussed what everyone, with the possible exception of Musinga, recognized as true. Musinga was a bad driver. Yet, because Dr. Bickel had thought he'd taught Musinga to drive, Musinga thought of himself as a good driver. The fact that he always rode and never drove these days merely served to convince him of his driving prowess. As now. When Dr. Bickel had told Musinga to go to Rugeri and fetch the white Madami, Musinga had told Kulu he would let him come too. Then Musinga had climbed in the back seat and Kulu had moved behind the wheel. Now here they were nearly to Rugeri and for days to come Musinga would go about telling how he had driven to Rugeri for the white Madami. Even the people who had watched them drive off, seeing Kulu himself crouched over the wheel, would say, why, yes, it was Musinga who drove to Rugeri to fetch the white Madami.

Without turning, Kulu swung his eyes to the right and watched Musinga standing beside the car in his best, in fact his only, white duck

pants and cotton shirt. Now Musinga took his shoes from the back seat.
Raising first one and then the other bare callused foot from the dusty
road, he pulled on the shoes with an expression of suppressed pain. Next
he took out his white smock and put it on slowly, buttoning each button and smoothing the frayed lapels. Closing the rear door and opening
the front, he hid his likembe under a rag on the floor. Finally, with a
flourish Kulu never hoped to imitate, he took his spectacles from the
pocket of his white smock and placed them on his nose. Kulu turned
his head and looked at him with admiration. Musinga gazed at him
sternly. Then he got in beside him and gestured imperiously up the road.

"The white Madami," Kulu said as he let out the clutch slowly and
shifted from first to second, "maybe the Doctor will take her as a wife."

Musinga frowned. The wise men of Dibela said that Dr. Bickel was
dying. Musinga had seen the signs himself, and he told himself he loved
Dr. Bickel and his heart would be sad when the old man died. Although
the wise men of Dibela were enemies of Dr. Bickel, Musinga had agreed
with them that the Doctor would die. In some conversations he even
had described Dr. Bickel's pain with exaggerated writhings that had de-
lighted the wise men. Musinga felt he acted wisely, for after Dr. Bickel
died, he, Doctor Musinga, surely would become the head of the hospital
and have a power that made his heart swell with expectation. Yet even
with that vast power he'd have to get along with the wise men of Dibela.
So it was well to agree with them, not only that Dr. Bickel was dying,
but even as to *why*.

It was tempting now to tell Kulu, who never conversed with the wise
men, that Dr. Bickel was dying. After he died, Kulu would think how
wise Musinga had been to have known it in advance. But Kulu would
spread it around the compound and some stupid one might ask Dr.
Bickel if it were true he was dying. Dr. Bickel would fly into one of
his rages and learn Musinga had said it. Then Dr. Bickel might send
him away from the hospital forever.

Musinga was greatly pleased with his cleverness in not telling Kulu
that Dr. Bickel would soon die. Meditating on his cleverness, he said,
"Dr. Bickel is too old to take a wife."

Kulu, who was young and unmarried, did not believe that any man
ever could be too old to take a wife. Besides, he'd said that merely to
see if Musinga would say that Dr. Bickel couldn't take the Madami because he was dying. Everyone said he was. Kulu fervently hoped this
was not true, though he feared it was. How strange, he thought, that

Musinga, who claimed to know everything, did not know that Dr. Bickel was dying.

"The white Madami won't stay here long," said Musinga. He hoped that was so, and his own tone of conviction made him feel it was.

"It's said that white madamis smell bad," Kulu said.

True, Musinga thought. But he said, "How would you know? You're from the hills. You've only been in Dibela a couple of seasons and you'd never get to Rugeri if I didn't drive you once in a while, as now."

Kulu decided not to argue the question of who was driving. He said, "I've seen the Bwana Administrator's wife and one other who was passing through Rugeri with her husband. But I haven't been close enough to smell them."

"I've seen many white madamis," Musinga said.

He had seen two. But as the man Dr. Bickel had chosen to be what he called his "number-one boy," he dared not confess his ignorance of white madamis. He knew that Kulu waited for him to say whether white madamis smelled bad. But the question suddenly confused him. The subject of women, both white and black, became depressing. Women were the cause of all trouble. He had sent his own wife back to her father for barrenness and still was trying to collect the five goats he'd paid for her. He didn't really care about the goats. He only wanted the divorce to be legally final, for she had been a troublesome woman, nagging him all the time.

That, it was said, was the great trouble with white madamis, quite apart from their awful whiteness, like the whiteness of antelope bones bleached long in the sun. They nagged you intolerably to do this and that and the other all at the same time. Aieee, the prospect of this unknown white Madami coming to Dibela and confusing everything and nagging him was more than he could bear. What would happen if he told Kulu to turn around and drive back to Dibela, where he'd explain that the white Madami had failed to appear at Rugeri? But she surely would come anyway and there would be great trouble. He took off his spectacles, which made his nose itch and which he did not need, but which were necessary to the dignity of his position. If only he had time for a tune on his likembe he might feel better.

But there was no time for music. Already they had turned off the road from Dibela onto the main road. Here was Rugeri. Musinga put on his spectacles and sat straight, his expression severe, as Kulu drove faster. Chickens and goats fled before the car and the children ran to the road from the lines of huts, shouting, "Jambo! Jambo!" Kulu grinned and waved to them, acting like a child himself, until Musinga told him sharply, "Try to show some dignity. Remember whom you're riding with."

They passed the store run by the Greek and the barracks and huts of the askaris and they came to the park of mango trees where a score of prisoners in striped shirts were lazily cutting grass with sharp pangas while one blue-uniformed askari carrying only a stick watched them boredly. At one end of the park was the red-brick jailhouse. Near it stood the court, which appeared incomplete to strangers because it was simply a long thatched roof raised on red-brick columns with a dais at one end where the Bwana Administrator sat and dispensed justice a couple of mornings each week. At the other end of the park lay the Administrator's bungalow and his office, two sprawling stucco buildings shaded by flamboyant and raffia palms and copal trees. Beyond stretched the bush, for this was all there was to Rugeri.

A sentry wearing khaki shorts and shirt and rolled leggings lounged before the administrative office in the still heat of early afternoon. Seeing the car turn off the main road, he braced himself and stiffly moved his rifle to rest arms. Then, seeing it was an old scarred car carrying two fellow Africans, he relaxed disgustedly.

"What do you want?" he asked as the car stopped and Musinga stared at him coolly.

"I am Doctor Musinga and—"

"Doctor my cousin's goat," the askari said. "You're one of the boys of that white doctor at Dibela and what do you want?"

"I see the army still enlists only the stupid," Musinga replied, unmoved. "I am Doctor Musinga and I've come to fetch the white Madami."

"The white Madami never would ride in that thing." The askari spat toward the car.

"I also have an order here—" Musinga began fumbling through his pockets—"for petrol."

"There is no petrol," the sentry said. "There may never be any more petrol for any but the army. Don't you know there's a war on?"

"War!" cried Kulu. "What war?"

"War!" the sentry mimicked him. "What war? The war's been going for more than a moon. But up in Dibela they never hear or know anything."

"Where's the war?" Kulu was excited. "Is it near here?"

"It's over the sea," the sentry said. Then, ominously, "But they say it's coming here soon."

[12]

"You never told me about it," Kulu said accusingly to Musinga.

"I've been very busy recently," said Musinga, who was only mildly interested to learn there was a war. He frowned at the sentry. "Now where is the white Madami?"

The sentry nodded toward the Administrator's house. "You'll have to wait."

Henri Lecomte, Administrator of the vast Rugeri District in the eastern Belgian Congo, generally had one glass of wine at lunch. Today he had drunk three. He was certain that his wife had noticed. But he wondered if she knew why.

Let's face it, he told himself, you never expected to be charmed by a Protestant missionary woman. Let's also face the fact that you're a decayed hulk of tropical bones. Finally let's face the fact that she is a Protestant missionary woman. After facing all these bleak facts Lecomte still found he was enjoying her company.

His thoughts had no connection with the story he was telling about a rogue elephant that had troubled his sleep long ago when he had had a post far down in the equatorial forest. He was rather proud of this ability to let his thoughts wander away while his voice flowed on effortlessly. It had taken many years of living in the bush with Marie, his wife, to acquire it. Probably there were days on end when he did not actually give a thought to the words he poured on Marie.

She sat across the room from him now, fat and passive, hands folded in her lap, gray hair wilted, red veins etched across the cheeks of her broad Flemish face. If only he didn't feel so sorry for her. Not for himself—for her.

It was impossible not to compare her with the missionary nurse, this Miss Cade, Miss Rachel Cade, who had remarked during lunch that she'd been in Africa since 1932. Seven years. So she must be about thirty years old, although she didn't look it; many of these Protestant denominations lured missionary women into their tropical predicaments at surprisingly tender ages. Seven years, and she still had not succumbed to some moist-handed preacher or doctor. Succumbed to marriage, that is. More interesting, thought Lecomte, it was doubtful if she had succumbed to un-Christian, extramarital passions.

Lecomte, who prided himself on being no idealist about human conduct, was certain of this. It was an absurd certainty to have concerning anyone, he knew. Yet he was certain of it and he did not know why any more than he knew why he had such a great facility for judging the inscrutable characters of his many thousands of African charges. It was intuitive, and there was nothing to be gained in pressing the intuition. He simply knew that Miss Cade was—well, virginal. Not virginal from choiceless necessity, the outraged mother of old-maidenhood. Virginal, rather, by choice, embracing that strange fate which the sensualist in Lecomte never could fathom, despite his effort to fathom everything. Thus, he was sure, if anyone ever told Miss Cade that she was a beautiful woman she would laugh aloud—not in cruel mistrust of the speaker's motives, but at the total irrelevance of his remark.

He wished he could stop thinking so intently about her. But how could he? For she sat there, listening and smiling and sometimes laughing at the droll points of his story which he himself heard only distantly, like a muted phonograph recording. She sat with slim legs crossed, occasionally swinging one sandaled foot. (Was it possible his story was running a trifle long?) She was slender and well formed and rather tall. But the extraordinary, the incredible thing was that Africa seemed to have done nothing to her. Physically, that is. Her dark hair curled clean and naturally (yes, magnificently, thought Lecomte) against the chair's white antimacassar which Marie had painfully worked in petit point. Her bare legs and arms were tanned, as if she'd spent her time with the rich planters on the Atlantic beach far down at Moanda instead of dispensing pills in the bush. Yet the finest, the ultimate characteristic with which one would choose to live (thought Lecomte) was her face. It was strong-boned—strong and rather broad cheekbones, strong and broad forehead, strong and straight nose. Her full lips were set gravely, but the habitual expression of her gray eyes was humorous.

Probably her hair was too long and untrained to be fashionable. Her brows she left alone. She did not (of course you had to keep remembering she was a missionary) wear rouge. She wore a plain gray chambray dress, a clean loose dress that only her body unconsciously adorned. An impossible dress in Europe, but here so sensible that it conclusively proved she knew the African bush. So she demonstrated outwardly what Lecomte knew inwardly: she lived knowledgeably and by choice.

Abruptly Lecomte ended his story, the distant recording of his voice stilled. He leaned toward her, quite aware of his long, loose, sorry figure in shorts and short-sleeved shirt: thin, bony legs and arms, ash-gray hair, great blade of nose curving into the mustache. Without transition he said to her: "But why Dibela?"

She smiled. "But why not Dibela?" Her voice was habitually pitched low, her French excellent, with only a trace of American accent.

[14]

So, thought Lecomte with satisfaction, she followed him readily even though they had not mentioned her destination in the past half hour.

"It's a terrible place." He did not mean to be cruel, but he knew she was accustomed to facing facts. "The road is impossible. It's out in nowhere. The people are among the most backward in the district."

"That's reason enough," she said. "I mean if the people are—backward."

"Why, Henri, Dibela is the prettiest place I've ever seen," Marie said, unable to measure the quality of the woman and fearful he would frighten her.

"Of course it's *pretty*," he said impatiently. "Most of Africa is *pretty*."

"The way the mountains rise up," said Marie.

"The mountains." Miss Cade stirred and smiled thoughtfully. "I look forward to seeing them. Dibela lies in their shadow, I understand. Maybe that was my selfish reason in wanting to go there when our headquarters decided to send a nurse to help Dr. Bickel." She sighed suddenly. "The Mountains of the Moon. What a beautiful name. It's really too bad they couldn't appear on the maps by that name instead of as the Ruwenzori."

"Ruwenzori isn't a bad name," Lecomte said. "As you know, in Swahili it means the Rain Maker. Apparently Stanley was the first white man to see them. At least he claimed to be the first. He camped for a good many days somewhere in this district before he glimpsed the flash of snow through clouds. You'll sometimes go for weeks without ever seeing the glaciers and perpetual snows of the summits. They're almost constantly wrapped in clouds."

"Snow," she said softly. "Snow here only a few miles north of the equator. I've always loved snow-capped mountains and I've spent all my life in flat country. I was born and raised in Kansas where it's very flat."

He smiled wryly. "You'll have your mountains at your door, Miss Cade, rising to nearly seventeen thousand feet." He wished to stop talking about the accursed mountains, but he heard his voice running on. "For centuries before Stanley the mountains stirred the imaginations of Africans. As long ago as the second century Ptolemy placed them quite accurately on his map of Africa. He named them the Mountains of the Moon."

She leaned toward him intently. "And by that name they're best known to this day. I think that's somehow wonderful. They fascinate me."

"Don't be fascinated, Miss Cade. We Belgians are not. The mountains are cold and dangerous and covered with clouds." He intended scorn,

[15]

but he heard his tone of wonder. For the mountains had absorbed more of his thoughts than he cared to remember.

"That's interesting," Miss Cade said. "I would have guessed you loved them."

A small bubble seemed to burst in Lecomte's heart. For an instant he was madly in love with her. She understood him. It would be possible for her to understand everything about him.

But he said gravely, "You do not love mountains, Miss Cade. You respect, fear and study them. But you do not love them."

"So," she said, "they are not as great as people."

He sank back in his chair, reaching around blindly for the cigar he'd left burning some time ago on the ashtray there somewhere. He knocked the cigar to the floor and picked it up and stuck it between his uneven yellowed teeth and stared hard at Rachel Cade.

She looked at him levelly. He knew (alas, alas) that she meant the unpassionate divine love of mankind that the Christians always talked about.

"You have not—" he took the dead cigar from his teeth and looked at it—"asked what I think of Dr. Bickel."

"No, I haven't."

He raised his eyes alertly. "You are interested?"

"Yes."

He smiled. "But you would not ask me."

She smiled too. "No. I'd depend on your telling me anything you think I should know."

"And then make your own decision after you meet the man. Very wise. So I shall be unpolitic and gratuitously offer my judgment for what it's worth. Because I think you'll find him difficult. I have. He's really not a missionary type at all."

"So I've heard," Miss Cade said.

"He's a scientist type," Lecomte continued. "He should be subsidized by one of your American foundations instead of by your church. On the rare occasions I see him he's always complaining about his lack of equipment and help. He's wrapped up in himself and his own interests. He hasn't organized a school out there or—well, influenced the people."

Miss Cade frowned. The frown made her look tired. Lecomte thought of the hundreds of kilometers she'd traveled over the impossible roads from Stanleyville in a car rented from the government for the journey. He thought of her riding with that inept African driver and staying in the impossible guest houses along the way and then being left here in

Rugeri, her journey still uncompleted because the Mission Society had paid for the car to come this far and no farther. He pitied her, and he said, "I don't mean to depress you."

"I'm not depressed," she said. "But you only tell me substantially what they say back west at headquarters. I'd merely hoped to hear that they were wrong back there." She smiled faintly. "But it seems they're never wrong at headquarters."

"Oh, they're often wrong at all headquarters," Lecomte said cheerfully. "They've been wrong about me at my headquarters for a long time. Many years ago, when I was very young, I committed a—hmm—an unpolitic act. Headquarters never forgot. And so today I govern Rugeri instead of a province."

Miss Cade smiled. "I'm sure they misjudge you at your headquarters, Monsieur Lecomte. But tell me something more about Dibela. A mission was established there some time ago, I understand, long before our people took it over a year and a half ago and sent Dr. Bickel there."

"That was even before my time here," Lecomte said. "My predecessor, the first Administrator ever sent to Rugeri, muttered about it to me before he fled this post. As I understood it, Dibela was opened by an Englishman. All the English are eccentric, I believe, but this fellow must have been unusually so. To go away off there, I mean. Why couldn't he have stayed right here in Rugeri and started himself a pleasant little mission? We have none, you know. Ten kilometers to the south we have a Catholic mission run by Father Gilo, whom you'll meet eventually."

"A very fine man," Marie Lecomte said firmly.

"A fine man." Lecomte nodded.

"Henri and I are Catholic," Marie said.

"Marie is a Catholic," Lecomte said. "I am nothing."

"You are Catholic," his wife said.

"I am nothing. But to continue with my story. This Englishman, a holy hair-shirted type with a little smattering of medicine, I understand, went off to Dibela, dragging his wife with him. It must have been about 1921 or '22. Just a trail then and a dugout to take you across the river. Well, they went and they lived in a hut out there and finally they bribed some of the people to help them build a big thatched structure that was to be both their church and hospital. It's still standing, doubtless rebuilt several times since with hired labor. But none of the people would join the church and none would take the Englishman's medicine. Instead of pulling out, as any sensible Belgian or Frenchman would have done, the Englishman apparently just became more stubborn. He made

[17]

life miserable for my predecessor until the government had its prisoners build a bridge across the river and widen the track a little to make it a kind of a road. I guess the Englishman thought it would be easier for God to get to Dibela if there were a road out there—"

"Henri!" his wife said sharply.

"Well—" Lecomte smiled dolefully at Miss Cade—"he wasn't a member of your particular church. At any rate, he failed altogether to get a single person to take his medicine or worship his God. He did amazing things. Somehow from somewhere he got the parts of a small hand-driven sawmill and dragged them out there. He worked it himself and maybe bribed some to help him. Really he must have been an amazingly difficult man not to get one African to like him—but, as I was saying, he sawed boards and built a very comfortable bungalow for his wife and himself and had the sense to make the foundation of brick so the termites wouldn't destroy it. It's still standing there. Bickel lives in it. And then he built another small cottage, heaven knows why or for whom. Maybe just to give himself something to do and to stop from going mad. All this was over the course of four or five years, you understand. Then his wife died and he buried her God knows where, because I've never found a trace of a grave. And finally he wandered off toward the mountains . . ."

Lecomte's voice trailed off. He really had told her too much, he thought. What a fool he was with his wagging tongue!

"He wandered off toward the mountains?" Miss Cade stared at him questioningly.

"Yes. And he never was heard of again."

"Never was heard of again?" She looked incredulous.

Why had he ever started to tell this abominable story? He would not tell *why* the Englishman went. But he knew. Oh, he knew all right. Just as he knew about Bickel. But he wouldn't tell her *that*. That was Bickel's story to tell, and it would be better if she never heard it. It would be better if she stayed a few weeks in Dibela and quietly went back west. In fact, it was time he took it upon himself to write to her headquarters and explain in detail the hopelessness of Dibela.

"But what was his name?" she asked.

"Who? The Englishman?" He shrugged. "I don't know. My predecessor told me, but I've forgotten it. I suppose it's somewhere in the records. But what does it matter? He's dead. The hyenas have eaten him."

"Henri!" his wife said.

"The hyenas have eaten him," Lecomte said coldly. "The man is dead and gone. The people still understand the low Swahili language he introduced. And the things he built with his hands still stand, patched. But that's all that remains. The sawmill is gone. I've found parts of it a hundred kilometers away. A saw tooth on a spearhead. Once a bit of blade with a Birmingham imprint serving as a latch on a door of lashed logs. It was in a village up north where they were afraid of lions."

"What a depressing story," his wife said.

"It's an African story," Lecomte said.

"What I find so hard to believe," said Miss Cade, "is that he could make absolutely no impression on the people. It seems to me that Africans are the most impressionable of people, the most receptive—"

"You are a missionary," Lecomte said, "and you are, therefore, the most optimistic of women. The people are not that way everywhere. There are many places like Dibela. But you have not yet been in a Dibela."

She raised her chin. "I've worked in Liberia and at four posts down Congo before I went to headquarters. I know that the grandparents of these people were cannibals who didn't understand the wheel. But I still believe that Africans . . ." Her voice died and she smiled wryly. "Well, I'm sure Dr. Bickel has made some advances since he came out here."

It would be better if she learned for herself, Lecomte thought bleakly.

She swung to her feet. "Why should I wait longer? Dr. Bickel was told by letter to send a car for me today."

"I'll drive you to Dibela, Miss Cade." Lecomte rose slowly.

Her glance passed over him briefly and out through the folding doors, which were opened wide. "Thank you. That's kind. But I imagine that's Dr. Bickel's car out there now."

"And Bickel himself?" Lecomte looked out at the old Ford and then turned to her, scowling. "Not even the courtesy to come himself. We'll put your luggage in that car and you will ride with me."

"No." She extended a hand, palm forward. "Thank you, no, Monsieur Lecomte. I'll look forward to you and Madame paying a visit to Dibela at some future time."

It was not always a pleasure, Lecomte thought regretfully, to have one's judgment of another proven accurate.

II

Rugeri lay (and indeed still lies) on a low escarpment of the high country which rolls to the Ruwenzori. Where the road to Dibela plunged east off the escarpment one could see, on a clear day, the dim blue mass of the mountains shouldering the clouds forty miles away. It happened to be a remarkably clear afternoon in October when Rachel left the Rugeri hills. Staring through the windshield from the back seat of Dr. Bickel's Ford, she saw the dim mass of the mountains far across the plain. Impulsively she said in Swahili to Kulu, "Stop the car, please."

"Stop the car," Musinga said.

But Kulu already had stopped. Rachel pushed back one of the bags piled beside her and swung out quickly. She crossed the road and stood at the edge of the escarpment looking east.

There was a glint in the sky above the bulwarks of the mountains. Instinctively she held her breath, wondering if she had glimpsed the snows of the Mountains of the Moon. But it was gone. She heard her breath rush out in the stillness, and the vast distances seemed to press physically upon her. You are in a state, she thought. And then, alertly: Why? But no logical reason came to her.

Before her the rolling plain stretched east, vast lion-colored islands in a green sea. The forests swept around the Rugeri hills, hugging them like two sinewy arms that grew thinner as they extended on across the plain until, surely in the imagination, only their fingers touched the mountains.

She turned abruptly and saw that Kulu and Musinga were standing in the road. Kulu was gazing at the mountains. But Musinga, who had introduced himself as Doctor, was looking at her.

"The Madami sees the mountains," he said.

"Yes," Rachel said, "they're beautiful."

She knew they found her remark strange and doubtless would laugh about it later. For they live with them, she thought, and it's difficult to call anything you live with beautiful. Remember how strange you thought it long ago when that visitor called the sun going down over the wheat fields of Trego County "beautiful"?

"The mountains are beautiful," Musinga said, nodding.

"The mountains are beautiful?" asked Kulu, puzzled.

There was the difference between these men, Rachel thought as she stepped into the car. Musinga did not believe a word of it but pretended assent. And Kulu did not understand but could be taught. She'd met them only fifteen minutes ago and already she'd formed opinions she'd guard meticulously against their catlike sensitivity, opinions she'd freely amend or discard when tested by longer experience. Musinga obviously was "number-one boy" to Dr. Bickel and Kulu obviously "number-one boy" to Musinga. Why, then, would she pick Kulu? Dr. Bickel must have had a good reason for having picked Musinga. Yes, she must be wrong. But then, looking ahead as they jounced down the sharp switchbacks of the escarpment, she noticed that Musinga's spectacles were not ground lenses at all. They were merely glass, clear glass.

It was a rough ride, the roughest of the many hundred miles of bad roads she'd traveled in these past days. But it was not tedious to her because the country changed gradually after they crossed a rickety bridge over a black still river where a hippo sank from sight.

The road climbed from the river through great liana-tangled mimosa trees. Quite suddenly the mimosa gave way to palmyra and mock date trees, and soon there were no trees but only the tall elephant grass and mock sugar cane. So they entered one of the lion-colored islands Rachel had seen from the escarpment, but the land was not flat as it had seemed from the heights. It pitched like the sea under a small boat and swelled steadily toward the mountains. When it seemed the savannah would go on forever, they dipped into the green forests of watercourses again, and then out onto another tan island and—eventually—into the green again. As they traveled, the trees of the watercourses grew ever smaller, smaller, for the land rose constantly toward the mountains, changing subtly but inevitably until it became a country such as Rachel had not seen before. The dense tropical forests where she had spent her years in Africa pall on one before one takes them for granted, but she knew that this country would not pall on her, she knew she never would take it for granted.

There were few people visible along the road or in the tiny villages through which they passed, and these few were not friendly, Rachel noticed. In the villages the children stared but did not shout "Jambo!" and the men sitting in the tiny palaver houses turned and stared at the passing car but they did not reply when Rachel waved. The bare-breasted women, bowed under loads of faggots and matting grass, shrank into the tall reeds of the roadside when they heard the car. The men stood aside too, though they did not shrink but stood openly and gazed impassively. Nearly all the men were hunters armed with bows and spears, their bows longer than those of the forest peoples, their spears longer, too, and heavier-tipped. The hunters were strongly built men, many wearing only breechcloths, and their foreheads and cheeks were tattooed. The old hunters looked fiercer than the young men, perhaps because they had known war; but they stood passively by the roadside now, yielded to the inevitability of peace. Some of the hunters carried braces of francolin and one had a small topi slung over his shoulders, so it appeared to be a land of plenty. If the people were not hungry, why were they not friendly?

She observed, too, that while these were a strong people, many bore the marks of disease. Yaws spread unchecked here, she saw, noting multiple cauliflower eruptions of the skin on many and eroding and bulbous tertiary yaws on a few. Some of the old women had cataracts and in one village she saw a youth hobbling from the effects of meningitis. There was, she thought, much work to be done here.

As they went east the mountain mass rose into mist before them. The sun was declining at their backs and it seemed to Rachel they were entering deep shadows, so heavily weighed the massive mountains on her imagination. Now the road ran straight between shimmering curtains of elephant grass, the mountains a wall ahead. At last it crossed a small river brawling translucently over rocks like the mountain rivers of America and unlike the rivers she had known in the lowlands of Africa. So they came nearly to the end of the journey.

It was a parklike land, scattered with round thatched huts and many manioc fields and fig and mango trees. Cultivation and tall grass and the spent limits of the forest came together here, all seeming to strive to touch the mountains and all (up ahead there somewhere) finally repelled.

Now the people came to the edges of the road from their shambas at the sound of the car, some waving and all straining to glimpse the strange visitor, the white Madami. They were speeding up the long yellow slant of road in the quickly fading light, Kulu honking the horn and Musinga nodding gravely to the people. In the dusk there was a long thatched roof and a whitewashed building, a bungalow. This was the mission, this was Dibela.

But Rachel was not looking at the buildings. Her mouth fallen slightly open, she gazed up at a huge limbali tree that towered into the evening sky. A limbali here, she thought in wonder. Its great trunk, probably sixteen feet in diameter, rose like a muscular dark arm from the dust of the compound and, far up, its vast spreading branches lay over the mission like a gentle hand. A limbali harder than oak, a prince of the equatorial forests, that had seeded and rooted and thrived far up here in the high country where its mere survival was incredible. It challenged the mountains. It would enable her to bear the weight of the mountains pressing down on her.

She stepped to the ground slowly as a man came toward the car. Short, thickset, aging, he walked with a curious hesitation, as if he might turn away at any moment and not bother to come to the car. His closely cropped hair was gray and his face itself looked gray in the failing light. Suddenly he halted and stared at her, gray brows and the deep lines of his blunt face seeming to shoot upward in surprise. She could not understand why he seemed surprised, for surely he was Dr. Bickel and certainly he had expected her.

Then he came on, saying in a weak voice that nevertheless bore an echo of sternness, "Welcome to Dibela, Miss Cade."

"I'm glad to be here, Dr. Bickel." She extended her hand. His hand, like his voice, was weak. Looking at him, hearing his quick breathing, she knew with dismay that he was ill.

"The boys will fetch your bags," he said. He looked up at her, eyelids suddenly slitted. "Did you bring the medicine I ordered?"

"Yes." She turned. "It's this case—"

One of his hands touched her bare arm coldly and she almost recoiled. "*All* of it?"

"Why—I suppose so, Doctor. I brought what Dr.—"

"Never mind, never mind—" He wheeled, calling in Swahili, "Musinga, Musinga, fetch that case to my house quickly, quickly." Then he started off, pointing in the opposite direction, saying over a shoulder to her, "That's your house, Miss Cade, the boys will show you, I'll expect you for dinner shortly . . ." And he was gone.

She stared after him, furious. To accept this assignment, to come this far, and then— She strode toward the tiny thatch-roofed stucco cottage he had indicated, her anger dissipating in depression so profound she feared that she might cry. Climbing the two steps and crossing the tiny empty porch, she paused in the screenless doorway of her cottage. Then the tears welled in her eyes, while she blinked frantically. For the one room was awful. A cot with torn mosquito netting, a triangular-legged

[23]

African chair, a table on which stood a candle, a bottle of water, a chipped enamel basin and a fragment of towel. And that was all, except for a tiny lizard that scurried across the floor in the twilight.

She dashed a hand across her eyes, paced the length of her cell to the screenless window, and when she turned and faced the doorway her eyes were dry. She tried, without much success, to smile at the two young men who tottered onto the porch with her luggage.

"How are you?" she said calmly in Swahili. Then she walked toward them, hand extended. "I am Miss Cade. What are your names?"

They gaped at her. One turned and fled. But the other touched her hand and said, "I am Kosongo, Madami."

She looked at him closely, at his broad shoulders and calm intelligent face. "I'm glad to meet you, Kosongo. Would you please fill the basin with hot water at once."

When he had gone, she stood for a moment, tongue touching her lips pensively. Then she opened her smallest bag and took out matches, flashlight and two candles set in small weighted sticks. She lighted the candles, for it was nearly dark. Across the doorway and two windows she drew the burlap curtains which, she noted, were filthy and would have to be replaced. Turning to the bag, she took out soap and washcloth, comb and brush, a bottle of cologne and a silver-backed hand mirror. Cocking her head slightly, she arranged these articles on the table, moving them about until their symmetry pleased her. She picked up the comb and brush and sat down in the chair. Leaning her head to one side, she loosened some pins and let her hair fall. Then, closing her eyes and smiling faintly, smiling both at the sensuous pleasure and at herself for succumbing to it, she brushed her hair with long strokes.

She was still brushing it when Kosongo called outside that he had the hot water. She held her hair back tightly at the nape of her neck, trying to make herself look as severe as possible, then told him to come in. He poured the water in the basin without looking at her and she thanked and dismissed him. Pinning up her hair again, she slipped out of her dress, and, standing before the basin in her slip, she bathed carefully. She was drying herself with a clean heavy towel from her bag when she heard a heavy step on the porch and Dr. Bickel called, "Miss Cade! Miss Cade!"

"I'm dressing," she said coldly. "What do you want?"

"Where—" his voice sounded choked with fury—"where is the nitroglycerin I ordered?"

"I don't know where it is!" she cried. "I only brought what Dr. Spencer

[24]

told me to bring and I don't know anything about your nitroglycerin or anything else. Now tell me where and what time I'm supposed to eat and go away and leave me alone."

In the silence a jackal yapped somewhere. Her eyes widened in surprise at her outburst; she wondered if she should apologize now or later.

Then Dr. Bickel said, "I'm sorry, Miss Cade. I understand how you must feel. You take your time and I'll just sit here on the steps and wait for you."

She didn't answer him.

"Miss Cade," he said.

"Yes."

"Where are you from in the States?"

"Kansas—originally. Trego County, Kansas."

"I'm from Nebraska," he said. "Originally." She thought she heard him sigh, or possibly it was the wind in the limbali tree. "A place called Four Rivers, though nobody ever could locate more than two around it." Surely he was smiling out there in the darkness.

Before she reached Dibela she'd thought she'd wear a clean dress and put on stockings for dinner. But after he'd walked away, she'd decided not to bother. Now she took out stockings and a fresh dress.

"I guess this looks pretty impossible to you," said Dr. Bickel.

"No," she replied. "Rough—but not impossible."

"I haven't done a very good job here," he said.

She paused, puzzled by his admission, as she started to roll a stocking up one leg.

"I wouldn't say that," she said. "Maybe I can help with some things you haven't had time to do."

"I haven't done enough—well, practicing. And I haven't done any missionarying. But I did a little researching before I lost interest."

"Research?"

"Yes. On malaria."

"Oh," she said. "Is there much here?"

"Practically none," he said vaguely. "So I gave it up." He paused. "I took up mountain climbing. And that's what killed me."

She sat motionless, feeling chilled.

"At least I guess that's what did it, though some of the natives around here have other ideas. I have angina, Miss Cade."

Her hands trembled momentarily before she could control them, before she could control a nameless fear of being left alone out here. She told herself she should only be concerned for him, and she was ashamed of her fear. The trouble was, she thought, that she did not know him. She began dressing faster, her hands fumbling in her desire to get outside quickly and come to know him so that she could be concerned for him and not for herself. She must learn everything quickly before—before—

"We'll certainly get some nitroglycerin here quickly." She heard her voice, calm, as from a distance. "If Dr. Spencer had known you were ill he'd certainly have made sure you got the nitroglycerin, Dr. Bickel."

"If Dr. Spencer had known," he said dryly, "he'd have recalled me from here."

"And you would not want to leave here?"

"I should," he said indistinctly. "I haven't done any good here—or in any other place. I . . ." His voice trailed off.

She heard herself rattling on as she dressed quickly, trying to reassure him, trying to make him understand things would go better now that she was here.

"You must take a long rest, Dr. Bickel. Don't you agree?"

He didn't answer her.

"Well, you must," she said.

There, the last button. She started toward the doorway, then paused and turned back to the small bag on the floor. From it she took a tiny vial of French perfume she'd bought in Brazzaville long ago in a moment of folly. She rarely used it. Now she opened it. A touch on either hand for Dr. Bickel. A touch on her chin for herself.

She blew out the candles and went outside, blinking at the sudden darkness. Apparently he had wandered off. Overhead one star gleamed through the great limbali tree, and hyenas sent up their *yooo-eee-yooo* cries toward the mountains.

There was a shadow on the ground at the foot of the steps.

"Dr. Bickel!" she cried and sprang to him.

He was dead.

III

SHE KNELT beside his body, holding one of his lifeless hands in both of hers, and stared up through the branches of the limbali at the single gleaming star.

"Oh, God," she said. "Help me."

Wind stirred in the limbali and there was no answer.

"Help!" she cried, and while none of them understood English, all understood the tone of desperate plea, and they came running, dim shapes in the darkness.

She staggered to her feet and said in Swahili, trying to make her voice calm, "Dr. Bickel is ill. Fetch a stretcher from the hospital and carry him to his house."

There were a half dozen of them milling in the darkness. She could make out Musinga and Kulu and Kosongo, and first Kulu and then Musinga ran toward the dim bulk of the big thatch-roofed building while the others chattered inanely. Kulu returned quickly with the stretcher. She grasped Dr. Bickel's body firmly by the shoulders and told them to lift the feet.

One shouted, "He's dead!"

They shrank from the body in the darkness and she could smell the sudden pungent sweat of one near her.

"Take Dr. Bickel's feet," she said.

Two ran off, but she could make out Kulu and Musinga and Kosongo and one other remaining. Then, hesitantly, Kulu reached forward and lifted Dr. Bickel's feet onto the stretcher. Musinga picked up the head of the stretcher jerkily and Kulu the foot and they went off in the darkness, Rachel and the others following.

A Coleman lamp burned on the bungalow porch and another had been lighted in the big room where, to judge from the disorder, Dr. Bickel had done everything but sleep. Rachel swept a pile of magazines off a cot and told Musinga and Kulu to lay the stretcher there. She walked slowly about the room, stepping over a pair of dirty corduroy trousers that lay where they had fallen, and came at last to a long wooden table which stretched almost the width of the room. It was piled with books and notebooks and papers. At one end stood a microscope, uncovered, with a pile of dirty slides beside it. At the other end of the table was a big black bag such as country doctors used to carry in the States. She opened the bag, took out a stethoscope, and returned to the body on the cot.

Listening carefully, she moved it slowly over his chest and wrists. He was dead. She drew a blanket over him, covering his face. Removing the plugs from her ears, she turned, glimpsing a dark face at a window, and then addressed the four in the doorway:

"Dr. Bickel is dead. Call all the people of the mission together here at once."

They disappeared, and she toured the room again slowly. She noticed that two places had been clumsily set at a small table where Dr. Bickel apparently had intended they should dine. She touched a packing case sent from headquarters; its lid was ripped off, but its Swahili Bibles and texts had not been unpacked. She opened the door of a large tin medicine cabinet and frowned at the careless disarray of bottles and vials. What sort of a missionary and a physician had Dr. Bickel been?

She closed the door and turned. Her eyes widened at sight of a gun rack she had not noticed before. Two rifles and a shotgun, an amazing armory for a missionary. She stepped to the rack, which did not have a lock, and saw that he'd carelessly piled great mounds of packaged ammunition into a crate beside it. There were a Springfield .30-caliber rifle and a beautiful Westley-Richards .425 and a Purdey 10-gauge shotgun. She lifted out the Westley-Richards and carried it to the lamp and opened its box magazine expertly. At least he kept his rifles clean. But why the armory and why the strangely shaped ax leaning against a wall? An ice ax; she remembered seeing a picture once. Ice was on the mountains, and he had said— She looked about alertly as she replaced the Westley-Richards in the rack. A coil of rope on the floor and here on the long table a book on the Duke of Abruzzi's ascent of the Ruwenzori from the east. More books on mountain climbing. With a strange despair or desire this man had turned to the mountains.

Sinking on a bench, Rachel rested her elbows on the long table and covered her eyes. It would take days to straighten out this mess. And then what? Dibela, it seemed, had existed precariously with a doctor; without one it was unlikely it could exist at all. Send for another? Inwardly she smiled bitterly. There was not another. There never were enough, but now, with this war breaking out in Europe and likely to spread everywhere, the denomination knew it would have to retrench rather than expand its mission program.

She remembered Dr. Spencer calling her into his office at headquarters a couple of weeks ago. She was his operating nurse whom he prized (someone had told her) more than his married daughters in the States. He was her father whom she prized because it seemed to her she never had really had a father. Dr. Spencer, turning his glasses in his fingers and staring out a window, told her that Dr. Bickel at Dibela had been begging for an assistant. The word Dibela, that most remote and easterly of the denomination's wide-flung missions in West and Central Africa, interested her. "We've decided," Dr. Spencer said, "that Dr. Bickel should have help at Dibela." Dr. Spencer never ordered his small staff of women nurses to special posts, except in emergency; he mentioned opportunities which they almost invariably accepted, causing them to feel they were volunteers and so making them content with their assignments. He was not ordering her to Dibela, she knew. He was telling her there was an opportunity and she was free to go.

Basically, she knew, he was not talking about Dibela at all. He was talking about Ralph Morgan. And Ralph was a subject that each knew was painful to both. In the ten months Ralph had been at the station he'd proven himself an able physician. People liked him and his wife, Ann, and their baby, Timmy. Rachel liked them. But certainly she hadn't realized Ralph was in love with her until that afternoon he was driving her back to quarters through the rain when he suddenly stopped the car and seized her hand and told her he *had* to talk to her. Thinking he had some problem with the job or Ann, she told him this was as good a time as any. (You're so *dense* sometimes, she told herself afterward.) Then, leaning toward her, sweating, he inundated her with words, telling her he loved and needed and wanted her. She was shocked. But not angry. Certainly not afraid. She kept thinking, Oh, poor Ann, poor Ann that he should be this way. And then she thought, Poor Ralph. She pitied him deeply because she knew these things were always happening, people could not constantly control the direction of their passions. For a moment she felt a part of her withdraw out into the rain and look in at Ralph and Rachel sitting there, and the part out there in the rain thought, Send Rachel off in the bush with him and let him have his way with her and that will get it over. But she knew it wouldn't, it wouldn't. It would merely be the first step of tragedy—for him, for her, for Ann and Timmy, for the whole widespread cause and system of the mission which, like the ancient Roman Empire, could be no stronger than its weakest link. That was why you lived by a code, a code that was sensible rather than severe. Adultery was not evil because Christ had said so; He had called it evil because He knew its effects. Yet the part of her that seemed to be out in the rain realized it was not just common sense that withheld Rachel in the car from bedding down with Ralph. She simply had no desire for it. And not just with Ralph. It had been the same with others, far back to a time when a quick flowering of desire had withered in a cold climate of circumstance.

So she'd told Ralph kindly that it was impossible. But neither then nor later did he accept her answer as credible, so fanatically did he worship at the altar of his desire on which he wished her to sacrifice herself. She discovered that one could not refuse a man like Ralph and go on pleasantly, as though nothing had happened, as though one had graciously declined to join a club. She tried to find ways of avoiding him, but it is impossible to avoid an associate in a jungle hospital. When all other means failed, he settled on the method of quiet derision. "Your fear will ruin you," he would murmur, coming up on her when no one was near. "I'll bet somebody scared you once and just because of that you're going to stay frozen and turn old and sour and not know why." She would back from him, defenseless. Except once, when she'd been holding a bottle of alcohol, and had wheeled on him, hating him suddenly, staring at him contemplatively, so that he had known she might smash the bottle across his face, and he'd scurried away.

It wore on her. She began to wonder if he didn't analyze her correctly. For she not only knew the facts of life; she had exposed herself to certain popularized ideas of psychology. She knew that sex was a natural, necessary and even a delightful (it was said) fact of life, and since she loved life, how did it happen that she had avoided sex? Since she pursued courage and dreaded fear, might he not be right when he said she was afraid? She searched her memory for the beginnings of fear, and when she could not recall it, her mind still was not at rest. For she knew that fear is the most phenomenal sensibility; one can bury its seeds at sundown and gaily pick its flowers for one's friends in the morning.

Then she remembered that one incident in Trego County when she was sixteen. The pain, the fear, the humiliation. Could that be it? It must be. Then why, just now, had she been unable to remember it? Perhaps memory never should be buried. Basically a cold and frightened woman, though she never thought of herself as cold or frightened. Maybe that was why so long ago with Dick her desire never had caught step with circumstances or propriety or whatever you wanted to call it until their engagement had not seemed to be terminated but had simply drowned in her own tears. And then Africa. And then? Not search and not expectation, but once in a while the dim hope she might meet a man, a doctor, one who would change all this, one with whom she might run a hospital far off somewhere, loving and living and doing this work that was more important to her than any on earth. Certainly this man and this way of life had nothing to do with Ralph Morgan.

When Dr. Spencer had told her of the opportunity at Dibela a couple of weeks ago, he turned suddenly from the window, put on his glasses, and gazed at her solemnly. "How have things been going for you, Rachel?" He knew about Ralph, she realized. In the past weeks she'd forgotten or tried to ignore that in the isolation of a mission one knows almost everything that happens to everyone else. She looked away and did not answer him. Then he said quietly, "I know it's been hard for you, Rachel, and I respect you for the way you've handled the situation." He snatched off his glasses angrily. "You don't have to go to Dibela. In fact I don't *want* you to go there. Do you understand?" She did. He was offering Dibela because it was the only place of his command where he could send her without throwing his ever thin line off balance. He could not send Ralph anywhere, gladly as he would sacrifice him over her, his best friend and operating nurse, who would play pinochle with him until midnight and administer a spinal anesthetic accurately at six in the morning. So his sacrifice was really greater than hers, for he would be left in the equatorial bush bereft of a pinochle partner while she went to the cool highlands of the Mountains of the Moon.

"I understand," she said, "but I'd like to go to Dibela." Oddly, as soon as she had said it, she was eager to go, her ever quick imagination building and shaping the new station as the culmination of these years of service. Then Dr. Spencer looked at her strangely and said, "It'll be a pleasant change for you for a few months." He was guileless, a good and possibly a great man, but he did maintain a few prerogatives of comfort in his position of command. One of these was Rachel Cade, an undemanding daughter, who made life easier and more pleasant for him. He would not cast her to the wild dogs simply because young Dr. Morgan had let his instincts get out of control.

"For a few months?" she asked, trying to stifle a tone of disappointment. He nodded, and then he explained, slowly breaking down his customary reserve of doctor to nurse, of commander to subordinate.

"Dr. Bickel came out here too late in life," Dr. Spencer said. "He was always vague about his past, but he'd practiced in the Midwest and then something happened, I don't know what. Apparently he got bitten by the tropical bug and somehow he talked the people in New York into sending him out here and even into guaranteeing him the Dibela post, which he'd heard about somewhere, heaven knows where. It had been closed for a long time, and never was operated by our denomination. So he talked them into letting him reopen it as our mission." He stared at Rachel. "I've never had a chance to get up there. But one of our New York inspectors went through a year ago and he said it was a mess. Now Bickel's due for retirement in a few months. Then we'll close Dibela."

Rachel smiled wanly, not trying to hide her disappointment. "So I'll have a short stay in the high country—unless something happens." Dr. Spencer nodded, and then he said, "Why do you look sorry?" She could not explain to him.

But later she explained, or at least described her emotions, to herself.

She used a medium that had become not a habit but rather an infrequent necessity with her. A diary, she thought of it, though it was not an assiduously written daily record of names, places, weather and events. The small imitation-leather notebooks in which she'd written for several years contained gaps of days and often weeks. Some of the gaps represented periods of exhausting work; others marked periods of indifference when she doubted that she'd ever bother to write a line again. But she always did resume, sometimes sparely and at other times almost floridly expressing things which she could tell no one, not because they were scandalous but because she was sure they would be trivial to everyone but her. She often scratched out words and entire sentences, hunting the exact words to express what she intended. She read a great deal, critically, and she came to take great pleasure in trying to express herself as well as did those writers she admired. (She liked specific books rather than writers; she worshiped no literary cult.) Occasionally she wrote a few lines of unrhymed poetry of which she was ashamed.

Thus, after talking with Dr. Spencer that afternoon, she returned to her quarters and wrote:

Today I learned that I shall go to Dibela. My foolish imagination, always too volatile, flamed at the thought. I have heard there is a great need among those peoples near the mountains, and apparently their wants are not being fulfilled. Yet see the human vanity! I had a quick, vivid mental picture of my life here being like one of our great equatorial clouds at the beginning of the rainy season: a pillar, shaped by seemingly careless winds, which rises in splendor from the plains un-

til it forms a head and moves purposefully. Dibela, I thought, was the head of my cloud. Then Dr. Spencer said I won't stay there long, and it was as if the splendid cloud had begun to dissipate and would end formless. I must remember that vanity is the cardinal sin. I must not think of my "career" or of the pleasure of seeing new country, the high country, the Mountains of the Moon. I must remember that the people have enormous needs everywhere on this continent.

Now, looking around Dr. Bickel's cluttered room in Dibela, she thought, The cloud has dissipated even sooner than expected. Insects ticked against the Coleman lamp. Kulu and Kosongo and two others stood in the doorway watching her.

She rose from the bench and asked, "Where are the others?"

Kulu said, "This is all, Madami."

"All?" She strolled toward them. "This is the entire staff of Dibela?"

"The others have gone off," Kulu said.

So, she thought, these are all I can trust.

"Where is Musinga?"

Kulu looked at the floor. At last he said, "Musinga has gone to tell the people."

He must mean the people of the village, she thought. She had told them only to notify the people of the mission. Let it pass.

"What are your names?" she asked the two with Kulu and Kosongo.

One flashed a smile and said, "I'm Guta, your cook, Madami."

Your cook, she thought. She smiled and said, "I'm glad to meet you, Guta." She looked inquiringly at the other, who was short and broad-shouldered, with a broad, almost flat nose.

He stared at the floor. "I'm Mzimba."

"I'm glad to meet you, Mzimba. What do you do in the mission?"

He looked up at her defiantly. "I'm the carpenter."

"How many others went off?" she asked Kulu.

"Two, Madami."

"So they were afraid because Dr. Bickel had died," she said slowly. "What cowards!"

They stirred uneasily and did not look at her.

"Because, as you know, there's nothing to be afraid of. You show there isn't by staying. I think you're all fine, good men."

They grinned at her. Then Kulu said, "Musinga isn't afraid, Madami. He just went to tell the people."

Let it pass, she thought.

[33]

She had them carry the stretcher with Dr. Bickel's body into his bedroom. It and the kitchen were the only other rooms of the bungalow. The bed was a large walnut four-poster which the nameless Englishman must have dragged here somehow years ago. She closed the door. The body could not lie there awaiting inquest, undertaker and clergyman. Headquarters must be notified immediately. But headquarters was a thousand miles away. Oddly she realized she was glad. But why?

"Kulu," she said, "have you ever driven to Rugeri at night?"

"I can drive, Madami," he said quickly, "but someone will have to walk ahead with a torch. The lights of the car don't work."

It occurred to her she might feel afraid, cut off alone here, and then she realized happily that she was not. She controlled a smile. "And you can't fix the lights, Kulu?"

"I don't know how," he said. "Wanga in the village could do it. He was a soldier for a while and trained as a mechanic. But he's angry and won't fix the Doctor's car."

"Dr. Bickel must be buried here," she said slowly. "Tomorrow." She turned to Mzimba. "You will prepare a box."

"A box?" He could not or would not understand.

She realized it was some tabu, a fear perhaps of losing some of his own spirit in the box containing the white man's spirit. In a year and a half hadn't Dr. Bickel been able to infuse some idea of Christianity into even these who were loyal to him?

The hospital, she thought suddenly. In the midst of this she'd forgotten the hospital. They must have run off and left the patients. Snatching up her flashlight, she said quickly, "Show me to the hospital."

They went with her, feet padding close beside her in the darkness. The beam of her light stroked the woven mat walls and the great thatch of the long building. It was strange that no night lights burned inside. She passed through the doorway and swept her light over rows of empty cots.

"The patients!" she cried. "Where are the patients?"

"There are no patients, Madami," Kulu said softly.

Panic mounted in her. She could understand much, but the absence of any patients was incredible. Something was wrong here, more deeply wrong than she could comprehend.

At that moment she heard the signal drum, resonant and then fading in the night. Signal drums were illegal after nightfall.

She felt the sweat start on her palms and she told herself, Don't be silly, this is Africa, this isn't Hollywood in Africa. She remembered how they'd laughed at that movie about Africa a couple of years ago where the "natives" attacked the hero and his girl. But now she thought of the gun rack; she was glad she'd learned to use a gun. Silly, silly, silly! To turn a gun on our people? She was striding through the darkness from the hospital, the boys padding close behind her. The drum had stopped talking. There was no sound but the *ka-wack, ka-wack, ka-wack* of frogs somewhere, friendly as a spring evening in Kansas.

Then, faintly, came the answer of another drum. Her neck chilled and she gripped the flashlight tightly. If only she could read the hollow language of the drums. But she didn't need to. She knew they were discussing the death of Dr. Bickel.

She halted under the limbali tree and calmly told the boys to fetch her luggage from the bungalow to Dr. Bickel's house. They left her, hesitantly. She snapped off the light and walked with studied slowness through the darkness toward the glow of the Coleman lamp. When she reached the porch she no longer was afraid.

As she entered the house her glance fell on the packing case. It was, she noticed, about six feet long. And Dr. Bickel was a short man. Troubled, she thought, How callous. No tears for him, no sadness, only haste to get him under ground. Oh, it shouldn't be that way for anyone. He didn't deserve it, for he'd been a kind man sitting out there on the porch before he died.

Crossing the room to the long table, she began turning over papers and opening notebooks. The papers were yellowed and blank; there was nothing written in the notebooks. Blank, like his life here. Nowhere was there a clue, even a cryptic "Send my effects to Four Rivers, Nebraska." He was simply gone, his life but not his work completed.

When the boys set down her luggage, she told them to unpack the case of Swahili Bibles and texts. She watched them, noting their care with the books.

"Can any of you read?" she asked Kulu.

"No, Madami."

Guta served her a dinner of lukewarm soup and fried potatoes and an indistinguishable meat. The coffee wasn't bad, but she told herself she'd have to spend some time in the kitchen with Guta if she had time. Time? There never would be enough to accomplish the things that needed doing here, even if she could stay. And possibly, somehow, she would find a way to stay in Dibela. If it was God's will . . .

She strung a mosquito netting over the cot and extinguished the lamps and undressed in the dark. Pulling on her pajamas, she crept under the net and lay for some time listening to the drums talk.

Her sleep was troubled by dreams, and once she dimly heard the faint music of a dance: bleat of gourds and honk of conch shells and the throbbing of drums. Dawn seemed a long time coming.

She was fully dressed before she noticed a small object on the floor beside her cot. Picking it up, she examined it curiously. It was a small bit of curled animal skin containing a tiny pebble. It was, she knew, a medicine man's charm intended to destroy her. At first she was amused. Then, suddenly, she was angry. *They* would not drive her from Dibela.

She found a length of string in one of her bags and, threading the charm, she tied the string around her neck. Then she went to the kitchen to show Guta how to prepare a decent breakfast.

When Guta saw the charm hung about her neck, he howled in anguish and ran from the kitchen.

IV

MUSINGA AWAKENED in the shade of a mango tree, his head throbbing. Memories of last night returned slowly. He had gone with word of Dr. Bickel's death to the hut of Muwango, the chief medicine man. Then he had joined the dance, shuffling, leaping, strutting. He had drunk much pombe. Suddenly he retched at the memory of the thick banana beer, but his stomach was empty and nothing would leave him, not even memory. Ah, yes, and then he had come out here somewhere, perhaps under this very tree, with Nioki.

He looked around, but she had gone. Yet there, on the other side of the mango, was his loin cloth. Staggering to his feet, he bound up his loins and rested dizzily against the tree. But where were his pants, his shirt, his shoes and smock and spectacles? Gone! Lost in last night's happiness. For what was now an agony had been a happiness then as the wise and great men of Dibela honored him for bringing the news that had been promised long ago. Dr. Bickel had been struck down for the well-known reason. No white could stay here now; this was the land of the people.

So he must go. Go in the early morning, they had told him, and warn the white Madami to leave. Aieee, he would go now. But he must go as Doctor Musinga, and how could he go as Doctor Musinga without pants and smock and spectacles? He hopped in an anguish of indecision until his head throbbed so painfully that he moaned and clutched the tree.

At first he only felt the eyes, but then he saw them, watching him from the elephant grass. An unblinking pair of eyes in a bodiless, leathery face that hung in the elephant grass. He didn't try to make out who it was, for it didn't matter. It was one of *them*. How long had *they* been watching him?

He groaned, for he must go. And then he went, tottering, down the path through the elephant grass, feeling the eyes following him. Too soon the path emerged from the tall grass into someone's shamba. The village stretched ahead of him. Women stopped their pestle grinding and watched him; children stopped playing and watched him; two old men in the palaver house leaned forward and watched him. Their eyes drove him on like whips. Aieee, all remembered what he now wanted to forget. They remembered that he was Doctor Musinga on his way to take over the hospital.

He halted. What would happen to Doctor Musinga when the whites had gone? Wouldn't he become Musinga again? There was something puzzling here, something he'd like to lie down and think about for a day or two. But a procession of women and children and dogs had formed behind him so that he couldn't lie down. He had to go on toward the distant towering limbali tree. When he walked faster, the procession walked faster. When he halted, the procession halted. It swirled like the eddies of a river, swelling with streams of others who flowed from distant parts of the village, and, like a river, it moved with a low wordless murmur.

Now he walked slowly around a corner of a hut and there was the compound under the great limbali tree. There were Mzimba and Kosongo digging a hole under the tree, standing to their thighs in the hole, digging reluctantly. What were they up to? And there was Madami, wearing pants, standing over them. What magic was this? Oh, his throbbing head. There was Kulu cranking the car. Its motor caught with a roar and Kulu ran around to push down the thing that would stop the roaring. What was he doing?

"Jambo, Musinga." Madami looked at him.

Now he must tell her. Now the crowd murmur grew behind him and

[37]

Madami was looking at the crowd that spread along the edges of the compound. Suddenly he saw the death fetish tied about her neck and he knew that someone had delivered it to her in the night. He shrank from her.

"Musinga," she said, "U mzima?"

Was he well? she asked him. That was strange. He felt awful. But he would tell her he felt fine. "Ni mzima, Madami," he muttered.

Mzimba and Kosongo had stopped digging. They stood in the hole and gazed fearfully from Madami to the crowd. Kulu had made the motor quieter and stood by the car, looking from Madami to the crowd. Slowly he walked from the car and stood beside her.

"What are the people doing here, Musinga?" asked Madami. "What do they want?"

His lips were dry; he could not look at her. But finally he muttered, "They want you to go away, Madami." And once he had said it, he felt braver. He raised an arm and pointed dramatically toward the road from Dibela.

The crowd, impressed by his gesture, murmured approval.

"So you are of the crowd," Madami said. She did not sound angry or afraid. She simply sounded disappointed. Unreasonably, he did not want to disappoint her, but it was too late now.

"Musinga," said Madami, "you have been drunk and now you're getting over your drunkenness. But you feel awful. Your head throbs."

He fell back a step, shrinking from her. How did she know? What was her magic?

"But I'll give you something to make you feel better." She turned and walked swiftly into the bungalow while the crowd watched silently.

If the crowd had not been there, he would have run. Kulu and Mzimba and Kosongo looked at him, but he stared vacantly over their heads. Then Madami was back with a bottle of white pills and a gourd cup of water.

"Here, Musinga," she said, "take two of these and you'll feel better soon."

He fell back another step. So she would poison him to prevent his taking command of the hospital.

"Musinga," she said dryly, "are you afraid to take a couple of aspirin from our own hospital?"

A voice trumpeted in the crowd and people stood aside to let old Muwango, the great medicine man, come forward. He stood there, withered and bony under his baboon-skin cape, shaking his rattle and calling, "Ikiwa mtu atakuja akakuambia kama anayo dawa ya ugonjwa huu, usimsadiki!"

It was a saying well known in Dibela for a long time: "If one comes and says he has medicine for your disease, don't believe him." Muwango was trying to help him out, Musinga knew.

Madami raised her head. "You," she called to Muwango, "do you have a better medicine?"

"Aieee!" he shouted to the crowd, prancing back and forth and shaking his rattle. "This foolish one asks if I have a better medicine." He slapped a hand against his narrow chest. "I cure everybody of everything. I am Muwango, the wisest of the wise."

"All right, Muwango, wisest of the wise," said Madami, "cure Musinga of his headache."

Muwango, wisest of the wise, strode from the crowd to the shade of the limbali tree. Three times he circled Musinga, shaking his rattle deafeningly, and suddenly and deftly he knotted a thong around Musinga's head so tightly that Musinga almost howled with pain. But since this was Muwango and since this was a cure, he did not howl. Muwango thrust his face close, fixing him with enormous eyes, and said, "You are better." His head throbbed badly, even after Muwango removed the thong. But since this was the cure and the people watched, he nodded.

Madami smiled at him oddly. "So your head has stopped aching, Musinga?"

"Yes," he said. "Yes!" he cried so the crowd could hear. Muwango howled with glee and the crowd murmured its approval and a few shouted.

"Very well then," said Madami, "you won't need aspirin." She poured the water from the gourd and slipped the bottle of pills into a pocket. "Now—" she turned to Kulu—"you will drive off on your mission, Kulu."

"Yes, Madami," he said and started toward the car.

"And Mzimba and Kosongo, we must dig this hole much deeper," she said.

They stared up at her for a moment, and then they slowly began to dig again. It was infuriating, thought Musinga. They acted as if nothing had happened, as if they didn't know he had taken command. But had he really taken command? Oh, his aching head! And that Kulu, acting as if he were number-one boy. That was the most insulting slap of all.

"You, Kulu!" he cried wrathfully.

Kulu turned.

"Don't you touch that car!"

Kulu grinned. "I serve Madami," he called.

"You serve me!" cried Musinga.

"But you do not serve Madami," said Kulu and climbed into the car.

"Try not to damage the roots of the tree any more than you must," Madami said to Mzimba and Kosongo. As if he were not here at all.

Uncontrollably he hopped a couple of times, but it hurt his head so that he stopped. The crowd murmured and Muwango shouted incoherently and the mattocks of Mzimba and Kosongo sounded *chuck-chuck-chuck* in the hole. He looked from Madami to the crowd and he knew he was the loneliest one in all the land. He stood here in the shade of the limbali with the people all around him and he ached with loneliness.

The car with Kulu at the wheel jerked to the road and then stopped. There came the drone of an approaching car, growing louder. It flashed beyond the row of huts that lined the road and swung into the compound, the driver sweeping impressively to the shadow of the big tree. The people murmured and then were still as from it stepped the Bwana Administrator.

Rachel did not realize tension had mounted in her until that moment when Lecomte strolled from his car in fresh khaki, smiling and nodding to her and tapping his crop, that wand of authority, against his leg.

"Miss Cade," he said, "it looks as if you're putting on a pageant here." He extended his hand and bowed over hers and murmured, "Allow me for the benefit of the players," and kissed her hand. "It will impress the people." He smiled. "And I rather enjoy it myself, though I'm not as graceful at it as I once was."

She took a deep breath. "I was just sending Kulu to you with a message. Dr.—"

"I know." He nodded gravely. "Dr. Bickel is dead."

"But how— Oh, the drums last night."

"Yes, the local radio." He gestured toward the crowd. "But what's all this?"

"I don't exactly know," Rachel said. "But I gather it's a delegation requesting me to leave Dibela."

"The stone-heads," growled Lecomte. "The hopeless stone-heads."

"No."

"Yes!" he said sharply. "They're just as they were fifty years ago except they've given up cannibalism—in general. I'll send a squad of police out here until—"

"Until?" asked Rachel.

His shoulders slumped. "Until, I'm sorry to say, Miss Cade, you leave Dibela. I'd be happy if you'd come back to Rugeri and stay with me—with us. But as you know we just can't have whites leaving places immediately some blacks say they must go." He looked at Musinga. "Who is this standing center stage?"

"Musinga," Rachel said, "Dr. Bickel's number-one boy."

"What's he trying to do?"

"I'm not sure. I'm only sure that he doesn't know exactly what he's doing himself. His most pressing immediate problem, I judge, is a bad headache from drinking banana beer."

"You, Musinga," Lecomte snapped, "come here."

Musinga came to them slowly, head lowered, and there was no sound from the people.

"What's bothering you?" asked Lecomte.

"Nothing, Bwana," Musinga said meekly.

"Did you tell Miss Cade to leave Dibela?"

"No, Bwana Administrator," Musinga said to Lecomte's feet. He glanced at Rachel's feet. "Maybe the Madami didn't understand."

"The dialect's a little difficult," Rachel said dryly.

"You know this could mean a few seasons in the jailhouse," Lecomte growled.

Musinga moaned and clutched his head.

"Do you want some pills now, Musinga?" asked Rachel.

He moaned again and nodded.

"Take the aspirin and go sleep it off," Lecomte said.

Rachel shook three aspirin from the bottle and handed them to Musinga. He tilted his head, closed his eyes, and swallowed them as the crowd murmured.

"I wonder how accurate a story you're telling me, Miss Cade." Lecomte looked at her with amusement.

"Accurate enough." Thoughtfully she watched Musinga collapse under the limbali and fold his arms over his head. "I suppose it's your duty to—to view the body."

Lecomte nodded. "I'm everything here. Great white father and coroner too." He called to his green-uniformed driver who leaned against the car and spat contemptuously toward the people of Dibela. "Summon Chief Buderga!" As he turned toward the bungalow with Rachel he glanced at Musinga. "I'd say you need a new number-one boy."

[41]

Poor Musinga, she thought. But he must be reduced because he could not be trusted. "I already have one," she said. "Kulu."

"For the short time you have left here."

On the bungalow porch she paused and faced him. "I won't be leaving here, Monsieur Lecomte."

His *"Comment?"* was incredulous.

"I have a feeling that I won't leave."

"A feeling!" His tone, his shoulders, caricatured her so aptly that she smiled. "Feminine intuition, I suppose. Well, Miss Cade, I'm sure that when your telegram reaches headquarters they'll immediately order you to close Dibela and return."

She did not answer him as she led the way into the bedroom. He looked at Dr. Bickel's body. Briefly she told him how he had died.

"There's a small cemetery south of Rugeri," he said slowly. "At the mission—the Catholic mission. It is—uh—consecrated ground—"

"I think," Rachel said, "we should bury him here. Under the limbali tree. This morning."

He nodded. "That is wise. I considered bringing Father Gilo with me this morning. He's a good fellow. Of course, he's Catholic—Franciscan—"

"And Dr. Bickel was Protestant. But not, I'm sure, a bigot. It doesn't matter, Monsieur Lecomte. Although I never have been ordained, I can read a little service." She shook her head. "This haste to get him under ground—" She turned away. "I can find no record of any next of kin— But it's the way it must be done."

"Miss Cade!" He was standing close to her, his voice suddenly sharp. "What's that thing around your neck?"

She smiled. "A fetish. It was left by my cot last night. It's intended to cause my death."

Lecomte swore and then apologized. "Buderga will have to answer to—"

"Monsieur Lecomte." She touched his arm lightly. "Don't be an alarmist. You've been in Africa a very long time and I'm sure you've received such gifts many times in backward areas."

"Yes, but—"

"Then sit down for a moment and have a cup of coffee before we—before— Guta!" She stepped to the kitchen door and asked him to bring coffee, smiling at him as he eyed the fetish about her neck. When she turned, Lecomte was looking at her. Admiringly, she realized, before he set his expression in official disapproval.

[42]

"We were discussing my—intuition about staying here." She sat down. "I plan to do what I can to help my intuition."

He examined his soiled bush hat critically. "Do? What will you do, Miss Cade? Pray?"

She frowned at his tone of irony. "I'm not much given to praying—formally. I'm sorry to say that, but I'm not. I'm more given to sitting quietly with my eyes open and hoping. So I've been hoping that a way can be found to keep this station open. Without a doctor, if there cannot be one—at first."

"But why?" He stared at her.

"It shouldn't be necessary to tell you why. You know the state of the people here—illiterate, many diseased, ridden with superstition—"

"Of course." He raised his hands in a gesture that, she thought, a man named Pilate must have used. "I know it as if I had read it in a book. I shake my head and say, 'Too bad, too bad.' I'm against it, as I'm against ignorance and poverty and disease everywhere. But what can I do about it? How can I let it affect *me*?" He leaned toward her. "Why does it affect *you*, Miss Cade?"

She had heard this sort of argument before. It had been advanced by friends in Kansas City several years ago when she'd announced her intention of coming to Africa. She never had thought of a ready answer.

Now, her gaze falling before his, she said, "Perhaps just because I was born to be—affected. Also I like this place. I like that great limbali tree. I—I like the sense of the mountains rising there. Monsieur Lecomte, has anyone climbed the mountains from here?"

He raised a hand. Censoriously, it seemed to her, as if he would delete her question. "No." His tone was brusque. "It's impossible. Forget about the mountains, Miss Cade." He smiled faintly. "Let me say one thing. I'm glad you don't indulge in sanctimonious cant on why you want to stay here. You candidly admit you want to stay because you like the country. Doesn't that—" his voice grew gentle—"make you what nearly all of us whites here in Africa are? An adventurer."

It was true, she thought. At least it was partially true. And even the partial truth troubled her. She did not want to be a mere adventurer, using Christianity as a boat and medicine as the sails that carried her far from a monotonous existence in the States in quest of—what? Excitement? She wished to be—what? Not fanatical. No, she wished only to be pure in purpose, to be—dedicated to a cause so great that the comforts of the flesh, the small triumphs of the personality would fade to their proper insignificance.

[43]

"Come now—" She knew by his expression that he understood her thoughts; yes, he was a fine and understanding man. "Come now, Miss Cade, it's not so bad to be an adventurer. But let's call ourselves instead— explorers. Explorers achieve, don't they? And adventurers only enjoy." He sighed. "But I fear we're talking in air. For in a week or so you'll leave and return—"

"No," she said firmly. "I'm not sending a telegram from your office at Rugeri. I explain it in the note I was sending you by Kulu. I'm mailing a letter to headquarters. I wrote it this morning. Kulu has it."

"But a letter won't reach your headquarters for a week—ten days."

She nodded. "Exactly. That's what I mean by helping my intuition. In the letter I was able to explain—to—to suggest."

He smiled slowly. "Fighting for time, eh? As they're doing in Europe now. If that's what they're doing. And that's another thing, Miss Cade— that war. I think it will go on for a long time and envelop the world. Certainly it will affect us here. It will be a reason you cannot stay here. Here in Africa we'll be cut off. There won't be a doctor available for Dibela. There won't be medicine . . ."

But, she thought, there still would be confused people like Musinga asleep out there under the limbali tree. There would be ill people like that obviously syphilitic youth out there in the crowd that had pressed near the Administrator's car.

Lecomte's uniformed driver suddenly stood at the foot of the steps with a tall, finely proportioned man who wore the amulets of power and whose broad strong face bore an expression of calm assurance.

"Pardon me." Lecomte rose and strolled to the head of the stairs. He looked down at Chief Buderga coldly. "Jambo, Chief. Why are the people here? Is there no working in Dibela today?"

Buderga's gaze fell and he did not answer.

"Pardon me," Rachel said, passing Lecomte and descending the steps. She extended her hand. "I am Miss Cade. I'm glad to meet you, Chief Buderga."

His large eyes met hers quickly and away, to the fetish about her neck and away. Slowly he touched his hand to hers.

"Please come in and have some coffee with the Administrator and me." She took him by the arm, feeling his resistance, as she led him up the steps. Lecomte was looking at her in astonishment. "It is not a wise idea, Miss Cade."

"I think it's an excellent idea, Monsieur Lecomte. I'm sure you don't treat other chiefs this way."

Guta stood there, his eyes wide, the tray shaking in his hands. "Thank you, Guta. Bring another cup at once." She took the tray. "Please sit down, Chief Buderga." She nodded to a chair, and he lowered himself into it cautiously, reluctantly. She poured a cup of coffee and handed it to him. He took it with both hands, in the universal African gesture of courtesy that recognizes the acceptance of anything in only one hand as a contemptuous act. His politeness pleased her and she thought, these too are fine people and there's just one thing wrong, some one thing I do not yet understand . . .

"Chief," said Lecomte after he had carefully taken the cup of coffee in both hands from Rachel, "your signal drums were beating last night. In the darkness they were doing a great talking while good people slept."

For a long time Buderga looked at the floor. At last he said, "Young men often do not sleep well. I've told them they must sleep better. I've told them it's forbidden to disturb the night with drums."

"And there was much dancing, I understand," said Lecomte.

"Aieee, the young men." Buderga shook his head.

"And today there is much idleness."

"Aieee," said Buderga.

"And in the night someone brought a gift to Miss Cade."

Buderga almost, but not quite, glanced at the fetish.

"She wears it now," said Lecomte, "to show her contempt for such foolishness. Do you think it will cause her death, Chief?"

"Aieee." Buderga peered sadly into his cup.

Rachel sipped her coffee and said, "There is good coffee grown here in the higher lands. Drink, Chief Buderga." She saw the sweat bead his forehead, and somewhere in the distant crowd a voice wailed. Oh, their fear was incredible. How had it begun? How could Dr. Bickel have failed so badly?

Buderga closed his eyes and lifted the cup to his lips with trembling hands. He opened his eyes wide and gazed at the Administrator. Then, closing them again, he threw back his head and drank the coffee. He coughed and set the cup on the floor.

"Why don't the people take the medicine of the hospital, Chief Buderga?" She could have bitten her tongue at the impetuous question, knowing the folly of asking one of these people the *why* of anything. Who, what, where, when they understood. But *why* was a question of civilization; perhaps it was the beginning of civilization, carrying with it the seeds of civilization's destruction. Yet they had a civilization too, an old and complex civilization rooted in this tropic husk of earth and bearing immemorial laws. They had a *why* if only she could be given the time to understand it.

"Why?" demanded Lecomte heavily, knowing the folly of the question as well as she, and yet suddenly impatient.

Buderga fingered his belly. "It is said they have a bad medicine."

It is said, thought Rachel. Would she ever learn who said it and *why*? But she was going at it badly, she knew.

"It is good medicine," she said. And then, smiling when he looked at her, conveying friendliness and a trace of mystery, "We shall see."

The mystery of her "We shall see" quickened his interest, she realized. Mystery was, after all, a common denominator of all civilizations, as food and love and sleep.

They looked up, then, at the sound of a car. In a moment a dusty Chevrolet swung into the compound. "Father Gilo," Lecomte said, rising. A short, fat man clambered out of the car. He wore sandals and white habit. Seeing Lecomte, he waved and plodded toward the bungalow, smiling at the Africans. His face was burned by sun, and within its roundness, thought Rachel, were the strong lips and nose of a thin man, a disciplined, an ascetic man. But his roundness, his mild blue eyes, the thin fuzz of blond hair that rose like a diadem above his broad brow reminded her of country priests she had seen in the Rhone Valley on her one trip to France. Now he stared at her in frank amazement.

"Henri," he said to Lecomte, "there is always something new in this country."

"Georges," said Lecomte, "this is Miss Cade, the—the new nurse. Father Gilo, Miss Cade."

He smiled and clasped her hand firmly. "My drum-talker must have failed me. He understood that Dr. Bickel—that—"

"He was right," Rachel said. "Dr. Bickel died last night a few minutes after I arrived."

Father Gilo bowed his head and crossed himself. "I'm sorry. I did not know him well, but I came to see if I could—do anything."

"You're most kind," Rachel said. "I—we—" She raised her hands helplessly. "He told me he had angina. And then he—" She looked toward the limbali. "We're going to bury him here this morning."

After she introduced Father Gilo to Buderga, the Chief suddenly turned and left.

"Rude fellow," Lecomte said, watching him go.

"I don't know," Rachel said. "I think he has a lot of dignity. If you will excuse me, I'll change. And then I think—"

"Yes." Lecomte looked at Father Gilo. "It is better that we do it now."

Rachel changed into a dress quickly. When she came out of the bedroom, Father Gilo looked at her reflectively. "Henri tells me you want to stay here, Miss Cade."

She smiled. "Yes. And now I suppose you too will tell me how impossible it is."

Father Gilo shook his head. "To the contrary, I hope you can stay. This country needs as many of us as possible."

Us, she thought with a small inward burst of pleasure. So he recognized there was not just one church or order that could do what needed to be done here. He had none of the un-Christian designs of empire that sometimes marked both Catholic and Protestant in this land.

"I'm glad," she said. "I'm so glad you feel that way, Father Gilo," and she moved toward him warmly, instinctively. Then she paused, blushing slightly, realizing she had been too—feminine. For, while he continued to smile, the thin ascetic face within the round benign face had suddenly taken control and he was not looking directly at her but at some invisible point just beyond her.

"There's a great need here at the foot of the mountains," he said. "We've often thought that we—at our mission—might come into this country. But we don't have anyone to send and the need is great below Rugeri too. Besides, your church has— Well, I won't say this is *your* country. But we do not want to proselytize when there are so many vast areas where there is—nothing."

"And I'm afraid," she said, "there's been nothing here too." She looked at Lecomte.

"Let us proceed," he said gravely. "If you'll permit Father Gilo and me, we'll—" He nodded toward the room where Dr. Bickel's body lay.

Awkwardly she explained about the packing case. For an instant the whole grim necessity seemed too ghoulish. She suddenly felt distraught and helpless. Then she was ashamed of herself. She was, she thought, trying to improvise emotion for a situation in which she basically felt nothing. Dr. Bickel was nothing to her, a voice in the night talking about Nebraska, and yet . . .

An hour later, when the wrapped body had been laid in the case, when Lecomte had made sure that the grave was much deeper than she would have thought necessary, when clouds had obscured the sun and rain was imminent, she stood on the porch looking at the people who still waited silently. Then, for one instant, she fought back tears and fingered the slips of paper she had inserted in the Bible.

[47]

"Now," Lecomte said gently behind her.

She went down the steps, looking straight ahead at the limbali, clutching the Bible in her right hand. Behind her she heard Lecomte catch his breath as he and Father Gilo bore the packing case, the frail coffin that would rot too quickly in the humus of limbali roots. They were trying to carry it gravely, decorously and they must have staggered on the steps. She did not look back.

Under the tree stood Kulu and Guta and Mzimba and Kosongo and Lecomte's driver. Yes, and even Musinga stood there, a little apart, yet staying and not joining the murmuring crowd beyond that stared at the strange rite of the people from the distant places. They watched her and she felt a great inadequacy. A missionary? She knew only certain familiar parts of the Bible and the finer points of theology always had puzzled her. She was, she thought, just a woman volunteer from Trego County, Kansas, a nurse, as Dr. Bickel had been only a man volunteer from Nebraska, a baffled stranger in this alien land. And now he was dead and she did not know what to do about his immortal soul.

Lecomte and Father Gilo, sweating, rested the box by the open grave. She opened the Bible to the place she had marked, to the fourteenth chapter of John. Suddenly she realized she was facing not the crowd but the mountains invisible in mist. But she did not turn, she faced the mountains as she read in a voice that gained confidence slowly:

"Let not your heart be troubled (said Jesus): believe in God; believe also in me. In my Father's house are many mansions . . ."

When she had finished the passage, she turned to the 121st Psalm:

"I will lift up mine eyes unto the hills: From whence cometh my help? My help cometh from the Lord, who made heaven and earth . . ."

Then she closed the Bible and nodded to Father Gilo, who prayed. And when his prayer was ended he and Lecomte took the ropes which Lecomte had lashed about the box and they lowered the box into the grave. Then Father Gilo dropped a handful of brown earth onto the box and said something in Latin she did not understand. He made the sign of the cross and stepped back. And Kulu, as he had been told, stepped forward with a spade and began to fill the grave.

So it was done, she thought, as it began to rain. Then she thought that nothing was done.

They followed her silently to the bungalow. During lunch it seemed that they could think of little to say. After lunch Lecomte lighted a cigar and strolled out on the porch and stared at the gray pouring rain.

"I think we should be going, Miss Cade," he said. "The road is bad in rain. I'll send a couple of policemen out. They'll be here by nightfall—I hope."

She shook her head. "Thank you, no. No police, Monsieur Lecomte."

He cleared his throat. "The grave. It should be watched—for a while."

"I know. We'll watch it."

"I mean," he said, "at night."

"I know. We—Kulu and the rest of us—will watch it."

"But—"

Father Gilo rested a hand on Lecomte's arm. "Miss Cade can take care of things, Henri," he said gently.

"There's just one question I haven't asked you, Monsieur Lecomte." Rachel looked at him steadily. "Have you any idea why the people wanted Dr. Bickel to die?"

He looked away. "Some superstition," he muttered. "No, I don't know, Miss Cade."

He was not telling the truth, she thought. But why? If it were for a reason he thought ridiculous, wouldn't he tell her? Then could it be for a reason he vaguely thought was valid?

She put on a raincoat and walked through the rain with them to their cars. Waving once as they drove away, she turned to the limbali. Kulu stood beside the grave. He wore a poncho and rested on a long hunting spear.

"The spear," she said as she approached. "You have a spear, Kulu?"

"Yes, Madami."

"Who told you to bear a spear?"

"The Bwana Administrator told me to guard the grave, Madami. I am guarding it."

She nodded. "Rest for a while, Kulu. Come in and eat before you guard again."

He followed her through the rain to the bungalow. On the porch she turned to him.

"The people believe Dr. Bickel died because he was being punished, don't they, Kulu?"

"Yes, Madami."

"What did he do that he should be punished?"

Kulu looked away. At last he said, "He tried to climb the mountains, Madami."

V

As THE DAYS PASSED, Rachel pondered what Kulu had said. His answers to her further questions were vague. He was not consciously trying to hide something from her, she believed. Rather, she must have asked about a tabu. And, she thought, it usually was futile to ask anyone, either "primitive" African or "civilized" Caucasian, about the reasons for a tabu. Why, for example, did Europeans consider it ill-mannered for a man to step through a doorway ahead of a woman when neither knew what catastrophe waited beyond? And why, by the same sort of illogic, should these people not consider it in the worst possible taste to try to climb the mountains?

She discussed the matter at length in her diary. Why a tabu? Did it not seem natural that a people living at the foot of high mountains should want to climb them? And then she read in one of Dr. Bickel's books on Mount Everest that in times past the Tibetans had been afraid to climb the mountains soaring above them. So, if it were a tabu, it was based on a common human instinct.

But the question that interested her most was whether Dr. Bickel had known he was defying a tabu when he set out alone for the mountains. Had he gone purposefully, or had he merely blundered to the mountains as he seemed to have blundered into everything he attempted here? She remembered what Lecomte had told her of the nameless English missionary who had wandered off toward the mountains and disappeared. He must have reinforced belief in the tabu when he disappeared. And then Bickel, dying of angina, which perhaps was induced by the strain of trying an ascent. She asked Kulu how far he had climbed. Kulu said he did not know, but it could not have been far beyond his own village, a day's walk up the spurs, because he had become lost and returned in a few days.

She thought of these things most often in the evening. In the darkness, as insects ticked against the Coleman lamp or rain fell, she wrote in her diary or read or mended her clothing. Whenever she saw something rather pathetic in herself sitting alone by a lamp, out here back of beyond alone, without husband or child or even property, she'd ask herself what was a better place or circumstance. Not Kansas City, where radios blared by open windows and neon lights scarred the night. Not the wheat fields, those limitless acres of dark silence, where someone—who? where is he going? who?—passed on the lonely road, whistling in the night. She'd take this, the cries of jackals and hyenas, the dance drums, and, on two consecutive nights, the grumble of a wandering lion. Perhaps Lecomte was right, she thought. Perhaps she was only an adventurer.

The hopelessness of her situation grew more evident to her with each succeeding day. She kept busy, but business became, she thought, only a means of disguising hopelessness. She brought physical order from the chaos Dr. Bickel had left. She untangled his personal interests from the hospital interests, placing his books and effects aside and organizing a neat dispensary of medicine. With Kulu and Kosongo and Mzimba and Guta she cleaned up the hospital and waited for a patient. She called on Chief Buderga and was received coldly. She walked through the village and the people turned from her. Musinga would not talk to her. He seemed unacceptable to the four loyal men, though he still ate with them and passed his days mournfully playing his likembe under the limbali. Yet he also was unacceptable to Dibela now. He lived in limbo.

Kulu she trusted above all. He was the most intelligent, the most courageous. He was the only one who would stand guard alone at night over Dr. Bickel's grave. Everyone at the mission understood the reason for the guard. There were animals, yes; but there also were men. It was not easy to fathom the reasons that sometimes led men to dig up the graves of the dead in a place like Dibela. Usually they dug up the body of a beloved strong man and ate the putrefying flesh to attain his strength. But occasionally they dug up the body of an enemy. That was why Lecomte had said a guard must be posted for a couple of weeks.

One night, about a week after Dr. Bickel died, she took a cup of hot coffee out to Kulu when he was on guard beside the grave. His teeth gleamed when the beam of her flashlight touched him.

"It's a long night, Kulu."

"Yes, Madami." He rested his spear against the tree and took the cup of coffee in both hands and thanked her.

"In another week we shall end the guard."

"Yes, Madami." He drank and sighed. "You will be here, Madami?" It was the first time he had questioned the future.

"I shall be here, Kulu."

"I'm glad."

[51]

And that was the first time she'd heard him express an opinion about anything.

"The hospital needs patients, Kulu."

"Yes, Madami. I've thought that if I could get sick you could cure me and then you'd have a patient."

She smiled. "But you're more important to the hospital well, Kulu."

"I have thought that too, Madami. So I shan't be sick. I've never been sick. But maybe, Madami, I could pretend to be sick and everybody would say, 'Ah, that Kulu is dying,' and then you could give me a pill and I'd get all better and everybody would say, 'Ah, the Madami gave Kulu good medicine,' and then others would come to get the good medicine."

"No, Kulu, we cannot do that."

"No, Madami."

"Do you know why?"

"No, Madami."

"Because it would be dishonest. One cannot do a bad thing—a false thing—in order to accomplish something he hopes will be good. It's like— There was a man whose children were hungry in time of famine and he stole a goat from the shamba of a friendly neighbor. He killed the goat and told his wife to cook it. She cried out at what he'd done. For, unknown to him, the neighbor had been giving his wife the goat's milk to keep his children alive. They lived for a few days on the goat meat before the children died of famine."

"That's a good story, Madami," Kulu said. "I'll think of it all night. Perhaps Madami knows some other fine stories."

"Yes. I do," Rachel said slowly. "Tomorrow after lunch we'll all get together and I shall tell you a story. And then—tell me, Kulu, would you like to learn to read?"

"Yes, Madami." His voice rose in excitement. "Oh, yes, I would."

So the next afternoon Kulu and Kosongo and Guta and Mzimba sat before her under the limbali. In the clutter of hospital possessions she had found chalk and a small blackboard which she propped against a stick driven into the ground.

"We're going to learn to read," she said. "It will take a long time, but we shall learn. Then we can know fine stories and the true tales of other people. Now, you are Bantu—and, as you know, Bantu means 'The People.' You are a great people—"

"Aieee," Mzimba said involuntarily, nodding his head. "Excuse me, Madami."

[52]

"That's all right, Mzimba. Any of you speak up whenever you wish."
Kulu raised a hand, palm out, to the level of his chin.

"Yes, Kulu?"

"We are great, Madami? But our skins are black."

"That makes no difference, Kulu. You are a great people."

They murmured and nodded to one another.

"There are millions of you. That is, you are numerous as the grass of the plain. You live here on the plain and far down into the bush to the great western ocean. You live to the north of the mountains and south of the mountains and you live beyond the mountains."

"Ah!" Kulu's eyes widened. "Beyond the mountains, Madami?"

"Beyond the mountains, Kulu. Dibela is not the whole land." Stooping, she raised a pinch of dust. "Here is Dibela." She let the dust fall to the ground. "Here is the land." She gestured to the compound.

They nodded, understanding.

"In the beginning all were brothers—" She paused. Where would she lead them now? She should have prepared for this. She was not a teacher. She was a nurse. But now she must teach. "All sons of one Father. God."

In the shade their eyes strained up at her whitely.

"You have heard of God."

They stared at the ground.

"You have not heard of God?"

At last Kulu raised his head boldly. "We have heard of God, Madami. He lives in the mountains."

Her neck chilled in the afternoon heat. In the mountains? Of course the Bantu knew there was a God, as did all people everywhere. But they preferred not to think of Him, even as the most civilized preferred not to think of Him. Yet she had not heard before that He dwelt in the mountains.

"God is the Father of us all," she went on slowly. "He is kind and loving."

They were looking at her skeptically. Kulu raised his hand to his chin again, and when she nodded to him, he said, "Tell us a story about God, Madami."

Now she remembered what friends of hers, the best missionary teachers, had told her. It was easy to explain the stern God of Moses to the people, for they understood His harshness. He was the passionate tropic God of famine and pestilence and storm and the stalking lion. But it was difficult to explain the God who sent His understanding Son to earth.

She glanced up, almost desperately, as if help might come from the

[53]

thick branches of the limbali. A green dove rose from the tree and was immediately invisible in sunlight. Theological authorities doubtless would disapprove of what she now would say.

"God is the Father. He walks on earth at all times, everywhere, though He is not visible, listening to all people and looking into their hearts to see what lies there."

They looked about and then at her, searchingly. And, seeing she was not being humorous now but was speaking with the authority of knowledge, they believed her. She was sure they believed her.

"One day when God was walking through the earth," she continued, "He became discouraged with the way people had forgotten His existence. He said to Himself, 'I shall send a Son to earth in visible form to explain to them there is much evil in the land.' Indeed the land was bad. There was much killing and stealing and eating of one another. So God's Son was born on earth and His name was Jesus, the Christ."

Kulu raised his hand. "Pardon me, Madami, but this Jesus the Christ, was He a black man or a white man?"

How had she been led into this? She was only a nurse, a woman from a Kansas farm.

"That is an interesting question, Kulu. It happened many years ago and the color of His skin does not matter now. The white people say He was white. The black people say He was black. You would be wise to think of Him as coming to earth with black skin. For God, His Father, is Father of both black and white. So He was born and grew to manhood and performed great acts of wisdom and understanding—acts we shall read about when we have learned to read—and He told stories which I shall tell you while you're learning to read. Still, many people would not listen to Him and finally they grew angry with Him and they killed Him."

"They killed Him!" exclaimed Kosongo.

"They killed His body. He could have avoided it, but He chose not to be a coward."

"And God, His Father, let them kill Him?" asked Kulu.

"Yes. Because God understood they could not kill His spirit. You see, some of the people with whom He lived and worked understood His great teachings and they carried His words on and they spread throughout the earth. Now His spirit and His teachings are abroad in the land. They are candles of wisdom and truth against the darkness of the world."

"It's a sad story," said Kosongo.

"It's a good story," Kulu said. "It is like the brave hunter who is slain by the leopard. The good hunter's spirit grows stronger." He looked at Rachel alertly. "Madami, then you come here with the good spirit of Jesus the Christ?"

"I do," Rachel murmured.

"And it's against the spirit of Muwango, the medicine man?"

"Yes," she said slowly, "against his spirit. But the struggle is not of the flesh. Do you understand?"

"I understand, Madami."

She knew that he did. Looking at their faces, she knew that Mzimba and Kosongo would understand, though it was doubtful if Guta ever would. Guta already had improved in his cooking and he would grow better under her instructions. But, she thought, he never would understand about the spirit.

"Now let us begin to learn to read," she said, taking a bit of chalk from a pocket of her slacks and turning to the blackboard. "Listen to the letters as I form them. *A* . . ." She pronounced it in the Swahili, *a* as in the English *father,* though not quite as deep, and she began to form the magic letters.

The letter *D* was a crooked man leaning on a staff and the letter *B* was a crooked man on a crooked man leaning on a staff. When Madami pointed to those letters on the board, Kulu identified them and stepped back, smiling outside and singing inside. He could identify all the letters Madami had written on the board, but he'd better not or the others would think he was bragging.

Madami stood there, one hand in a pocket, her great spirit shining from her eyes and her soft hair trembling in a soft breeze as if God the Father or Jesus the Christ were passing near. Now it was the third day of the great lessons under the limbali tree. The afternoon rain had drifted west on its constant circling and sun shone on the bright world. Looking up and away east, he saw the glint of sun on snow, far up there on the mountains. Madami didn't see it, and he wondered if he should interrupt the lesson to point it out to her, for she always was asking him about the mountains. But he'd better not—there, the snow was lost in clouds again —for he did not like to talk about the mountains to Madami. It reminded him that he had not told her the—story. Someday he would. Someday, someday. He didn't want to discourage her, though he knew the story wouldn't discourage her. Still, he didn't want to do anything that would help make Madami leave. For when she went he would have to go with her, following her out into the strange world to serve her always. He did not want to leave this land, his home. But if she went, he would go too. Madami did not seem to know it, but she needed somebody to protect and care for the needs of her body, that worship house of her great spirit. If anybody ever tried to hurt her, like they did Jesus the Christ, he would kill them. He could do it. Until Madami came here he did not know who he was. That is, he had forgotten. He had thought he was Kulu, a country boy who came to the city of Dibela and became a houseboy, an instrument of Musinga's. But now Madami made him realize he was Kulu of the lower mountain slopes, climber to the cloud line in defiance of his father, strong runner, mighty hunter who had slain a leopard.

Faintly, from the sleeping hut behind Madami's house, came the plaintive notes of Musinga's likembe. He should hate Musinga for the way he'd treated Madami, but he couldn't. Poor Musinga, the dogs barked at him in the village and the old men spat on the ground behind him. He was nothing. But when he, Kulu, went through the village the dogs did not bark nor the old men spit. They shunned him because he was of the mission, but they did not hold him in contempt as they did Musinga.

Ho, look who was coming into the compound now, walking slowly, walking with his head down. Wanga, wearing his tattered shorts, last remnant of his soldiering days. Wanga, with a body deceptively strong, like the thin wires in the belly of the car, but with no spirit these seasons since he came back to Dibela and got a wife who worked his shamba. Now Wanga halted several yards from Madami and looked at her doubtfully.

"Jambo, Wanga," Kulu said. "This is Wanga, Madami. Wanga was a soldier and he came back."

Madami strolled to him and touched the hand he reluctantly raised to hers. "I'm glad to meet you, Wanga. We're learning to read here under the limbali. May I help you in some way?"

Wanga looked at the ground and then defiantly at her. "I do not like this hospital. It is not like the good hospitals I've seen in other places. Your doctor did not cure my son. He died. He made bad medicine."

"Perhaps no one could have cured your son, Wanga."

"They could have cured him in Stan." He looked at her proudly. "I have been in Stan. I have been a soldier. I'm sorry I came back."

"Perhaps we can try to make this a better place," Rachel said.

"This is a bad place," Wanga said. "I'm sorry I came back. Now I have no place else to go."

"Would you sit down with us?"

Wanga shook his head. "Now my other son is sick too. I think he'll die

[56]

because I saw a man die with this once in the west. It is here." He laid a hand on his belly. "These fools like Muwango can set a broken leg or arm. They can do quite a few things. But they can't do anything about this." He slapped his belly. "Can you, Madami?"

Kulu watched her intently. He knew she was thinking that here was the great opportunity. Cure Wanga's son and others would come to be cured, she thought. She did not know that Wanga was not in much favor here and few would want to imitate him. Still, she must cure Wanga's son. Why did she hesitate?

"I'm not a doctor, I'm a nurse," she said. Oh, Madami! Are you afraid? Why say you aren't a doctor? Breathe your great spirit into the boy, prick him with magic needles and cure him. "But I'll look at your son," she said to Wanga.

Then she was striding toward the bungalow. The whole world was in motion to the music of doves in the limbali. The earth turned lightly under Kulu's feet as he followed Madami. She came out of the bungalow with Dr. Bickel's bag, the bag Kulu had seen her pack with strange things. She looked at him, not really seeing him this time, as he took the bag from her at the foot of the steps. First went Wanga and then Madami and close behind her he walked with the bag. Behind him came Kosongo and then Mzimba. Only Guta failed to follow; he ran off to chase a straying goat from the garden. But the word spread like grass fire in the dry season, and the village streamed behind, children and women and men and dogs and goats, while chickens fled for shelter.

Once Madami looked back and frowned and hesitated.

He smiled at her to give her confidence. "They come to see the cure, Madami. When you cure the child they will be in awe."

"But Kulu—" her voice rose, as in pain—"I do not know if I can cure the child."

"You can, Madami."

So they came, at last, to Wanga's hut at the edge of the village. Madami followed Wanga, stooping low, and Kulu followed Madami, out of the sunlight into the darkness. Wanga's wife was crouched in the kitchen corner. When she saw Madami she wailed and covered her head with her cloth. It smelled bad in here.

The boy lay on a pallet in one corner. He was a thin boy about seven years old named Tibu. He lay on his side, his knees drawn up, his eyes wide and white in the light from the doorway. The death look was on him, Kulu thought, for he did not moan or cry but simply lay quietly in the way children wait for death when it is certain. Madami knelt beside

[57]

him, smiling and murmuring something, the words not mattering but the tone important, for children only understand tone when near death. Ah, he had seen many children die, and he knew. The doorway was blocked with people and there were faces at the tiny window.

"The people must stand back," Madami said.

Kulu went to the doorway, pushing Kosongo and Mzimba before him, saying quietly and with an authority all accepted, "Stay outside, stand back." When he returned, Madami had placed a thing in the boy's mouth and somehow she made him turn on his back, but when she made him straighten his legs, he moaned and tears filled his eyes. Finally she took the thing from his mouth and went to the light and studied it. Then she came back and moved her hands over the boy's belly until she pressed a place on his side and he screamed.

Still on her knees she looked up at Wanga, her face drawn in the dim light, and she said, "Your son is very sick. I'm certain he has—" A word neither Kulu nor Wanga understood. "He will surely die if this thing is not cut out of him. I have never cut this thing out of anyone. I've helped many times when doctors have done it. I know how it is done, but I never have done it. If I do it, the boy very likely may die. If I do not try to do it, he almost definitely will die. Do you want me to do this cutting, Wanga?"

Wanga took a deep breath and stared at his son. Then he said, "Yes, Madami, do it."

Informers at the window called the word back to the people and there was a great murmur.

"Quickly, Kulu," Madami said, "send Kosongo and Mzimba running to the hospital to fetch a stretcher."

"Quickly," he shouted to them as they ran off. Only then did foreboding begin to churn in him. He wished to discuss it with Madami, but he couldn't. It was too late. It would have been better if she'd simply told Wanga that Tibu would die, for then she would be credited with wisdom. Now, if Tibu died—and the death look had hardened on him—she would be blamed. No matter what she had told Wanga about the risk, she would be blamed.

"Kulu." Her voice was intense. Impulsively she laid a hand on his arm as no one ever had, so that her spirit entered into him, and a sweetness as of mountain flowers flooded the sour hut. "You are the only one I can depend on, Kulu. You must do everything I say. Will you listen and do exactly?"

"Oh, yes, Madami." The words came out as lightly as breath.

"Go to the hospital. Fill the vat with clean water and start a fire under it. Wait for me there."

He went, slowly at first, and then running, skimming the earth with bare feet as he had not in too long now, until he reached the hospital. There, his breathing unlabored, he filled the vat and carried fire from Guta's kitchen to the hospital kitchen.

He was waiting in the doorway when the procession entered the compound led by Madami, with Kosongo and Mzimba carrying Tibu on the stretcher behind her. They laid him on a cot as Madami directed. Her face no longer was strained. She seemed to forget the people who boldly surrounded the big thatched building, chattering noisily. She concentrated on mysterious acts, telling him to follow her with a tray of things as she went to the boy's cot. He held the tray while she pricked one of the boy's earlobes with a needle and let exactly one drop of blood fall onto a little piece of glass. He followed her to the enclosed room where she had placed the many mysterious things of medicine many days ago. Now her hands moved surely and she was looking through the tube thing.

At last she looked up and said vaguely, not to him but to herself, something in the strange language of her native land which must still be the language of her thoughts. Then she was still and her eyes were closed. She was, he thought, communicating with the good spirits, God the Father and Jesus the Christ. He had not really tried communicating with Them before, but now he closed his eyes and to his vast amazement and delight he saw Them clearly. God the Father was a huge, muscular, handsome man with satiny black skin sitting under the limbali tree smiling thoughtfully at His Son. Jesus the Christ was standing beside Him and had just finished saying something to Him. He looked like His Father, only He was younger, and the muscles under His black skin were maybe a little heavier than His Father's, as a younger man's should be. On His bare chest was the long spear scar where the people had killed Him when He was visible on earth.

The clear image behind his closed eyelids awed Kulu, and he was hesitant to speak to Them. Then, hearing Tibu suddenly cry out in the next room, he formed the words with his lips but didn't even whisper them. God the Father and Jesus the Christ, this is Kulu, he thought. He waited for Them to look at him, and when They did, smiling and nodding to show They heard him, he thought, Please help Madami to cure Tibu because her spirit is great and tender and will be crushed like grass if he dies. They nodded and smiled, and he meant to add something about Tibu but the image of Them was fading and his eyes were opening—they were open wide.

Madami was staring at him curiously. "What is it, Kulu? What's the matter?"

His hands, he saw, were trembling. "It was God the Father and Jesus the Christ, Madami. I just saw Them and spoke to Them and—"

"*What?*" Now she was looking at him as if afraid.

"Madami!" His hands rose pleadingly. "I *saw* Them, Madami, and it's going to be all right. They said it would be all right."

Unaccountably tears rose to her eyes and she turned away quickly and strode across the small room. She faced him. "I'm glad you saw—Them, Kulu." She started to say something else, but she didn't. "Now let's think only of the work we must do. Listen to what I say, Kulu. The two of us will carry the boy in here and put him on this table and close the door. Everyone else must stay outside. Then we'll scrub our hands in the hot water and we'll put on the rubber gloves and masks and caps here so the cut cannot be infected. And in the boiling hot water we'll put the instruments I have laid out here. Then I'm going to put in the boy's spine something that will make him feel no pain." She held up a needle with a glass thing on it. "Then I'll take this alcohol and cotton here and scrub his belly thoroughly all the way around. When I begin to cut, Kulu, you must stand exactly where I tell you across the boy from me and as the blood flows you must sop it away with the clean cloths whenever I tell you. It's very hot and my forehead will begin to sweat and I can't wipe it away because both hands will be very busy. We cannot let any sweat fall in the cut, either yours or mine, so be careful and do not lean over. Whenever I tell you 'wipe,' you run this clean towel across my forehead. I tell you all this in detail because you might not understand at the time. If anything falls, leave it on the floor. If the boy starts to move, stop everything else and hold his legs until I can—until—if I can— Then just do what I tell you, Kulu. I'll tell you these things and others as we go along, but I want you to understand." Turning, she busied herself with things. "Can you repeat any of this to me, Kulu?"

"Yes, Madami." And he repeated all that he could remember. When he had finished, she turned and warmed him with a radiant morning sun smile.

"Kulu, you are, as we say in my country, a good man."

Oh, he felt like a sharp-edged spear and in him was the fine lightness of the hungry hunter near his quarry. There was a little trouble making Wanga understand he could not come in the room with his son and there was a little trouble calming Tibu himself when they arranged the cloth hoop about his neck so that he could not see Madami cutting.

Then Madami began her work. Because she had explained, the strangeness of the operation did not disturb him. Soon he saw that this, like everything important, had a rhythm. Like dancing and hunting and feasting and love-making, it found a rhythm and he entered into it. She worked silently, gray eyes intent above the mask, wincing once when she began to cut and the blood flowed. He quickly saw how to stanch the blood and still let her find the way with the knife. Sweat beaded her forehead. With his other hand he cautiously dabbed at her forehead with the sweat towel. Then she moved her head impatiently and bent over her work. He saw the boy's entrails through the blood, a confused mass, and Madami worked more slowly in the confused mass. Once she dropped an instrument and exclaimed something in her native tongue and said harshly, "Wipe!" so that he snatched up the sweat towel as she seized another instrument from the tray. There was less blood and her eyes kept darting up toward Tibu's face. Once she stopped for an instant, as if to do something about his breathing, for it seemed slower and slower. Soon it would stop, Kulu thought, until he remembered the way God the Father and Jesus the Christ had looked at him. Taking courage from that, he nodded encouragingly to Madami. She looked at him, her shoulders slumping helplessly, saying to him with her eyes that she couldn't do anything about the boy's breathing. Then she worked on until the instrument thing like scissors pulled out something and Madami dropped it in the pail. For an instant he felt a little sick, as he always did at the thought of anyone losing any part of himself, but he remembered where he was and he did not let himself be sick. Now Tibu was breathing better and now, such a long time afterwards, Madami was stitching the cut.

She washed Tibu's belly with alcohol again and took up the thing with the tubes and tore off her mask and rubber gloves and listened through the thing to his heart. He was breathing, he would be all right as God the Father and Jesus the Christ had said. Still, Madami listened and listened while he stood there, afraid to take off his own mask and gloves. She took the tube things out of her ears and wiped her face with the sweat towel and fell back on a stool, shoulders low in weariness, watching Tibu breathe. Suddenly she flung her head forward into her hands and sobbed.

Kulu tore off his mask and said, "Madami, Madami, Tibu is all right."

[61]

"I know he is," she sobbed.

Then why did she cry?

VI

FOR THREE DAYS it rained steadily until the land was smeared and desolate. On the afternoon of the third day, Lecomte's sedan churned out of the muddy road into the compound. It was covered with yellow mud, as if it had rolled over on the road, and its motor died in an exhausted sigh. Lecomte climbed out dispiritedly after the driver. His boots and trench coat were spattered with mud.

Rachel, watching from the hospital doorway, called and waved to him. He slogged through the mud toward her, hands deep in his pockets, head lowered against the rain. It was the fourth time he had visited her since Dr. Bickel died three weeks ago. To have come so far in this weather, he must bear news, she thought. She did not want to hear it, for it could only be word of her recall.

"Miss Cade." He spoke as he plodded toward her, his expression dour. As he reached the doorway he wearily brushed a drop of rain from the tip of his big nose. "Get your things packed. You're leaving with me at once."

She stiffened. His coming here talking like a policeman! The things tropical weather did to the most affable men. She forced a smile. "Monsieur Lecomte, I found a couple of bottles of cognac in Dr. Bickel's things. I believe you need some."

His expression brightened. He actually smiled at her. "Miss Cade, you're a fine, wonderful woman. I'll drink a glass of your cognac." He glanced at Kulu who stood behind her in a white smock. "What's this? A hospital orderly?"

"My co-worker, Kulu. We have a patient, a recovering patient."

Lecomte's brows rose in surprise.

"Madami!" She knew the urgency that made Kulu interrupt now. "Madami, you aren't going away?"

"No, Kulu, I'm not going away," she replied, taking her raincoat from the peg beside the door.

"Now, Miss Cade—" Lecomte began.

"Monsieur Lecomte, I'm not leaving a sick patient, so let's have no nonsense about it."

"Nonsense?" He sounded incredulous, as if no one in memory had accused him of talking nonsense. And then he lost a struggle to withhold a smile, as if he secretly knew he'd been talking nonsense for years. "But there's no nonsense about the road from Rugeri. I have died a thousand times reaching here. The rivers are flooding, the road is a swamp. If I don't get you out now I may not see you in weeks."

Rachel looked at the sky and shrugged. "But I have a patient."

"What's wrong with the patient?"

"He's a little boy recovering from an appendectomy."

Lecomte's eyes widened and he fell back a step. "An appendectomy! But—"

"But," she said ruefully, "no more patients have come."

"My God, Miss Cade, you mean you—"

"Yes."

"But—"

"I know it's illegal and quite impossible," she said. "I'm sure I'll never do it again. I don't think I *could* do it again. But I had to."

"My God," said Lecomte. Then, "Pardon me." He fumbled inside his trench coat and handed her several damp letters. "Mail finally came for you. . . ."

She riffled through them hastily. Two from headquarters. But neither bearing the initials of Dr. Spencer. That was odd. The other letters, from the States, were inconsequential at the moment.

"I'm sure you'd like to read your mail," Lecomte said. "I'm going to see Buderga and have him put his men on the signal drum. I'll need the help of men in every village along the road to get the car through this mess to Rugeri. Then I'll dry out over that bottle of cognac in your residence, Miss Cade." He trudged off through the rain.

She tore open one of the letters from headquarters and glimpsed the date, two weeks ago, and the signature, *Yours, as ever, Ralph Morgan.* Her eyes widened as she read:

DEAR RACHEL [He'd been calling her "Miss Cade" in those last tense days at headquarters.],

I have just received your letter reporting the death of Dr. Bickel. [But she had written to Dr. Spencer.] Two days after you left for Dibela, Dr. Spencer was summoned hurriedly back to New York for a conference on what is to be done about the program as a result of the war in Europe. Obviously we'll have to retrench. Dr. Spencer left me in charge during his absence. In the few hours before he rushed off to Matadi to board a ship he said that you were to remain in Dibela until his return. [Good.] But the death of Dr. Bickel casts an entirely different light on the situation. Dibela is so distant and conditions apparently so primitive that it inevitably will be one of the stations which the New York conference will decide to abandon. [That's what he thinks.] So I know I am acting wisely when I direct you to close the operation there as speedily as possible and return here. . . .

Never! Accept defeat before she had really begun? Never. What did they know back there about the need of people like Kulu? Was Kulu to slide back into the abyss of the bush, with Kosongo and Mzimba and hundreds of others who had not yet even glimpsed the way out?

Kulu, standing beside her, looked at her now—and away—as if he read her thoughts as clearly as she read the letter. Beyond him Tibu smiled shyly at her from his cot.

She opened the other letter from headquarters. It was dated two days after Ralph's letter and was signed, *Love, Edith.* Edith Barney, her bungalow-mate at headquarters and surely her best friend in Africa. Sturdy, steady Edith. If she *had* to go back to headquarters before Dr. Spencer returned, Edith would make life bearable.

DEAR RACHEL,

All of us here miss you terribly and are thinking of you out there alone now that Dr. Bickel is dead. It was indeed sorrowing to learn of the poor man's death. Things just aren't the same here with you gone and then Dr. Spencer leaving for that sudden conference at home. He'll be gone so many months and in that time our medical effort is bound to suffer with you know who at the head.

Sometimes I almost wish I hadn't trained as a nurse, and I guess you do sometimes too. If I hadn't trained I could transfer out of the medical section and work for Rev. Prosser and just be a plain *missionary!* But then we volunteered as nurses in the foreign mission field and things have a way of working out. . . .

I'm just sticking my two cents in, Rachel, and believe me I certainly would like to have you back here in the bungalow at headquarters because we have such good times and don't get as *rattled* as certain parties we both know— I heard about Dr. Bickel's death, poor man, from Ann— You can be sure none of us ever hear *anything* with Ralph in Dr. Spencer's place. Ralph hasn't even gone to church the past two Sundays and as you can imagine Rev. Prosser is quite put out about it— Well, putting my two cents in, Rachel, I wouldn't be in a hurry to leave Dibela because nothing here is very good and it would be hard for you. *You know what I mean!!* I count on you to stay there just as long as you can. Bad times are coming for all of us with this war, but I think for your own sake the longer you can stay in Dibela the better it will be—at least till Dr. Spencer returns. My prayers and the prayers of many here are with you. . . .

She folded the letter carefully and pulled her raincoat about her and put on her old rain hat. She did not look at Kulu as she went out and picked a way through the compound mud, under the limbali tree, past the wooden cross marking Dr. Bickel's grave.

On the bungalow porch she paused, staring and yet not really seeing the gray waste, carelessly letting the rain drip from coat and hat onto the clean floor. There must be a way. There *had* to be a way. God help me, she thought. She took off coat and hat and hung them carefully. She placed the four, five, six letters on the big table and absently fingered through them again. An ad from a book club that had pursued her all the way to this place. An ad from what surely was a manufacturer of home appliances in Philadelphia; how had they ever heard of Rachel Cade?

A letter from New York, the return address on the back. It was from Mrs. Haricort, Phyllis Haricort. She sat down slowly and opened the letter, remembering that vigorous, ageless woman with the long, red face and short, sturdy legs. Mrs. Haricort had raised four children and buried a husband before she found happy release in the great Protestant world of causes and committees. She was, among other things, a member of the Foreign Mission Board. Though preoccupied with good works, she had maintained a sense of humor. She had come out here on a field tour at her own expense several months ago and fallen in love with Africa. Instinctively she had felt at home, more at home than in Montclair, she said, and had flung herself about so vigorously and carelessly that she'd contracted dengue. Rachel had nursed her through the fever. They had become fast friends. She was, Rachel thought, an admirable woman, perhaps the most admirable woman she'd ever known. And for some reason, Mrs. Haricort had insisted on treating *her* as an admirable woman. They had corresponded. Mrs. Haricort frequently sent gifts that were more valued than gold to a woman here—linen, combs, sheer silk stockings to be worn on special occasions or in moods of depression.

Now Mrs. Haricort was writing in her usual effervescent good spirits.

"It was wonderful to hear from you again. . . . The Denver conference may not have settled anything except the fact that I'm getting older, for I went on to Estes Park with the Caulfields and took a long hike by myself and slipped and fell halfway down a mountain and sprained my ankle. . . . You've been in my thoughts a great deal recently, my dear Rachel, I don't know why. . . . As I'm constantly reminding you, if ever there's anything we can do here which you and Dr. Spencer understand better in your wisdom than we here ever can hope to achieve in our ignorance . . ."

Suddenly she swung to her feet and seized stationery and pen from the shelf. Sitting down again, she began to write fast in even, flowing lines. Dimly she heard the signal drum through the rain. When she had finished one letter, she began a second.

After a while Lecomte came in, wet boots squeaking. She glanced at him as he hung up his trench coat and sodden hat. "Yes," she said absently, "the cognac."

"Yes," he said, sinking wearily on the bench on the opposite side of the table. He pulled at his wet scraggly mustache and sighed.

She brought one of the unopened bottles of cognac and a glass. "Do you drink water with this, Monsieur Lecomte?"

"Heaven forbid, Miss Cade." He glanced at the label and nodded approvingly. "I'll open it. But where is your glass?"

"I don't drink."

"Not ever?"

"Oh, I have once or twice. I'm not a fanatic about it. I just don't like it."

"Hmmm." As he uncorked the bottle with his knife, she resumed writing, bending her head low over the paper in the intensity of composition.

Aware finally that he was looking at her, she raised her head and surprised on his long, lined face a look that was—yes, it must be compassionate. He raised his glass. "Your health, Miss Cade."

"Thank you." She hesitated. "I must really seem rude. For I'd like to raise a glass and say, 'To yours.' But I don't like cognac and it would be—insulting to toast you in water."

He smiled and drank. "You express yourself very well, Miss Cade. I wish I knew English better so that we could talk in English. Then I think I'd find you expressed yourself even more eloquently." He nodded at her letter. "You're expressing yourself now."

"Yes." She glanced at the letter, signed her name and folded it.

"Monsieur Lecomte, I'm going to take you into my confidence. You're my friend. I'm going to make you my ally." Then she told him about Ralph and Dr. Spencer and how she had happened to come here. She told him of Dr. Spencer's return home and why she felt she could not go back to headquarters. "So I've written a letter to Dr. Spencer and to a woman friend in New York, a person who's powerful in our church. I have told her and Dr. Spencer rather glowingly about Dibela. I haven't exaggerated the beauty of this place—" she looked out at the dreary compound and smiled—"the usual beauty of it. I may have slightly exaggerated the—receptiveness so far. I've told them both I wish to stay here. I think they will see that I do."

Lecomte got to his feet suddenly. There was a cracked mirror on the wall, and he went to it and looked at himself. "Ah, me," he said to his reflection. He turned and strolled back to the table. "It was, I believe, the dramatist Terence who said some two thousand years ago that the most profitable study for a man is the study of his own face. I trust I have profited." He poured cognac into his glass. "Miss Cade, would you mind very much if I smoked a cigar?"

"Of course not."

He took a cigar of dark Congo tobacco from his shirt pocket and lighted it. "Miss Cade, this doctor now in charge at headquarters whose exact name you have so carefully edited from your conversation, as if he'd done a despicable thing in falling in love with you—is this doctor the only thing that keeps you in Dibela?"

"No," said Rachel, "I think, rather, he's a convenient excuse. I simply like it here and feel there's great work to be done and I want to stay."

"Alone?"

"Alone if necessary. But we need a doctor."

Lecomte sipped his cognac. "Let me put it this way. Supposing this nameless doctor, who had the good taste but bad fortune to fall in love with you, should assign himself to Dibela—"

"But he couldn't!" Rachel said in alarm. "He's responsible for—"

Lecomte waved his cigar at her. "This is hypothesis, Miss Cade. Supposing he were to come here. Would you stay?"

"Yes," she replied without hesitation.

"Alone—with him?"

"Yes."

"But what about your—ah—virtue?"

She smiled wryly. "I can take care of that. I can take care of the—annoyances if I know there's a real purpose to be served. And, frankly, I

[67]

feel there's greater work to be done here than back at headquarters."

"Purpose. Work." Lecomte looked out at the rain. "You use such words a great deal, Miss—may I call you Rachel?"

"Of course."

"And you may call me Henri, if you want to."

"All right—Henri."

"Well, Rachel, I'll confess that my bedroom is stuffed with books and I read a great deal. The only things I seem to enjoy any more are reading and traveling around in the bush. Maybe I've become just a bush philosopher. But at any rate one of my books discusses a word—" he said it in English—"compulsive."

"Oh, I understand. You think I'm compulsive. I understand the word and I don't think it bad at all. I'm sure all the saints and artists besides a lot of us common people have been that way. Compulsive."

"All right." Lecomte sipped cognac. "I won't belabor you further. I won't try to analyze you. I won't even say that you put perhaps too great value on your—virtue. I would merely point out, as a final remark, that there are many, many places in Africa where the people are more receptive to—ah—enlightenment than here in Dibela."

"But the hospital is here," Rachel said. "This is where somebody years ago had the vision and tenacity to set up the physical fact of a hospital. This is where I've been sent. This is where I've found Kulu and seen the—the basic outline of the struggle that goes by many names—black against white, or civilization against primitivism, or whatever some scholar in a study wants to call it. All right, so I've somehow emotionally involved myself here in Dibela."

Lecomte, dragging on his cigar, gazed at her solemnly.

"If I lose," she said, "it must be for some better reason than because a man back there at headquarters wants me to go to bed with him."

"Uh—" Lecomte took the cigar from his teeth—"yes."

"Now I want you to tell me something—Henri. Why are the people of Dibela so reluctant to accept us?"

He raised his glass and drank. At last he said, "They always were a fierce, proud people around here with their own fierce, proud gods. Years ago, when you were a baby, I fought through here myself. They gave me a platoon of Europeans and some African hangers-on from down country and said, 'Quiet things down up there, Lecomte.' I was young in Africa then and I only knew the European way of doing it by the book—a hopeless way, we know now. We came in and the people deserted the villages before us. We had to build thorn bomas at night against their spears and arrows and old Arab rifles. One of our men would be shot and so we'd burn a village. No torturing, you understand. I was young in Africa but never so young that I permitted torture." He shrugged. "That's the way they were."

"But that's the way they were in many places," Rachel said. "And they've changed rapidly. What, for instance, is this tabu about climbing the mountains?"

"What?" Lecomte looked at her sharply and then down at his glass. "So you've learned about that. Oh, I don't know. There was a British expedition up through here once, away back even before my time. I guess they caused some trouble." He looked up at her again. "Also there are the geographical facts. Anybody trying to climb the Ruwenzori doesn't do it from here. He'd go through Fort Portal over in Uganda, the way the Duke of Abruzzi went when he finally made it back in 1906."

"Did you know that Dr. Bickel tried to climb the mountains?"

He looked away. "Yes. I heard it on the drums."

"Did he know about the tabu?"

Lecomte shrugged elaborately. "We never discussed it. I came out to see him when the drums reported his return. He was sick, but he didn't tell me how sick." He frowned. "In his own curious way Bickel loved this place. He merely was obtuse about people. I think he wanted to die here."

And that, Rachel thought, was Dr. Bickel's epitaph. She stirred. "Monsieur Lecomte—Henri—have you ever wanted to climb the mountains?"

"*What?*" His amazement was only feigned, she knew. In his eyes was the hunger of a bushman who had seen the mountains and wished to climb them.

"Why didn't you?" she asked quietly. "Why didn't you at least try?"

"I didn't want—" His shoulders sagged and he looked outside where the rain had ceased to fall. "Yes, I wanted to when I was younger. But I never seemed to have the opportunity. And now I'm old and I don't have the strength." He glanced at his empty glass and got to his feet. "Now I'm only good for reading books and pottering along the roads and passing judgments on my fifty thousand black children." He looked about the room. "It would be pleasant to spend the night here with you."

"By all means stay," she said. "We'll fix a bed for you and in the morning—"

"Ah, Rachel." He smiled at her slowly. "You do not or you will not understand."

[69]

She understood then and flushed. She did not mind. He was a fine man.

"I'm an old man," he said, going toward the porch, "old and feeling a little sorry for myself at the moment. So old that there's nothing left for me to do but get in my car and take the road back to Rugeri." His back still to her, he gazed outside and said, "Now give me your letters for the good woman and the good doctor in the United States and make a list of things you may be needing here. When I come this way again I'll bring what I can."

She addressed the envelopes and stamped them. She remembered that she needed salt and flour and a new roasting pan from the Greek trader in Rugeri. As she wrote the items on a slip of paper, Lecomte called sharply from the doorway, "Come here! Rachel, come and see—"

She hurried to the porch. As suddenly as the rain clouds had come three days ago, they were evaporating and shredding. Golden columns of sunlight struck and lighted the earth. Here and there they seemed to strike red and white sparks, bougainvillea and orchids against thatched roofs and mud. Wind passed through the limbali, shaking the rain from it in a last silver shower; two green doves rose from its upper branches and flew purposefully north. With incredible swiftness the welding columns suffused the country in golden light. The clouds rolled up to the mountains like a vast curtain torn by enormous hands as a cock crowed victoriously somewhere in the village and a macaw answered proudly. Now the green shoulders of the mountains were exposed as Rachel never had seen them. Still the hands tore at the clouds, ripping and shredding them until she caught her breath. There was the gleam of snow, and there the whole mysterious wasteland below the glaciers. Then, at last, she saw the shining snowfields and two sharp peaks thrust against the blue sky.

"Well—" Lecomte's voice was low—"there are your mountains, Rachel." He faced her and said something else she did not hear. For she stood, transfixed, a hand pressed against her throat.

Gently he took the slip of paper and the letters to Mrs. Haricort and Dr. Spencer from her other hand. "Thank you for the cognac, Rachel. I'll post the letters and return with the supplies when I can. *Au revoir.*" He went down the steps quickly.

"*Au revoir.*" Her voice seemed a whisper as she tore her gaze from the mountains. Then she called, "*Au revoir, Henri.*"

Lecomte looked back and smiled. He walked on with an odd high step, as if, Rachel thought, he were stepping over fallen bodies. His driver opened the door for him. The car stuttered and started and turned heavily in the compound mud. Soon the sound of its motor was a distant labored hum.

But Rachel did not hear it. She sat down on the porch and locked her hands behind her head and gazed at the mountains. She did not hear Kulu; she sensed the presence of someone and knew it was he, standing at the foot of the steps.

When she smiled down at him, he said, "Madami sees the mountains?"

"Yes, Kulu, I see the mountains for the first time."

He stared gravely at the peaks.

"You told me once your home was at the beginning of the mountains, Kulu."

"Yes, Madami." He pointed. "There at the beginning. See, it looks like a dog crouching. There is the back and there the head against the mountain. My father's shamba is there at the dog's neck and the mountain goes up beyond."

Now she could see the lighter green of a mountain spur, the curving back and arching head and rough forepaw of a great dog. "There is a trail to your home—and beyond?"

"Yes, Madami. There is a bad trail beyond my village that went part way to the bamboo forests."

"That trail—" Rachel looked at him closely—"that would be the trail that Dr. Bickel followed when he—he tried to climb the mountains?"

"Yes, Madami."

"Did you go with him to show him the trail, Kulu?"

He shook his head. "He did not ask me, Madami. He asked some of the Chief's men and they would not go. He asked Musinga, and Musinga walked with him for half a day. Then Musinga said he hurt his ankle and he came back."

"And Dr. Bickel went on alone?"

"Yes, Madami. He was gone many days. He did not go very high. Only there—" he pointed—"where the green turns to brown. He got lost and fell sick and he had to come back. When he came down to a place near my village the people had to carry him back."

"Had he been sick before he tried to climb the mountains?"

"No, Madami."

Perhaps, Rachel thought, he'd suffered his first attack alone up there in the mountains.

"He should not have gone alone," Kulu said. "A man cannot climb

[71]

mountains alone, Madami. I would have gone with him to help carry the load, but he did not ask me and I dared not ask him."

"How long before he died did he try to climb the mountains, Kulu?"

Kulu looked at the ground thoughtfully. "Perhaps a moon, Madami."

One month, she thought. That would be it. That would be when he sent his desperate plea for help and medicine, though he'd still been too proud or stubborn to admit he was ill. Such a strange man. And yet, she thought suddenly, how strange my own determination to stay here would seem to most people.

"Had Dr. Bickel talked about the mountains ever since he came here?" she asked.

"No, Madami. Only since someone told him—I think it was Chief Buderga told him . . ." Kulu's voice died.

"Told him what, Kulu? That there was a tabu on the mountains?"

Kulu looked away. At last he said, "Not a tabu, Madami. A thahu."

"A thahu? A curse?"

"Yes, Madami."

"Do you believe in it?"

He looked at her unwaveringly. "No, Madami. Once I thought maybe I did. But now I believe in God the Father and Jesus the Christ."

"Tell me about the thahu, Kulu," she said gently.

"It's a long story, Madami."

She gestured to the chair beside hers. "Come and sit down and tell it to me, Kulu."

He climbed the steps and sat down on the triangular chair. For a while he gazed at the mountains, and at last he said, "I'll tell it, Madami, as it is told to boys at circumcision. I'll tell it as we are taught to believe it, but I do not believe it now.

"God, they say, dwells among the summits of the mountains. . . ."

Africans generally believe, Rachel knew, in the existence of God, a Supreme Being, the creator and dispenser of all things. But they do not worship Him until goaded to it by white peoples, preferring to leave Him alone and not draw His attention to themselves. So the God of the African legend who dwelled up there in the mountains would be an angry, vengeful God.

"Many, many seasons ago, even before the time of the grandfathers," said Kulu, "a white bwana came from the west to climb the mountains. He brought one or two other white bwanas with him from over the great western sea. And he brought a few black men from the west who carried the burdens.

"Our people were greatly disturbed when they learned that the bwanas came to climb the mountains. They did not wish these strangers to disturb God, who was peacefully running the world up there on the summits. They did not want His attention drawn to the people below.

"So the chieftains and medicine men met here in Dibela. They knew that eventually they'd be punished with death by other white bwanas if they killed the strangers and they could not dissuade them from trying to climb the mountains. Then a wise and strong young man, the only son of the most powerful chieftain, rose and said he would make certain the bwanas did not reach the summits. It is said his name was Bolambo. Bolambo said that he himself would go with them as their guide and take strong young men with him to help carry the burdens."

In imagination Rachel could see the expedition, with Bolambo in the lead, threading through the tall grass of the savannahs and filing up the mountain spurs.

"It is said there were bad storms in the mountains at that time and Bolambo and his men knew it was a sign that God had glimpsed their coming and was displeased. Bolambo urged the bwanas to turn back, but they would not. And so they climbed on into the land of perpetual mist and rain and sometimes they heard, above them, the howling of fierce winds. They forced a passage through the bamboo forests, where the gorillas live, and came at last to the strange moss land where the heather trees grow tall and the bright flowers flourish.

"Early one morning the mists sank around them and they saw they were in the high country. Above them rose the glaciers, blue-veined as the legs of old men, and the peaks of white frozen rain which were the color of goat curds in the rising sun. Bolambo and his men were afraid, for this was the home of God, and they did not look up lest they see and disturb Him in His mighty solitude. The mist rose again quickly, and soon they heard a rumble that the bwanas said was thunder. But Bolambo knew it was God speaking in annoyance that men should dare to climb to His place and look on Him. Bolambo knew that before the sun sank that day he must appease God's wrath for the sake of the people below.

"Bolambo led the way and the bwanas followed and the long column wound after them through the mist. The mist thinned and fell below them and the sun flashed blindingly on the frozen rain above them where God dwells in shining glory. Bolambo did not look up, but only ahead of him along the bank of a green and narrow lake which they were follow-

[73]

ing. Then he saw the means of doing what he must, and he went forward to it steadfastly.

"At those altitudes, it is said, there are deep bogs covered with a moss which appears to provide as firm a footing as the grass of the savannahs. Toward one of these marshes Bolambo led the way unfalteringly, and there was no sound but the heavy breathing of the bwanas in the thin air and sometimes a wail from one of the bearers who feared being led so close to the presence of God. The bwanas followed Bolambo confidently onto the bog and then their weight broke the moss and they began to sink slowly in the bottomless ooze. They floundered and cried out and behind them the long column of bearers writhed like a snake whose head is crushed. But Bolambo had not counted on the bwanas' bearers from the west coming to their aid. These men, who still stood on firm ground, threw ropes to those who were sinking and, one by one, they hauled them, floundering and cursing, to firm ground. Bolambo, the farthest out in the marsh, was the last to whom they hurled a rope after all of the others had struggled to safety. He had sunk to his loins, and even as the rope lashed across the moss within his reach, he sank to his waist.

"The rope lay where he could grasp it, but he did not. They called to him, and when he did not seize the rope, the bwanas cursed him and finally pleaded with him. Now all of Bolambo's men ran up, forming a dense crowd on the firm ground, and begged him to grasp the rope. They cried to him that he would become the greatest of their chiefs and they needed him above all men.

"He simply stared at them calmly without fear or grief or hatred, his palms extended upward on the moss, as he slowly sank to his shoulders. They knew then that he never would seize the rope, though they did not know why. Then one of them, his closest friend, whom others held from plunging into the marsh and dying with him, cried, 'Bolambo! Great Bolambo! Give us one message to take back.'

"Only then did Bolambo speak. His words came faintly, as he raised his head above the moss. 'Juana,' he said. 'Pendana. Sameheana.' And he sank from sight."

Juana, thought Rachel. Pendana. Sameheana. In the Swahili, "Know one another. Love one another. Forgive one another." A Christian message from a savage throat. It was incredible. It was a gilding of the legend. Bolambo, if there had been a Bolambo, could not have said it. Or could he?

"Great was the grief of the people," said Kulu, "when the young men

[74]

came running down the mountain crying that Bolambo was dead. And the women ran through Dibela wailing, 'Lo-o-o! Tumepata hasara kubwa!' Aye, Madami, they believed that they had suffered a grievous loss. But the medicine men could make no sense of the message. They made medicine and told the people they had talked to Bolambo's spirit and he had placed a thahu on the white bwanas that would prevent them from getting closer to God.

"Soon the bwanas and their bearers from the west came down the mountains. They had not reached the summits. So it was seen that Bolambo's thahu had been a strong one. The bwanas went away west, muttering against our people, and they never were seen in this country again.

"After they had gone the medicine men made medicine once more. They cast what is said to be the strongest thahu ever cast in our land. This is the thahu, Madami—and this is the end of the story: If any white ever tries to climb the mountains from this place his body will be racked by pain and his soul doomed to eternal suffering."

She heard him distinctly enough. But she could not tear her gaze from the mountains where her eyes sought a way up the highest slopes.

VII

ON THAT DAY in the following January when Lecomte realized what had happened, he was appalled. It was, he thought, the worst day in many years.

He was presiding that hot morning in the Rugeri court of justice, eyes half closed as he half listened to the involved case of a stolen goat. The larceny itself was simple enough; the involvement was of two enemy families which, in turn, involved two blood-enemy tribes. The goat, in short, was merely a minor incident in a saga of love and hate and incest and an interminable series of poisonings. Sometimes it seemed that in Africa a leaf could not fall to the ground without shaking the earth. Lecomte could not settle the case, he knew. He could merely prolong it. Solomon himself could not have settled it. And anyway, it needed a chronicler, not a judge. Shakespeare could have done justice to it, he thought. It would have absorbed Dostoevsky, though the Russian might have handled it too heavily. It really needed a collaboration between Dostoevsky and one of those composers of *opera buffa*—say, Rossini. Lecomte began whistling softly as he listened to the aged African with two filed teeth passionately accusing his enemies.

Then he saw Father Gilo standing at the entrance to the unwalled hall of justice. His lips were pursed in perplexity and sweat streamed down his round cheeks. He raised a forefinger and nodded to Lecomte, saying, in effect, "A word with you." The fan boy stopped passing the broad palm leaf over Lecomte's head and the court clerk, an *evolué* named Pierre Bunkeya, rose politely.

"Recess," Lecomte said, grasping the arms of his chair and pulling himself to his feet. The bailiff woke from a sound sleep and staggered up, leaning on his staff. Everyone in the crowded hall rose, and Lecomte went down the aisle to Father Gilo.

"Henri." Father Gilo placed a hand on his arm. "Has your adjutant reported on the drum message from Dibela this morning?"

Lecomte groaned. "Now what? What did you hear?"

"I'm always afraid my people misunderstand—"

"They never do," Lecomte snapped. "What did you hear, Georges?"

"That Miss Cade has started to climb the mountains."

Lecomte swore and did not bother to apologize. "François!" he roared across the park toward the administrative bungalow. The sentry, who had been dozing there, leaped to his feet and nearly dropped his rifle, and François stumbled out of the office without having bothered to put on his shoes. The sentry swung his rifle to port arms, as he had been taught, and trotted toward Lecomte with François leaping after him in great bounds.

Lecomte swore again. But already his anger was evaporating against that wonderful, beautiful, mad woman. Still, this time she had gone too far. This time she was courting death, an absurd and melodramatic suicide on the mountains which would, he was sure, defy an experienced mountaineer, let alone an inexperienced American girl.

François was babbling, yes, yes, yes, the drums had so spoken and he was so sorry not to have told Colonel Lecomte. (In moments of stress François invariably called him Colonel, although he never had been more than Captain Lecomte.) But, said François, he had not wanted to interrupt court— Oh, hell! The people were milling under the kapok trees, knowing this was a big show, and pressing close to the benign Bwana Administrator to learn what would happen next. The sentry, having nothing better to do, barked at them and pressed his rifle butt authoritatively against their ribs while they laughed because they knew him as a harmless fellow. Father Gilo was speaking, but Lecomte could not hear him in the confusion.

"Quiet!" he roared. And the people were quiet. "You were saying, Georges?"

"I went to see Miss Cade again last week. She told me that story about the mountains. It's a fascinating story— Have you heard it? It—"

"Yes, yes, I've heard it."

Father Gilo looked at the sky. "She seemed to want to tell me something else, but she didn't. I wonder if even then she was planning to try to climb the mountains and feared—"

"She'd better have been planning." Then Lecomte remembered having taken to Dibela a coil of rope, among other items she'd requested, just two weeks ago. A rope with which to hang herself! "She'll have to be brought back."

"I wonder," said Father Gilo to the sky.

"Well, I don't. I'm fond of that woman and I'd rather she didn't die."

"You don't mean, Henri, that you believe the people's legend about any white—"

"Of course not! I simply don't want her killed by a leopard or lost in an avalanche or— François! Send me Watu." Watu was the best African marksman in the district besides having other solid accomplishments.

"Colonel!" François raised eyes and hands to heaven. "Watu is sick."

Drunk again. "Rouse him from his sickness, François. If he can't be roused, put him in the back of the pickup truck. The rough road to Dibela will rouse him. Put his rifle in the truck with him and a couple of hundred rounds. Rations for him and two drivers—mine and the truck's—for one week. And rations for one soldier—Corporal Tuku. We'll leave in half an hour. There will be no court until I return." He started toward his bungalow, but Father Gilo plucked at his arm.

"I would like to go with you, Henri."

"Well." Lecomte looked at him dubiously. "Let's face it, Georges, you were not built for climbing mountains. And I'm going climbing."

Father Gilo smiled. "You may have been built for it, Henri, but the structure has somewhat deteriorated."

"Bah!" But Lecomte smiled.

"I don't plan to climb any mountains," Father Gilo said. "I merely want to follow you in my car and stay a day as—observer."

He meant as counselor, Lecomte thought. The priest had something on his mind. "Follow along then, Georges." He walked toward his bungalow, thin bare legs moving nimbly.

Marie looked up from her crocheting as he stalked in. She followed him to his bedroom as he shouted for his personal boy. As he threw clean clothing on the bed he told her what had happened. She was aghast, saying stupid, obvious things about Miss Cade's folly until he secretly began to build defenses for Rachel's action.

He took his favorite old 7.65-millimeter Mauser from the rack and a couple of hundred rounds from the locked drawer. While Marie, still talking, packed his canvas bag, he hauled out his bedroll and hurried his personal boy at the task of packing the tin safari box with canned goods.

It was almost an hour before the three cars, first Lecomte's and then the pickup and finally Father Gilo's, eating the yellow dust, rolled out of Rugeri. Lecomte, jouncing in the back seat, lighted a cigar and realized he was rather enjoying himself.

But as they drew near Dibela in early afternoon, heat and rough riding and the carefully mulled stark facts of the situation had depressed him. He looked ahead at the bastions of the mountains rising into clouds and laid a hand along a jaw, as if a tooth ached. There was no question but what she had started toward the mountains. He remembered the morning the drums had reported that Dr. Bickel had started toward them. Interesting and odd, he'd thought then, and gone about his business. And when, a week later, the drums said that Dr. Bickel, ill, was being carried back to Dibela, he'd thought, That's tough, if he wants help let him have Buderga request it. It was a calculatedly unkind reaction, he'd realized, but that harsh and bitter Bickel had always seemed calculatedly unkind himself. Ducasse, the Belgian coffee planter who lived south of Rugeri, had dropped by the office that morning; he'd heard the report from some of his people, and now Lecomte remembered how they had discussed Bickel's attempted assault on the mountains. But neither had made a move to go to his aid. Doubtless Father Gilo would have gone, for Bickel's insulting manner never had diluted Gilo's Christian charity, but the priest had been on a journey far to the south at that time. So, a couple of days later, Lecomte finally had admitted the existence of his conscience and made the long trip out here. And found what? Bickel, propped in a chair, curt and more bitter than ever because he had failed with the mountains as he had failed with everything else. No, Bickel hadn't wanted help from *him*. He had even refused to explain what ailed him. He'd simply given Lecomte an urgent request for aid and medicine to be sent back to his headquarters. A man standing in the path of the world with clenched fists.

Ah, but Rachel was different. Quite apart from the fact that she was lovely, she stood apart from the world and beckoned it to her. She not only was a woman he'd have been happy to die for in his romanticizing younger days; she made him almost forget that he was old. Oh, rot!

She had felt she *had* to climb the mountains. He understood that. He had followed her progress—rather, her lack of progress—in Dibela watchfully. There had been her miraculously successful operation on the son of that fellow who long ago had deserted the army and found his way back home; the fellow who had tried and almost succeeded but failed to evolve from the bush into the lowest level of this thing called civilization and so earn the proud appellation *evolué*. But Rachel's successful operation on the boy had not brought other patients to her hospital. In Dibela, as elsewhere in the world, the acceptance of medicine followed patterns of social snobbery; unfortunately the cured child's father was socially unacceptable.

In Lecomte's rare forays into the narratives of African missionaries he had noticed that almost invariably the good missionary venturing into a bad country had finally overcome incredible hardships by saving the chief's son or doing something equally melodramatic. Then the chief would say there was something to this white God and after a while the converts flocked in and the people sought shoes and the women bound up their breasts, both the pendulous and the beautiful—

The car bounced and he cracked his head on the roof and shouted, "Poli-poli!" at the driver, but the fellow slowed only momentarily.

Yet Rachel had not saved one of Buderga's sons; the Chief didn't even have a son, to his inestimable sorrow. No, she had merely saved a politically worthless child, the son of a man whom no one in Dibela would emulate. And so her hospital had remained empty while these obdurate people had resisted all her skillful blandishments: small gifts and a dignity of manner that nearly all Africans found irresistible, the appealing mystery of new medicine and the magic of learning to read. Dibela was worse than evil—it was unlucky. Yet Rachel, like Bickel and the nameless Englishman before him, had stubbornly refused to recognize its true nature. Having pushed in and taken up her position, she had then wittingly severed her escape route. For her friend, the woman in the States, and the good doctor who went home had written and assured her that she could stay there. And the bewitched doctor who had been so fatally attracted to her back at headquarters (poor chap) had also written, wrathfully telling her that she'd *have* to stay there now that he was in charge. Apparently the doctor's passion for her had finally turned to hatred when she violated the simple rule of power: Never go over your immediate superior's head. He'd received *his* orders concerning her from the doctor and the woman in the States, catching the barb and dipping it in poison before he hurled it on at Rachel.

It all demonstrated, Lecomte thought sententiously, a favorite theory of his: Progress, as whites understood it, was an illusion; primitive pride dominated mankind. "Poli-poli!" he shouted at the driver.

So they came, at last, to Dibela, cars rushing up the long yellow slant of road while the people gaped and began to hurry after them. They swung into the compound and fanned out in a military pattern that was quite unconscious but still defensive, as if they were defending the whole Western world against the encroachment of one village.

That fellow—what was his name?—Musinga, the one who tried to be of both worlds and so was of none, rose slowly from a chair on the porch. "You!" Lecomte cried at him as he climbed from the car. Musinga ran toward him, eyes wide and white. "What are you doing sitting on that porch, boy?"

Musinga halted and shrank. "Madami left me in charge of the hospital, Bwana Administrator."

"So you didn't go with her. Who did?"

"She left me in charge, Bwana Administrator. Kulu went with her and Kosongo and Mzimba and the one from the village, Wanga. They went off this morning."

Lecomte grunted. At least she hadn't gone alone. At least she had tried to organize the incredible expedition.

"Madami left a letter for you, Bwana Administrator. I was sitting there guarding it. . . ." His voice trailed off and his eyes widened as he looked at the corporal and Father Gilo and Lecomte's personal boy and the drivers. He fell back a step and the people streaming into the compound cried out as over the tailboard of the pickup clambered Watu, the mighty black hunter, whose fame had penetrated even to Dibela. Watu slung his rifle over a thick shoulder and walked heavily to Lecomte. Ah, it was a great show, the people said.

"The Bwana Administrator—" Musinga wet his lips—"has come to fetch back the white Madami?"

"What makes you think that?" snapped Lecomte.

Musinga shrugged. "The mountains are dangerous," he said to the ground.

"They expect you to bring her back, Henri," Father Gilo said quietly in French.

The full implication struck Lecomte as he strode toward the bungalow. It had occurred to him dimly on the way here, but he had banished the thought. It was an inconvenient thought, obtruding on his desire to protect Rachel and his function of running a quiet and orderly district. Imagine what they'd say in the higher administrative echelons if they ever learned he let an inexperienced white missionary woman attempt an unauthorized assault on the unassailable western flank of the Ruwenzori. But now, as always, he must view a situation on the scene instead of from headquarters. The people of Dibela expected him to bring back the white Madami. When he did, it would demonstrate what they had always known: the mountains were inviolate. So he would help sustain their basic belief which was the keystone of their piled superstitions. Thus he now allied himself with dark superstition against—what? Well, the enlightenment—yes, that was what it was—that Rachel sought to bring here. This, then, was why Father Gilo had come along. Gilo had seen the implications immediately and faced them fearlessly, not as an administrator—or as one who was more than a little in love with Rachel Cade.

His feet fell slowly on the steps. Musinga, bowing and fawning, took an envelope from the table and handed it to him. He opened it and stared, bemused, at the date, yesterday, and her *Mon cher Henri*. My dear Henri, my dear dear Henri. If only just once he could hear her whisper that. My God, Lecomte, but you're an ass!

"Fetch Chief Buderga here at once," he growled to Musinga. He read the letter.

> Early tomorrow morning I'm starting out to climb the Mountains of the Moon—or, to be more prosaic, the Ruwenzori. I hoped at first to start out secretly, but secrecy is impossible in Dibela. Before we have gone very far we shall hear the drums. And if I know you, you will be here within a day or two. I wish I could silence the drums. But I cannot. Perhaps some day the drums will be silenced here and we shall communicate one with another by more enlightened means.
>
> Henri, I fear you will appear here with bristling efficiency, determined to drag me back. I wish you would not, Henri. The reasons should be apparent to you. I'm sure they lie in your mind just below the flimsy administrative veil. Lift the veil for a moment and my reasons will be clear to you. I have failed to bring any enlighten-

ment to Dibela, except for the four mission men and this odd little man, Wanga. It is not pride or fear or anything at headquarters that makes me say I cannot give up and go back. My spirit has entered into this place so completely that I now feel there is nothing to go back to. In short, I do not want to go back. Given these facts, I can only go ahead. And the only way I can do that is to strike at the very foundation of the people's superstition. Once that is broken, there is some hope I may help them. The necessity seems unreal in part to me, but perhaps a certain unreality is inevitable wherever civilizations collide. I regret the necessity of dramatics— of having to climb a mountain. But sometimes only dramatics can accomplish a necessary end. Do not indulge in analysis of me or drag some psychological theory of a complex from your books when I remind you that the wisest man who ever lived, Christ our Saviour, sometimes found it necessary to resort to dramatics.

So I am going, Henri—I'll have gone when you read this. Do not follow. I have made sensible plans and taken reasonable precautions. Kulu, Kosongo, Mzimba and Wanga are accompanying me. They are good, strong, loyal men—especially Kulu, who was raised on the lower slopes and is fearless. Musinga and Guta I have left behind. We are carrying provisions for two weeks. I carry Dr. Bickel's Springfield, a weapon with which I trained long ago in Liberia. It will not be needed against men or mountain spirits, but for game if necessary. I've read everything possible on mountain climbing and the Ruwenzori. (Dr. Bickel somehow managed to collect quite a library on the subject.) I have hardened myself by long walks hereabouts in recent weeks.

We go first to Kulu's home, a long day's march. From there we go up. I have no absurd ideas of pushing to Mt. Stanley, which would be impossible for me to reach. I'm simply going up the nearest highest mountain to the place where God is supposed to dwell. Then I'll come down again and demonstrate that He is as much here in Dibela as among the high peaks. Not long after my return I hope to begin doing some good in Dibela.

If I need you, Henri, I shall send one of the boys for you. Enjoy Dibela in my absence. If restlessness overtakes you, do not go beyond Kulu's village on the spur. Wait for me there. Meanwhile, read a book under the limbali and do not think of me.

As ever,
RACHEL

He folded the letter and looked up blindly. At last he saw Father Gilo, wiping the yellow dust from his sweating face with a white handkerchief. The priest filled a glass with water from the bottle which Rachel must have filled and left on the table. He drank, gazing at Lecomte above the rim as he raised his head.

He set down the glass and said, "It's good spring water here."

Chief Buderga stood at the foot of the steps, not looking at Lecomte.

"Chief—" he tried honestly and failed to blunt the sharpness of his tone—"did Madami ask you for men to climb the mountains with her?"

"Aieee," Buderga said. "Yes."

"And you did not send them?"

Buderga shook his head slowly. "It is forbidden to climb the mountains."

"Who forbids it?"

"It is forbidden. It is bad. No one will go."

"You make bad medicine here in Dibela, Buderga."

"Aieee." Now he looked at Lecomte boldly. "But you come yourself to fetch back the white Madami. You do not want something bad to happen to her."

Lecomte took a step forward angrily—and halted.

"No." His voice was tight. "I did not come to fetch back Madami, Buderga."

The Chief gazed up at him in astonishment.

"I came to pause here a while. I may do some hunting hereabouts, Buderga."

The astonishment did not leave the broad, strong face.

"Now take your bad medicine and get from my sight, Buderga. And silence your drums!"

Lecomte turned on a heel and faced Father Gilo.

The priest smiled at him. "Henri, you really are a most intelligent man."

Part Two

VIII

AT NOON they rested under a giant mimosa tree beside a clear stream that rushed over crystalline rocks. Far off a baboon hooted. Then the bush belonged to the insects, humming, screaming, dripping like rain on the leaves, while birds were still and animals slept.

They had eaten small bananas and juicy yellow mangoes picked on the way and they'd drunk deeply from the cold stream. The men, except Kulu, lay in the ferns. He sat, eyes half closed, listening. It was too early for pursuit, Rachel thought. Lecomte would not yet have arrived in Dibela. And when he read her note, he might not follow. Oh, give him the good judgment not to pursue!

The mountains were far up ahead, high above the bruised sky. But they showed their first sign, the crystalline rocks of the stream there. For these were not volcanic mountains; they had been created in the great upheavals that formed the world. A few million years ago they'd tossed down a message which she, leaning against this great mimosa now, could read if she wished: the crystalline rocks that said, We are older than time. (Take care, she thought. Don't become the center of the universe. What was it the Quakers said? "Beware the Particular.") Yet she could not ignore the Particular of the ancient mountains in the heart of the ancient continent. By virtue of their age alone one could understand why some Africans should believe that here dwelt the ancient deity, not the Christian Mungu of the Swahili tongue, but the Nzame or Nzamo or Nzambi or Ndjyakomba or Anyambie of many old dialects. But she would show that no cruel God dwelt in the Mountains of the Moon—God willing. "Beware the Particular. . . ."

She must have dozed, for she started when Kulu said gently, "It is time, Madami?" It was indeed time, she saw by her wristwatch. One o'clock, and they had far to go.

"Hoaieee!" sang Kulu, shouldering her sleeping bag. On the sleeping bag was lashed Dr. Bickel's ice ax, and around the ax coiled the long

rope. Rachel swung on her knapsack and slung the rifle on her right
shoulder. The men were on their feet, spears in hands and bows and
sweat-blackened quivers of arrows over shoulders. Kosongo raised the
tin box containing her provisions onto his head and grinned at her.
Mzimba raised the tin box containing the men's provisions and groaned.
Wanga lifted the heavy extra pack onto his back. Each barefoot man carried shoes wrapped in his blankets for the rocks and snows of the summits. Somewhere an insect rasped, *con-trast, con-trast, con-trast.*

"Njoo!" grunted Kulu and started up the faint track that wound among
palmyra trees. She followed, and after her came Kosongo and then
Mzimba and finally Wanga.

Sweat ran down her breasts under the khaki shirt and formed on her
legs under the rough twill trousers. Shifting her bush hat and touching
her hair, she smiled wryly. Vanity, vanity. She had cut her hair yesterday,
cropping it short, hacking at it ruthlessly with scissors, forming a dark
and gleaming pile for Guta's ash heap. A sacrifice to the mountains. And
if she did not take care she would feel a trifle sorry that no one but she
could see and care what she had done. Vanity, vanity.

"Hoai!" sang Kulu, bowed under the weight of his load.

"Hoai!" answered Kosongo.

"Watu wasiokuja kazini jana . . ." sang Kulu, and then all chanted
rhythmically, "Ho—ai! Ho—ai!"

"Waende kwa Bwana . . ." sang Kulu, and the deep voices replied,
"Ho—ai! Ho—ai! Hoai, hoai, hoai!"

Let the men who did not come to work yesterday go to the master.

Now Kosongo sang, "Watu wasiokuja kazini . . . Ho—ai! Ho—ai!
. . . leo wasipate fedha yao kesho . . ." And the long, deep chant.

Let the men who are not at work today get their money tomorrow.

It was jazz, she thought, improvised and powerful, before enslavement
and the dirges of exile in the Mississippi Valley.

There were two men who did not come to work, sang Kulu, and one
was loved by a woman. And the other loved the woman, sang Kosongo.
Why didn't the men come to work for the master? Ah, one pursued the
woman. And the other was pursued by the woman.

Round and round. The circle of African song that knew no end, as
the turning of the seasons and the turning of the earth knew no end. The
time was slow because the march was slow.

But long ago on Bourbon Street in New Orleans the same kind of
music had been fast, she remembered. On a march to the mountains here,
time was truly a scythe; but in America time was always a mechanical

mower. She preferred not to think of New Orleans, but she kept thinking of it. She had gone there on a vacation from Kansas City. The man to whom she had been introduced—he was handsome—had taken her to one of the jazz spots and interpreted the music. He was a kind man. They had fun together and he tried to go to bed with her and she had wanted to because the engagement in Kansas City had broken up then—that's why she'd taken a vacation in New Orleans—but she hadn't let him go to bed with her. And far into the morning hours she'd lain wide-eyed and rigid in her narrow hotel room and thought of the kind and handsome man she had wanted to go to bed with but hadn't, wondering why she hadn't, wondering if that one painful incident in the wheat fields long ago had made the act of love forever impossible for her.

She had not thought of this in a long time, she did not want to think of it now. I shall lift up mine eyes unto the hills, she thought, and she felt sweat down her breasts and her legs.

"Ho—ai! . . . Ho—ai!"

The song had not ended, for it was endless. It was merely suspended, waiting for Mzimba or Wanga to pick it up. But Mzimba could not form lines of song in his mind and Wanga could not form them in his heart, so there was no singing until Rachel, desperately trying to forget New Orleans, called out almost breathlessly, "I shall sing one line," and Kulu turned and grinned at her and the men cried, "Aieee!"

"Watu wasiokuja kaini kesho watapata matata," she sang. They laughed delightedly at her line of song: If those men don't come back to work tomorrow, they'll get into trouble. But it did not delight Rachel, for she heard her voice clearly, as if another sang. It was, she thought, the throaty voice of a woman singing the blues.

They left the high grass and passed into a last thicket of the equatorial forest where no sunlight filtered. Silently they filed between buttresses of enormous palms which raised a mucus-colored scaffolding of enormous roots where hirsute spiders as large as one's hand scuttled. They emerged into light and climbed steadily through palmyra trees. Macaws screamed and monkeys chattered, flashing and swinging before them, alarming the unknown world ahead of their approach.

A coldness breathed on them, refreshing at first until its dankness seemed to putrefy. At last, Rachel knew, this was the beginning of the mountains. But she felt no exhilaration. The coldness ate at her until dissolved by the sweat of climbing. Still she felt numbed, though not

[87]

by cold, as they went straight up, and then up by switchback, twisting and turning, gasping for breath and pausing, and then pushing on.

At last Kulu halted and raised a hand. They stood on a ridge. On their right they sensed, but could not see, the towering mountains. On their left the light was failing.

Cupping his hands, Kulu shouted: "Ai-ooh!" His shout rolled, echoing, along the mountain wall. When it died, there came, quite close, an answering "Ai-ooh!"

"Come," Kulu said and plunged ahead faster.

In a few minutes a young man emerged from the gloom ahead. Grounding his spear, he raised an arm in salute and spoke in a dialect Rachel could not understand. He was tall, finely proportioned, naked except for a breechcloth and the amulets of power. His cheeks were tattooed and in the lobe of his left ear was fixed a leopard's tooth. He and Kulu shook hands with the old African grip of thumbs and talked quietly in their dialect. Then Kulu said, "Madami, this is my cousin, Kita, the mighty hunter and chief of our village. He speaks your and my tongue a little."

Kita studied her gravely as she extended her hand and said, "I'm happy to meet you, Kita." Kulu never had mentioned him, but she lied, "I have heard of your greatness as hunter and chieftain."

"Ah!" Kita smiled and met her hand in the thumb grip. "The white man who came had not heard of me. But Madami has. I could have taken him through the bamboo forests, but he would not hear me because I would not speak in a tongue he could understand. I speak so Madami can understand, because Madami speaks as I do. Welcome to our village. I shall take you on through the bamboo forests."

Kulu, obviously pleased, spoke animatedly in their dialect again. This was good luck. It was important, then, that Kita be an ally. But Kulu had said nothing to prepare her for meeting his cousin. It was strange. But, as they walked on, she realized that Kulu had not thought it necessary to prepare her. He had known she would instinctively conduct herself correctly. The village had learned by the morning drum rolling out of Dibela that they were coming. That, Kulu must have thought, was enough. Aided by God the Father and Jesus the Christ, Madami would do the rest.

The thin wrist of the ridge widened into a broad hand as darkness fell. Fires flared and there were the shadows, voices, smells of a village. People speaking the dialect she could not understand pressed close to see the woman with the strange white skin, and one bold child touched her arm. Kulu moved against the lights of fires, seeming taller and more assured than he ever had in Dibela.

They showed her to a hut where Kulu unrolled her sleeping bag and suspended her net over the head. Suddenly she was so tired that she gladly would have crawled into the bedroll. But she knew she could not. Fire was carried to the front of her hut and over the fire Kulu hung her personal cooking pot. As he worked he carefully explained he could cook dinner for her from the provision box or else she could join in eating Kita's food. It was, he said, a dish of yams and manioc and bushbuck.

He was pleased when she said she would eat Kita's food. Kita and other young men appeared. Women gathered around their own fire pot and from the periphery of darkness peered old men. She knew instinctively that the old men disapproved of change and the violation of the upper slopes, and she wondered if there had been some kind of revolution here that had brought young Kita to power over the old, disapproving men.

"Is your father here?" she asked Kulu.

"Over there, Madami." He nodded toward the shadows. "I spoke to him briefly, but he has no place here by this fire."

"May I discuss the legend with Kita?"

"Oh, yes, Madami, for he does not really believe it either, as our fathers did. He has been high in the mountains and he has seen no sign of God. You might tell him about God the Father and Jesus the Christ, Who are everywhere invisible. It would interest him."

She rose suddenly and went to the heavy pack which Wanga had carried. From it she took lengths of bright cotton cloth printed in Lugano, Switzerland, for the remote tropic trade. Going to Kita, she made a little speech, which Kulu quickly translated to the delight of all, and then she handed the cloth to Kita. His speech in reply was warm and lengthy and largely incomprehensible.

Taking her bowl, he dipped it in his own cooking pot, fearlessly violating the tabu that women should not eat from the men's pot. When an old man called to him from the darkness, he shouted an angry reply. Rachel asked Kulu what he had said, and Kulu murmured, "He says, 'This is not woman, this is the white Madami!'"

Not woman—but Madami. It was a troubling remark. She was only woman, an incomplete woman at that; she did not know who Madami was, except a symbol of power.

They ate, sitting cross-legged on the ground. When they had finished she told Kita, with Kulu helping in translation, that she had heard the legend. But she was going to the summit, she said, to prove that Bolambo's strange message was one of great wisdom: people should know one another and love one another and forgive one another. Kulu, standing behind Rachel, called her words to the people in their own tongue. The young men nodded, nodded, and somewhere one began to tap a drum.

Bolambo's message, said Rachel, was like the message of the true God of all, who did not live in the mountain peaks but was everywhere in space and eternal in time. God's spirit, she said, had entered Bolambo's heart before he died. Her voice rose and fell as they listened, and the tapping drum was joined by another that caught the rhythm of her story of God the Father and His Son, Jesus the Christ.

The drums bothered her. She tried to shut off their sound, and finally she believed that she had. Then, as she talked, she realized she was trying to listen to them instead of concentrating on her great true story. A young man rose and shuffled slowly out of the firelight. Another followed him, and they returned to the light, shuffling rhythmically, dark bodies gleaming in the firelight. Reed instruments began to bleat and the drums grew louder as other men joined the dance. The blare of a conch shell cut the reeds and Rachel was speaking only words, the great true story quite vanished from her thoughts, as she wondered, hypnotically, by what travail and magic a conch shell had come from a distant ocean to these oldest mountains in the world. Now the young women heaped wood on the fires and formed their own dancing line.

Rachel sat silently, a hand pressed over her mouth, staring fixedly at the dancers. Kita leaped to his feet, crying, "Madami tells a great story!" He began to dance, leading the mournful orchestra into a faster rhythm as he shuffled to the head of the line of men.

Beside her, Kulu's feet began to tap the rhythm. Suddenly he shouted in a strange voice, "A dance to God the Father!" and swung toward the dancers, clapping his hands.

She closed her eyes and pressed a hand against her mouth, thinking: What have I done? How have I created this terrible blasphemy? And then: Fast, fast as Bourbon Street. No! Then, resignedly: It is not blasphemy to dance to God if that is the way God speaks to one.

Rising, she went to her hut and undressed and crawled into her bedroll. But she could not sleep. The firelight leaped on the curving wall of the hut and the drums seemed to beat on her temples. The night was cool on the mountain, but no air penetrated the hut. She felt burningly hot, as with fever. At last, despairing of sleep, she flung herself out of the bag and pulled shirt and trousers over her underwear, thinking dimly that she'd carry the bag to some quiet, cooler place under the open sky. Dragging the bedroll outside, she stared at the dancers. This was no dance to God, she thought bitterly. Look at them, women naked except for their two small outer and inner aprons, breasts bobbing rhythmically. Men's faces distorted by earthly joy. The carnal smell of sweating bodies. What had she done?

There was Kulu, loose-limbed, laughing, lustful. Yes, lustful, as he moved toward a girl, whose teeth flashed in a smile at him. Suddenly the girl turned and ran and Kulu ran after her. They laughed as they raced into darkness.

IX

HER SLEEP was troubled by unremembered dreams. Yet she awakened at dawn, refreshed. Lying in her bedroll, looking out of the hut at the growing light, she suddenly thought: I am not going to climb the mountains.

She would go back to Dibela and she would go on back from Dibela to some jungle station. And if there was no tranquillity left in Africa for her, she'd go home, back to Kansas City, and from there on back to the ultimate end: the August stillness of a prairie town where maiden ladies sat alone, each behind her arborvitae hedge in the shade of dusty cottonwoods. She remembered that exact scene in a dream last night.

Kulu entered the hut quietly, bearing a basin of water. He was fresh from bathing in some mountain stream; she could smell the soap she'd given him. Feigning sleep, she watched him through slitted eyes. He looked—happy. Clean and happy. How could she begin to tell him how he had disappointed her? How could he have claimed to see the vision of God and then distort it into random lust for a girl whom he'd borne to earth in the night? She would say—

"Kulu!" A sharp tone.

He turned, smiling benignly. "Yes, Madami?"

It was not his smile that did it. It was her tone, the sharp tone of bitterly disappointed women which she'd heard in many places. Often, on hearing the tone, she'd thought, May I never sound like that. And now?

Birds sang in the trees. Nearby was the crunch of a woman grinding manioc with a pestle. There were the clear voices of men breaking a morning camp. And Kulu, standing there, smiling down at her, saying, "I have made coffee for Madami."

So— She faced the idea resolutely: Possibly she was frustrated and— yes, jealous that earthly joy had eluded her. Possibly—no, unquestionably she was deficient in Christian zeal. For she simply was incapable of chastising Kulu and turning back now. She would go on. It was man's condition to be carnal. And Kulu was a man. And she was—whatever she was, she never would raise the harsh voice of a bitterly disappointed woman.

"Madami?" Kulu looked at her with concern; he never had seen her so preoccupied. "Madami is well?"

"Madami is well, Kulu." She smiled wanly. "Now go and cook me fresh eggs for breakfast. We must start soon."

She bathed and dressed. When she came out of the hut, she saw the girl crouching by the men's fire, cooking manioc in palm oil. The girl glanced at her fearfully.

"Who is the girl, Kulu?"

"Ah, Madami, here is your coffee." He handed her a steaming cup. "The girl is of the village, Madami."

Rachel strolled to her. The girl stood up and backed away. She smelled, Rachel noted wryly, of the same scented soap as Kulu. So together they must have— "What is your name, girl?"

Kosongo, Mzimba and Wanga looked from Rachel to Kulu, laughing.

"Madami." Kulu trotted to her with the coffee. "She does not understand our language, Madami. Here is your coffee, Madami."

Rachel took the coffee and looked at him with amusement. "Then tell her I asked her name, Kulu."

"Her name is Giza, Madami, and she is of the village."

She must be a pretty girl by their standards, Rachel thought. She was fifteen or sixteen with firm young breasts and the darkest eyes she ever had seen. No scars or lesions anywhere visible. She overcame a temptation to ask to see the girl's mouth, as if the poor child were a horse.

"Tell her I think she's very pretty," Rachel said.

Kulu wet his lips but did not speak. Kosongo laughed and told Giza what Rachel had said. Giza smiled at her timidly.

"Kulu." Rachel sipped the coffee. "I think she would make you a good wife."

Mzimba, howling with laughter, fell over on his back. Kulu looked at Rachel with a troubled expression. "But Madami, I do not want a wife. How can I serve Madami if I have a wife nagging at me and children running all around and—and—" He brightened considerably— "I do not have the price of a wife."

"We could advance the necessary amount to the girl's father from mission funds," Rachel said.

Kulu said, "Owooo!" as if he had stepped on a thorn. Even Wanga laughed now. Rachel, fearing she was being cruel, stepped to the shrinking girl, and rested a hand lightly on her warm shoulder. "Now Kulu—" she looked at him—"tell Giza that I think she's a very pretty girl indeed."

Kulu muttered something to Giza and turned back to Rachel's fire. The girl understood, for she reached out impulsively and patted Rachel's arm.

Kita led the way from the village, swinging his long spear, striding so fast that the burdened men almost ran in order to keep up with him. Behind them filed a dozen young men who would go a half day, Kulu said, to honor their journey. And behind the young men ran children, laughing and shouting.

As they passed the last shamba at the edge of the forest, an old man with frizzled white hair hobbled into the path from a kapok tree. He gesticulated wildly and cried out. Kita shouted at him fiercely and raised his spear. The old man thrust his naked, bony chest forward defiantly and pointed at Rachel. Kita rested his spear point against the old man's chest and the column halted.

"What is he saying?" Rachel hurried around Kulu to Kita's side. "What is it?"

Kita did not answer as the old man fixed bloodshot eyes on her and poured out a torrent of words.

"Kulu." She turned to him. "What is he saying?"

Kulu looked at the ground.

"Kulu!"

"He placed a thahu on you, Madami." Kulu looked at her, troubled.

"A curse on me?" She smiled tightly. "What does he say?"

"He says if you go farther, Madami, you will be doomed to eternal suffering. He is a bad old man, Madami. I could run him through with my spear but it would cause bad blood between his family and mine. Pay no attention, Madami."

"Of course I pay no attention." Her voice rose and she lowered it. "But I would like to know his curse. Is it that I shall die?"

Kulu shook his head, staring at the ground. "No, Madami, he says that you shall live long, and as long as you live you shall be tormented. He says you shall live very long and suffer very long. He's a bad, crazy old man, Madami, and I shall run him through with my spear."

Kita suddenly whacked the old man aside with the butt of his spear. The old man fell to the ground, then raised himself on an elbow and pointed at Rachel, cursing her.

She bent over him and tried to raise him by his arms, but he shrank from her and rolled away in the grass, finally staggering to his feet and hopping off.

"Kita," she asked, "did the old man curse the white man, Dr. Bickel, when he started up the mountains?"

"Yes, Madami," he said gravely. "He said the white man would die."

"Let us go on," she said, stepping into the file behind Kulu. Kita hesitated. "Let us go on, Kita," Rachel said clearly.

The children, silent now, drifted back toward the village. The column filed into the shadows of the forest.

As they walked, Rachel thought, That old man's curse is meaningless. But unconsciously, she realized, she was examining herself. It was as if she had suffered a fall and were feeling herself to learn if any bone were broken. Then, consciously, she asked herself: What *could* happen to me to make me suffer? Wait. You must really believe in the curse to be thinking so hard. But why not think hard? What could happen to *me*? If life were long, life could be expected to be healthful. Then what could it be? If her effort failed at Dibela, she would go back. And if Ralph made it impossible back there, she could resign and go home. But where was home? She remembered the dream or thought-dream of waking: a prairie town with nasturtiums and cottonwoods in a yard hedged with arborvitae. Rachel Cade, old maid, the town trained nurse. Rachel Cade, with memories of Africa. Perhaps that would be the curse: to leave Africa, for Africa never would leave her. Africa was her only home.

What was the matter with her, taking a primitive old man's curse seriously? Only God could deliver a curse—if He would—but her God never would. "I shall lift up mine eyes unto the hills. . . ."

The trail climbed along the jagged edge of a deep ravine. Far below, visible occasionally through the dense green treetops, was the white-feathered course of a barely audible stream. From the rocky walls of the ravine grew clumps of giant bracken, thrusting over the void thirty-foot stems from which trailed lacy ten-foot leaves. Occasionally, as they worked along a narrow ledge, they saw the long twisting scar of the ravine rising ahead of them into mist.

Now she was glad she had trained for the journey with long walks around Dibela. Her pounding heart sometimes reminded her of Dr. Bickel, who must have been bent on suicide when he attempted this. As they climbed on, she tested each muscle, each breath for signs of weakness. Finding none, she was positive she would not fail, so that each step forward increased a sense of exhilaration in her. But the men? She kept counting them off. Kulu, rather reserved this morning while he puzzled over Madami's remarks about Giza, would certainly last. Kosongo would last. Mzimba sometimes troubled her with his tendency to moan and howl at the dizzy heights, but Mzimba was strong and Mzimba was social; he would rather die in company than try to return alone. She did not know what to think of Wanga, so quiet and absorbed in his own thoughts. Probably not even he knew why he had come on this strange journey; perhaps he had a dim loyalty to her for saving his son's life and a dim hatred of his town, Dibela. But at any time he might turn back without explanation, leaving an almost unbearable burden on the others. Kita might leave at any time too, she thought, for she instinctively doubted the tenacity of his gaily stepping warrior character.

Yet Kita kept on when the trailing honor guard turned back late in the morning. At noon, a dry stop, she carefully divided the water of her canteen among six cups and waited for Kita to say he was going back. Instead he said he would go ahead and find the night's camp.

As he disappeared up the trail, she asked Kulu, "How long do you think he will stay with us?" As soon as she'd spoken she knew it was the sort of question an African found incomprehensible.

"He will last until he tires of climbing, Madami," Kulu said.

She closed her eyes and smiled, rubbing her back against a kapok. "A most sensible answer, Kulu," she said in English. "Speculation is futile."

"Madami?"

She opened her eyes. "Yes, Kulu."

"Madami—" he chose his words carefully—"you think it good that I take Giza for a wife?"

"Yes, Kulu."

He sighed. "I do not think so, Madami."

[95]

"Today you do not, Kulu. Last night you did."

"Aieee!" He clapped his hands to his head. At last: "But last night was last night, Madami, and today is today."

"And tomorrow may be like last night, Kulu."

"Aieee!" He looked at her innocently. "I did wrong, Madami?"

Wrong? Of course he'd done a terrible wrong by all mission standards. For the standards were the Puritan and Catholic standards of the Temperate zones. The people must be monogamous and the women must cover their breasts; they must work hard and believe in the Christian God. One must ignore the basic reason for the Africans' polygamy: that a woman nursed her child for two years and dared not have intercourse in that time lest she become pregnant again and cause her milk to dry up so that the first child would die; and, since man was carnal, it was too long for him to wait. One must ignore the fact that to them a woman's breast was no more interesting a sexual object than a leg or arm. One must ignore the simple bounty of tropic earth which made idleness natural, even sensible, and caused the driving conspicuous consumption of Temperate man to seem unnecessary and even absurd here. One must never think of the Christian God as too abstract to fulfill their desire for tangible pagan gods.

But all this, she told herself, was evil thinking. They were the thoughts of one who had, as the stories said, "gone native." She must arouse herself and re-establish contact with the strong sources of her mission. Yet lethargy lay on her lightly, deliciously, as she stared at a strange bird with bright orange plumage perched on a bracken stalk and heard it sing two high sweet notes. Something was happening to her on the mountains. Some spiritual strength was evaporating. She had been absent too long from her own people, her own kind. And the odd thing (the deliciously odd thing, she thought, stretching her legs languidly in the ferns) was that she did not care.

"I did wrong?" repeated Kulu.

Now she would tell him of his great wrong. At least she would give him one small bromide on the virtues of celibacy. But she vividly remembered the drums and the firelight; she knew his great satisfaction in his new God. She could not say it.

"Think about it, Kulu," she said slowly. She wanted to quote a line of Scripture, but Scripture now would sound—hypocritical. "Think about it," she said.

Kulu knit his brows. He did not want to think about it. He wanted to forget it. If he had done wrong, he wanted Madami to tell him so that he could do penance. She understood that. But she also believed that he could not remain a child, dependent on her judgments. If he would embrace the new Western civilization he must also embrace the confusions of its individual thinking.

"Let us go," she said at last. Silently the men took up their burdens and resumed the climb.

The track was faint and sometimes overgrown altogether for long distances. But Kulu always found it again as they crept along the edge of the ravine. Once she complimented him on finding the way. He replied that he found it because Kita had blazed a trail. His honesty pleased her, but she did not find Kita's signs as she peered ahead.

As the afternoon wore on she judged they were well above five thousand feet and probably nearing six thousand. The rocks along the ravine edge, always formidable, became impassable. When it seemed they could not go farther, Kulu pointed silently to a bracken stalk which Kita had felled with his panga. They left the ravine and entered a dark green world of enormous ferns where there was no track, only the occasional blazes of Kita's panga. By her compass Rachel saw they were moving due south along the mountain flank. But direction seemed meaningless here and a compass useless.

They were like ants lost in an enormous field of tall grass, she thought. They sank to their ankles in spongy, humid earth. Sweat stung her eyes and she began to think of water. She touched her empty canteen on her belt and tried to think of other things. But she could think only of water, the cold rushing stream of yesterday and then the muddy water holes where cattle drank in Kansas. It seemed they were not moving. Where Kita had slipped through the dense clinging ferns, tunneling a way under their interlocked luxuriance, they could not follow with their burdens. Kulu, grunting, hacked at thick branches with his panga, forcing a few yards ahead, then backing away and turning in an easier direction, but always circling in the true direction and finding another of Kita's signs.

At last he halted and they stood, panting, in the green choking darkness of the great ferns where it seemed to Rachel that only a scream would free her from this prison. She stood, head bowed, eyes half closed, thinking of water and listening to her heart. Had Kulu finally given up?

He forced his way back past her, and Kosongo forced his way to the lead. Then the *chok-chok-chok* of Kosongo's panga began. They took a step forward. They moved a yard, two yards, three yards.

"Stop!" Kulu called hoarsely to Kosongo.

Rachel looked around at him dazedly. He was studying a tall slender bamboo which grew among giant ferns. He swung his panga suddenly and seized the bamboo as it fell. Methodically he searched its surface until he found a section bored by insects. He chopped off the section and, breaking off a hollow fern stem, he inserted it in an insect hole of the bamboo. Handing the bamboo to Rachel, he smiled and said, "Drink, Madami."

She drew thirstily on the fern stem. The water was cool and sweet. Forcing herself to stop drinking, she offered the bamboo to Kulu. But he shook his head and cut off four more lengths, handing one to each of the men and drinking from the last himself.

Then he said to Kosongo, "To the right." Kosongo plunged to the right.

In a few minutes Kulu called, "Left!" and Kosongo flung himself on another barrier.

They would have been forced back if the men had not brought their pangas, Rachel knew. Theoretically she led the expedition; she had tried to plan everything, but she had not thought of the heavy bush knives. Actually she did not lead the men. They led her. She was helpless. What they did, she would have to do.

It grew lighter, as if a cloud were passing from the sun. The great ferns parted high above their heads, exposing patches of leaden sky. Kulu resumed the lead and they moved faster along the steeply pitching mountainside, threading among the clumps of enormous ferns. She saw a balsamine with orchidlike flowers and a fifty-foot spur. Soon the exuberant balsamine were growing all about her, huge pale flowers lifted to the light, the air heavy with their sickly-sweet scent that reminded her of funerals and death.

It rained torrentially for several minutes. Her poncho was little protection against the downpour. Then the rain stopped and the earth steamed as they sloughed on. She imagined she could see them from a great height, tiny humans lost among the immense plants. She did not care. Lethargy dragged at her, more cloying than the gummy earth. She had tried to keep her rifle dry under the poncho during the rain, but now she didn't care if the rifle rusted. It was an unnecessary weight she'd gladly throw away.

"Ai!" Kulu halted and forced a smile at her. "Let us rest, Madami, before we go up." He pointed.

A faint track came out of the southwest and went straight up. She sank to the ground.

"The gun," Kulu said. "Does Madami want me to carry the gun?" When she shook her head, he said, "It's an animal track, Madami." Then, as she stared at him dully, he took his panga from his belt and hacked down a tall banana seedling, pointing it toward their path through the fern forest. "So we know the way coming back," he said.

Now she understood. He wanted her to tell him whether she wished to go on. He was not certain of her strength and undoubtedly it was much worse ahead. He was asking her to lead, for he'd sensed her spirit was faltering. Well, they were not going back. The thought was bravado, she knew, but it was a time for bravado.

"I understand," she said to him. Rising stiffly, she took a packet of salt tablets from her shirt pocket and gave him one and then handed one to each of the others who lay, exhausted, in the track. They licked down the tablets, staring at her moodily.

"Madami." Kulu beckoned her up the track. She went to him and stared down at a large, almost human footprint in the earth. "Gorilla," he said.

Oh, God, she thought and controlled an impulse to laugh hysterically. Oh, Tarzan! Neither she nor anyone she knew had seen a gorilla in Africa; they were becoming extinct and it was forbidden to kill them. Now here on the mountains was the imprint of a gorilla.

"Have you ever seen a gorilla, Kulu?"

"No, Madami. Only their signs. Long ago I had a cousin who went hunting gorillas and never was seen again."

The lethargy had left her. "Let's go on," she said.

They stumbled off the faint animal track toward the fire of Kita's campsite as it was growing dark. He'd made camp beside a spring and against a cliff face that glowed redly in the firelight. That afternoon he'd killed a small topi which he now was slowly roasting on a spit. He crouched on his heels before the spit, so preoccupied that he scarcely turned his head when they sank to the ground around him.

Rachel found her cup in her knapsack and drank thirstily from the spring, feeling the cold water numb her stomach, drinking three full cups until she paused and stared at Kita across the fire. A complete man, she thought, self-sufficient and unafraid. He could climb alone to the summit and return. They would not go far after he left them.

She was so exhausted that each move was painful. She wanted to crawl into the bedroll and fall asleep, but she forced herself to walk around the fire to Kita. She sat down beside him and admired the roasting topi. Guile. Yet guile was as necessary as strength if she would succeed. She was certain of that now. And what happened when guile was exhausted? What would she have to spend and give? It was a strange thought, she realized, persistent and yet seeming to lead nowhere.

Like many apparently self-contained men, Kita responded favorably to guile. His admiration of his own prowess increased in proportion to hers. While Kulu watched and listened and sometimes translated for her, Kita told of great hunts.

As he was carving the meat, a leopard sounded its *ha-ha-ack—uh, ack, uh—ack-ack-ack* somewhere on the mountain. But the cry did not stay Kita's hand. He simply said, "Leopard." They ate their fill of the pink tough meat sprinkled heavily with salt. Then Kita unwrapped a pipe from a bit of leopard skin and lighted it with a live coal held between thumb and forefinger. A strange sweet fragrance, unlike tobacco, enveloped them.

Kulu translated for her when she asked Kita if he had seen the gorilla signs today. Kita's look was withering, as if he had seen much more, but he replied politely that he had seen many signs, some fresh and others old. She knew it was foolish to question him. Probably he did not understand the kind of fear-talk that whites engaged in.

In a few minutes Kita drew from his blanket a bongo horn which encased a small pebble. Rising, he stepped to the limit of firelight and rattled the pebble toward the darkness. Gravely he walked the limit of firelight, rattling the pebble in the horn, while the men watched him dully.

So he was not above fear, Rachel thought. He rather disappointed her. His rattle, the gift of a sorcerer, was his expedient against bad influences. Her story last night of God the Father and Jesus, His Son, had been merely a good story to him. Like most Africans, he felt that evil alone existed and good was merely the accidental absence of evil. Everything, he believed, was hostile to man.

Kicking a huge chunk of wood onto the fire, he wrapped his blanket around him, lay down, and instantly was asleep.

As she went around the fire to her sleeping bag, something huge and black suddenly whirred at her from the cliff. She screamed and ducked. Another came, crying strangely.

"They are bats, Madami," Kulu called, hurrying to her. "Giant bats live here on the mountain but they will not hurt you. They live on fruit."

Without undressing she scrambled into the sleeping bag and drew it over her head. At last she raised her head and looked out. Crying weirdly, the giant-winged bats whirred over the fire and disappeared.

Everything hostile to man, she thought. Here on the mountains that was understandable.

X

At noon Mzimba said, "Madami, I want to go home."

"If you leave, Mzimba, you will get lost and die. We must stay together."

He rolled over on his face and groaned. Her logic was unanswerable.

"I'll go with him, Madami," Wanga said.

"Fools," snapped Kulu. "You're weak men from the plain. You cannot find your way back without me. What would you do when the leopard stalks you? How would you make a fire when the wood is wet?"

Wanga stared at him defiantly before his shoulders slumped.

It had been a bad morning. They had climbed straight up through dense forest, hacking a way through the matted undergrowth, climbing and sliding over fallen trees. They were bruised by rocks and scratched by thorns and finally the men had been forced to put on their painful shoes as protection against giant nettles and splintered fragments of bamboo deadfalls. Now the land had leveled in plateau, but nowhere through the clouds that swirled just above the green roof of their prison could they see a sign of release.

They must be well above seven thousand feet now, Rachel thought. But where did the plateau end? Kita's answers to her questions were vague. He had said it was not far to the great bamboo forests. But she was beginning to doubt that he had been here before. He, too, was restless, she noticed. At any moment he might turn back. He'd foraged ahead for game this morning and returned empty-handed. Even the game deserted this wilderness.

When they started on after the noon rest, however, Kita still was in the lead, slashing at clinging liana and thicket unwillingly, but still slashing. It rained steadily. They slid down a muddy gulley and hauled themselves up a farther bank and crawled under huge fallen trees and slid down another gulley. There, by a common tacit consent, they dropped their burdens and lay still. Only Rachel was standing. Looking at their mud-spattered bodies, their half-closed eyes, she thought that this was as far as they could go. But it was not as far as she could go. Some fanatic strength stirred in her body. The necessity was clear. If they turned back now, she would leave Dibela. If she left Dibela, she would leave Africa. Would that be the eternal suffering of the curse? Of course, she didn't believe in the curse. Face it, she told herself, standing there in the rain, you *do* half believe in the curse and may God have mercy on your soul for half believing in it.

"Njoo!" she said to Kulu.

"Yes, Madami," he gasped. "In a moment, Madami."

Kita croaked harshly to Kulu, and Kulu crawled along a rotting log to him. In a moment he returned, his muddy forehead creased in a frown.

"Kita wants to go back now, Madami."

Mzimba and Wanga would go with him. If they returned, the temptation surely would be too great for Kosongo. And so, she thought bitterly, ended one more attempt to climb the Mountains of the Moon. She realized suddenly that she would give anything in her power to force them to go on.

"What does Kita want?" she asked Kulu in a low voice. "What can I give him that will make him go on and help us?"

Kulu frowned. "I don't know, Madami." His voice fell. "But if there is anything, you must not give it to him until he has gone as far as you both agree." He slithered along the log to Kita again and they talked together. When he returned, he was shaking his head. "It cannot be, Madami. Kita says if you will give him your gun and much ammunition and teach him to use it he will go as far as you wish, even to the summit. But our people are forbidden to own guns."

So that was all. A great sense of relief rose in her. A mere rifle. She did not know what she'd expected, but a rifle was nothing. Of course he could have it. And if Henri Lecomte ever heard of it, she'd talk her and Kita's way out of the problem.

"It's a pact," she said levelly to Kulu. "Tell Kita that he must climb to the summit with us and return with us to your village. There I shall give him the rifle and many rounds of ammunition and show him how to use it. But there will be no more bargaining. There will be nothing more. A pact is a pact and this will be the end of it."

Kulu stared at her. "Madami," he said worriedly. "Madami—" He did not know what to say. "Madami—"

"Tell him, Kulu."

Kulu crawled along the log and told Kita. Then Kita rose, smiling, and cried, "Njoo!" Slowly the men dragged themselves to their feet and they went on.

As light faded, they staggered from the anaconda winding of the wilderness. The change was too sudden for them to comprehend immediately, as if they suddenly had found release from inevitable death. Before them rose a strange country from which gray clouds rolled. They stared, motionless, watching the clouds roll back until they glimpsed a dim white peak.

The peak faded and Rachel's gaze fell to the strange country, a green and brackish land of what seemed giant toadstools and spikes and weaving moss. A nightmare land. She closed her eyes, thinking that this was not just the surface of the Mountains of the Moon, but the surface of the moon itself. Its utter silence seemed physically to squeeze them so that instinctively they moved closer together before its oppressive weight.

"Njoo!" muttered Kita and walked on.

They followed him across green moss that turned black as the light failed, and they wound among lichen-bearded podocarpus trees as the cold rose numbingly. When only a few minutes of dim light remained, Kita halted and began slashing at a podocarpus with his panga. The sound echoed on the mountain. Frighteningly, Rachel thought. The silence should not be disturbed.

She stood numbly, with Kosongo and Mzimba and Wanga clustered close behind her, staring at Kita and Kulu cutting the podocarpus branches. Ceasing suddenly, Kita drew a cigar-shaped package of leaves from his leopard-skin pouch. He unwrapped the leaves carefully until a smoldering chunk of moss was exposed. Squatting, he breathed on it and it glowed in the darkness. Fire caught the dry inner husk of podocarpus and leaped up. Kosongo sighed in relief.

If they talked at all that evening, Rachel did not remember it. She ate a tin of corned beef and a couple of hard biscuits, washing them down with scalding coffee, and then she put on her extra sweater and crawled into her sleeping bag.

A strange sound awakened her. It was early morning and she was numb with cold. It came again, a human scream that ended in an animal roar. About her rose the dim shapes of the men, faces stiff with cold and terror as they groped for their spears.

"Gorilla," Kulu said faintly.

Kita was on his feet, his spear raised. "Sidalaba!" he cried. She did not know the meaning of the word. She reached for the poncho in which she'd wrapped her rifle each night, but the rifle was not there.

"Sidalaba!" Kita cried again, shaking his spear at the mountain. His face was contorted into a fierceness she never had seen on any face, a strange mixture of pride and fear and cunning and anger.

"My rifle." Her voice was calm. "Where is my rifle?" Then she saw it at Kita's feet. She muscled out of the sleeping bag and her hands found her boots while she stared at Kita and the men looking fearfully from him to the mountain.

"Kulu." Her voice was calm. "Fetch me my rifle."

As Kulu stooped to pick up the rifle, Kita struck his arm with the edge of a hand. Kulu snarled at him in the strange tongue and Kita snarled in reply.

"Kita!" she cried sharply.

His eyes on Kulu, he spoke rapidly.

"Madami." Kulu did not turn; he stayed, half crouching, eyes fastened on Kita. "Kita says he must have the rifle now. He says you must show him how to use it and he will kill the gorilla on the mountain."

"Nonsense." She made her tone affable. "We have a pact—"

So swiftly her eyes could not follow, Kita swung the point of his spear against Kulu's throat.

"Do not move, Kulu," she said tensely. "Ask Kita why he has lost the use of our tongue and cannot speak to me."

Unmoving, Kita spoke to Kulu in his own dialect.

"The blood is on Kita," Kulu said at last in a strangled tone. "He cannot speak in any tongue but his own until he has slain the gorilla that defies him. It has been said that one man of our village someday will slay a gorilla and he will be the greatest hunter of all time. Kita says it will be he."

"Tell Kita," Rachel said slowly, "that I know a greater story. Tell him it has been said that we shall pass unmolested through all dangers to the summit. But if—" her words fell slowly—"we seek trouble, trouble will destroy one of us. Let Kita give me my rifle, as we have made our pact, and we shall go on."

Kita spoke rapidly again to Kulu.

"Madami." Now he was truly frightened. "Kita says he goes to meet the gorilla, as it has been told one shall do. Kita says he will first kill me and then the rest unless he goes with the rifle." His voice rose. "He means it, Madami."

"Very well." It was hopeless. "Tell him he shall have the rifle."

Kita spoke.

"And you will teach him to use it, Madami?"

"I shall teach him." Before we turn back, she thought, leaving Kita here on the mountain. Before I turn back to Kansas.

Kita spoke again.

"He says," Kulu said, "that he will lead you on to the summit after he has slain the gorilla and recovered his tongue and become the greatest hunter of all time."

"Very well."

Kita grounded his spear and Kulu backed from him.

Was Kita, she suddenly wondered, so different from herself? When he proudly sought to meet his fate against a gorilla, was he really very different from her, proudly seeking her fate against the mountains? Wearily now: it seemed so long ago that the reason for climbing the mountains was apparent to her. The good reason of overcoming superstition so that she could perform good works which needed to be done. Now the reason was dim and lost—foolish and naïve even—in the immediate grim struggle against the mountains.

"Madami." Kulu stood beside her, trembling. "He has gone mad, as my cousin went mad and sought the gorilla and never was seen again. Show him how to use the gun and let him go on. We shall go back, Madami. We must go back. The way is easy. Let us leave this place. If we go on, we'll die."

"Start the fire and cook breakfast, Kulu."

Kita gazed at her watchfully as she took a cartridge clip from her knapsack and moved toward him. He picked up the rifle by the barrel and handed it to her trustingly.

"Beware, Madami," Kulu called as the others clustered around him, chattering.

"So you've lost your tongue, Kita," she said dryly.

She suddenly was incapable of hating him, even though he had destroyed the expedition. Certainly she did not fear him. For, she thought, in him was something of her own madness. The morning cry of a gorilla aroused in him a desire for supremacy even as this hateful mountain (quite ignoring the good forgotten reasons that had made her turn to it) had become a personal enemy she must conquer. Race, climate and twenty centuries of so-called progress had failed to make much difference between Kita and Rachel Cade.

"You cannot possibly learn what I'm going to try to teach you, Kita," she said in English, gripping the rifle.

She paused, thinking, I'm destroying him. If he had not come and been tempted by the rifle; and if she had not let him be tempted by her fateful bargain yesterday; if—if— It would be her fault if anything happened to him, for she had brought the temptation of the rifle. Now he must learn to use it quickly, and he could not learn to use it at all, let alone skillfully. He was not acting in the way whites said Africans acted, as if black skin prescribed a traditional conduct. Whites would say she had failed to maintain control. Supremacy, the whites called it. Yesterday in the muddy gulley when he had threatened to turn back, she should have pointed her rifle at him and told him to move on. Then he would have respected her (the whites would say). But she'd been incapable of it. Soft? Perhaps that was it. There could be no softness or understanding on the mountains. Their immovability demanded irresistible force. So perhaps she had failed in her appointed role of supremacy. And, as a result, he had failed in his appointed role of docility. She had destroyed the established order of life in this country. She had gone too far by not going far enough. For such an error in such a place nature exacted the penalty of destruction.

Wearily she passed a hand across her forehead, thinking, Let him learn, while she knew she should be thinking, Let him die.

She pulled back the rifle bolt and inserted the clip and drove the bolt and released the safety and raised the rifle. He stared in fascination, his spear held loosely. By swinging quickly, she could shoot him between the eyes. It would not surprise anyone—except Kita. The rest probably expected it. Kulu, who had sweated the death sweat before Kita's spear, surely expected it. In this country almost anyone—Lecomte, for example —would have done it. But Kita's eyes were not fierce now; they simply were bright with growing interest in the weapon. She was shocked to think that even theoretically she had considered killing him. As she turned slowly she lined in the rifle sights a small silent bird on a podocarpus limb. She hesitated and passed on to a dead branch fifty yards away. She pressed the trigger. The branch plummeted to earth as the sound crashed and echoed across the silent mountainside.

"Aieee!" wailed Kulu. But Kita shouted triumphantly.

As the morning light grew and the mist rolled back, she showed him how to handle the weapon, loading and unloading, demonstrating bolt and safety and trigger and sighting, until the crucial moment when he loaded the rifle and fired and missed a distant tree.

"Let us eat," she said. During breakfast the men carefully sat apart from Kita. He sat with crossed legs, the rifle across his thighs, oblivious to them as he stared up the mountain.

At last Rachel said slowly, "You have ears though still no tongue, Kita. Surely you have wisdom to be so great a hunter. In your wisdom you see that you're not yet ready to hunt the gorilla with the rifle. Wait until your skill has increased." She rose. "Now give me back the rifle and we'll go on to the summit. We'll pass unharmed through the gorillas if we do not try to harm them. You can return later to hunt them when you've learned to shoot."

Kita swung to his feet, as if he had not heard her. He reached in her knapsack and drew out a half-dozen cartridge clips. Stepping a few yards away, he clumsily but methodically loaded the rifle, remembering the safety, as she had showed him.

"Madami," Kulu whispered, "let's go back now."

But she paid no attention; she watched Kita. He revealed, she thought, the same kind of awkwardness and naïveté with the rifle that she had demonstrated when she had quit her natural life and organized this expedition to the mountains.

Kita raised the rifle and fired without flinching. He hit the tree. He ejected the shell and fired again and missed the tree. He released the remaining live cartridges and then clumsily reloaded them and set the safety, carefully pointing the rifle in the air and squeezing the trigger to make sure it was set. He put one clip in his pouch and the remainder in his arrow quiver and rolled his belongings in his blanket. With bow across his shoulder and spear in his left hand and rifle in his right, he started up the deep mossed bank toward the highlands.

"Wait!" Her imperative tone made him pause and slowly turn. "We'll go with you, Kita."

"No!" cried Kulu. "Madami, no, no, no!" And the men shouted, "No!" and Mzimba flung his bowl on the ground and lay down, kicking at the moss and crying, "No! No!"

Her body felt rigid, as if it would break but never bend. "Listen to me! I command you in the name of God our Father to follow me!" Dimly she thought, It's not my voice. It was as if someone she did not know had delivered a curse, taking the name of God not in vain but in vanity.

"In the name of God our Father?" Kulu looked at her dazedly.

"Come," she whispered, stooping and gathering up her knapsack.

Mist pressed them in its morning amber as they climbed fast over slimy moss. Kita ranged far ahead, seldom in sight. Rachel followed, sliding and slipping and occasionally falling, but never losing his footprints in the moss. The men trailed badly, often out of sight. Kulu brought up the rear now, a drover instead of a shepherd, pushing the others ruthlessly, snarling and jabbing his spear at them, an erstwhile friend who had become their bitter enemy.

Frequently he shouted, "Ma—dami!" And she would call back through the mist, "Aye." He would shout, "Slower, please, Madami." And she would call back, "Aye." But she did not slow her pace. Before nightfall they must press through the strip of bamboo forest that lay ahead, leaving behind them that dreaded land where the gorillas feasted on tender shoots. On the day after tomorrow she must reach the summit and start down again. Their food would not last more than four days longer. They would be hungry before they returned to Kulu's village. If they returned.

For now, as she climbed alone, she pondered death. And she found, to her surprise, that she did not fear it. Purposefully, recklessly, she cast out the balance of judgment. She accepted the fact that here on the mountain she had become fanatically obsessed by the single idea of conquering it. At some lower altitude she'd left caution and enjoyment of comfort. There was no good thing left in life except to reach the summit. Only by reaching it could life ever be good again. The gorillas were not the great danger; the great danger was simply exhaustion or a broken leg. The gorilla, she told herself, was a shy vegetarian who did not pursue man. The gorilla had a thick vestigial skull that could repel a clip of .30-caliber bullets. If a gorilla loomed through the mist now they would gaze curiously at each other across the chasm of eighty thousand years and turn from each other. And if the gorilla did not turn away— It was better to die here on the mountain than to return to life's slow erosion.

As she climbed, she sought some nourishing bit of stoic thought. She found, bemusedly, that she could not remember any lines from the Bible that would strengthen her. No fragment of poetry returned nostalgically. At last she sank into the moss to wait for the men to come up, remembering a bit from the Second Part of *Henry IV*:

"*By my troth I care not; a man can die but once; we owe God a death. . . . No man's too good to serve his prince; and let it go which way it will, he that dies this year is quit for the next.*"

No man's too good to serve his prince. But who was the prince she served? God, she thought hastily, the Christian God whom she had formally worshiped in church for as long as she could remember. Wasn't it God who had given her the call, as they said, to come to the foreign mission field? Well, yes. But also there had been the fascination with far-off lands and the breaking up of the engagement to Dick, whom she had loved (could she have? yes, she must have loved) so devotedly. Now, in this wilderness where rain drip-drip-dripped from a tumescent primeval growth that might in some centuries-long evolution become a tree, why did God not inspire her? Why was she inspired to die rather than live? Why did hope of life come not from God but from a primitive old man far below who had cursed her with a prophecy of long life?

She buried her face in her hands and heard hoarse breathing and the heavy slogging of feet. Looking up, she stared at the men as they flung down their burdens and fell in the moss. Only Kulu stood, resting on his slender spear.

"Madami," he said, "let us stay together now as we go through—" He pointed ahead.

The mist boiled up and there came the pale lemon glow of sun, lighting the moss lands and silvering the limits of the bamboo forest. For a moment she was suffused by a sense of unearthly beauty until she felt again the ache of muscles and the old hopelessness at going on.

But in a few minutes she got to her feet and said, "Let us go."

There was no sign of Kita as they approached the bamboo forest. His tracks in the moss had disappeared completely.

"It's my fault we lost the tracks, Madami," Kulu said. "I know where I lost them. We were climbing fast, and I should have gone back and followed them."

"No," Rachel said. "I saw his direction." She pointed southeast. "He went toward the thickest part of the forest. He has gone his way. We'll go ours."

They walked slowly, softly, staring at the bamboos before them. From the top of a slender tree came the warbling warning call of a sunbird. Then Rachel saw it, a beautiful bird of dark metallic green shot with iridescent purple. Wind passed through the bamboos, rattling their branches.

"Aieee!" Kulu padded beside her on bare feet. "Behold how God the Father goes before us, clearing the forest of all dangers. See, the sunbird is still, watching us."

She glanced at him and saw he no longer was afraid. Close behind them the three men walked side by side, listening to Kulu. If only her faith were as strong as his. Yet where had he found it? From her, he would say. And she thought, No, Kulu, not from me.

"Madami," he said, "let's sing the American song now as we go into the forest."

She did not want them to sing it. It was childish, and she did not want them to be childish. She regretted teaching it to them, but they'd said they wanted to learn a song of her native land in her native tongue. And so she'd found herself teaching them the childish song that so many missionaries taught their people in English, the song that vaguely disturbed her whenever she heard it sung in the great mission compounds of the equatorial forests down west. It was a children's song, and while Africans might be childlike, they were not childish.

"Please start it, Madami," Kulu said.

She began to sing huskily and the others joined her, drowning her voice so that she stopped singing as they trudged toward the forest.

"Ja-sus loves me these ah knew,
For da Bee-bul tells me sew.
Lee-tul ones to Heem ba-long,
Dey are wake, but Hey is strong."

"Yas, Ja-sus loves me," sang Kulu.
"Yas, Ja-sus loves me," sang Kosongo.
"Yas, Ja-sus loves me," sang Mzimba.
Together they chanted, "Da Bee-bul tells me sew."
"Aieee," cried Kulu, "let's sing it again."

Now they were in the bamboo forest, panting on the steep climb, but still finding breath to sing. Their voices echoed in the open glades where sun fell through the silver leaves and mottled the ground in leopard's spots. They saw the droppings of gorillas and Kulu began to sing again and this time Rachel joined him strongly, smiling confidently at the others as they moved in stumbling phalanx.

In less than an hour the forest grew more open, its trees smaller, and soon they left it behind them. Its upper branches spread below them like a silver lake, but still they climbed on without resting into the strange land of the tree heaths. They kept looking back toward the forest, until, well into the afternoon, they collapsed on a high knoll. For fully ten minutes they lay still, gasping and sweating.

The crash of a rifle, rolling across the highlands, brought them to their feet. They stared far down at the forest shining in the sun. But there was no sound, no movement on the sun-drenched land. Then, far down in the forest, came a bull-throated roar whose echo seemed to grunt along the ridges. Again a rifle crashed, nearer this time. And again. But Rachel could see no movement along the distant curling edges of the shining forest.

Suddenly Kulu cried, "Madami, look!" He pointed south of the place where they had left the forest, but she saw nothing. "Look, Madami."

Then she caught the gleam of sunlight on metal and made out a figure moving. It was a man running. Kita running. And from the forest behind him came another figure, squat and black, closing the gap between them in huge leaps. Kita halted and turned. She saw the flash of rifle fire, but the thick black figure bounded on. Kita dropped the rifle, as its sound reached them, and crouched low with raised spear. The gorilla seemed to leap over the spear, snapping it like a match, driving down onto the man. They rolled over and over soundlessly until they disappeared, as if the mountain had swallowed them, and there was only the forest gleaming in the sun.

Rachel covered her eyes and swayed dizzily. As from a great distance she heard Kulu's urgent tone, "We must go on quickly, Madami."

She tottered after him, seeing his figure dimly before her, waiting and waiting for another sound to rise from the forest. Yet when it came she was unprepared for the human quality of its victory cry. At first her heart leaped and she thought, Kita. But it was not Kita, she knew, as the roar grew deeper than any human voice, sounding the triumph of many thousand years.

Kita's death was her fault. She suddenly found herself sitting down, unable to go farther, thinking, It's my fault he died.

"Madami," Kulu said urgently, "we must go on faster now."

She stared at him and beyond him at the mountain.

"Please, Madami."

At last, slowly and painfully, she got to her feet and followed him.

XI

CLOUDS ENVELOPED THEM again that afternoon as they passed through a lifeless moss land of leafless tree heaths. Even the tree trunks were wrapped in tumid moss, like wet gray fur, and from every branch trailed fantastic beards of gray lichen.

The men had stopped complaining after they saw Kita die. They were resigned to death, Rachel thought. They were simply going, following Kulu and her, like men walking in sleep across a nightmare landscape. They did not have consuming desire to reach the summit. Actually they never had expected to reach it, she realized now. They simply had come out with her because they liked her and had been willing to gambol on the mountains for a few days. They did not think God dwelt among the highest peaks. They did not understand either proof or disproof of any idea because they were just beginning to understand the nature of an idea. Now they had passed beyond the limits of fatigue and fear and were simply going, without expectation of returning home.

That night they camped under a cliff. It seemed to Rachel they had been climbing for weeks, but she realized it was only the fourth night since they left Dibela. She had intended to make notes on the journey. But as she sat before the fire, the pencil stub in her fingers refused to mark the notebook page. For what could she write that was not already burned into her mind? She never would forget each step of the way. . . . Her eyes closed and her head nodded.

The next morning they climbed into a new, more frightening land where solid earth disappeared. Thick groves of giant senecio about twenty feet high grew from the morass. When Kulu stepped forward cautiously along a rotted fallen senecio trunk, it suddenly disintegrated under him. He lunged for a growing senecio, embracing it to support himself. But it broke in his embrace and fell, plunging him into the moss-covered morass. By the time he'd uncoiled the rope and thrown it to Kosongo, he had sunk to his waist.

Rachel, pulling on the rope with the men and shouting encouragement to him, remembered the death of Bolambo in the legend. At least it was based on the facts of life on the mountains. Kulu remained calm. Was he, too, resigned to death? Or did faith in God the Father still buoy him? Now this was strange, she thought, staring at him. It did not especially matter to her what he believed. Strange—and terrible. As his faith increased, it seemed that hers grew indifferent.

"Madami," he said, as he wiped the black stinking ooze from his legs, "we must find another way."

They worked along the edge of the senecio swamp to a flank of thick wiry helichrysum bushes as tall as a man and crowned with pink and white everlasting flowers. They lunged into them, hacking a path with pangas through the stalks. Above them darted hundreds of crying swifts. It rained, and they still could hear the invisible swifts crying above them in the rain as they slashed through the helichrysum. The swifts suddenly were still and there was no sound but panga and rain.

About noon they came out of the helichrysum into a green world of moss where mist swirled. At times they could see only a few yards in any direction, and again the green land was visible for a quarter of a mile as the mist rose. The mountain seemed to be smoking. Then Rachel saw ahead something like the quiver of flames. She halted. The smoking mist curled down and the flames leaped up. They were giant poinsettia. Strange steel-blue flowers flared on arm-thick candlesticks of lobelia. Something whirred over Rachel's head and she paused. A tiny bright-blue sugarbird clung with fluttering wings to a lobelia stalk and pecked at the flowers.

The mist pressed closer around them as they went on. Now moss-covered rocks and trailing giant green heather began to assume familiar shapes. Like people she had known, Rachel thought vaguely. There was— She could not place the name. But there and there and there were familiar people, chained in the smoke and flames of hell. She shook her head, as if that would shake away the fantasy. She held the compass in her flattened hand, trying to concentrate on its points, trying to cast off the illusion that was more exhausting than fatigue. If she ever identified any of the dim shapes, she might never leave here. She commanded herself to stop it, but her imagination would not obey.

In the brooding silence even the innumerable brooks were hushed as they fell down the mountain in deep moss-lined trenches. It was the world before the time of man. To return to it was almost more than mortal nature could bear.

Then she saw Kulu toss a helichrysum flower. It lay on the green moss like a bit of crumpled white paper. In a few moments he dropped another. When the mist lifted momentarily, she looked back and made out a trail of everlasting flowers strewn across the moss land, and she remembered that Kulu frequently slashed bush and tree with his panga. So he expected to return home.

Late in the day, when it should have been growing dark, the light began to increase. Suddenly, as if they had ascended from a tomb, they were in sunlight. Over them arched the forgotten blue sky of Africa. Ahead of them, so near that it seemed she could touch it, a glacier filled a valley. Beyond the glacier soared the snow-capped peak of the mountain.

Kulu cried out and the men murmured.

Staring at the peak, snow yellowed by the setting sun and black rock escarpments towering sheer above the glacier head, Rachel knew they could not climb it. They simply lacked the skill and strength. Only if she were actually bent on death would she attempt it. Now, up here in the sunlight under the good blue sky of Africa again, reconciliation with death seemed madness. There, below the glacier, curled a long lake, like the lake of the legend. And there, to the left of the glacier, rose a lesser peak. Perhaps she could make it. Tomorrow she would try that lesser peak. She did not want to die.

They camped in a shallow cave that looked out on glacier and mountain peaks. Their fire was small and the night cold. Wind whined over the rock ledges. Twice in the night Rachel woke, startled by the rumble of avalanches. On the first waking, when she looked out at the brilliance of stars from her sleeping bag, she thought how the earth was still forming. And she found the thought pleasing. But on the second waking, when she thought of the cold and endless forming of earth, she felt a poignant loneliness. To lie alone upon the Mountains of the Moon was no better than to lie alone upon the moon. Here now, she told herself. Then, alertly, she thought that the voice of her consciousness had a spare, dry, spinster quality. Spare, dry, spinster, she thought, and turned uneasily in the bedroll, trying to think again of the cold and endless forming of earth. But she could only think that in caves such as this, fierce and hairy men and women had created with fire and passion and stone and cruelty the beginnings of the race.

Morning light awakened her. The fire had been rekindled. The men moved stiffly, coughing and spitting, their breath frosting in the cold wind off the mountains. She considered what she would say while they ate. When they'd finished, she addressed their love of rhetoric.

[114]

"Kulu," she said, "I shall speak now."

"Aye, Madami." He looked at the others and they were still, watching her.

"You have been brave, good men," she said, "and because of you we have come to this place."

Wanga grunted in satisfaction.

"We are now among the mountain peaks." She pointed. "The ignorant people of the plain have said that God hides up here ready to vent his wrath on man. Do any of you believe that now?"

They shook their heads and Kosongo said, "No, Madami."

"You are here. You see." She hesitated. "God is everywhere. He has come with us all the way."

"Is He going back with us, Madami?" asked Mzimba.

"Of course. Why should He bring us here and then leave us?"

"Foolish one," Kulu said to Mzimba.

Mzimba ignored Kulu. "Are we going back now?"

"We are going back tomorrow morning—if all goes well. Today, right now, Kulu and I shall cross the valley here and climb the peak to the left. You will wait here at the cave for us. Gather lots of wood and light a big fire there on the ledge if we are not back by nightfall." She rose. "You can watch us most of the time, climbing up that face. If anything should happen to us, it will be because we were careless or stupid. It will not be the work of God. Remember that. If you should return without me, tell it everywhere that God is everywhere, a kind, forgiving God—and not a cruel, frightening God living in the mountaintops. Remember where you have been and tell it everywhere to the people."

Suddenly embarrassed by her rhetoric and thankful that none of her kind was present to hear it, she fastened on her canteen and said, "Let's go, Kulu."

They moved fast across the valley below the glacier, picking a way over and around huge boulders. By eight o'clock, when the sun had driven the mist down to the cloud level through which they'd climbed, they reached the foot of a large rockfall.

Kulu looked up at it dubiously. "It is not difficult, Madami. But it is dangerous."

"It's the only way," she said.

"Aye." He hitched the coiled rope over his shoulder and suddenly removed his shoes. Tying them around his neck, he climbed agilely over the loose, rotten rock, using the ice ax as a balance.

She followed cautiously. One sliding stone could start an avalanche that would hurl them to death. And what was she proving by climbing on now? This last push to the summit above was for conscience. This was so she could tell the world, I climbed to the summit and I have returned, whole and unharmed. For conscience? Or was she merely sinning the mortal sin of pride in trying to reach the highest place? Now she could say—if she lived—I, I, I climbed to the highest place which none other could reach.

They paused at the head of the rockfall. Her heart pounded, and she gasped for breath. Above them soared creviced black rock. Wasn't this enough? Hadn't she now proved all she wished to prove?

Kulu watched her. He waited, she knew, for her to say, "Now we'll go back." But she stared up at the creviced cliff face and said, "Do you think you can climb to that ledge and lower the rope to me?"

"Yes, Madami."

He hung the coiled rope about his neck and fastened the ax to his belt. He went up slowly, muscular black legs and arms moving against black rock in the lemon light of morning. His hands and feet found holds in what seemed smooth rock, and he pulled himself on slowly. She watched him, her mouth open as she gasped the cold thin air. If he fell now, he would be killed—or, worse, be injured and so die slowly in the wilderness. She would call him back. But her voice choked and she merely stared at him as he hung, motionless now, like a fly stuck to a wall.

"Kulu!" Her tone was faint with fear for him.

"Madami?" He did not move.

"Come back. It cannot be done." The utter absurdity of the whole attempt overwhelmed her and she suddenly wrung her hands.

At last he said calmly, "I cannot come back, Madami. I must go ahead."

His left hand groped upward blindly and swept in a wide arc. It found a hold. He moved again, his body swinging outward and then in. For a long moment he held to the new position. Then he climbed on faster and drew himself over a ledge. He stood up and looked down at her, white teeth gleaming in his black, sweat-shining face.

"Wait, Madami," he called. He disappeared, and it was fully ten minutes before he came into sight again. The rope sang down at her feet. He had tied a careful slipknot in it; now he was taking a turn around a jut of rock with the other end. She put the noose over her head and under her arms, holding all her weight stiff-armed on the rope as he began to pull. She swung her legs, and her booted feet found the cliff face. Quickly he drew her to the ledge.

He grinned at her as he recoiled the rope. "This way, Madami." They climbed along the wide, twisting ledge until it ended suddenly over the abyss. But to the left was a curious tunnel formed by huge stone blocks jammed across a gulley. Water trickled down the gulley and its rocks were sheathed in ice.

Again Kulu told her to wait. Slipping, grasping, clinging, he pulled himself into the semidarkness and disappeared. In a couple of minutes the rope lashed down. She tied it around her and stumbled up the tunnel.

The light increased and grew blinding as she emerged into the white world of a snow slope rising toward a sky that suddenly was bluer than any she had ever seen, even in Africa. Kulu, grinning, gestured toward the snow slope like a showman to a stage. "The rain that is white, Madami."

Stooping, she picked up a handful of the soft snow, remembering suddenly the melting snows of spring in Kansas when the wind quartered to the south. She remembered— It didn't matter. She smiled at Kulu.

"We're lucky," she said and nodded toward the summit. "The day is clear for us. We can find our way up and back."

"God still goes before us," Kulu said.

She looked up. Beyond the wide snow slope towered a black chimney of rock. That was the summit, the attainable summit.

So they went up, the rope stretched loosely between them, Rachel leading now, legs sinking in the soft snow that chilled her to the groin. On their right the glacier widened as they climbed. Far behind them the great churning sea of clouds rolled outward toward the distant plain, lost in the gray infinity of space. Once, on some invisible slope, they heard the groaning of the earth itself and then the muted roar of landslide. Perhaps, Rachel thought, they walked over dangerously thin snow which bridged deep crevasses. But they had neither time nor skill to move cautiously and test for danger. They were simply going, driving or driven, straight up by geometric line toward the fixed point of black chimney through snow that lay blue in shadows and orange along the sun-warmed hummocks.

They had left the tunnel at nine-forty by her watch. At eleven-fifteen she flung herself down on a slab of rock at the base of the chimney. It was a long time before she could calm the beating of her heart and sit up. She traced the downward ribbed march of the glacier and saw, far down and beyond it, a thin gray plume of smoke where the men waited at the cave.

"They watch us, Madami," Kulu said. "They add wet moss to the fire to send up smoke and tell us that they see us."

"We haven't much time," she said. "We must be down by nightfall."

They rose and worked their way around the rock base slowly until Kulu, in the lead, cried out joyfully. The smooth rock became knobbed and broken. Its breaking in some eons-old past, Rachel saw, had left an easy stairway to the summit.

They climbed the last few hundred feet rapidly until they stood in a strong wind on a broad slab. This was the summit.

Not far off, connected to the chimney base by a serrated ridge of snow and ice, rose the main peak. Clouds curled from the west around its shoulders and poured through distant gaps like water through a broken dam. Dimly she made out another peak, and then another, shining evanescently in a momentary shaft of sunlight and then disappearing. These, then, were the summits of the Mountains of the Moon. And she stood upon her attainable summit among them.

"Madami." The wind snatched at Kulu's voice. "Should we not give thanks to God, as you do down in Dibela?"

"What?" Kulu seemed to stand so far from her. "Yes. Yes, Kulu, of course." She closed her eyes and her lips moved. At last she found her voice. "Thank you, God, our Heavenly Father, for bringing us here safely. Thanks be to Kulu and all the men for the strength to come here. Bless them all with unswerving faith. Bless Kulu."

She opened her eyes and saw Kulu, his eyes open, staring transfixed at the sky.

"Well," she said in English, "I guess we'll go back now."

XII

THE DRUM TOLD the story. It thundered in Kulu's village at nightfall and was heard in Dibela where the drum-talker and his assistant leaped to their feet in the palaver house and raced to their post and stood, heads cocked and listening, as the people came quickly and watched. The drum was heard along the mountain flanks, in villages where people had accepted some of the new white order, and by remote clans gathered within thorn bomas where the white faces still were called by the old savage name of red faces.

In Dibela, Chief Buderga himself crawled from the hut of his youngest wife, where he had been about to perform an act of personal importance, and came to the drum post. The people cleared a path for him until he stood beside the listening drum-talker and assistant drum-talker. When the drum died in Kulu's village, the drum-talker in Dibela announced the message and the people murmured and Buderga walked away abruptly to the hut of his youngest wife.

Then, hunching over his huge and craftily hollowed log, the Dibela drum-talker told the talker in Kulu's village that he had heard. He paused for a moment and then imperiously told the listeners of the plain to hear the word, sent by the Bwana Administrator himself, to be passed on even though night had fallen. So the word spread in the night to Rugeri where François, the *evolué*, was informed as he cut out another picture of Leopold, King of the Belgians, to adorn the newspaper-covered stucco walls of his adobe cottage. After making one of those ponderously slow decisions that invariably pleased him, he took the word to the Madame Administrator who crocheted and rocked in her house, having had no word from the Captain Administrator for ten days now. And the word spread beyond Rugeri. Others eventually took the message to Father Gilo and his assistant, Father Schwartz, as they played chess in what they sometimes wryly called their monastery; and to Ernest Ducasse, the coffee planter, who was just finishing dinner with his tall, strong, freckled wife when he heard the drum and learned the message from his number-one houseboy.

The Ducasses, avid hunters, had planned to spend a pleasant evening jack-lighting antelope that had been raiding the new plantings on the southern hundred hectares, but the message somehow made them decide to drive down and see the Gargantiers, who were green colonizers but hard-working. Madeline Ducasse said it was a shame she'd never gone to see the American Protestant woman but it was God's own distance to Dibela, and Ducasse said he'd never seen her himself but inferred from Lecomte that she was a delicious dish quite worth uncovering. He rose from the table, rolling his eyes with mock lecherousness, so that his wife laughed boisterously and smacked his backside hard.

Thus, on one night, was the word spread and discussed in huts and palaver houses and great white houses over many hundred square miles of the land.

The word was that the white woman of Dibela, accompanied by four men of her village, had climbed to the summit of the Mountains of the Moon and returned safely.

That was all there was to the message. It was a simple factual bulletin. But it was the sort of fact that would nourish the commentators of many palaver houses for many days while people brought them beer. (Everyone recognized that a commentator did his best interpreting of events when supplied with beer.) The commentators would lay the fact of the ascent against the background of the legend. In the far-off places, where the new order had brought some stability and prosperity and the legend had weakened to the point of disbelief, the commentators would say (as long as the beer lasted) that it was a triumph for the new order and the old gods were dead. But in the places nearer the mountains, especially in Dibela, where the new order had thus far failed and the legend still had strength, the commentators would say (as they sipped their beer) that a curse lay on the white woman and that the process of her destruction would soon begin.

Lecomte knew all this, of course. As he turned from the drum post in Kulu's village and walked through the gathering darkness he was thinking how the word would be received to the limits of this land, larger than most ancient European duchies, which he ruled in the name of his king. Yes, it strengthened the new order, and that was his purpose here on this vast equatorial husk of land. But then he found himself thinking again of the thahu, the curse, that had been laid on Rachel Cade by the old man who had disappeared now as completely as if the mountains had swallowed him.

When he'd arrived in Kulu's village several days ago to take up the supporting position, as Rachel had requested, the people had told him a thahu had been placed on her. A vulture had flown low over Kita's shamba a few minutes after they left to assault the mountain and its shadow had been seen by several on the hut where Rachel had slept. Thahu, ha! Lecomte had snorted and stomped the ground and wriggled his mustache ferociously at them. But the local medicine man, a very old man with filed teeth who huddled in a baboon-skin cape, resting storklike on one scrawny leg before Lecomte, had looked at him shrewdly and known (Lecomte could tell he knew) that the great white chieftain believed in thahu.

For he did. True, he believed in God. That is, he believed in a God unrecognizable to practicing Catholic or Protestant or Jew or Moham-medan. Only an idiot could live long close to earth and animals and fail to believe there was a God who created order. Most definitely the universe was not energy in riot. But Lecomte's God was not as concerned for the welfare of the higher primates as was the God of the Catholics and Protestants and Jews. His God, like a brilliant general, was following through an established plan. And, like a brilliant general, He didn't mind sacrificing men since His manpower supply was inexhaustible. Thahu was as natural a part of order as death itself, for thahu was one of the preliminary steps to death.

So he had gone apart with the medicine man, whose name was Kalanumu and who turned out to be quite a decent old fellow, and they had talked at length in the local dialect. Lecomte had asked him why the nameless old man placed a thahu on the white Madami. Kalanumu replied that the man had nothing personally against the Madami but was simply abiding by the truth of the legend, which said that no white should climb the mountains from this place. The old man, Kalanumu said, was simply practicing his religion; somebody should do it, and he had taken it on himself when no one else in the village did. Lecomte told Kalanumu he understood this; he was surprised, he said, that Kalanumu had not done it himself. Kalanumu shrugged and said he was getting old and lazy and, while he had no contact with whites, he'd heard enough about them to believe it could get mighty troublesome if you placed a thahu on one of them. True, Lecomte said firmly. Be-sides, Kalanumu said, he was pretty sure that a real strong, bad thahu had already been placed on the white Madami down in Dibela and this one by the old man up here was just an extra. Maybe so, Lecomte said, explaining that he probably could do something about the Dibela thahu but was powerless over this one up here. Couldn't they get the old man back and try to do something about calling off this particular thahu? Kalanumu replied that he couldn't get the old man because he believed he'd gone off to die somewhere after performing this last great work in the name of his faith. Besides, even if he could get him back, it had been such a bad thahu, with the old man personally confronting Madami, that it would be necessary to have Madami herself participate in the purification ceremony. Would she consent to that?

"No." Lecomte had shaken his head sadly. "No. No."

Kalanumu sighed and said, "It is indeed a bad thing to put a thahu on a white. For they do not know how to remove the curse."

Lecomte's candor concerning thahu had won Kalanumu's respect and they became good friends during the days Lecomte waited there. He gave Kalanumu tobacco and a length of iron chain, and Kalanumu offered him his choice of maidens with whom to bed. Lecomte thanked him profusely, but said he had a wife in the capital and when he wandered in the bush any more it was as the bachelor elephant wandered, without the dragging penis of the heated herd. Kalanumu remarked that this was an interesting and unusual attitude for a powerful white chieftain on tour, and he assured him that the proffered maidens were clean and free of the running disease. Again Lecomte thanked him and said his heart was set on a little hunting while he tarried here. So Kalanumu had told him where he could find eland, and Lecomte, accompanied by his mighty hunter, Watu, and several young men of the village, had gone off for a day and returned with three of the massive antelope.

There had been a great feast, in which the whole village had gorged on grilled haunches and filets of delicious eland. After they were filled, Lecomte and Kalanumu lay down on adjoining mats and smoked and talked in what assuredly is the most civilized deportment after a heavy dinner. Somewhere on the dark mountain sounded the cry of a leopard, followed by the hearty cursing of baboons at being disturbed by their most feared enemy.

Lecomte and Kalanumu talked of hunting and the old days when it had been legal to be warriors. Lecomte said he understood the attraction of warring, having indulged in it himself, but he couldn't understand eating your enemies. It was what you became accustomed to, Kalanumu said philosophically, explaining that while there wasn't much nourishment in it there was powerful excitement. Not that he had ever engaged in the pastime himself, he added piously. His lie was understandable, Lecomte thought. He changed the subject out of deference, though regretfully, for his insatiable curiosity about the orderly universe extended to cannibalism as naturally as to all other matters, and he had yet to meet a former cannibal who would rationalize the practice intelligently for him.

The worst thing about the outlawing of war, Kalanumu said, was that it had left the young men restless and idle. They had nothing to do but hunt, and even hunting palled on a man. The women, as always, had their shambas to tend and huts to build and children to bear and raise. But what had the men? Lecomte tried to explain that there was this new thing called commerce or business, known as shauri in the Swahili tongue. Shauri was for women, Kalanumu insisted. Some of the men had tried it, carrying hides and skins (that is, women had done the actual carrying, but men had conducted the column) all the way to the white trader's in the capital, Rugeri. They had gotten little for their pains and most of that little the men had wasted on a strange deadly beer which the trader sold them and which made the men think they were warriors like their grandfathers once had been. Many had been cut up with spears and pangas and several had ended in the jailhouse by order, Kalanumu said slyly, of the great white chieftain who now lay sociably on the mat adjoining his.

Yes, Lecomte thought sadly, he had sent so many fine men to the jailhouse when the one man who should be sent there for all time was that conniving, grasping bastard, Theomopolis, the dirty Greek trader who consistently outmaneuvered him. Some day he would nail him and send him into permanent exile, no matter if this land were without salt and cotton fabric for ninety years.

The next venture into business at Rugeri had been largely conducted by women, Kalanumu continued. Women, having no pride and being concerned with trivialities and given to haggling, were the natural ones to conduct this thing called business, Kalanumu said. They went to Rugeri with a couple of the most passive men and refused the trader's offers. Finally, when it was dark, they sent the trader the most comely young woman so that he might lay with her for the night. In the morning they obtained better prices. Kalanumu turned his head from Lecomte and spat to express most eloquently his view of business.

Ha, there were laws about that! Lecomte considered rising and having the young woman called to him so that he could begin preparing a case against Theomopolis back in Rugeri. But he was full of eland meat and the world, he thought, was full of miscegenation. He stretched languidly on the mat and stared at the sparks of many fires leaping into darkness.

Euuu, groaned Kalanumu, nothing good happened to the men of the village any more. A few had gone away west and never been heard from. Then, a few seasons ago, Kulu, who now served Madami, had suddenly walked off down to Dibela and gone to work for the white madman who had recently arrived there. Wasn't that a strange thing for him to do? asked Lecomte. Strange indeed, said Kalanumu. Kulu, a circumcision brother to one of his own sons, had been an able hunter and fearless bushman. In the good old days he would have become a warrior captain. He was so shrewd a youth, Kalanumu said, that he'd considered apprenticing him into his practice. And then one day, without a word to anyone, this shrewd Kulu had gone down to Dibela and stayed there, working like a woman for that mad white man who had so many thahus

[123]

cast on him it was a wonder he could rise from his mat every morning. Now Kulu had taken up the heathenish ways of the white Madami. Defying the great strong medicine which had fed his spirit all the days of his youth he now had turned to assault the mountains.

Warming to his subject of erring youth, Kalanumu said that Kita had sucked of the same hyena teat as Kulu. There was a madness in him, as in all youth today, because he could not follow the old true path of the warriors. A chief's son, he could not wait to become a chief. When his father died and the elders met to confer on his successor, Kita had gathered the young men and they'd marched in on the elders, utterly defying all known standards of conduct, and Kita had announced he was chief. When Kalanumu had protested that the very impetuousness of his act marked him as unfit to rule, Kita had threatened him with his spear and dared him to cast a thahu on him. Kita cried that he did not believe in thahu. Ah, said Kalanumu, rubbing his belly, there was a madness loose in the world these days which people breathed and so fell mad, even as people sickened when they breathed the smoke of the volcanoes far to the south.

"But did you cast a thahu on Kita?" asked Lecomte.

"Yes," said Kalanumu. "Of course. A very bad thahu. The vulture that cast its shadow on the hut where Madami slept also shadowed the hut of Kita. And the morning of the day you came here his wives found the dung of a hyena near his hut."

The worst possible sign, thought Lecomte.

"His wives came to me," said Kalanumu, "begging me to remove the thahu, promising to do anything if I would remove it, for it is said he is strong to lay with and his wives are happy."

"And you did not remove it?" asked Lecomte.

"No. Of course not. I do not think Kita will return from the mountains."

Lecomte shivered. The night was growing cold, he told himself. Kalanumu reached out his old left claw and laid it gently on Lecomte's right arm. "Do not worry, friend Bwana. I shall tell you something which I know even though I never have seen you before or been to your capital —since it has been your capital. No one in this land has ever cast a thahu on you. No one ever will. You have always the strong medicine of the respectful heart."

"I'm not thinking of myself," Lecomte said.

"You are thinking of Madami."

"Yes."

"Why, Bwana? Do you wish to lay with her and she will not let you?"

"No." Lecomte was very still. Then, knowing the futility of lying to Kalanumu, he said, "Yes. Perhaps that is it."

"You could force her," Kalanumu said. "Once when I was young I forced an unwilling young woman and I remember it was a great pleasure."

"No. You just said I have the strong medicine of the respectful heart. The respectful heart does not act so, Kalanumu."

Kalanumu sat up suddenly, exclaiming, "I see! You whites also have your own kind of thahu. You have given me much to think about, friend Bwana."

Now, walking from the drum post toward the big fires of the dead Kita's shamba, on the evening of Rachel's return, Lecomte remembered his great concern for her during the days of waiting. He had, of course, brought along a book, *Le Côté de Guermantes*, which he'd read twice and planned to read again. But Proust had failed him this time. He could not concentrate on reading while he waited here in the foothills. Rather, he thought of the magic of African medicine and the men he had known who had been both blessed and cursed by it.

Like most lore, it contained much absurdity and some wisdom. Its greatest practitioners were profound psychologists, as profound as their greatest white brethren in Europe. Some of their work was utterly inexplicable. But could it, he asked himself, work on a white? The question was rhetorical. He had seen it work too often to doubt there was something—what would you call it?—some area of African knowledge and experience that had totally eluded him all these years on the continent. There was, for example, that Englishman, the engineer, years ago way down country. Symington, that was his name. A cool, intelligent chap, bent on completing a job and cursing the wogs who hindered his progress. Black magic? Symington always hooted with laughter and slapped his thigh when that subject came up. One morning Symington awakened in racking pain, his right side paralyzed. A mission doctor, a good one, came to his quarters and examined him carefully. Not a thing wrong with him medically, the doctor said. Must be that a thahu had been cast on him. For the doctor, a devout Christian who had spent a long time in the country, believed, of course, in thahu. Symington had cursed the doctor thickly. But a day later he had piteously begged Lecomte to do what he could to get the curse taken off him. And, after time and the cost of several goats and diplomatic negotiations of the highest order, the witch doctor who had placed the thahu on Symington had removed it. Symington rose from his bed and finished the job as quickly as he could and fled the country. A believer. But it was doubtful if Symington, in his distant Manchester or London or Blackpool, ever told relative or friend about the time he was cursed in the Congo. He knew what they'd think or say: "Symington's one to pull your leg. . . . Poor chap must have had a touch of fever. . . ."

For those who knew the element of truth refused to voice it. Even I, thought Lecomte. No one ever had heard him expound on the truth of thahu. The old hands who'd lived back of beyond knew he believed, of course, for they believed too. They never discussed the matter with the white tourists who touched the isolated white islands of the black sea: Stan and Leopoldville and Elizabethville and Nairobi and the Cape. But sometimes, on those rare occasions when they came together over gin and ice in some dim bar that passed as luxuriant to them, one would guardedly remark: "Heard an interesting case the other day . . ." Another would say: "That reminds me . . ." Oh, they didn't swear and beat the bar about thahu. They merely remarked on it from the sides of their mouths, as members of a secret brotherhood give one another the sign in passing. They were sensitive men, all of them. They did not wish to outrage the sensibilities of those who believed all the world's knowledge flowed from the fount of European experience.

To believe in thahu one must be prepared to believe so many strange things. That this was the greatest continent and belonged to its own peoples. That mere man's existence was incidental to the beautiful, balanced, pulsing life of dark forest and yellow plain shimmering in the haze of sun. That pain is the rule of life, to be borne with fortitude; and death the destiny of life, to be faced always with equanimity. That communication is a vast mystery, probed more deeply here than the whites ever could dream in their vaunted babbling and traveling among one another, for it was true that elephants conversed with rumbling stomachs, and vultures suddenly appeared in an empty sky the moment carrion touched the ground, and a man might cause a distant enemy to fall ill and die.

Yet what did Rachel Cade know of all this? Nothing, Lecomte thought as he strode silently. Yes, she'd spent years on the Continent, but always in the confines of mission walls. Now, for the first time, she'd come over the wall and faced Africa nakedly and even defied it boldly. (You are, he suddenly thought, thinking like an African. It has conquered you and you never even scratched its face.) But he couldn't mention any of this to her. He could neither warn nor prepare her, for she would turn him aside with hearty white laughter.

Thinking these things, which still preyed on his mind, he had waited restlessly in the village. At last he'd maneuvered on the lower wall of the mountain, following her trail upward for one day and seeing the awful choking ambuscade of forest that formed the mountains' first line of defense. By his fire that night he'd pondered whether the root of the legend and the curse against whites lay in the very harshness of the mountains, whether they had become tabu because they were so dangerous, and whether from tabu had come thahu. But no chain of events moved so logically in Africa; deviousness was the rule of survival in the bush, and so it was a devious culture. The next morning he'd sent Watu farther up to scout for half a day, and then they had turned back to the village. He had told himself he might miss her if he went higher, and then he wondered if he were afraid to go on himself. His next maneuver was tactically good—and helped to pass the dragging time. He'd posted scouts from the village at every possible strategic point one day up the mountain with orders to report to him immediately at the first sign.

And so, at noon today, a runner had burst from the forest, shining with sweat, crying an ancient war note, heated to feverish warrior pitch by the suspense and delight of maneuvering on the mountain.

"The Madami comes!" he shouted hoarsely. "Kita is dead!" And there was riot in the village.

Lecomte lunged up the mountain, Watu trotting to keep up with him. Scrambling, sweating, gasping, he'd gone up and up until he'd heard the distant croak of voices that incredibly turned into some kind of marching song as around a rock face there stumbled a strange file of three, four, five men. He'd paused, thinking frantically, Where's Rachel? And then he'd seen her, walking behind Kulu, a sun- and dirt-darkened, crop-haired creature in tattered khaki whom he'd at first mistaken for an African.

"Rachel!"

She halted. Slowly, with a strange hesitation, she raised an arm in salute. Then she came on faster and he was racing toward her, so that they were like lovers in the last reel of an old melodrama. He saw her thinness that really was a new hardness. But then she smiled, and the old soft smile in the new hard face seemed almost more than he could bear.

He did not bother to extend his hand with the old formality. He simply passed his arms around her, feeling her pathetic thinness and

[127]

smelling the smoke of many campfires in her dirty hair as she rested a cheek against his. She sagged, leaning against him; she would have fallen if he'd stepped back quickly.

"Henri!" Her voice was pitched lower than he remembered it. She patted his arm and, summoning a reserve of strength, she disengaged from his embrace.

"Did you make it?" he asked, clinging to her hands and staring at her. "Did you reach the summit?"

"Yes," she said. "We made it."

Oh, God, he thought.

Now, as he reached the tumult of Kita's shamba, Kalanumu approached him.

"You understand, friend Bwana, that Kita is dead because of my thahu."

"Yes," Lecomte snapped.

"The mad young one there does not seem to think so." Kalanumu nodded toward Kulu.

Kulu stood on a log, a great crowd clustered around him, while Kita's three wives wailed in mourning before their huts. Kulu was saying:

"Now I have told you how Kita died, my people. It was as a brave but foolish hunter. It began when he raised his hand against Madami and took the gun from her. He said he was to become the greatest hunter by slaying the gorilla. He would not listen when she told him he lacked the skill. He would not listen when she said he could pass with us unmolested to the summit. So he died because he was foolish and would not listen to the wisdom of one who was with God the Father."

Kalanumu took his rattle from the folds of his great baboon-skin cape and shook it loudly. The people murmured and looked around at him.

"Who am I?" he cried.

"Kalanumu," said a man. "Kalanumu the great medicine man," said another.

"Aye, it is I, Kalanumu the great medicine man."

"Kalanumu," Kulu called over the heads of the people, "go away, old man. Go back to your hut and eat your gruel."

Lecomte shifted his weight uneasily. There was no sense in the boy courting trouble.

"And you, young babe," Kalanumu said to him without asperity, "go suck an old mother's teat." People laughed and Kalanumu shook his rattle for silence again. "I tell you now, so that you may not forget, Kita died because I placed a thahu on him."

The people looked at one another, nodding and murmuring, and turned from Kulu.

But Kulu cried, "Old sorcerer, old Kalanumu whom I respected much in childhood and respect as a man now, though not your medicine, hear me."

"I listen, young babe," Kalanumu said contemptuously.

"I say it was easy to place a thahu on Kita," said Kulu. "Kita's blood was hot and he constantly pursued death. Sooner or later it must have turned on him. And now you take the credit with your thahu."

Kulu's logic pierced Kalanumu, Lecomte saw. And it pierced him. He wondered, How deeply has this Africa corrupted my intelligence? Have I grown very old that I choose the wise old bachelor over the strong young male? Now, consciously, he took a step away from Kalanumu, staring at him.

Kalanumu shook his rattle at Kulu. "Do you defy me, child of this village and circumcision brother to my son?"

"Aye, I defy you," Kulu cried passionately above the wailing of Kita's wives, "I defy you and your false gods."

"Again I ask you, Kulu of this village, do you defy Kalanumu?"

"Again I tell you, old Kalanumu, I defy you and your false gods. God the Father and Jesus the Christ His Son are with me. For They are everywhere. I have been to the summit of the mountains and I have seen that no angry God of Kalanumu dwells there. I do not fear you, Kalanumu."

Kalanumu spat in his direction. "I place a thahu on you, Kulu."

Kulu smiled. "Make it your worst one, old man. Pluck the eyes from a live goat and pour its urine in my father's beer. I do not fear you. I go with God the Father and Jesus the Christ His Son. When I suffer and when I die, it will be because They will it. Not you, old fakir."

He stepped from the log and the people made a path for him. Instinctively Lecomte stepped toward him. As instinctively, he paused. Then, glad of the consciousness that suddenly lighted the dark recesses of his mind, he walked to Kulu and took his hand and rested his other hand on Kulu's strong shoulder.

"Son," he said and hesitated as Kulu smiled at him. He did not know what to say. Then he said, "I am with you. Let us go find Madami."

They found her seated, cross-legged, before a large fire outside Lecomte's hut. Watu and the corporal had quickly raised a hut for her alongside his. She had bathed at a spot in a nearby stream which Kulu had showed her. She looked fresh and lovely, even lovelier, Lecomte thought, than he remembered her.

"The hair is becoming," he said, sitting on the ground near her.

She touched the short gleaming coils of hair at the back of her head in a feminine gesture. "You like this better than the long?"

He shrugged. "I wouldn't say that, Rachel. I simply like it."

"What was all the noise about?"

"Kulu was haranguing the populace."

She looked sharply across the fire toward Kulu and beckoned him to her. "What were you telling the people, Kulu?"

He told her what he had said. Except, Lecomte observed, he did not mention the thahu. So Lecomte told her himself, while she listened intently, how Kalanumu had cast a thahu on Kulu.

"You rather more than half believe in thahu, don't you?"

It startled him. He moved uneasily. Then, "Yes, I guess I do."

She stared into the fire. "You know, of course, there's one on me. I haven't minded so much for myself, but now this thing about Kulu rather worries me." She smiled. "So I guess I believe just a little bit in a real bad thahu myself. I know Dr. Spencer thought there was something in it. He studied everything about it he could and said it had something to do with autosuggestion. Well—" she shrugged—"I think a strong person can defeat it. I'm certainly not worrying about it."

"No, don't worry," Lecomte said, and then he thought that the mingling of two cultures certainly made a confused hypocrite of a man.

While they ate, she described the ascent of the mountains to him. By the time they had finished, she was nodding sleepily.

Looking at her, thinking of her great beauty and strength, Lecomte felt his heart pound faster. He blurted something inconsequential, trying to cast aside the thing he wanted to say. And then he felt instinctively that now was the time to say it. He must say it now or forever be silent.

"Rachel?" His voice sounded thick.

She looked at him.

"May I come into your hut and lie with you tonight?"

She opened her eyes wide. She had, he thought, stopped breathing. "No," she said. For an instant he thought she was going to add, "Not tonight." But she didn't. "No," she repeated firmly and swung to her feet. She stared down at him and smiled faintly, as if to say they were and would remain friends, good friends. "I'm tired," she said in a remote voice, "very tired." She moved toward her hut and glanced back at him. "We must leave for Dibela in the morning. Good night, Henri."

XIII

A SEASON of unusual dryness came to the western plain. The sun burned on Dibela, browning the land until the elephant grass stood brittle and the leaves of the limbali hung limply in the heat.

There were devastating grass fires in the huge game preserve to the south and the game drifted north and east toward the mountains, seeking the green grass of the plunging watercourses which were fed by the eternal springs and snows of the mountains. The zebra moved in small circling herds, their strange barking audible in Dibela at sundown. After the zebra drifted the many varieties of antelope, hoofs stepping tentatively, heads raised alertly. The huge Cape buffalo forsook their drying wallows and grazed eastward, surly faces raised toward the mountains. Behind them skulked the predators. The filthy hyena, friend of no one, was seen often near Dibela now. The chilling cry of the leopard was raised frequently in the night. Scarcely a night passed that a roar or a cough did not mark the passing of lions prowling north and eastward toward the mountains behind their quarry. And in the wake of lions padded their friends, the jackals and little foxes who would feed unmolested on the lions' kills. Even a huge old bachelor elephant, outcast of a herd, was seen near the village, accompanied by two young males, his students. The elephants aroused excitement and there was much talk in the palaver house of an elephant hunt, but by the time the hunt was organized, the elephant, wise and old and seeking only peace on his last long odyssey, had led his charges far to the west.

Hunters ranged after the game with bow and spear. But as the days passed and the choicest game passed, they went out less frequently, and soon they did not go at all, but stayed indolently in the village while the women tilled the land. With the coming of the dry season, Rachel observed, disease increased. Many were shaken by malaria or went about with open tropical ulcers and other suppurating sores. There was an increasing incidence of yaws, and, from time to time, there were deaths from causes unknown to her.

She had just a month of peace after she returned from the mountains, she noted later in her diary. They were good days. The heat was not oppressive to her, for it was unlike the steaming jungles down west in their dry seasons. This, she thought, was scarcely a dry season at all, but the people were attuned to their own climate which worked its seasonal lethargy on them.

She rested and waited while the people of Dibela waited for the thahu to begin its work on her. She set everything in order in the hospital (where, she admitted to herself, everything already was in order) and she waited for patients. She slept long, though seldom deeply. She lounged in an old canvas chair on the bungalow porch or in the shade of the limbali. Occasionally she thought that she now lived in the dreaded image of her Midwestern spinster, the fading bougainvillea her tropic arborvitae, as she read from her scant library or wrote in her diary.

Often she grew restless. She increased the length of the Swahili lessons in reading and writing and Bible which she held daily under the limbali. Now the class included Wanga and his son, Tibu, and Musinga. Ah, Musinga, she often thought as he stared at her owlishly through his clear glass spectacles which he had miraculously recovered somewhere in the village. She had returned him to grace and granted him the title of First Assistant Orderly, which swelled him with self-importance quite as much as had the old abandoned title of Doctor Musinga. The others were amused by him, as ever, but he accepted their amusement resignedly now; like many men of all races, he assumed the role of buffoon because it seemed the only place available to him in a society he urgently required. Was he, she often wondered, merely an outcast of the village or did his mercurial instincts reflect the development of a changing temperature in Dibela toward her? Surely in the eyes of the people the thahu grew weaker with each passing day that found her living in health and happiness.

But books and Bible lessons and gentle behavior could not always fill the void of restlessness while she waited. Then, accompanied always by Kulu, she went abroad with guns. It was an experience she had not enjoyed since her first year in Africa when the congenial white staff of the Liberia hospital had enjoyed hunting in the bush. In later assignments there had been lack of opportunity or official disapproval of missionaries wantonly taking animal life as if they were rich, bad, white sportsmen banging around in Kenya. But now, having returned from the summit of the mountains and often remembering the loss of the Springfield, she took an interest in Dr. Bickel's guns. She stripped and cleaned his Purdey 10-gauge shotgun and the Westley-Richards .425. Carrying the Purdey, while Kulu padded behind her with the Westley-Richards, she often wandered far from Dibela, shooting francolin and guinea fowl and sand grouse. On the way home she'd sometimes break open one of the flat yellow boxes of .425 cartridges and fire on target until she became adept with that excellent rifle.

Kulu was her eyes and ears in the bush, as in Dibela. He showed her the migration of the animals and how to track them. One afternoon he led her, creeping, up a ridge and pointed into a draw where a handsome black-maned lion was curled seventy-five yards away. She placed the lion's ear squarely in the leaf sights of the Westley-Richards, noting with pleasure the steadiness of her hands as she held her breath. But she did not squeeze off the shot. To Kulu's astonishment she lowered the rifle and crept away. Oh, she was pleased with herself for not shooting the lion. This, she thought, was the way she had been before she climbed the mountains: reluctant to destroy any life, even the harmless gray spider that spun its web on her chair. This killing of birds was not good, she thought. She should stop it. And she did for a few days. But again she grew bored and longed for the heat of the bush and the blood-curdled sky that arched the plain at sunrise and sunset and the expectancy of the draws and the precise movements of leading francolin and grouse on the wing. She missed the fresh bird flesh, she who had been content with yams and vegetables and drab soup and canned corned beef and an occasional tough compound chicken. She enjoyed eating the tender white meat of francolin with mustard pickle which she made herself by an old Kansas recipe with cucumbers she had planted weeks ago in Guta's garden. For she had a sharp appetite these days and she ate heartily, without gaining weight. She was hungry, hungry, hungry for something that eluded her, some strange appetite that francolin meat and mustard pickle almost satisfied.

She had visitors in those days of waiting. Father Gilo came, bringing with him Father Schwartz, whom she had not met before. It seemed to her that Father Gilo watched her pensively and that Father Schwartz frankly disapproved. When they had gone, she studied her face in her hand mirror. She looked—different since she'd climbed the mountains. Perhaps, she thought, it was her hair, which she had decided to keep short. But that wasn't altogether it. She looked—younger. She looked thinner and fitter and—maybe the word was harder. She looked vaguely like somebody she had seen somewhere, but she did not look as she remembered herself so long ago at headquarters. It didn't matter, she told herself, for not in a long time (she was quite sure) had she much cared how she looked. Yet she often found herself stealing looks at her reflection in the mirror as the days passed.

Ernest and Madeline Ducasse, the Belgian planters, came to visit her. "We just came to take a look at the white girl who climbed the mountains," Ducasse said, beaming at her. "And we might stay over for a day of hunting," added his wife. "I don't suppose you hunt." Rachel said, "Well—" And then Ducasse saw the Westley-Richards in the rack and whistled in surprise and suddenly they were friends. The Ducasses, who hunted with a handsome set of Tanganyika lion hounds they'd brought along in their car, stayed three days. At Rachel's invitation they slept in the cottage across the compound and hunted days. On the second day Rachel went with them. On the third day she went with them and killed a steinbok. When they had gone, she was lonely.

Lecomte came, bringing his wife and mail and supplies from the Greek trader. They sat formally on the porch while Guta served tea and little cakes in the formal manner Rachel had taught him. They talked of this and that, Lecomte's brooding eyes carefully refraining from meeting Rachel's, his manner so formal that it seemed quite impossible he was the same Lecomte who had wanted to lie with her upon the mountain. She wanted him to understand she was not annoyed. They were, she wished him to know, the same good friends. But she couldn't get through the this and that of the conversation.

Marie Lecomte wondered if Rachel had seen the airplane yesterday. No, she said, she hadn't. Passed too far west, said Lecomte, and remarked on the growing habit of the embattled British to fly airplanes over neutral Belgian Congo. Not that it would be neutral long, he said. When the roads of Belgium and France were thoroughly dry the Germans would end the strange, bloodless, distant war and Belgium no longer would be neutral. Marie said she wished he wouldn't talk like that, and Lecomte compressed his lips while Marie asked Rachel if she liked gardening. At last they rose to go. As Marie started toward the car, Lecomte muttered, "Ducasse tells me you've turned into a hunter. You need a permit, you know. Here." He handed her an envelope and murmured, "Be careful, Rachel," and followed his wife toward the car. Rachel wished again that she could make him understand they were the same friends as ever. Next time, she hoped, he might leave Marie at home.

The letters, like the Lecomtes, were vaguely unsatisfying. She was disappointed there was not another letter from Dr. Spencer. Edith Barney's gossip about life at headquarters was downright dull. Strange, Rachel thought, that the idea of going back there was so repugnant now. And Phyllis Haricort, writing from New York, was somehow annoying with her blithe chatter. Then Rachel told herself, What an ungrateful wretch you are to be annoyed at that fine woman.

She sat down slowly and stared up at the limbali. What was wrong with her? She had lost her old composure since she climbed the mountains. And it was not caused by any African thahu, she thought. She had lost her composure because she was unable to begin fulfilling her purpose here. That was why she wandered about the country shooting. Each shot only served to emphasize her purposeless way of life. And Phyllis Haricort annoyed her because Rachel's letters had led Phyllis to believe she was fulfilling a great purpose in Dibela. She had, she realized, worked her way into a position from which she could not escape.

It happened undramatically just a month after she returned to Dibela from the mountains. Kulu padded up the bungalow steps early that morning, his eyes wide, his voice barely containing his excitement.

"Madami, a patient has come to the hospital!"

She swung past him wordlessly and strode across the compound, walking faster until she was almost running. A young man stood at the door of the hospital, watching her. Beyond him, at the edge of the compound, stood a silent crowd.

"Jambo." She smiled at him. "What is your trouble?"

"I have a bad sore, Madami," he said indistinctly and pointed to a large, suppurating ulcer on his left leg. "Can you cure it?"

"Yes," she said. "Not in one day. Maybe in this many." She held up the fingers of her right hand. "Maybe in this many." She also held up the fingers of her left hand. "Come." She started ahead of him into the hospital and paused, looking at the crowd. "Invite your friends to come with you."

The young man called to the crowd, mentioning names and beckoning. Slowly, reluctantly, several moved from the crowd toward him. Rachel greeted them warmly and invited them inside. The men followed, looking about cautiously, but the women stayed outside. Musinga dashed in, pulling on his white smock and fingering his spectacles. Kulu, the Chief Orderly, buttoned his smock carefully and told Musinga to wash his hands.

While Rachel washed her hands, she talked to the young man. His name, she learned, was Tiza. She did not ask why he had decided to come to the hospital.

Tiza sat on a cot with his left leg stretched out while his friends stood back watchfully. He did not, naturally, show his pain when she applied alcohol. The edges of the wound were not hard and she doubted it was cancerous; rather, it was a typical tropical ulcer caused by a combination of bacterial infection and nutritional disturbance. On the granulation tissue of the ulcer floor she carefully applied ointment and then deftly bandaged it.

"Lie in your hut today, Tiza, and rest," she said. "Do not touch the bandage. Come back tomorrow morning and we'll put a new bandage on it." She pointed to the ulcerous legs of two of the watching men and smiled at them. "Will you let me treat your wounds?"

They looked at Tiza and then at each other. Finally one stepped toward her slowly with downcast face.

When they had gone, she looked at Kulu, her eyes shining. He smiled and said, "Madami is happy again."

Yes, she was happy, she thought, as she paced among the empty cots and pallets. The important thing was to work again. She thought about it through the day, and that evening she wrote in her diary: *To work again is so much better than to caress this fabulous land with wandering feet.*

That evening, too, Kulu came to her with word of why Tiza had come to the hospital. Tiza was tired of his ulcer. He had gone to Muwango, the medicine man, and asked for a cure. Muwango had given him a remedy, but Tiza had noticed that Muwango himself had a bad ulcer which he tried to hide under his cape. What sort of medicine was this? Tiza had asked his friends. A thahu on the white Madami? She went about healthy and happy, didn't she? How could a man who could not even cure his own ulcer cast a potent thahu on the white Madami?

So it was a young man again, rising from no special experience, who asked the pertinent questions. The young ones, Rachel thought. They seemed to breathe a fresher air than the old ones.

The next morning Tiza and his friend returned. Rachel cleaned and dressed and bandaged their ulcers. Two men and a young woman with bad sores followed them. Musinga danced about excitedly, but Kulu watched and learned and helped.

In the afternoon, while class was being held under the limbali, Muwango came to the edge of the compound. He sat cross-legged on the ground and ostentatiously made medicine with fire and the bones of a goat. But not many watched him. They watched the class and murmured in astonishment when first Kulu and then Kosongo read from the little magic things in their hands loudly enough for all to hear.

Muwango made such loud medicine that many had to come near the limbali to hear Kulu and Kosongo. After a while Muwango grew very angry and picked up his medicine bag and hobbled away. As everyone knew, Muwango was getting old and he had a bad ulcer.

XIV

Now GOOD DAYS came in the shadow of the limbali. As Kulu went about the compound he often sang to relieve the pressure of his joy-swelled heart. Sometimes Madami heard him and smiled. But he did not sing for her; he sang for himself. He did not need to sing for her, he knew, because she had her own mute joy-hymns. He sang for himself because she was happy again and because God the Father and Jesus the Christ were now very busy in Dibela, stroking through the limbali and moving over the people's shambas and walking in and out of their huts, touching them and saying, "Go now to the hospital and let Madami help you."

And the people came after Tiza's ulcer had dried and healed and he walked again without pain or limping. Then they were very busy indeed at the hospital as the people wound across the compound in a long, patient, neck-craning line, young and old, men and women and children and naked, oily, wet-nosed babies slung on their mothers' backs.

Madami organized things very carefully inside the hospital, making even Musinga work, and elevating Kosongo to the position of Second Assistant Orderly. She had Mzimba build a long table in the hospital with a long bamboo rail a few feet in front of it. Behind the rail stood first Musinga and then Kulu himself and then Madami. Behind them on the long table were the medicines and the bandages which Madami had taught them to make. Kosongo, pleased with his new office and white smock, stood at the doorway and sent the people, one at a time, to the bamboo pole, telling them to place the sore leg or arm on the pole, before Kulu if this were the first visit, or before Musinga if it were a later visit.

Musinga would unwind the old bandage and drop it in a pail. That was all Madami would let Musinga do; she had to watch him carefully, silencing him when he told friends they were cured and enemies they were dying until he finally learned that the good attendant must not speak when on duty. After the patient's bandage was unwound, or if it were a first visit, the patient moved along the bamboo rail to Kulu. It was his happy duty to clean the wound, as Madami had taught him. She would look carefully at the wound and tell him what dressing to take from the table behind them. Then she would apply the dressing and bandage the wound. As time passed and the patients increased, crowding through the doorway where Kosongo valiantly tried to maintain order, Madami taught Kulu how to apply the dressings himself, thus saving time.

Madami always said a few words to the people. She learned their names and asked how matters went on their shambas and inquired after their eldest and youngest relatives. Some who suffered from illnesses other than tropical ulcers she would ask to sit down and wait. She would treat them when she had the time. Oh, it was fine to stand beside her and see her shining eyes as she talked and worked. The interesting thing was that she loved everybody, and everybody realized it and so loved Madami. At first Kulu doubted that she understood this. For some who loved Madami most stood before her silent and unsmiling, Kulu knew, while others who loved her less chattered and chuckled like francolin at sundown. But then he began to see that she even understood how the hearts of some people naturally contain love as easily as a gourd contains water while the hearts of others naturally hold as little love as a banana leaf holds water. And it made no difference to Madami in her attitudes toward people except sometimes to make her a little sorrowful for the flat hearts.

Kulu constantly thought that Madami was cast in the image of God the Father. Every hour of the day she proved His existence by the things she did. God loved all people equally, and so did Madami. Not all whites were like Madami, of course, just as all Africans were not alike. The white priest was like Madami in the gentle way he talked to you on his rare visits. The Bwana Administrator was almost like Madami, but not quite; he treated you well, Kulu knew, because you were Madami's strong right arm and he cared for Madami; but he saw Musinga's flat heart without forgiveness and treated him contemptuously. And the big white planter and his big white wife were not good at all when they came to hunt; they were, Wanga said, like nearly all the whites away west. They disliked Africans and even trained their dogs to dislike

Africans and during their visit they'd shouted, "Boy! Boy! Boy!" all day long, demanding this and that. In the west, Wanga said, all African men were called "Boy!" in loud tones. When Kulu asked Madami about this, she said it was true that nearly everywhere in Africa, from the place called the Cape to the city called Cairo, whatever the language, you would hear that English word "Boy!" Madami said, "When you hear it, Kulu, you must understand and forgive."

The good feeling of the compound gradually extended through Dibela and beyond to other villages of the plain where people heard of Madami's cures and filed in to throng the shade of the limbali. It seemed, then, that the days were too frail to bear the great spear of work. Madami no longer went hunting. At first Kulu missed going out with her and show-ing her the land and the game. From the day they had set out for the mountains and his toes had touched good earth again he had felt old stirrings which he'd missed those many past moons in Dibela. His hunt-er's smell had returned to him and life had regained the fine balance of the monkey that stands on one foot in the highest wind-tossed mango tree. To have climbed to the highest place with Madami was a great triumph, and one triumph demanded others, so that he had been restless when he returned to Dibela.

Curiously, Madami had been restless too. It troubled him, not for him-self, because he could take care of himself, but for her. For this, he dimly knew, was the way a thahu began to work. He could not explain it even to himself, let alone to Madami. But when a real bad thahu was cast on you, it lived with your desires. And usually your desires eventually gave you trouble—the running disease, a wife, a bellyache, death from care-lessness when, like Kita, you wished to do something you couldn't do. And when the evil fell, people said, Thahu. That, at least, was a part of it. There were other mysterious things about thahu. But he'd figured out that much by himself, as had several young men he knew who took un-kindly to their village teachings. He knew, or at least he felt, it was bet-ter to defy a thahu, as he had defied Kalanumu's, than to shrink from it. No, he was not worried about the thahu on himself. But he had been vaguely worried about the thahu on Madami when she returned from the mountains and seemed so lost. It was as if she had fulfilled some desire on the mountains which could not be fulfilled again. And that, of course, was the making of thahu.

But he was not worried now. For these were the good days when he remembered God the Father and vowed not to forget Him again. The things he had showed and taught Madami on the mountains and in the hunt were nothing compared to the good things of the hospital Madami now taught him. He would forget the mountains and the hunt and his village; he would live forever under the limbali with God the Father and Madami His daughter.

Madami had to teach Kosongo to help on the ulcer line so that she would be free to heal other patients. Ah, it was a proud day when she made Kulu head of the ulcer line so that she could work on other patients, trusting him to consult her on only the most difficult cases. It was necessary to put Mzimba on the door, a job that helped him regain self-respect. For Mzimba had caught the running disease from Nioki. When Madami found it out she had held her head. Then she ordered Mzimba to bring Nioki to her. He dragged her, kicking and screaming, to the hospital and sat upon her stomach, with head politely averted, while Madami did what was necessary to Nioki. Nioki ran out, still screaming, and Madami told Mzimba he must drag her back tomorrow. Mzimba said he would, but as he started away, Madami told him to stay. She said he must be cured too or leave the compound forever, and she did what was necessary while he bellowed in mortification. He crept off and lay all afternoon in a corner of the sleeping hut, his face to the wall, until the smell of Guta's cooking aroused him to eat. He told Kulu his shame was as great as if he had been turned into a hyena and he never could face Madami again. But he did and he was cured and he loved his new job and now he lay only with the clean wife of a circumcision brother who was detained in the jailhouse for trying to steal an empty petrol tin in Rugeri.

Such incidents as the mortification and curing of Mzimba absorbed the thoughts of Musinga and Kosongo, but Kulu saw them as Madami did: trivial to the great and growing complexity of the work. She made Wanga a member of the hospital staff, specifically assigning him the title of Chauffeur when he demonstrated that he loved as well as drove the Ford. When the car was in an ill humor, Wanga would lie with it happily for a whole day until it was purring and chuckling like a young wife. And since he kept it in good humor most of the time, there was increased passage to and from Rugeri.

Madami was forever writing letters requesting medicines and bandages, which trickled in to the Bwana Administrator's, and there was increased buying at the trader's. The Madami Administrator interested herself in preparing bandages and the Administrator came to Dibela frequently, smiling like the morning sun at all the hospital activity. Madami herself rarely went to Rugeri, for she was too busy. Sometimes she sent Kulu when there was a matter that required the co-operation of the Bwana Administrator. But usually she sent Wanga, who had become much happier. Madami always permitted the car to be filled with persons who had legitimate business in Rugeri. Ah, it was surprising how many citizens of Dibela suddenly developed legitimate business in Rugeri.

It was, in fact, the opportunity of riding to Rugeri that led Chief Buderga to abandon his aloofness and come to inspect the hospital. He remarked favorably on the work to Madami and then asked for a ride on the next passing to Rugeri. On the appointed day he arrived in the compound with his youngest wife and Muwango. Wanga said later it was a wild ride with Buderga yelling and his youngest wife screaming and old Muwango making medicine on the front seat. Upon returning, Buderga informed Madami he would go to Rugeri each time the car went. But Madami gravely informed him that he would not, that the ride was free to any common citizen of Dibela with legitimate business. Talk in the palaver house, even among many of the oldest commentators, was that Buderga had lost much face. Muwango, too, had acted foolishly, the commentators said, in succumbing to the new medicine of the car. But Wanga said it was simply a matter of old Muwango having a passion for riding in the Ford; in order to have a ride he had convinced Buderga his barren youngest wife might finally conceive if she rode in the Ford to Rugeri, after—of course—Buderga had performed the necessary act.

The truth was that whatever the old ones of Dibela thought, the times were slowly changing. Kulu knew this and he wondered if Madami saw it as clearly as he. It was happening in many quiet ways. For instance, the afternoon Swahili class grew too large for Madami, and to his surprise and joy she split the class and made him the teacher of one group. He studied very hard, just as he practiced very hard at doing the things she taught him in the hospital. She used him, too, to help with the services she held on the first morning of every seven days. It was the day of rest, as God the Father had ordained when He worked hard for six days to create the world and then rested on the seventh. On this morning of the seventh day, which for some confusing reason actually was now the first day of the Christian week (Madami said), the people gathered under the limbali in fine weather or in the hospital during rain to hear her tell stories about God and Jesus. They were good stories of ancient Bible times and equally good stories of what God and His Son were doing on the plains and in the mountains during these present times. The people came increasingly to hear the stories of the good life until the hospital would not contain them nor the great limbs of the limbali shade them.

Madami taught them to sing songs and to pray, which was the Christian way of bowing your head and closing your eyes and trying to catch a glimpse of the heel of God the Father or the loincloth of Jesus the Christ as you talked to Them.

This praying was indeed a great medicine, Kulu felt. Usually he was too busy to pause by himself during the endless business of the days and get a good glimpse of Them. But on the seventh morning there was time enough and sense of leisure, as in the old days in his village, so that he often had a blissful, warming look at the Father and His Son while his eyes were closed. They always smiled and nodded or waved to him, but They never spoke and he never wished to trouble Them with his own trivial matters.

For a time he considered asking Them, when he saw Them, about the thahus on Madami and him. But as he thought about it, he could see it would be impertinent, like asking a friend if there were a stolen goat in his flock. Certainly it would be irksome to Them to be asked about a thahu when Their very presence in this country showed that thahu was dead. No, They never should be asked trifling questions; They answered questions before being asked. With deeds. And the deed was that Madami and he were happy and the work growing greatly in Dibela.

But slowly, as the moons waxed and waned, he came to see that he would have to ask Them a question. He came to it slowly because they were so busy and the sense of change was on them all. The change extended over all the world, it seemed, in the places Madami drew for them on a green coconut which was the strange shape of the world. (Aieee, what a world this was, so enormous that it made your head swim when you saw that you could walk for a full moon and only cover one fiber of the coconut.) There was change away up on the coconut, Madami said, in the land of the Bwana Administrator where now lived the earthly king he represented. Now the northern fatherland, *Belgique*, had been invaded by fierce warriors, and there was war everywhere. So great was the world, and yet so small, that because of such events as this it was hard to get petrol and medicines away down here on the coconut at Dibela. This, then, was the way of the world: stones dropped in a still pool which rippled the farthest shore.

On the seventh morning, the prayer morning, after he learned this news, he did not see God the Father and Jesus His Son when he closed his eyes. It was understandable. They must indeed be busy these days, hurrying off to remote parts of the coconut and trying to make Their presence felt on the shambas of the northern warriors. Oh, those northern warriors must be bad ones, for Madami admitted when he questioned her that they professed to believe in God and His Son. Yes, the hearts of God and Jesus must be sore at this betrayal, and while They did not take the earthly course of vengeance, it might help if a few men like himself were sent against the northern betrayers. He mentioned this possibility to Madami, but she firmly said, No, his place was here with her. Having offered and his offer having been rejected, he was content to stay. In fact, he wanted to stay with Madami.

On a later seventh morning when God the Father and Jesus hurried through, he saw Them again. Their faces were drawn with sorrow and They looked weary from much travel and work. The question already was forming in his mind. But neither then nor on later seventh mornings did he have the heart to ask Them a favor.

The favor was to send them a doctor here in Dibela. For Madami had made him understand there were certain things she had not been trained to do. Some things she could do very well and heal the people, but there were other things she could not do. She could not, for instance, make Chief Buderga's youngest wife fertile so that she might bear him a son. This would have been a great medicine which would have impressed Buderga immensely, for he was fond of his youngest wife and would have nothing to do with another woman. By so impressing Buderga the last resistance to the changing ways might be wiped out. Then, indeed, would the people see the power and love of God the Father and Jesus His Son. When he pointed this out to Madami, she said there were white doctors who might be able to work this cure on Buderga's wife, but she lacked the skill. Then why didn't They send a white doctor to perform this cure?

Madami shook her head sadly. Because, she said, God and Jesus worked only through the world as it was. And as the world presently was, there simply was not a doctor available to come all the way to Dibela. Besides, said Madami, it was not just Buderga's wife they must think of. She was far less important, said Madami, than innumerable others whose lives could be saved and made fruitful by the presence of a doctor.

Oh, this worked on Madami and she grew increasingly troubled by the things she could not do. The people, too, were puzzled. But Kulu now cared less about the people than about Madami, who would sit up all night by candle in the hospital with a patient she could not possibly save. Yes, these things she could not do worked on her and she grew tired and needed rest. But she could not rest, she would not leave the side of a patient in the hospital and let death take him.

So, at last, it happened on a seventh morning when they bowed their heads in prayer and each prayed silently. Kulu had not planned it would happen that morning under the limbali. He simply closed his eyes, as usual, and quite suddenly God appeared in His accustomed image and then Jesus came around the limbali and They looked over the people's heads, speaking briefly Each to the Other.

Then, amazingly, Kulu heard Their voices. God said, "Son, there's much trouble in the world and I am weary." And Jesus said, "Yes, Father, so am I. It would be good to go apart for a few days and rest." God said, "Yes, it would, Son, but there's too much to do. Even here in Dibela." Then God turned slowly and looked directly at Kulu and said, "You spoke to me, Kulu?"

"Yes, yes," cried Kulu, dropping to his knees, "God the Father and Jesus His Son, there's something I'd ask You. Please send Madami and us here in Dibela a doctor to help the sick."

And God smiled and said, "We'll see what we can do, Kulu."

Then he felt Madami shaking his shoulder, her strong fingers gripping him hard. He opened his eyes and stared up at her, amazed at her baffled and almost angry expression.

"Kulu!" She didn't know what to say to him.

"Madami!" he cried. "I saw Them. I saw and talked with God the Father and Jesus His Son just now and I asked Them—"

"I know. I heard you. We all heard you."

The people were murmuring and rising in excitement to get a better glimpse of Kulu on his knees. Kosongo called, "What happened, Kulu?"

Kulu got to his feet shakily, his face radiant as he turned to Rachel. "Madami, They say They'll see what They can do about sending us a doctor!"

This was too much, she thought in despair. There was so much frailty here, but please, God, spare me Kulu. If he started seeing fantastic visions, there was no one left. "We shall sing," she called in an authoritative tone. "Kosongo, you lead us."

After the service she told Kulu to come to the hospital. She took his temperature, but it was normal. She felt his pulse, but it was normal. She studied the pupils of his eyes, but they were not dilated. She asked him if God had spoken to him recently before this morning and he said no.

She asked him other questions about the routine of the hospital, but he answered normally.

She smiled at him wanly. "Go and eat a hearty meal and sleep the afternoon away, Kulu."

"Yes, Madami." He looked at her, his brow furrowed. "You do not believe I saw God—"

"Yes," she said quickly. "Yes, of course I do, Kulu. Things will work out. Now go and rest."

"And you, Madami? Will you rest too?"

"All right," she said at last.

She walked slowly under the limbali to the bungalow. It was good to sit down. She picked without relish at the tough stewed chicken Guta served. Then, to pass the time of eating, she took out her diary and leafed it idly, regretting the busy days when she had had so little time in which to write. Now it would soon be a year since she came to Dibela. The diary told the story, its blank pages as eloquent as all her scribbling.

After eating, she lay down on the living room cot and looked out at the lowering sky. Rain began to fall and she slept. She awakened once, hearing the rain, and found herself thinking that persistent thought of many months now: If I hadn't climbed the mountains, would it really have made any difference? The change would have come anyway. And now this is about as far as I can go alone.

Annoyed with herself for refighting the old battles, she flung over on her other side and closed her eyes, listening to the rain, sinking slowly into sleep.

Four mornings later, as she came from her bedroom, she heard the throbbing of airplane engines. The plane seemed to be coming straight toward Dibela through the misty rain. She hurried to the porch and looked up, listening. There was something wrong with the plane. It had a coughing sound, like an old lion near death.

People were running in the compound, looking up and shouting, "Ndege! Ndege!" Yes, iron bird, she thought dully. She stood rooted there as the drone grew to a hacking roar, passing low and invisible overhead, flying due east toward the mountains. Then, in the grayness of mist, she glimpsed orange flames. It was flying directly into the mountains. Instinctively she screamed a warning, and then clapped a hand over her mouth. The flames disappeared and the hacking roar faded. There was silence and then a distant explosion, like the firing of a huge gun. And then silence.

[145]

Now Kulu was beside her and the others were running toward them. She directed them calmly. They needed many men. And she needed her first-aid kit. She seized her raincoat and old hat from the peg, and then she was hurrying, almost running, up the eastern track through the elephant grass toward the mountains. Kulu hurried behind her. After him streamed scores of men.

When they'd gone about a mile, she left the track and climbed a low ridge. She stood on the ridge, gazing eastward toward the mountains, trying to pierce the misty rain. She could see nothing. There was no smoke, no flame in the tattered veils of rain. Yet certainly the plane had crashed over there toward the mountains. She'd heard the explosion only two or three minutes after it passed over Dibela, but a few minutes by air meant a half day's walk. It might take days to find the plane; or it might never be found in this wilderness.

She could turn back now, she thought, and let the men go on. But if she turned back, the men would soon lose enthusiasm for trying to follow the trackless ndege. There was no spoor, no excitement of the chase. To some of them it must already seem an illusion that a ndege had passed over Dibela, and why were they running after a footless ndege anyway?

So she returned to the track and led the way on east, and after a while she realized that the old excitement at going toward the mountains was rising in her again. Somehow it was less important now to find the site of the crash, which doubtless no one had survived, than to be going toward the mountains. If she had not come this way once before, she would not be coming this way now. For the sound of the footless ndege seemed illusory; moving across the country toward the invisible mountains was the only reality.

Kulu, who understood that she believed the plane had crashed, used his hunter's instincts. At his command the men deployed from the track, spreading in a ragged line about two miles wide, each man within hail of another. And at his command the line finally pivoted on the track and left it to swing farther northward in the direction of the plane's flight.

In early afternoon Kulu suddenly halted and said, "There's a sign, Madami." He pointed ahead and to the left. Vultures circled under the low clouds. Someone yelled to their left and they forced a way through tall grass until they reached the crest of a small rise where Tiza stood pointing into a draw beyond.

The smoldering fuselage of an airplane lay at the end of a great charred sluice of earth strewn with bits of wreckage. One of its wings had been torn off and still burned slowly fifty yards from the fuselage.

[146]

Scores of white marabou and black vultures stood, croaking, or flapped about, waiting for the molten heat to cool.

No sign of life, Rachel thought, and at that instant there was a faint scream.

"Aieee." Kulu sprang forward and Rachel raced beside him down the long charred track where the plane had bounced and skidded in flaming fragments.

"Higgins!" a man's voice cried commandingly, and Kulu and Rachel halted. "Okay, Higgins, o-kay!"

Surely it was an American voice, Rachel thought dimly. And then the scream of excruciating pain again from the grass to the right. Kulu pointed and they ran again.

A man lay there. She closed her eyes. Not a man now, but a protoplasm burned and swollen unrecognizably. An enormous blister from which life still screamed horribly.

"Jesus!" It was another voice. A man had halted his painful inching through the grass toward the unrecognizable body and stared at her dazedly. In one sweeping, penetrating glance she saw he was a dark-haired man with blue eyes, his forehead gashed by a cut.

"Jesus!" the man said again.

She dropped beside the stinking, peeling, hairless blister, crying, "You'll be all right! All right, all right!" Thinking, as she fumbled the first-aid kit from Kulu's hand, Oh, why can't he die now! The sightless eyes from which the lids were burned rolled in their sockets. He heard. He answered with a wordless gargling sound.

She tore open the kit, wondering what to do, where to begin. Behind her the other man crawled a little closer, gasping. When she turned to the horribly burned man again, he was still, peeled lips parted over even white teeth. He was dead. She knew he had died at that instant, but still she mechanically applied ointment on his face, staring at him in horror.

"No point in that now," said the man in the grass behind her. "He's dead."

"You don't *know* he's dead," she cried in sudden unreasonable anger. "He's dead."

"How do you *know?*"

"I know all right. I'm a doctor."

[147]

XV

"His name was Higgins," the man said. "Peter Higgins. I'm sure it was Higgins. I recognized his voice. Higgins, the navigator."

"There may be others," Rachel said, rising quickly.

"No others," the man said. "I was thrown clear. So was Tibbett. I was with him when he died. Never regained consciousness. Then I heard Higgins and I started crawling to him." He lowered his head to the ground and his voice was muffled. "Been crawling all day it seems."

Inanely she thought it was so good to hear English again after all these— What was it? Years? Months? And not just English, but American.

"You," she said numbly. "You're hurt too. Let me—"

"A busted leg." He raised his head and winced. "Shaft of the tibia, I think. And maybe a rib or two." He looked beyond her and suddenly shouted, "Get those goddamn filthy birds away from Tibbett!"

But as she started to tell Kulu to drive off the birds, they rose, flapping slowly, before the men running to the wreckage.

"Madami," Kulu said, staring at the injured man, "is he—"

A doctor. Yes, she thought dazedly, the man had said he was a doctor and the implication had not yet sunk in to her. Oh, she was dull, dull, dull from being so much alone. He had said he was a doctor and just four days ago Kulu had had a— *No,* visions were impossible. It was coincidence. Sheer coincidence. But a doctor. *A doctor to Dibela!*

She did not answer Kulu's incomplete question. Instead she bid him set the men to digging a deep grave.

The man had spoken again. She stared down at him abstractedly and suddenly she dropped on her knees beside him. He started to speak again, but she interrupted him. "You say you're a doctor?"

"Yes. There were eight of us. I was in the tail and it broke loose and I fell free. There were eight of us, I said. It's a De Haviland Albatross. I mean it was an Albatross. Who are you?"

"My name is Rachel Cade and I—"

"Rachel Cade." He tried to smile. "That's a funny name."

[148]

"Yes, I guess it is rather."

"Where am I?"

"You're an American," she said firmly.

"You're damn right I'm an American. But where *am* I?"

"Near a place called Dibela."

"Dibela where? I mean is this Kenya or—"

"It's at the foot of the Ruwenzori. You were flying right into them."

"Never heard of the Ruwenzori," he said. "I was only a passenger, bound for Nairobi and Johannesburg."

She noticed then that he wore the torn, soiled remnants of some blue uniform. "You say you're a doctor and an American, but you wear a uniform, don't you? What—"

"Whoa!" He gripped her knee and smiled. "You tell me first where I am and then we'll have the proper introduction, Rachel Cade."

"I told you." Then, realizing how provincial one could become living in Dibela, she said, "This is the eastern edge of the Belgian Congo just a little north of the equator."

"That pilot!" he said. "That dumb bastard Harris—" He released her knee. "I'm sorry, Rachel. I see it bothers you when I speak so harshly of the dead. But he was perpetually lost. We came down the west coast to Leopoldville. That's where we left this morning. They decided to send us away over to Nairobi, God knows why, and Harris kept running around thunderstorms until he fouled himself thoroughly and— Oh, the hell with it. I'm alive and young Harris never again will see the dim gray spires of Oxford."

She inched backward, repelled by this self-centered male animal lying wounded in the grass while the bodies of his friends awaited the vultures.

"My name is Paul Wilton. I'm an American." His blue eyes caught and held her backward inching. "I'm a surgeon, a captain, assigned to the R.A.F."

She leaned toward him suddenly, resting her weight on her palms. "Does the leg hurt?"

His left hand lightly touched her cheek before she could move back. "It hurts like hell, Rachel."

"I guess we'd better set it here," she said.

"Hey! Are you a doctor?"

"No, but I'm a nurse. I'm the one who will have to set your leg if it's ever going to be set because there's no doctor within two hundred kilometers."

"Jesus," said Paul Wilton.

[149]

Rising, she called to a couple of men who were searching around the wreckage to cut poles and weave grass for a stretcher.

"You must be a missionary," he said.

"I'm a nurse," Rachel said. "I work as a nurse for the mission department of my church."

"Do you believe in it? The missionarying, I mean." He frowned. "That's a stupid question. You're here and here I am and I'm damn—I'm very grateful to you. At this place you're from—what's its name?"

"Dibela."

"Do you have X-ray at Dibela?"

"Heavens, no! I don't think you realize how remote we are here. So I'm going to set and splint your leg."

"Okay, Rachel. I've also got a pain in my chest. Here. Above the left clavicle."

"Have you spit blood?"

"No."

"Then stop worrying," she said. "We'll look you over at the hospital. We can't give you radioscopy, but we'll tape you up, if necessary, and after a while you'll stop worrying."

"Goddamn," Paul said slowly, "I like you."

Kulu, cutting elephant grass for a stretcher, looked up. "God?" he said in English to Rachel.

"I'm sorry," Paul said. "Honest, I won't say *that* either. Who is the—the bright young African?"

"His name is Kulu. He's quite the finest person I've ever known. He wants to be your friend. I hope you'll remember that and treat him as a friend. And I—I rather wish— Well, he wouldn't know anyway."

"You rather wish what?"

"I wish he wouldn't know that you're a doctor."

She took iodine from her first-aid kit and cleansed the gash on his forehead. When the men had finished making the stretcher, she told them to move him onto it. He raised his own weight on muscular, hairy arms, as they lifted him gently. He was a strong one, she thought. Before they came, when he dragged himself away from the wreckage, it was doubtful if he'd cried out in pain or terror.

Kulu and Tiza carried him some distance from Higgins's body. As Rachel cut open his right trouser leg, she glanced up at his face. He was not exactly handsome, but he had a strong, an interesting face. His nose was blunt and his square chin had a curious childish cleft and over his left cheekbone was an old crescent scar. He left her with a strange sense of unreality. He was here, tangible enough. *But who is he?*

"It's going to hurt for a minute," she said.

"I know," he said grimly. "At least, so they tell me."

His hands gripped the poles of the stretcher tightly as she carefully examined the fracture. "You're lucky," she said. "A simple fracture. Shaft of the tibia."

"Then set it," he said in a strained voice.

She set the break and splinted and taped it. Sweat beaded his forehead, but he made no sound. When she'd finished, he said, "Thank you, Doctor."

She smiled up at him. "You're welcome, Doctor."

Suddenly he turned his head and retched and vomited. "Sorry," he muttered. "Sorry." He closed his eyes.

She cleaned his chin with her handkerchief, murmuring sympathetically, until he opened his eyes and said, "I have nine cigarettes left and I think I'll smoke one now." He drew a flattened pack of Player's and a lighter from a breast pocket.

"Rest a bit and smoke," she told him. "Then we'll head for Dibela."

As she walked slowly toward the burned-out fuselage of the airplane, she thought, I don't like him. And then she thought, But I've been away from the world so long that I'm incapable of judging him. After all, he was a doctor. But he was not and never could be a doctor for Dibela. They must take him back to Dibela and then hustle him off to Rugeri as soon as possible. This was an official matter. There was a war on and he was a soldier and—

Looking up, she saw Kulu.

"There are three bodies, Madami, counting that one." He pointed back toward Higgins. "And more in there." He pointed to the twisted, smoldering steel. "Fire destroyed them in there, Madami. They cannot be buried."

"Then we'll bury the three," Rachel said. The dim gray spires of Oxford, she thought. She returned to Paul and told him they were burying the three immediately.

"Carry me down there," he said.

Kulu and Tiza carried his stretcher.

"I didn't know any of them well," Paul said impassively. "I was just a passenger. So that is the end of that."

Rachel frowned at him, thinking, The end of what? Life should not be this cheap. Eight men flew east from Leopoldville this morning and now one says, "That is the end of that."

Almost angrily he said to her, "Well, isn't it?"

"I don't think so," she said and turned from him.

When the bodies had been lowered into the hole she stepped forward and the men gathered across the grave from her. She recited the Twenty-third Psalm in Swahili, and then, sensing Paul Wilton's gaze fixed on her back, she recited it in English.

"Let us pray," she said in Swahili and most of the men, as they had learned to do, bowed their heads.

"God the Father," she said, "look with mercy on the lives of these men who left us today. They were brave men dedicated to a great cause. Strengthen the loved ones they leave behind them, we ask in Thy name. Amen."

As the men began to fill the grave, she turned around. Paul Wilton, staring at her, took another one of his precious cigarettes from his pack and lighted it with steady hands.

As they carried him down the last slant into Dibela, the misty rain stopped falling and the sun broke through. He looked up at her walking beside his stretcher and smiled.

The people shouted as those streaming back to the village met those running out to meet them. A youth was blowing a conch shell and another was beating a drum. But what, Rachel wondered dimly, was there to celebrate?

When Kulu and Kosongo carried Paul into the hospital operating room, he looked about curiously. "Clean," he said. "Orderly. You run a good show, Doctor."

"All it needs, Doctor, is a doctor," she said.

When he pulled off his torn shirt and T-shirt, the whiteness of his muscular body surprised her. It was so long since she'd seen a white body. Not that color made any difference, she told herself. You're a nurse and a body is a body. It was strange that his should make her feel ill at ease.

"Now let me examine your chest." She fingered each rib. When she pressed above the left clavicle, he said, "Ouch." She tapped it and put on the stethoscope and asked him to breathe deeply and exhale slowly. "The râles are very slight," she said at last. "Maybe a little lesion. But I'm positive nothing's broken. Shall I tape it?"

"No. Let it take care of itself. Bandages make me itch." He grasped her left hand suddenly. "Rachel Cade, you're a terrific person."

"No." She tried to free her hand.

"Yes," he said. "Now tell me. How many of you people are there here?"

"There's Kulu," she said, "and Kosongo and—"

"No. How many whites?"

"Just me," she said.

"My God!" He pressed her hand. "You know, you could almost make a guy believe there is a— Well, it doesn't matter. What I want to say is, thanks for saving my life." He looked at her left hand in his. "I knew you weren't married. You don't wear a ring."

Truly a male animal, she thought. An injured man who had miraculously escaped flaming death, noticing whether his rescuer wore a wedding band.

"Observant cuss, aren't I?"

"Yes." Her tone was disapproving. "Do you always go around observing such things?"

"Sure." His lips had a way of curling back defensively at such a moment. "I'm always noticing whether a beautiful woman is married."

He had a strange capacity for arousing despair in her. But why should he? How could he? He was just a man passing through. But he was a doctor. And these past months a doctor, any doctor, even Ralph Morgan, had begun to assume the stature of a god to her. For, despite her long experience, she had not truly realized before the wonderful things that a doctor could do in a place like Dibela.

"Rachel," he said, "might you happen to have one teensy bit of internal alcohol on the premises? Frankly, chum, I could use a drink."

"Yes," she said slowly. Of course, being a man, he'd like a drink after what he'd been through. "Yes. There's a little cognac." She started away and paused. "Is—is— Well, I've been away from everything so long I'm curious— Is this word 'chum' new slang or—or something?"

He stared at her solemnly. "It's British English. In Britain now everybody's 'chum.' War stuff, I guess. Annoying, isn't it?"

"No," she said quickly, "I didn't mean—"

"I know what you mean, Rachel." He smiled at her. "You like a person to mean every single word he says. But in the sad bad outer world today hardly anybody dares say what he means. If they did, nearly everybody would go slit his throat." He looked out at the growing darkness. "Rachel, my desire for survival knows no bounds. Now I'm getting hungry."

"Then you shall eat."

"But first I'll drink."

"All right."

"And you will eat and drink with me?"

"I think," she said, "that like most doctors, you're going to be a difficult patient." Then she smiled. "I'd love to."

She did not intend to take such a long time. But there was so much to do. And all of it was a pleasure. She told Kulu and Kosongo to move the Bwana to the coolest corner of the hospital and make him comfortable, setting up a woven screen to give him privacy. And she had to send a message to the drum-talker for the Bwana Administrator in Rugeri: A plane had crashed. (The talker never would be able to transmit the word "British.") Seven men were dead. One was saved and lay injured in the hospital. All was well. Come tomorrow. Next she had to listen to Kulu extol the great manly virtues of the new Bwana Birdman. Then she hurried to the bungalow and gave Guta strict orders on dinner for two to be served hot in the hospital when Madami sent word. She wanted a shower, and she stood too long under the sieved drum. Tonight she would wear a dress. And stockings. (It was a shame how long she'd been wearing shirt and slacks.) And the suede shoes with high heels. Would he think her foolish for dressing? But how would he know she didn't dress this way every evening? What a mess her hair was. And then there was the perfume which, she suddenly feared, might have evaporated. But it hadn't.

When she started off through the darkness with the Coleman lamp, she suddenly remembered the cognac. She ran back for a bottle and a glass, but decided to bring two glasses. Not that she would drink any, she thought.

"What were you doing?" he asked petulantly when she finally reached the hospital. "Making gin in the bathtub?" Then he smiled at her as she hung up the Coleman and turned it high. "Hey! Something from Paris, eh? Turn around, gal, and let me look you over."

She didn't turn, of course. This old chambray! But it was nice to hear him say it. It was nice not only to remember but to live again in contact with someone of your own kind. Yet he was not really her kind, she thought. He was an American, but he was unlike anyone she'd ever known.

"Cognac," he said, taking the bottle from her and turning it in his hands. "Rare old cognac. It's not that I have to have a drink so bad. It's that I have to have a cigarette so bad. I have seven mashed Player's left in this pack and I can't stand a drink without a cigarette. So, since I'm going to have a drink—" He looked up at her. "Do you follow me?"

"Yes." She felt a trifle breathless. "Yes."

"Okay." He splashed cognac into a glass and held it out to her.

"Thanks," she said quickly, "I don't drink."

"Neither do I." He poured a larger amount in the other glass. "Except in extraordinary times. And these are extraordinary times, Rachel. Times, as the poet or somebody said, that try men's souls." He thrust the glass toward her again and she took it hesitantly. He raised his glass. "Cheers, Rachel." He sipped his drink.

Slowly she raised hers and a little cognac burned her throat.

"Good gal. Good cognac. Find yourself a chair and sit down."

Kulu had placed a canvas chair near his cot. Kulu had social imagination. She sat down slowly, watching Paul take a bent cigarette from the table and light it ritualistically, inhaling deeply and exhaling slowly.

"It's not a Camel nor even a Chesterfield," he said. "But at least it's a Player's. What do people smoke around here?"

"Some kind of dark, strong tobacco. A lot of them smoke pipes."

He studied her thoughtfully. "Now I want to hear the story of your life. Start here and word backward or start at the beginning and work forward."

"There isn't much to tell—"

"When they say that there's always a lot to tell. Look, I'll interview you, like a newspaperman. Miss Cade, why did you come to Africa?"

She looked at the glass in her hands. Suddenly the glass seemed to waver and she realized she was staring at it through tears. What in the world was the matter with her? What in the world was the capacity of this man for arousing despair in her?

"Hey." He leaned toward her and touched her hand. "I'm sorry, Rachel. Honest, I'm sorry. I didn't mean to—to say anything that—"

"You didn't say anything." She raised her chin and her voice broke. She dabbed at her eyes with a clean lace handkerchief. "What an adolescent I am. It's just that somehow you manage to make me feel so—odd. I mean you make me feel as if I've been living away off from—from reality for so long."

"Rachel," he said gently, "let me tell you about reality. This is reality right here. That up there in Europe now, and I guess back home in the States too—that's—nightmare. There's nothing left of Europe. The krauts have taken France and Belgium and Holland. They're a strange new race

[155]

of machines. They aren't men. By one slight miscalculation in the machine they haven't taken Britain too. But they gave us what Roosevelt or Churchill or somebody calls the Battle of Britain. We won it. It's practically over. But I'm a fugitive from it. Sure, I wasn't one of those kids who won it in the sky. I was just one of the guys on the ground who helped piece 'em together every morning and evening to go back for more. They call me a surgeon. Surgeon, hell! I've been playing psychological wet nurse to a bunch of kids who were doing something I had neither the skill nor the guts to do."

"But you've been doing something important," she said. "You didn't *have* to do it. You're an American. You could have gone home."

"Yeah." He sipped his drink and looked at his cigarette. "Well, to give you my story on a postcard, I graduated from Johns Hopkins and I interned at Bellevue. I took two years of resident surgery and then—well, I took up an offer of a year at a hospital in London. It was good training. Then the war came along. And while I sometimes think I hate the British, I purely love 'em when they're in a war—especially against Germans. So I joined up, as they say. And here a couple of weeks ago they decided to send Old Wilton, as they call me—I'm thirty-four and that's frightfully old in the Royal Air Force—they decided to send Old Wilton down to South Africa on a junket to examine a lot of young raw material and decide if it's fit to be shot up over Europe. They have a very high standard in the R.A.F. on the physical material they'll let get shot up over Europe. So—here I am."

Thirty-four, she thought irrelevantly. Two years older than I.

"And that's my life story," he said. "Almost my life story. Any questions?"

"No."

"Not one?" He smiled at her, knowing her mind was crowded with questions. "Wouldn't you like to know something else? I mean like— Well, I prefer my steak rare and I'm single and I have no use for religion. Hey, you run a Protestant place here, don't you?"

She told him about the mission she served.

"And you believe in it, of course?"

"Of course," she said. And then, because she thought she sounded smug, she added, "I'm not exactly your idea of a missionary. I haven't organized a formal church here. I don't feel I'm—wise enough. I'm a nurse. I was the operating nurse for the chief surgeon back at headquarters. He went home and hasn't come back. I— Well, I'm proud of my profession and I'm fond of the people and the country and I feel there's much to be done here for them."

"That's good," he said slowly. "That's real. That being an operating nurse, I mean. You must be a damn good one."

He asked her technical questions. She answered, but not alertly. Watching him, observing his eager interest in the profession, she wondered, Is this all there is to him? His interest in medicine was genuine enough, she saw. But was that *all* there was to him? Since those first moments near the plane, he'd presented a mask to her, the mask of a self-centered man concerned only in his own survival. His manner was—hard-boiled. With him, to be tough was all. Well, the circumstances that had made him thus were no concern of hers. He was here now, but he would soon be gone.

Yet he was not without subtlety, she realized. For, under his casual questioning, she found herself telling him of her training in Kansas City. What made her become a nurse? Why, it was the only thing she'd ever wanted to be since she was a child in western Kansas. Had her parents helped her toward her goal? No. There had been only one parent anyway. Her mother had died when she was six.

He brought it all back to her. The strong dam she'd carefully built to preserve herself against the floods of memory crumpled like cardboard under his questioning. She was carried away as she talked. Despite her valiant efforts, some of her bitterness must have been apparent to him. Rufus Cade, her father. Rufe Cade, farmer, with strong hard hands curled like the roots of old grapevines and a mind as narrow as a stem. David and Joseph, Dave and Joe, her older brothers, whom she hadn't heard from or scarcely thought of in years. ("Git goin', Rachel, an' git me s'more hotcakes.") Cook and bake and sew and clean; tend the garden, tend the hens, tend the men. She might have been there yet if her father hadn't married again and if Sam Claymont hadn't— Having Nellie Mc-Comb for a stepmother was bad enough. But the really bad thing had been letting Sam Claymont take her down by Simpson's Creek. From two bad events at the age of sixteen came the one good resolution to get out. So she had gone to Kansas City, her father letting her go finally because she told him she could get a housekeeping job and would send home money. She never sent back a cent, and it was too far and too expensive for any of them to come looking for her. In Kansas City she had gone to Mrs. Wentworth, the woman the local pastor, Reverend Davis, had written to, and it was her good fortune to be rescued. Mrs. Wentworth not only was of the church; Mrs. Wentworth was kind. So the church had become meaningful to her, and its people had become her people. Her life had become inextricably joined with it as she wound through school and training and her frustrated engagement to the fulfillment of Africa. Sam Claymont had not created a (what did the psychiatrists call it?) trauma. By causing her to believe that pain was the bedded conclusion of married slavery in Trego County he had driven her out. He had done her a favor.

Life is strange that I should now be sitting in the middle of Africa talking to a man thrown from the sky, remembering the slavery of America and saying:

"I guess you'd call my childhood emotionally underprivileged." She made her tone dry.

Paul understood dryness. He grinned at her and reached for another cigarette.

By that time Guta had served dinner and carried away the dishes and brought them coffee. They had wandered to and from the story of Rachel Cade, with Paul always bringing her back to it until she had told him— well, not everything, certainly not about Sam Claymont—but almost everything. She had told him about Ralph Morgan because Paul was determined to learn why she stayed here alone. She had told him about the enjoyment of reading poetry. She had told him about climbing the Mountains of the Moon. There was nothing, almost nothing, left to tell him.

She sat now, relaxed, after pouring forth so much. The fact she had talked to him was less important, she knew, than the fact that she had talked to someone, an American, who understood the language of her thoughts.

He exhaled cigarette smoke and looked at her. Tolerantly, knowledgeably. He knew she had not told him the whole truth, for he knew that the whole truth was usually unbearable to one's vanity. There must be certain unbearable truths about him, she thought. That was why he turned a tough exterior to the world.

Now she waited for him to tell her more about himself, matching his own brief, dry understatements with hers. But he did not. Perhaps, she thought, he had no dismal Trego County of his own. Yet he was thirty-four, and that was rather old for one with the medical experience he had mentioned. There must have been a gap of years before he entered medical school. How had he filled the gap? She waited, carefully refraining from questioning him.

But he did not talk about himself. He was absorbed now only in her climbing of the mountains. He found it so incredible, she knew, that she wished she hadn't told him. Yet she could understand. Sometimes it was incredible to her too.

"Why?" he said wonderingly. "That's what interests me. How you did it is amazing enough, Rachel. But more than that, I wonder why."

"I told you," she said defensively. "It seemed the only way I could break through this superstition of the people and—"

"I know." He nodded, staring at her broodingly. "You understand the situation here far better than I ever could. But you know what I think? If you'd waited a little longer, the people would have begun coming to the hospital anyway. You did a magnificent thing, Rachel. But it wasn't really necessary."

She wanted to bury her face in her hands, for he merely said what she had often thought. The memory of the climb lived vividly with her as a great experience; why would he not let it seem significant too? But she did not bury her face. She merely brushed at her forehead.

Suddenly, not far off, a lion roared in the night.

Paul stirred. "What's that?"

"A lion."

Again there was a roar. Another lion, a female, Rachel thought.

"What's he up to?"

"There's more than one. There may be a pride of lions circling 'round."

"What's a pride of lions?" Paul asked.

"A family," Rachel said. "A male and his females and their cubs. The male usually feeds first on the kill. After a while he lets the female join him."

"That sounds fair. After all, he's the boss."

She smiled slowly. "There's just one thing. Almost always the female does the killing for him."

XVI

Lecomte arrived in the early morning. He sprang up the bungalow steps, calling, "Rachel!"

[159]

She came toward him, smiling, with two cups of steaming coffee. "I have a doctor for the hospital," she said.

"No!" Lecomte dropped in a chair and took his cup in both hands.

She told him in detail what had happened. When she finished, he looked at her strangely and said, "The man—this doctor—will have to return to duty when he can travel?"

"Naturally," Rachel said. "But I hope that when he can walk a bit I can persuade him—" she looked abstractedly at the highest branches of the limbali—"to perform just a few operations that are badly needed here."

Lecomte fingered his chin, drawing the exact shape of an imaginary goatee. "Let us go see him," he said and got to his feet.

Paul was asleep. He lay on his back, one hand clenched on his chest and the other curled loosely against his cheek. He seemed to be smiling. Rachel often wondered afterward whether it was his smile that suddenly made her think he was handsome in the way a rare small boy shows intimations of future handsomeness. When he awakened, she knew, he would not seem as handsome to her. Just as few small boys ever actually grow into handsome men.

"My God," murmured Lecomte, "he's very handsome."

The words "très beau" pierced her as she stood, rooted, gazing down at Paul. Her right hand stole to her throat and she thought, Beau Wilton. That was how she'd been thinking of him without being able to find the word. Beau in the American sense of magnolia romances, meaning: dashing, cavalier, selfish. . . . Oh, nonsense!

She lowered her hand from her throat and said, "Paul." To her annoyance, his name came in a cautious whisper. "Paul," she said firmly.

The hand on his chest tightened spasmodically and he opened his eyes. He smiled, but she liked better his faint smile of sleep. Lecomte arched his brows curiously at her.

"Paul," she repeated, "this is Monsieur Lecomte, the local administrator."

"Bonjour, mon ami." Lecomte stepped forward with outstretched hand. "Comment ça va?"

"Good morning." Paul accepted his hand and looked at him steadily. "Do you speak English?"

"Uh." Lecomte stared down at him, a frown gathering. Then he said in English, "Very badly."

"But your English is better than my French." Paul released his hand. "So let's speak English."

Lecomte bowed and looked at Rachel. He did not like Paul Wilton, she knew.

"I suppose you want information," Paul said. "Well, I'll tell you what I know."

Lecomte sighed and drew a small black notebook from a shirt pocket. He leafed the pages leisurely, caricaturing an ignorant policeman by licking his thumb and scowling until Rachel laughed. They looked at her with surprised expressions, Lecomte's feigned and Paul's genuine.

"For heaven's sake, Paul, don't act so stuffy British." She rested a hand on Lecomte's arm. "This is Henri Lecomte, my very good friend, a sensitive artist of life, a lion of the plain and a leopard of the mountains."

"I like that," Lecomte said to her in his heavily accented English. "A lion of the plain and a leopard of the mountains. Gilo would appreciate it, I think. But I know no one else to tell it to."

"And I like it." Paul grinned suddenly. "In fact, I like everything about this whole situation. Henri, chum, if you'll speak English for two minutes I'll try to speak French for two. Hey, Rachel, when do I get coffee?"

"Kulu," she called.

"Yes, Madami."

"Two coffees for the two Bwanas, please. Pese."

"What does 'pese' mean, Rachel?"

"Hurry."

"If I can learn a dozen words a day I'll be talking this Swahili pretty good in a month."

"You expect to be here a month—Paul?" Lecomte looked at him gravely.

"At least a month. Maybe longer. Wounded birdman and all that, you know. Knocked out of the war in the wilds of Central Africa while on mission." He grinned. "May get the D.S.O. or something. Poor chap had a frightfully rugged time. Only survivor of terrible crash. Crawled for days through tiger-infested jungles."

"No tigers," Lecomte said. He stared at Paul, shaping an imaginary goatee on his chin again.

"Okay. No tigers. Only beautiful white madamis." He smiled at Rachel. "Good morning, Rachel. I forgot to tell you that you look beautiful this morning."

Lecomte sighed heavily. "The two minutes are almost ended, Paul. It will soon be time to speak French." He shook his head. "It took me some time to call Rachel anything but Miss Cade. And you—" He shrugged. "*Eh bien!* You Americans! In any event, you think you will be here a month."

"When you report this," Paul said slowly, "and I know that's why you're here—"

"Yes. The word will go on the telegraph from my office today. Provided the telegraph is working. It's a very temperamental line."

"When you report it," Paul said, looking at Rachel, "you can say it will be at least six weeks before I can be moved. Maybe more. Broken leg. Head injuries. Internal injuries. It's internal injuries that always gets 'em. They never can figure just how internal an injury can be."

Lecomte rubbed his nose and looked at his notebook.

"Now," Paul said, "I'll give you all the information I can. . . ."

After Lecomte had recorded Paul's remarks about the flight and the crash and the victims, he closed his notebook. He sat for a while, drinking coffee and questioning him about the war in Europe. Then he left to investigate the crash, taking Kulu and a large number of Dibela men with him.

"A nice guy," Paul said.

Rachel tightened her lips. He sounded so patronizing. Yet what did she want him to say? How could she expect him to know, on a first meeting, what a true friend and fine man Lecomte was? This, she thought, was a result of her living so obsessively close to this remote land that it came to fill the whole wide world for her. She could not expect Paul to see it immediately and to understand the importance of one like Lecomte who loved it as much as she.

Lecomte returned from the scene of the crash in midafternoon. Rachel walked to his car with him. He moved tiredly, silently, his head bowed. At the car he turned to her and extended his hand.

"Take very good care of yourself, Rachel. I'm not worried about your handsome doctor. He'll take care of himself. I shall not call again until you need me."

The next morning Paul sat up on his cot and watched the line of patients file into the hospital. He said nothing when Rachel showed him cases of ulcers and yaws.

A young woman carrying a baby entered and walked hesitantly toward Rachel, ignoring Mzimba's shouted directions to go to Musinga first. She had a large goiter. "Madami." The woman touched the swelling in her neck and stared at the floor.

"What do you do about things like this?" Paul asked.

[162]

"Nothing." Rachel was relieved to hear him speak at last. "What can I do?" She looked at him. "The woman knows I can do nothing. Her husband has asked me about it. But now he's heard you're here and he wonders if you're a doctor."

Paul grunted. "Tell her to step around here."

Rachel took the woman by an arm and led her to Paul's cot.

"Ask her how long she's had it."

"That's no use," Rachel said. "I'll try. But there are no calendars here. Time is not like it is to us. She will say whatever she thinks I want her to say." She turned to the woman. "Did you have this before your child was born?"

"Yes, Madami."

"Did it come to you after your child was born?"

"Yes, Madami."

"Have you had it a short time?"

"Yes, Madami."

"You have not had it a short time, have you?"

"No, Madami."

She turned to Paul. "That's hopeless. What else do you want to know?"

He fingered the growth on the woman's throat. "It could be simple goiter. Ask her if she sweats a lot. No, that's pretty silly. Ask her to hold out her right hand."

The woman did as Rachel told her.

"No tremor," Paul said. "Doubtful if it's thyrotoxicosis. You notice the mass is changing shape even while we're looking at it. That means it's very vascular. What would happen if this woman were operated on and she died?"

Rachel looked at him. "You would lose some face in Dibela. But it wouldn't last long. You'd gain it back with something else. This woman's husband thinks her goiter is unsightly. Otherwise he wouldn't have sent her here. Probably she's losing strength and so is a poorer wife. If she died, he would mourn her officially—and get another wife."

Paul smiled grimly. "You're speaking of how the husband feels, of course. Not how you feel."

"Of course."

"You would like the woman to lose her goiter?"

"Naturally. Wouldn't you?"

"Naturally." He paused. "Tell the woman to come back in a week. By that time I'll be standing on this leg—or know the reason why. Perhaps I can do something for her."

[163]

Rachel suddenly felt ebullient. She tried not to smile. It would be better, she thought, if she acted as though she naturally expected he would help her with some difficult cases before he left. Reaching to the table, she picked up several tiny pebbles from a pile and counted seven into the woman's hand.

"Throw away one each sunrise," she told her. "When the last is gone, return here with your husband."

"Yes, Madami." The woman left.

"What's that routine?" Paul asked.

"A pebble thrown away each day. Then she will know and remember when to return."

"Good God!" He stared at her incredulously. "If time is so meaningless and these people's memories so short, what's the use of—of—"

"Do you insist on knowing the I.Q. of all your patients, Doctor?" she asked sharply.

"Ouch!" He smiled at her. "Of course not. But—"

"The woman is a person if not an Einstein. She suffers and she has a soul. If her life is dreary, her child's can be better. But if she dies, the child will die too. For she has at least a year longer to nurse him. There are no prepared formulas available to orphaned infants in Dibela."

"All right," he said. "Okay, Rachel. I'll do what I can. Hey!" He pointed to a middle-aged man wearing a loincloth who limped through the door. The inside of his upper right thigh was badly swollen and discolored. "Let's take a look at him."

Rachel beckoned to the man. He approached slowly, looking away from them, conveying to Rachel a sense that he was completely disassociated from himself.

"Let's see this, chum."

The man turned his leg without Rachel speaking, as if he understood English.

"This could be sarcoma of the femur," Paul said. "Or it could be osteoma, though osteoma probably would be smaller. An X-ray could decide. And we don't have X-ray. Again, it might be epithelioma. But I'd say sarcoma of the femur just because that's the commonest. Ask chum here if he's hurting bad, Rachel."

"Again I'll try, but I don't think we'll learn much, Paul. The way these people endure pain is amazing."

"If it's the stage of sarcoma I think it is, he certainly is amazing. I saw a very brave army colonel scream like a baby with this. Somebody ought to do some research on primitive stoicism— Ah, the hell with it. Ask our chum if he hurts."

"Are you in pain?" Rachel asked the man.

"No, Madami."

She shook her head at Paul. "He says no. He would lose great face to admit pain. But you see his eyes. They're away out there, disassociated from his pain."

"Of course I see his eyes. Poor devil. What would be his lot if he lost a leg?"

"It would be a bad lot. A man doesn't last long here without two legs and two arms. His people will feed him, but he dies of pride."

"I could try it," Paul said thoughtfully. "If it's sarcoma of the femur, a hard, spindle-shaped growth encircles the bone. Usually the lower end. But not necessarily. And maybe the bone—" He frowned. "Ask this man if he would rather lose the leg than to have it the way it is."

Rachel shook her head. "You cannot ask him that. He's not able to decide. I don't recall seeing him before. He must be from another village. All he knows is to try to keep his legs and arms and endure the pain and accept death. You can't ask these people to make decisions like that— yet."

"What do you mean—yet?"

"I mean maybe someday when—when life here is a little more—"

"Civilized?" he asked scornfully. "Hell, it's better this way before they've discovered neuroses."

"You don't believe a word of that," she snapped.

"No," he said slowly, staring at her. "No, it's just another of my con lines, I guess. I guess I'm just trying to avoid making a decision."

"But you *have* to make a decision," she said.

"All right." His voice rose. "Give him seven pebbles. Wait! Give him five. I'll somehow—goddamn this leg— Give him five."

Instinctively she touched his arm. He was a good man.

He looked down at her hand and up at her face. Then his lips curled back from his teeth in that defensive smile. "Where's he from and what's his name?"

Rachel asked the man and he answered her in a remote voice.

"His name," she told Paul, "is Wamaza and he comes from Tuka, which is a tiny clan village seven or eight miles from here."

"So he walked it with sarcoma of the femur," Paul said wonderingly. "Doesn't he have relatives or something here so that—"

"He'll stay here in the hospital," Rachel said. "He'll have a pallet and we'll feed him and—"

"Good." He nodded. "Do you have money enough to feed and care for everybody?"

"The money comes in," she said. "There's a regular payment from headquarters. Enough to pay the men and do the necessary things." Turning to Wamaza, she explained carefully that he was to stay here and in a few days they would try to cure his leg.

By noon Paul had seen thirteen patients with a variety of diseases on whom he said he would operate. Kulu and Musinga and Kosongo and Mzimba watched him worshipfully. As if he were a god, thought Rachel. It troubled her. For he was so humanly imperfect. He would leave soon and the people here never would understand why he left.

Kulu drew her aside. "Madami, the Bwana is a doctor?"

"Yes, Kulu." She did not look at him.

"He's the Bwana Doctor, as God the Father promised."

How could she explain to him that his seeing visions was a weakness and that Paul's presence here was a coincidence, unrelated to an ever-loving God? And yet, she thought, *is* it? In explaining away all visions and all prophecies did Western rationalism explain away Kulu's vision and Paul's arrival? Yes, she thought, it *had* to. It could admit no exceptions without destroying its careful structure. All exceptions had to be called coincidence—and so be incredible. The fact that life moved by coincidence was no concern of the inexorable rules of rationalism. Yes, this all had to be coincidence. Someday she would have to convince Kulu that it was merely coincidence. Otherwise he would utterly confuse his own desires with the unfathomable designs of God. That, after all, was why it had been necessary for man to invent rationalism.

"You must understand one thing, Kulu," she said slowly. "And you must make the others understand. The Bwana Doctor cannot cure all these people. Some will die. And you must understand and make the others understand that he will not stay long with us. He's a soldier in the northern war and he must return to it."

"Yes, Madami." Kulu smiled at her. "But I think he will stay much longer than you believe."

She started to speak impatiently to him, and then she checked herself. At least he was expressing a thought in disagreement with hers. A few months ago he would not disagree. Disagreement was progress. Even as Kulu had learned to say what he thought instead of what he believed she expected of him, so others in time would learn. Kosongo was learning. Mzimba was learning. Even Musinga sometimes gave signs of learning.

They carried Paul's cot to the shade of the limbali near the whitewashed wooden cross marking Dr. Bickel's grave. Guta served lunch to Rachel and him there. Afterwards Paul lay back, his eyes half closed, staring up into the cool green shadows of the great tree where doves murmured sleepily. Hens clucked and rubbed their feathers in the compound dust. Somewhere a macaw talked to himself.

He turned his head to Rachel and smiled. "They know I'm a doctor, don't they?"

She told him hesitantly about Kulu's experience of six days ago.

He shook his head. "Hallucinations. He seems like a smart young guy too. I can't imagine his hallucinating."

"Maybe he wasn't." Her voice sounded remote. Whenever she sat under the limbali it seemed that a part of her took refuge in its upper branches.

"Don't tell me you believe in visions," he said.

"No," she replied, "I don't."

"Then you agree it was hallucination."

"Yes, I guess it must have been hallucination." She stirred. "Of course it was hallucination."

"Right," he said with a note of triumph. "At least we agree on what's real and what isn't. Lying here under this big tree is real enough. It almost makes me wonder if I know what I want after all."

"Do you know what you want?"

"Of course I know. I want to be successful. Which means I want to be rich. I want to be an able, rich surgeon." He raised himself on an elbow. "Sounds childish, doesn't it? But it's the truth and this strikes me as a good place to tell the truth. I know there are a lot of physicians who don't care about being rich, and I respect them—if they're able. And I know a lot who want to be rich, and I respect them—if they're able. It's ability that counts." He lay back. "There, I sounded off."

"Well, don't apologize about it," she said without asperity. "So you want to be rich. So you must have been poor."

He yawned. "Small town poor. I grew up in a place called Pendennis, Ohio. Being Pendennis poor is worse than New York Lower East Side poor. On lower First Avenue you can always walk up to Sutton Place and get an idea of how you can hope to live someday. But on the south side of Pendennis you can only see the freights go through." He stretched his arms and yawned again. "But I'm not being bitter. You understand that, don't you?"

"You poor man," she said abstractedly, "you just don't feel you can afford any emotions, do you? Not even bitterness."

He sat up so abruptly that he winced. "Emotions? You mean you think I'm—cold? You mean—"

"I mean you used the word 'con' this morning. By that I presume you mean a con game, a counterfeit to conceal the truth." She smiled faintly at him. "That's all right. We all indulge in it more or less. But I do think you're a much better person than you give yourself credit for being. Your joining the R.A.F., for instance, when you could have sailed safely home to the States and started becoming a rich, successful surgeon."

"Oh, that." He lay down again and let his arms trail relaxedly from the cot. "That was just—well, I figure we'll all be in this thing eventually and I might as well get in early, even before the Americans join up, and get myself a soft berth on the ground floor."

"Nonsense," she said. "You didn't figure anything. You just knew the British were in a tight spot and you wanted to help. Just as you wanted to help when you saw the patients this morning. I appreciate it more than I can tell you."

"That?" he said. "Now that—well, what the heck, you saved my life. . . ."

She didn't listen to him. She thought, Someday somebody's going to love him terribly just because he is the way he is. Then, suddenly: I could love him. The thought shook her and she stirred uneasily in her chair. Of course you couldn't, she told herself. He'll leave soon and you will stay and you'll never see him again. So think of other things. Keep him as distant in your thoughts as he is in the flesh.

"You must have worked very hard," she interrupted him, her voice annoyingly unsteady.

"Naw," he drawled. "I worked around. Times haven't been so prosperous at home these past few years. I guess you know. Took me a while to get through school. I worked in a steel mill in Gary, Indiana, for a while. I was an oil rigger in Texas and saved my money. Stuff like that. But I got through— Hey, what's that green bird?" He pointed.

She looked up. "A dove." When she lowered her gaze she found he was staring at her strangely.

"Rachel." He hitched himself onto an elbow. "Rachel, I—"

Kulu stood there and behind him stood Chief Buderga, carrying a spear. Kulu was speaking, but she seemed unable to hear him. She was wondering what Paul had been about to say.

Buderga stepped forward and presented the shaft of his spear to Paul.

"He's giving it to you," Rachel said quickly. "It's a gift. Shake his hand."

Paul shook hands with Buderga and accepted the spear. He looked at Rachel. "Jolly trophy for the town house, what? What's the angle?"

"Wait."

Budgera spoke at length on his pleasure in having the Bwana Doctor Birdman in Dibela. At last, like a well-trained lawyer, he made his plea: Could the Bwana Doctor Birdman make it possible for his youngest wife to conceive a child?

Rachel translated, and Paul asked, "Has he ever sired any kids?"

"Six daughters by two wives. But he's most concerned about his third and youngest wife. He's fondest of her."

"Until she has a child," Paul said. "Then, I suppose, he'll take a fourth. So now it's gynecology. Do you realize I'm no genius, Rachel? Suppose it doesn't work."

"Then it won't work," she said. "Do you want to give her an examination this afternoon?"

He shrugged. "Okay."

"The Bwana Doctor will examine your wife if you bring her to the hospital now," Rachel told Buderga. "He does not know if he can help. He will see."

Buderga bobbed his head and almost ran from the compound.

"Anything special I ought to know?" asked Paul.

"You'll find she's undergone an excision. All girls around here undergo it when they're ten or eleven. The labia majora and clitoris are removed and—"

Paul swore in surprise. "Then they can't enjoy married life very much."

Rachel felt herself blushing. She rose, aware that he was staring at her, aware that he realized she was— What was he thinking as he stared at her?

"Uh," he said, trying to keep the surprise from his face and managing only to look amused. "Well, Rachel, I— Well, damn it, isn't that true?"

"I suppose so," she said. "I—"

"You *suppose* so?"

"I *suppose* so," she repeated coldly. "But the men feel it keeps them— faithful and—and content to find the deeper satisfaction of marriage in—"

"The *deeper* satisfaction of marriage?" He grinned at her.

"In bearing children," she continued doggedly, "and working and maintaining a stable family." She started toward the hospital.

He cupped his lips and called in the metallic tone of a loudspeaker, "Dr. Wilton wanted in surgery, Dr. Wilton report to surgery."

He acted such a fool, she thought. And then, suddenly, she smiled. For it was pleasant to have a man pretending to be a fool around here.

They ate dinner together at her bungalow that evening and they talked until midnight when she told him, "I have a surprise for you."

He looked at her alertly. "Don't tell me. Let me guess. You're moving me out of the hospital. I'm staying here with you."

"Not exactly," she said. "You're out of the hospital. But you're living in the cottage across the compound. I've had it cleaned up."

"But it's lonely out there." He gestured toward the insect-ringing darkness. "I'm scared of being alone in the dark."

Always *kidding*, she thought. Never serious. And yet his very lack of seriousness about anything except the ill was a pleasure. She said, "You won't be alone. Kulu says he will sleep in your doorway. Kulu has decided that in addition to all his other duties he's going to be your slave." She called Kulu's name, and he and Kosongo padded silently into the ring of light. "The Bwana Doctor is ready to be taken home."

"The Bwana Doctor isn't ready," Paul said. He looked at her. Then he said slowly, "But the Bwana Doctor will go."

Yes, it was a pleasure to have him here, she often thought in the following days. He would perform some desperately needed operations before he left. But sometimes she thought she would have enjoyed his presence for a few days even if he had not been a doctor. For he made the little things of life count again. To eat with him was to dine instead of picking at food in loneliness. His first bath, administered by Kulu and Kosongo while all three laughed and shouted in stentorian voices, he made seem as important as a baby's first bath. He rocked her with hearty laughter when he clowned in a shirt and pair of pants that had belonged to Dr. Bickel. They were so absurdly too small for him. Her delight matched his when she stayed up nearly all night and lengthened trousers and altered a shirt to fit him. The shirt was necessarily bereft of a collar and had a large stripe of insert down the back. But he was so grateful.

The greatest satisfaction came, however, when he and Kulu and Mzimba made crutches and he struggled off the cot and walked a few steps. Each day he stayed a little longer on the crutches and walked a little farther. On the seventh day after his arrival, though not on the fifth as he had hoped, he said he was ready to try an operation. Under his pantomimed directions Mzimba had built an odd contrivance which looked something like a ship's crow's-nest. It would enable him to stand restfully while he operated, he said.

So, on the seventh day, he operated on Wamaza from Tuka under a local anesthetic. Rachel stood opposite him and Kulu stood at Wamaza's head which was protected by a sterilized towel over a hoop so that Wamaza could not see the operation. Rachel tried to think only of the importance of this operation to Wamaza, but she found herself admiring Paul. Oh, he was deft and able as even Dr. Spencer had not been. She kept telling herself she should not think thus. But she was an able and experienced operating nurse, and she could not deny the fact of his skill unfolding before her eyes.

Wamaza suffered from sarcoma of the femur, he tersely told her as he showed her the cancer. "It's hopeless," he muttered, sweat beading his forehead. "A failure." But he did what he could and sewed up Wamaza's leg and they carried him back to the cool corner of the hospital. Paul was too exhausted to operate on the woman with the goiter.

They were deeply depressed at dinner that evening. But the next day he hobbled cheerfully to the hospital and successfully removed the goiter from the woman's neck while her relatives whimpered in the shade of the limbali. In the afternoon he operated on Buderga's youngest wife, removing a series of large cysts. Afterwards, sagging back against his brace, he muttered, "She might someday just happen to have a baby."

The next day he was able to perform four operations, and the following day there were five. The word spread on the plain and there was great rejoicing. Each morning the waiting line of the ill grew longer.

On the evening of the fifteenth day after the Bwana Doctor came to Dibela he hobbled up the steps of Rachel's bungalow and lowered himself onto the blanket-covered cot. He sprawled there, his eyes closed, his hair wet from the shower.

At last he said, "Rachel, let's tap that bottle of rare old cognac again. I need it." He fingered in a pocket and opened his eyes and smiled at a bent cigarette. "My next to last Player's."

She brought the bottle of cognac and two glasses and pulled a chair close. She didn't want a drink, but she knew the importance of sipping a little with him. She knew the importance of his being here, a doctor or not.

He poured a little in her glass and three fingers in his own. He held up the glasses and said, "Sit beside me while we drink this."

Unhesitatingly she moved to the cot beside him, leaning back against the grass cushions and sighing relaxedly. He turned to her, holding out her glass. As she reached for it, he moved it. His face was close to hers. She felt his breath and closed her eyes. His lips moved against hers, softly at first and then crushingly, and she felt a strangeness pass through her body that made her tremble. She opened her eyes and he was gone. But he was merely setting their glasses on the floor. His arms were around her and the strangeness passed through the length of her body again as he drew her to him.

She moved. Her hands pressed against his chest, gently at first and then fiercely. She was standing, swaying, trying to smile down at him. He was looking up at her expectantly.

"No," she whispered. "No."

"No?" His voice was edged with anger or passion.

"No." She backed from him until the table was between them and he seemed far away. "You'd—you'd better have your drink," she said unsteadily. "I don't want any."

"Okay," he said. "Okay!" Sweeping one big hand to the floor, he lifted his glass and drained it. Then, getting heavily to his feet, he limped to the porch and shouted, "Kulu!"

"Yes, Bwana Doctor," Kulu cried in English as he ran across the compound.

"I'll have dinner over there!" Paul waved toward his cottage and limped down the steps. He did not look back.

XVII

She sat at the table and stared out at the sky which had been cleansed by rain a few hours earlier and now was a deep shadowed blue in the declining sun. Guta moved silently between table and kitchen, removing her untouched food. Kulu crossed and recrossed the compound to and from the cottage which lay outside her line of vision.

Foxes barked on the plain and dogs answered in the village. *Now see, now see, now see,* said the doves in the limbali.

Out of her numbed thoughts rolled the question. *What's the matter with me?* For the matter was with her, she thought. Not with him, not with him. He wanted her. *I want him too. At least I wanted him.* So the trouble was with her that she had repulsed him. But why? And yet why not? She was the sum total of her disciplines and she could not just— But she could. This good life in Africa had not been one of discipline; it had been one of choice. Now, when he kissed her, he made her wish to choose otherwise.

She waited tensely for the sound of his returning steps. He would come and say—what would he say? It really did not matter, if only he'd come back and simply *be* here in this low, wide, open room with her. Now she saw it. All these past days she'd waited on his coming and going, drawn quite out of herself whether he was present or absent, thinking constantly of how he looked or the things he said. Secretly critical of him, yes; harshly critical of his imperfections. But now she saw it was his very imperfections that made him human—and so necessary. This, then, must be the much-maligned emotion called love: not admiration of inhuman perfection, but all-absorbing devotion to human imperfection. Yet must two bodies complicate its purity of feeling?

And why not? Was it really as bad as it had been that time so long ago in Trego County? I must not think this way, she told herself, almost forming the words with her lips. I must not think this way. She rose and walked slowly about the room. She tried to think of something to do. And there was nothing to do. It never had been this way before. Always there had been something. But now she knew what nothing was. And that, she thought, was why she must not think this way again. For he would go and she would stay and they would not see each other again. But if this thing went further, his presence would be here forever and she would not be able to forget him. And that, given the place and the circumstances and the troubled time of war in the world, was what she must do and would do: forget him.

She reached out for a book, any book, and opened it in her lap and stared sightlessly at the page as the light faded. When darkness had almost settled, Guta came in and asked in a surprised tone, "Madami wants the lamp lit?"

"Yes, please, Guta," she said.

He had lighted the lamp and left when she heard Paul's halting steps. She gripped the book tightly and tried to compose her face. But she

[173]

moved forward in her chair and turned her head, eyes straining into the darkness until she could see him limping into the circle of light.

"Hi." He did not look at her.

"Hi," she said in a low voice.

"Sorry I made an ass of myself."

"You didn't." She tried unsuccessfully to make her tone light. "Forget it."

He looked at her gloomily then. "The trouble is, Rachel, I can't forget it, I won't forget it. I—" He sat down carefully, hands folded on the head of the stick which Kulu had cut from the limbali. He rested his chin on his folded hands and stared at her. "I think it would be a good idea, Rachel, if I pushed along."

Her right hand stole toward her throat. No, she thought, there's so much for him to do here yet.

"I think you'd better set in motion whatever has to be done to get me out of here. A message on the drum to Lecomte, I suppose. It'd be a good idea if I started back from here tomorrow."

She could not say a word to him. Her lips parted, but no words came. Yes, it was better if he left quickly.

At last she said faintly, "All right."

He lifted the point of the stick from the floor and let it fall gently. "We had—how many operations scheduled tomorrow? Three?"

"Yes."

"I'll finish them before I go." He paused and then looked up at her. "But that's all. I won't do any more."

"All right, Paul," she said quietly.

"I *have* to go." His voice rose. "Do you understand?"

"Yes, Paul, I understand."

He got to his feet. "G'night."

"Good night, Paul." She did not rise. She stared at her hands locked in her lap until she heard his footsteps and cane receding.

Then she turned out the lamp and went into her dark bedroom. She undressed in the darkness, dropped her clothing carelessly on the chair. She lay down, not bothering to lower the netting around the wide bed, and then she cried.

She awakened at dawn, swinging her legs from the bed with an exuberance habitual on recent mornings. When her feet touched the floor, she remembered that this morning was different. She sat on the edge of the bed, staring at her feet for fully a minute. At last she rose slowly and the day began for her.

She was standing drinking coffee and staring vacantly out at the rain when Wanga came up the steps and removed his pride, that visored cap dug from some dark bin of Dr. Bickel's. He smiled at her.

"Madami, I took the car without your permission before you were up. A runner came from a place a dozen kilometers along the road to Rugeri. I know him, he is an honorable man whose uncle received new life from the Bwana Doctor. He said his nephew was dying and could not come to the hospital. I went to Kulu at the Bwana Doctor's house, but Kulu could not get the Bwana up. He is very tired from working so much, Madami. So I drove to the place and we put my friend's nephew in the car and brought him here to the hospital. Will the Bwana Doctor look at him, Madami?"

"Yes." She put down her cup. "Yes, he will. You used good judgment, Wanga."

She drew her raincoat over her shoulders and crossed the compound through the rain. Already, despite the early hour, a line of the sick was forming under the eaves of the hospital. They called out to her, "Jambo, Madami. Jambo!" And she thought, There's so much to do, as she greeted them.

The boy lay on a pallet in the foul smell of his vomit. His belly was distended hugely. He was possibly twelve years old. His forehead was clammy with sweat, his eyes withdrawn into the orbits. His father, sitting beside him, looked at Rachel beseechingly. The boy smiled and said, "Jambo, Madami. Will I die?" He retched suddenly and brown, stercoraceous slime oozed from his lips.

She wiped his lips and said, "You will not die if we can help it, son." Kulu came in at that moment and she called, "Kulu, fetch the Doctor quickly."

"Oh, Madami." He shook his head and then she saw his expression was troubled. "He is hard to rouse this morning. He does not want to get up."

"Is he sick?"

"No, Madami, but—" Kulu shrugged and spread his hands in the eloquent gesture he had picked up from Lecomte.

She strode out of the hospital, not bothering with her raincoat, and crossed the compound to Paul's cottage. He lay in his bed, staring at the ceiling.

"Please get up," she said sharply.

He looked at her and smiled faintly. "Why?"

"Because a very bad case has been brought in. A boy. I think he has general peritonitis."

He rubbed his temples. "I thought we agreed that today, after I performed these last three, you'd—release me."

She had a sudden clear picture of the boy in the hospital asking, "Madami, will I die?" And then she thought, I'll never release him. Every day he stays means at least one more life saved, one more soul that will live on to the better days that must eventually come here. And, knowing she would not release him, she felt at peace.

She said, "Perhaps you did not hear me. There's a boy in the hospital with peritonitis and you are a doctor."

"I heard you," he replied, nettled. "I'm coming." He started to throw back the sheet and paused. "I'm in the nude. You'd better turn and run, Rachel."

"No," she said, "I won't. You still need help in dressing and I—"

"Beat it, Rachel, will you please?" He grinned at her. "I'll be over in a couple of minutes."

She went out with a sense of contentment, as if the problem of his leaving were settled forever.

Kulu met her under the limbali as he walked toward Paul's cottage. "He will not get up, Madami?"

"He is up, Kulu. Fetch him some hot coffee, please."

He looked at her in amazement, as if she had performed a miracle. And then he smiled, as if he too believed a problem were settled forever.

She had just measured the boy's temperature at 104 when Paul limped in. He smiled at the boy while he felt his pulse, and then he said to her, "Probably we don't have the equipment, but we'll try."

They moved him into the privacy of the operating room where Paul ran a rubber decompression tube through the boy's nose and into his stomach. He told Rachel to prepare a salt solution and take a blood type, meanwhile showing Kulu how to work the manual suction tube to decompress the stomach. Then he rigged an intravenous feeder for the saline solution. Gradually the boy's abdominal swelling decreased. Paul worked silently until about nine o'clock when he said, "We'll go ahead now."

The operation lasted two hours. He removed the foreign matter from the peritoneal cavity and closed a series of perforations in the intestinal tract. When the boy had been sewed up and his father had given a transfusion, Paul sat down.

"I believe," he said, "I could use that cigarette." He took the last be-draggled Player's from a pocket, smiled at it, and lighted it.

"We've *got* to find you cigarettes," Rachel said.

He blew a stream of smoke in her direction and studied her specu-latively.

"Kulu," she called, "where's Wanga?"

"Here, Madami." Wanga stepped through the doorway.

"Wanga, there's a list of things on my desk in the house that need fetching from the trader's. Kulu will get it for you." She took a slip of paper and a pencil stub from a pocket and wrote in French, "Ten pack-ages of cigarettes, Player's or the mildest possible," and handed it to Wanga. "Leave at once and come back at once."

"At once, Madami?"

"Pese, Wanga."

"Yes, Madami. I'll be back as soon as I can."

"Where's he going?" asked Paul.

"To Rugeri to get supplies," Rachel said.

His brows rose. "I could ride with him."

"But there are three operations yet to do today," she said.

He rubbed his chin and then he smiled slowly. "Yes. Three."

She watched him as he rested on an elbow, enjoying his cigarette. At last she said, "What would you like for dinner tonight?"

He looked at her for a long time. Finally he said, "Oh, let's have something different. Let's have canned corned beef."

It was dark and raining heavily by the time they finished the day's work at the hospital. Paul said he wasn't going to bother using her shower; he was simply going to stand outside with a cake of soap and have a refreshing bath. "I shall arrive promptly at eight," he said.

He did. He limped up the steps a few minutes after Wanga returned from Rugeri.

She stood waiting for him expectantly, her hands behind her, as he shook himself out of Dr. Bickel's raincoat.

"Nothing like getting home after a hard day at the office," he said.

That was what it really was, she thought. If only— She moved her hands quickly and said, "Here," handing him a blue package of ciga-rettes.

He took the package slowly, and read aloud, "Tabac Congo Belge."

"Not Player's," she said regretfully. "They didn't have any."

[177]

He took her hand. "Rachel, I— Rachel, you're a wonderful girl. I—"
He kissed her hand lightly.

"Is there anything you can do with cognac?" she said, turning.

"You can drink it."

"I mean, we don't have any ice, but I wondered if you can do anything to make it—more palatable."

"No, baby. You can only learn to like it."

Baby! She examined the word thoughtfully as she uncorked the cognac. She had always thought of it as the way paunchy, bald-headed men addressed peroxide blondes in cheap hotel rooms. Yet she liked his calling her that. She liked anything he wanted to call her because he was—right about these things. She remembered his sureness, his deftness in the hospital and she thought, I'm lucky because he's right about these things.

"Whoa!" he said. "Leave some for yourself."

She faced him quickly. "Paul, would you mind terribly if I—if I didn't have a drink with you tonight?"

"Of course not." He took his glass and sat down in a chair. "Tabac Congo Belge," he read, and opened the pack.

"Paul." She sat down on the edge of a chair. "Paul, you can smoke all you want because I had Wanga get ten packages of them today."

He looked at her oddly. "Ten? Well—wonderful. Thanks." He raised his glass. "To you, Rachel." He sipped the cognac.

She watched him light a cigarette. There was something about the way he did it that made her wish she could enjoy smoking herself. "It's sort of strong, isn't it?"

"Uh." He cleared his throat. "A little. But good. A good cigarette."

"But it's not a Player's."

"No. But neither is a Player's a Camel. It's all relative."

She listened suddenly to the heavy splash of rain, as if she caught a sound above it. "Yes, relative," she said at last. "You have to take what you can when—"

"No," he said quickly, almost harshly. "That's a lousy, stupid philosophy even to an unphilosophical guy like me. That take what you can get when you can get it. I don't believe in that sort of thing."

He lied, she thought. She knew he lied. But what did it matter? She had been sent a doctor and she was making what use she could of him while she had him. Wasn't that true? Well, on one level. But there was another level, the level of just liking to sit here with him listening to the rain.

They did not talk much. There didn't seem much to say. At first her quietness obviously bothered him. But soon it relaxed him, and they sat, exchanging few words, listening to the rain, until she said, "Would you like more cognac?"

"No, thanks." He looked at her. "Maybe we should—save it."

"There's another unopened bottle I didn't tell you about."

He smiled. "Holding out on me?"

"Paul."

"Yes."

"There are two more bottles."

He threw back his head and laughed in a way she had not heard him before. She liked to hear him laugh that way. She wished he would do it more often.

"Would you like to eat, Paul?"

"Sure. I'm starved."

She went to the kitchen and told Guta to serve the soup. During dinner they said little, and it troubled neither of them, Rachel saw.

Now, she thought as she drained her cup of bitter coffee after dinner. *And I'm glad.*

She rose and excused herself and went into the bedroom. She undressed, slowly at first and then quickly. Her hands fumbled and she trembled as with a chill. She put on a robe and went to the door.

He sat looking out at the darkness, smoke rising from a cigarette in his fingers.

"Paul."

He turned his head, the cigarette motionless in his raised hand.

"Paul, would you please come to bed with me?"

She did not wait to hear what he would say. Turning quickly, she took off the robe and lay down. She saw the lamp go out in the other room and she heard him enter quietly and close the door behind him.

Soon he was lying beside her, his arms around her, his lips against hers. He smelled, she thought, like honey. And then, crazily: Could honey still the frightful knocking of her heart? He was gentle. He smelled of honey. She had not known it could possibly be like this.

She slept. When she awakened at some time that didn't matter he was asleep on her arm, his head on her shoulder. She wanted him again and her free hand moved up his leg flung across hers. Instantly he was awake, murmuring to her. She wished he'd say, "I love you." But he didn't.

Later, still awake, she thought that she couldn't expect that. She could only expect that he'd stay in Dibela a while longer now. And then

[179]

she thought, But that's not why I want him to stay. He must stay because she never could stop wanting him now, wanting what he had taught her to want, what she had asked him to give. Not for the sake of the sick people of Dibela, but for the sake of Rachel Cade.

"Paul!" She drew him to her.

XVIII

WHEN HE COULD WALK easily, they walked toward the mountains one morning. It was Sunday.

"Even here in the middle of Africa you'd know it was Sunday," Paul said. "I don't care where you are, Sunday is always different. It's quieter everywhere."

They followed the track that wound through the elephant grass and eventually became the trail to Kulu's village. She went ahead with the shotgun slung over her shoulder and he followed, carrying the Westley-Richards and a knapsack containing a folded blanket and sandwiches and a bottle of cold tea. It was his idea to take the guns.

"I wish I could shoot a lion," he said. "I'd like to have my picture taken with a foot on the body of my dead lion."

Her throat constricted. Something for his mantel, she thought. A snapshot to show the boys at the officers' club and to pass along the bar of a London pub. She must not think this way. She had not thought thus in nearly four weeks now. He had said nothing to make her think so. He simply was here, as she was here, with time suspended by their close proximity. Somewhere, remotely, a war rolled on, and now almost four weeks had passed since he'd ceased to think of leaving Dibela. The pages of her diary were blank since the day he'd performed the first operation in the hospital. Then, she dimly remembered, she had written something rhetorically hopeful, something about Dibela at last having a doctor. But the events since that time she never could inscribe on any page; they were the incommunicable secrets of her own heart.

She could count the passage of time only by Sundays, and this was the third Sunday she had failed to read from the Bible to the throng under the limbali. That task she had assigned to Kulu. Task? It once had been a pleasure, but now she could not bring herself to do it. Was it a symptom of guilt? Once, in the darkness of a rainy night when she'd awakened beside Paul, she had thought over the Sermon on the Mount, trying to spell out her sinfulness. "Ye have heard that it was said by them of old time, Thou shalt not commit adultery: But I say unto you, That whosoever looketh on a woman to lust after her hath committed adultery with her already in his heart." And she looked with lust on Paul by day and committed adultery with him by night in the unsanctified union of their bodies. There had been a time when she believed in God the Father and Jesus Christ, His Son on earth, and while she had not ceased to believe, she could not relate Christ's teachings to what was happening to her in Dibela. If this was lust, then lust was a tender love for Paul that transported her out of her own body in attenuated unearthly joy. If this was lust, then lust was merely sitting near him and watching with him the heavenly patterns of clouds and rain and sky and sun. But if this was only lust, as the sad-eyed white missionary preachers of the bush would say it was, she would not read from the same Book as they to the people gathered under the limbali. No, it was not guilt. She felt no guilt. She felt only an uncontainable joy of living. She could not read from the Book because somewhere between her and God stood the figure of a sad-eyed, grim-lipped preacher whom she did not care to brush aside in her present happiness. So she did not read from the Book. She let Kulu do it.

The people knew. The people thought it a great joy. The Bwana Doctor had taken the Madami for a wife and they worked together in the hospital from dawn to sundown and lay in the house from sundown to dawn. They made great medicine under the direction of the new, kind God, causing the ill to grow well and the dying to live. Occasionally they failed, but, as Kulu told the people, they failed for reasons known to God which He chose not to reveal. Yes, Rachel thought, the people knew. And so Lecomte, carefully absenting himself from Dibela in these weeks, would know. For he knew the events of his domain as thoroughly, and as casually, as the lifelong inhabitant of a house knows the nature and location of his furniture. She did not care. Without bravado, she did not care if the whole world knew that she loved Paul Wilton and he reciprocated her love.

Now, leading the way along the track on that Sunday morning, she thought there was only one thing she never would want the world to know. She would not want it to know he had failed to tell her, *I love you.*

[181]

Yet he loved her, she knew. He merely did not tell her now because he was uncertain whether he would love her a year hence. He was an earth wanderer, traveling from no fixed point, detained but never irrevocably involved in the wars and loves of mankind. A tinkerer really, an extremely able tinkerer of the human flesh who held the human spirit in carefully concealed awe. But uncommitted to anything. Saying with Ecclesiastes, "There is no remembrance of former things; neither shall there be any remembrance of things that are to come with those that shall come after."

Time could not contain love any more than a dipper could contain a flowing stream. It came, it was here, but it was never gone. Time was helpless before it.

Now it was here, she thought. On this Sunday morning a golden hawk crossed the blue sky toward the mountains. Francolin cut and swerved ahead of them with simpering cries. The tall grass throbbed with myriad life under the warm sun. The humid earth drew her feet to a standstill. She turned suddenly and saw him clearly, his eyes not seeing her immediately but turning from sky to earth in a grave search. What did he hunt? He did not know. Perhaps only Africa, which was both too huge and too elusive for him ever to catch.

He looked at her questioningly.

She wanted to say, "Paul Wilton visits Africa." But she knew it would hurt him. For it would penetrate to the heart of his nature, a nature of which not even he altogether approved.

"Those partridgelike birds are francolin," she said, like a guide to a tourist.

"Oh?" He knew that was not what she had intended to say. He waited, but she turned quickly and went on.

They climbed a low hill and he saw clearly for the first time the bulwarks of the mountains rising to their perpetual clouds. The view excited him, as she seldom saw him excited. Like a small boy, he wanted to know how she possibly could have climbed there. And she, intoxicated briefly by his wonder, could not think of a word to say to him.

She felt a heady evanescence, as if she were a pretty young girl standing on a little hill in a summer dress. She wanted to rise on tiptoe and spread her arms and cry, "It's all mystery, mystery, and it must never any of it be explained." But she looked down at her muddy boots and her khaki slacks and then she gazed across the green-spotted yellow plain.

She said, "There are so many mysteries. Stay here. I'm going down the track, down there into the draw, and I'm going to lie down for a moment in some nice dry spot. Stand here. Watch me. And watch the sky. See, the sky is empty now. I mean the big upper sky. Watch and see if vultures come. And when they come, try to see where they come from. Do they rise from the ground? Do they come from nowhere?"

She went down the draw and found a place to lie down. She watched him, outlined on the hilltop. In a moment she saw him gesticulating wildly. Shading her eyes against the sun, she saw vultures circling high above her. She stood up, and he hurried down to her.

"It's incredible," he cried, still excited. "I swear I watched everywhere. And in a moment they were there, come from nowhere. Look." He pointed up. There were no vultures. "Where did they go?"

"I guess they just flew away."

"But where?"

"Just—away."

They went on, following the track as it sought and held to the highest ground, for it was an old war track, passing close to mango groves but never entering them. At last, as Rachel had remembered, the track abandoned its warring origins. It dipped and meandered among palmyra trees and at last, as she remembered, she saw the giant mimosa tree where she and the men had paused when they climbed the mountains. She heard the stream, and soon they saw it, plunging whitely over crystalline rocks.

"We stopped here," she said indistinctly, "when we started for the mountains."

He looked at her. "Why don't we stop here too? I'm starved." He started ahead of her across the stones which had been laid in warrior strides long ago. He paused and smiled and held out a hand. She did not need it, but she took his hand gratefully and followed him across the stream to the shade of the mimosa.

"It's noisy here," he said. "This yelling creek." (She liked the way he called it "crick.") "Let's go upstream, up there under those trees. What are they? Palms?"

"Palmyras," she said. "And that's another mystery. They're an East Indian tree. How did they get here? How did they spread over Africa? Do birds fly from east to west halfway around the world? Were there early voyagers who—"

"Mystery," he said, hooking a thumb in his rifle sling. "I'd like some solutions instead of so many mysteries."

She looked at him steadily. "You can't solve some things. Maybe it's better you can't."

He frowned. "Sometimes I don't follow you, Rachel. Of course it's better to solve any problem. There's always an explanation. The vultures, the palmyras—"

"All right." She barred his way upstream. "Take us. We're a problem. How are you going to solve us?" Momentarily she was sorry that she'd said it, for his gaze fell and his feet shifted uneasily. He must be wondering why she wanted to spoil a perfect day. Did he remember that a woman spoiled the first paradise? But then she was glad she had said it. For it would have to be said sometime and this first saying would help later. Maybe.

"Problem?" he said vaguely, sparring for time while he tried to think of something, anything that would—how did the saying go?—take him off the hook.

She took him off the hook. She smiled brightly and said, "No problems, then." She turned. "Let's go upstream."

"Well," he said, hitching the rifle on his shoulder. "It's okay, is it? To go up through this grass, I mean. Let me go ahead. You can't tell what sort of varmints are around here."

She smiled over her shoulder at him as they walked. "But I can tell. There are scorpions, snakes, lizards, mice, spiders. There are lions, leopards, buffalo, baboons. They're busy spinning, crawling, hunting, eating, sleeping, mating. Living, that is. They hear us coming now with our great crashing. And since they know we don't come to destroy them, they move away from us and let us live too."

The stream curved, its brawling fading behind them, and finally it widened in a broad translucent pool. Green, animal-cropped grass grew to the edge of the pool, and overhead the palmyras spread their broad fans to the sun.

"What a place," he said and leaned the rifle against the smooth straight bole of a tree and swung the knapsack off his shoulders. "I could stay here forever."

She looked at him quickly. "Could you, Paul?"

"I sure could."

She shook her head, her eyes seeking his insistently. "I mean could you stay here in Dibela, in this country, as long as you shall live?"

His gaze faltered before hers.

"Could you, Paul? Could you, so help you God?"

"No," he said quietly. He raised his eyes to hers. "No, I couldn't. And neither could you."

"But I could," she said, her voice lower than his. "I shall."

"Stay here forever?" he demanded incredulously. "But why? What is

[184]

there here except always one more African standing in line with one more pain in his belly? Sure they're your friends because you do something for them, you give them good medicine. But what do they *do* for you? Sure, they flatter you and—" he made his tone dry to show her he was not trying to hurt her—"you're a kind of a queen around here, you know, and there aren't many places left in the world where anybody gets treated like a queen. Oh, they bring chickens and eggs in gratitude. But, Rachel, what do they *do* that could make you want to stay here indefinitely?"

She rested her shotgun against the tree and faced him. "They give me a full life. And they—they hold out the hope that life could be fuller. I mean—" She looked away from him, across the pool. "Medicine is only the beginning. At least it should be. I've failed at that. There should be —a church. And there—"

"A church!" he said scornfully. "Praying and preaching and every man cut down to one wife and—"

"There should be a church, Paul. There should be a good school. And there should be someone to teach them improved agricultural methods. They waste the land. I can see it, but I don't have the time or the skill to—"

"Civilization," he said bitterly. "You want to bring civilization to paradise and spoil it."

"But civilization is what you want to go back to," she said gently.

"Sure, because I was brought up to expect it. Because it's all I know. But I wouldn't wish its complications on a dog."

"Only on yourself." She took a deep breath. "So you will go and I shall stay. And—" with great effort she kept her voice steady—"I don't think either of us ever again will be quite as happy as we are on a Sunday noon by this nameless stream above Dibela." She smiled for him.

"Listen—" He seized her hands roughly. "Look, Rachel—" He squeezed her hands harder.

She listened for what he might say, but he did not speak. She looked at him, but his gaze did not meet hers.

At last he said, "Rachel."

"Yes, Paul."

"Look."

"I'm looking, Paul."

"When I leave here, you leave too. Resign. You have a passport. Get a ship to England. I'll help you get a visa. They need skilled nurses like you in England now. You can get into service. . . ."

It sounded so absurd that she wanted to laugh. Yet it sounded so sweet that she wanted to cry. Resignations, passports, visas, connections, wires pulled. Flee with me, my love, across the border. Let us sail together beyond the western sea. Meet me under the clock in Piccadilly Circus a year from next Christmas Eve at midnight. This was—the great liaison, the plotted trysts of Don Juan or Madame Bovary. It was, apparently, the best that he could do. It was not good enough.

"Oh, Paul." Her arms were about his neck, her face pressed to his chest. She felt the hotness of tears. "You're so sweet. But no. That can't be. You know it."

"Listen, Rachel." He grasped her arms and she could hear his quickened breathing. "Rachel—I love you."

Stunned, she blinked up at him through her tears.

"I *love* you," he repeated fiercely.

He had said it. He did not need to say it again ever. It was enough. Her tears flowed and she leaned against him. If he had not held her she would have fallen.

"And I love you," she said at last. "You know that." Of course he knew. She had said it often enough in moments of passion. But now he had said it too, bringing to her a strange sense of completion that made her life suddenly seem purposeless because it had arrived at a destination.

Now where? She stepped back from him. What now? Since each knew, what could their knowledge do? The initiative still was his, as it always had been and always would be. Oh, he didn't need to say or do anything more. This was enough. Still he stood there, blinking in the glare of the sun on the pool, wondering what to do with his self-knowledge. Poor Paul. She stepped to him and kissed him on the lips.

"It's a lovely day," she said lightly. And it was a lovely day, she thought, the loveliest of them all. "Shall we eat?"

He shook his head. "Not right now. I—I'm not hungry right now. Let's—" his eyes searched the land shimmering in the sun—"go wading."

"It's too deep for wading."

"Then let's go swimming."

"All right."

He looked at her, his lips smiling, his eyes grave. "That's what I'll never forget about you, Rachel. The way you— Okay, Rachel, let's go swimming." He began unbuttoning his shirt. "And afterwards?"

Her heart quickened and she smiled at him faintly. "All right."

"Right here?"

[186]

Could there be a better place anywhere than here in the heart of this shimmering land? Here between earth and sky, between water and tree. In this place where he said he loved her.

She said, "Right here."

He smiled at her. Then, slowly, a frown gathered. "You're taking care of yourself, aren't you?"

She could scarcely hear him. She was listening to her heart and the noon song of insects. "Yes," she said vaguely.

"I mean you're all *right*," he said.

"Of course I'm all right."

"Do you understand what I mean?" he insisted.

"Of course I understand. I tell you everything's all right."

They came home at sunset, walking hand in hand, idling in the blue ground shadows and staring up at the red and gold cumulus of the western sky. Jambo, jambo, jambo, through the village, among the smiling white teeth that lighted growing darkness more warmly than the cooking fires. Jambo, jambo, jambo, children and dogs running before and behind them, voices calling greetings in the sudden fall of night.

They crossed the compound, and Rachel's hand suddenly tightened its grip on his. Lecomte awaited them. She saw the outline of his head against the Coleman lamp.

"Oh, Christ!" Paul muttered. He halted. Then he went on slowly.

He was limping, she realized. Oh, he should not do that. She wanted to tell him to stop limping, but her mouth was dry and she could not speak. Kulu emerged from the darkness. He did not speak to them, but stood there. Silently Paul handed him the rifle and knapsack and shotgun, and Kulu silently disappeared. Then they were climbing the steps, Paul limping.

Lecomte took a cigar from his teeth and stared at them soberly. At last he said in English, "Hello."

"Hello," Paul said.

"Hello, Henri," Rachel said.

"Taking a little walk," Paul said. "Trying to limber up this leg."

Lecomte's stare was cold. He was, thought Rachel, a soldier looking at a soldier. And there was a war on. Whatever the necessities of Dibela and her own flesh, the fact at large in the world was a war. And this man beside her was a soldier and that man watching him knew the fate of his country depended on men such as he. She could see it clearly, as from a distance. There was another dimension to Lecomte she never had considered before. He was a patriot, such a patriot that it never had been necessary for him to mention the name of his king or his country. But the man here beside her was—Paul, a physician and an American caught up in a foreign war which, as he had planned it, never would deeply commit his personal life. Yet here he was committed. It would be all right if only he wouldn't limp before Lecomte.

"A long walk." Lecomte got to his feet. His expression softened when he looked at Rachel, taking her in with a swift encompassing glance. "It's good to see you, Rachel. I arrived early this afternoon and I thought I'd wait."

"I'm glad you did," she said quickly. "Have you eaten?"

"Yes." He smiled wryly. "Your boy finally fed me. I'd say I wasn't— what's the word?—too popular here. Your boys seem to think I've come to—" he nodded toward Paul—"take away."

Her right hand flew to her throat. But Paul said calmly, "Well, have you?"

Lecomte shrugged and took an envelope from his pocket. "I came to deliver this." He handed it to Paul.

Paul tore it open, read it expressionlessly, and thrust it in a hip pocket.

"What is it?" Rachel asked him tensely.

"From His Majesty's somebody or other. Ordering me to report to Stanleyville as soon as possible for further transportation back to wherever they decide I'm to go. His Majesty—" his tone was sarcastic—"has further need of my services, it seems."

"His Majesty is the King you chose to serve," Lecomte said mildly. "Is it possible there's nothing back there, ignoring the war, that calls you? No wife, no . . ."

Wife, Rachel thought dully. What did Henri mean? Did he mean that he knew Paul was married or—

"I am not married," Paul interrupted Lecomte. "I have no wife."

He was a man speaking the truth, Rachel knew. And she saw that Lecomte knew too. What was wrong with her to—suspect? It would not have made any difference anyway. But her sudden pang indicated that she must secretly hope what she never before had consciously considered: that he would ask her to marry him.

Lecomte was speaking, his sharp mind circling and coming upwind on his quarry. "So I came today because I had to come some of the distance anyway. There's an *evolué* who wanted me to marry him." He sighed elaborately. "They do not give me enough to do. They also burden me with marriages."

[188]

He had made his point, Rachel thought. She glanced stealthfully at Paul.

But if he understood, he did not show it. And could you blame him? Lecomte was poised before him now like a trap. He was accustomed to avoiding traps. In the process, of course, he was accustomed to avoiding nearly everything else. But the important thing here, on this evening, was not what Lecomte said or Paul said. The important thing was that she'd take the cash of Paul's telling her *I love you* today and let the credit of marriage go.

"You've informed the necessary people that I'm—recuperating?" Paul asked Lecomte.

"Of course. I've informed them twice. And they have informed me that I'm to provide you transportation to Stanleyville."

"Whenever I can travel," Paul said.

"Whenever you can travel," Lecomte said.

"That will be in a few weeks."

Lecomte rubbed his nose violently. "See here, Doctor—Paul. Let us speak in confidence. You are doing a great work here. I wish you could stay in my district forever. I know that Rachel wishes that too. But we know that cannot be. I must give headquarters a date. It will be easier for everybody everywhere. What shall I tell them?"

"A month," said Paul.

A month, Rachel thought. It was not long enough. Or was it—too long? It was a strange thought, random, seemingly circling from nowhere, like the vultures of the sky. But it was persistent. It was incredibly true for some incredible reason she could not define. And then she thought, A month gives us time to quarrel.

"Three weeks," she said.

They gaped at her.

"Three weeks," she repeated, and her eyes filled with tears.

"Rachel, baby," Paul said, "don't let your sense of duty—"

"Three weeks!" she cried and strode blindly into the bedroom and slammed the door behind her.

XIX

SHE REMEMBERED the three weeks for many years. She and Paul worked hard. They loved passionately. The rains came early and the compound was a warm bright island in a chill gray sea.

But Father Gilo made his way through the rain to Dibela. He visited them in the hospital and he came and sat with them in the living room. At last he said in his slow fragmentary English, "I wonder, can I do something in Dibela as *padre?*"

"As *padre?*" asked Paul.

"As priest," said Father Gilo. "I am Catholic. You are Protestant. But—"

"I am nothing," Paul said.

"You are—" The priest studied him searchingly. "You are *le bon docteur,* the good doctor, my son. You are a fine man. Our Miss Cade is a fine woman."

Rachel saw the muscles of Paul's jaw tightening.

"So I wonder," Father Gilo continued slowly, "is there anything I can do as priest?"

"No." Paul got to his feet. "Nothing, thank you, *padre.* I have to go back to the hospital. Good-by, Father Gilo." He snatched up his raincoat and walked out into the rain.

As Father Gilo watched him go, tears came to his eyes. Rachel thought in surprise, He's really a very sentimental man.

"I'm sorry, Miss Cade," he said in French. He stood up and looked at her with compassion.

Reaching out, she touched his arm gently. He must be making a great religious sacrifice to be willing, as a Catholic, to marry a Protestant and a nothing who had been living out of wedlock. But he really didn't understand, she thought. Oh, he comprehended all good and evil, but he never could have loved or been loved in the way that Paul and she loved. On him, on this good man, should compassion fall. Not on her.

"Thank you, Father Gilo," she said. "Thank you for coming to visit us."

"Call on me at any time," he said. "If there is ever anything . . ."

Soon after he left, Paul returned. He paced the room restlessly. He talked abortively of this and that. Finally he said, "You're all right, aren't you?"

"Of course. Why?"

"Well, I don't know. I— You know what I'm talking about, don't you?"

"Of course. Everything's all right."

He looked at her sharply. "Everything's all right?"

"Yes, Paul. Everything is all right."

He stood up and then sat down again. "Look, baby."

She smiled at him. "What—baby?"

"About this priest. Father Gilo. I know why he came and I know what Lecomte meant back that Sunday night when— The hell with it." He hitched his chair near hers and took both her hands in his. "I'm saying this badly. What I want to say is—will you wait around for me till this damn war is over?"

She fought tears, and lost. She nodded.

"Because I'm going to wait around for you, Rachel. I don't know whether I'm coming back to Africa or you're coming back to the States or we meet in—I dunno—the middle of South America. If there's still a South America left after this mess." He squeezed her hands hard. "But we're getting together."

"Getting together?" she asked dully.

"We're getting married," he said.

"When?"

He frowned at her. "What's the matter, baby, aren't you listening to me? We're getting married after the war."

Dimly she remembered Dick, that boy whose identity hadn't mattered to her in years, saying, "After Mother's had a chance to adjust to Father's death." But that was long past. And this was nearly past. She mustered a bright smile for Paul.

"After the war," she said to him, hoping she sounded the correct eager note of a child promised a gift for next Christmas. "We'll write each other." She must be very careful not to sound hysterical.

"Yes," he said. "Naturally."

Undoubtedly he meant every word he said, she thought. Undoubtedly he loved her. He just wasn't a self-committing man. He really hadn't consciously thought of it, but he knew he'd go many places and meet many women before— Oh, stop it!

[191]

"The damn thing is," he said, "I haven't got a single personal thing left to give you. You picked me out of the bush. . . ."

And you leave me to the bush, she thought. Stop it! Listening to him, she felt so terribly sorry for him. He was acting a charade and believing, like a child, that every word and gesture was unalterably true. Why couldn't she believe in "after the war"? Because he had only needed to come in after Father Gilo left and say in his inimitable curt way, "We're driving off to Rugeri tomorrow to get married." But he hadn't. Well, let him believe in "after the war." And she would try to believe in "after the war." When belief failed her, she'd always have memory.

So time ran its inevitable course to the inevitable day. On that last morning her courage faltered but did not fail. They rose early, as a man and a woman nearly always do when the man is going to war. They wanted parting to last forever and yet they wanted to get it over quickly.

Morning light was still a faint and curdled yellow above the eastern mountains, but a huge crowd had gathered in the compound. It milled silently under the limbali and flowed to the road, for the word had spread that the Bwana Doctor was leaving for war again.

When Rachel and Paul stepped onto the porch, they paused in amazement at the size of the crowd which surged silently toward them in a solid black mass through the gray light. A murmur grew in the crowd, and suddenly a woman wailed. The crowd sighed. Here and there people began to chant a lament. It rose and fell, like wind in the limbali.

I can't stand it, Rachel thought as she gripped Paul's hand tightly. Buderga came forward, accompanied by Kulu and Kosongo and Mzimba and Musinga and Guta and Wanga. He bore before him a great war shield with the whole skin of a leopard, a shield such as had been illegal in the land for many years now. And Kulu carried a long spear, a veritable lance plumed with the black feathers of a mountain eagle, such as had not been used since the great wars of the grandfathers' times.

Buderga spoke and Rachel translated to Paul in a high, strained voice. The shield was for the great Bwana Doctor to bear always on his left arm and to protect his strong heart when he faced the northern enemies. Might victory come soon to him so that he could return quickly to his home in Dibela.

Paul stepped down and took the shield and said, "Thanks a lot," and Rachel said behind him, "Keep talking, say anything." His lips were tight and his voice unnatural as he shook Buderga's hand and said, "I don't know what to say except that I'll never forget it here and I—I'll be back some day and all you guys take care of Madami while I'm away." This Rachel translated in strained tones as, "I am deeply grateful to you, Chief Buderga, and the people of Dibela. I love you all. I shall miss you. I shall return when I can. God the Father watch over you while I'm away."

"What did you tell 'em?" Paul asked her. As she started to reply a great joyous shouting rose at word of his return and men jumped like children, calling, "When will you return, Bwana?" So she did not answer his question.

Then Kulu stepped forward with the spear. His mouth opened, but no words came, and he bowed his head and wept. Paul touched his shoulder and then, suddenly, drew Kulu to him and laid his cheek on Kulu's in the sign of brothers so that the people shouted in happiness at this great good sign. He took the spear from Kulu while Kulu still wept and smiled at once. With his left arm through the shield thongs, he raised the spear in his right hand, waving its plumed tip high in the immemorial gesture of the warriors. The people roared, pressing in on him.

He shook hands with Kosongo and Musinga and Guta and Mzimba and Wanga. Hands clutched at him as the people tried to clear a path for him and Rachel to the car. He put the shield and the spear in the back seat of the car, the long spear thrust far out an open window with its black feathers fluttering in the morning breeze.

Now the people were shouting, "Kwaheri! Kwaheri, Bwana!" Goodby, good-by, good-by, Rachel thought dimly. She had so seldom heard the word since she came to Dibela. She started the car, for she was driving him. They were riding alone to Rugeri.

The Ford moved slowly, the people running alongside and behind and even ahead of it, out to the road and then west on the road. The people ahead fell to the sides and those on the sides fell behind as the Ford gained speed down the long slant from Dibela. But even after they'd passed the last shambas of Dibela they could see, when they looked back, that people still ran in the road behind them.

Paul lighted a cigarette with trembling hands.

For many miles along the road the people stood before every shamba and in every clan village, shouting and waving. "Kwaheri, Bwana! Kwaheri!" Even in the wild open country the road menders and the women bowed low under piles of faggots and the hunters departing for game turned at the sound of the car and smiled and waved and called, "Kwaheri, Bwana!"

No sullen faces now, Rachel thought. No faces such as she'd seen on that day so long ago when she first rode toward Dibela.

They tried to talk, but there was no satisfaction in it. They merely repeated phrases. "I'll drop you a line from Stanleyville," he'd say, and she'd say, "Fine, and I'll write you as soon as I know your address." He'd say, "Write to the one I gave you in England, don't forget, and I'll let you know the minute I'm somewhere permanent." But talk, she thought, was like a hollow rustle now, like the dry hollow rustle of grass before the rains came.

They arrived, too quickly and yet not quickly enough, in Rugeri. Past the thatched huts and past the trader's and the jail and around the park where the inevitable prisoners listlessly cut at the inevitable tall grass until they saw the huddle of administrative buildings. There drawn up in double ranks was Lecomte's small force of askaris. She stopped the car. A sergeant bawled an order and the men presented arms and Paul stepped out of the car woodenly. Lecomte stepped forward, from nowhere it seemed, and saluted Paul smartly in a way that recalled old reviews and an untarnished military tradition. Paul returned his salute, not as smartly, and the sergeant bawled again and the men grounded arms with precision.

Rachel forced herself to get out of the car. Lecomte bowed to her, his face still set in that unfamiliar military grimness which at some time must have been natural to him. Then he said to Paul in English, "The car is waiting."

"Yes," Paul said vaguely. "I have to transfer my things. That shield and spear and—"

"They are being transferred," Lecomte said and turned to the sergeant and told him in French to dismiss the guard. The askaris shouldered arms and faced left with a European high stomp and marched away.

Then Lecomte went off to make sure everything had been transferred to the government car and she and Paul were standing there and it began to rain. Paul's face was white and he bit his underlip.

"Rachel, I—" He seized her roughly and kissed her hard, his lips as hungry on hers as the first time he kissed her, and they stood locked thus until the rain was falling heavily. Then he broke from her. She saw his white face for an instant and then his face no longer was discernible to her.

She saw the government car pulling away, Paul sitting straight and alone in the back seat, the Dibela spear thrust out a window, its black eagle feathers hanging limply in the rain. The car disappeared and she

[194]

still stood there. Somewhere Lecomte said gently in English, "Steady, Rachel, steady."

She nodded vaguely in his direction and she got in the car and drove away. At the edge of the Rugeri escarpment, where the Dibela road rolled down to the plain, she stopped the car. She covered her face with her hands and her body shook in sobs. At last she raised her head and stared down at the plain buried under the wash of gray rain.

She told herself she would live on. I *have* to live, she thought. He had taken himself away. But he had not taken from her that thing he would have insisted on taking from her if he had known it existed. To take it from her dead would have been his demand, she knew. For she was certain that she was pregnant. She carried within her a part of him, their child. Even now, staring down at the gray plain which stretched in the rain as unfathomably as her own future, she would not have willed it otherwise.

Part Three

XX

ONE DAY in February, when the rains had abated, Rachel asked Wanga to drive her to Rugeri. She rode beside him silently, remembering this ride with Paul a month ago. Then, as she remembered, she had felt numbed. But now there was the loneliness that was unbearable until you bore it. There was the physical desire for him, that strange and late awakening, so unendurable until you endured it. There was the sense of emptiness that could not be filled even when you crowded the day and half the night with the innumerable parts of things that never quite made you whole. And there was, finally, the unknown, the child within her. When would it end?

In Rugeri she went to the administrative building. François, the *evolué*, told her Lecomte was holding court. But Lecomte had seen her from the presiding chair and recessed court. He hurried to the office in long strides.

"Rachel." He took her hand and looked at her searchingly. "I have some mail here for you."

She fingered through the letters quickly. Nothing from *him*. She smiled ruefully at Lecomte, who still watched her. "Nothing from Paul."

"You have not heard from him since he left?"

"Oh, yes. I got a long letter from him in Stan." She looked away. "May I speak to you privately?"

"Of course." He closed the door and gestured to a chair. Pulling his own swivel chair away from his scarred roll-top desk, he sat down, his hands spread on his knees. The *tock-tock* of an old Swiss clock on his desk was loud.

She gazed at him steadily. "Henri, I'm pregnant."

His hands tightened on his knees. The clock continued its slow destruction of time.

"I am—" she smiled wryly—"nearly two months pregnant."

He crossed his legs and swung a foot, his face impassive. "He did not know?"

"No. I didn't tell him."

"You didn't tell him," Lecomte said wonderingly. He started to pull a cigar from his shirt pocket and then thrust it back. "You—"

"I didn't want him to know. He would have wanted to take the child from me. The word I dread to say is 'abortion.' And I could not have stood his suggesting that. It would have killed everything between us." She tried to make her tone dry. "I could not have stood that. Our love couldn't have stood it."

"And you did not suggest marriage to him?"

"Of course not."

"You say 'of course' so casually, as if—"

"Of course," she said flatly, "because it would be an impossible situation. Forced gallantry festers. If he ever wishes to marry me it will have to be because he wishes to. Not because I'm pregnant."

"But, Rachel," he exclaimed, "you must think of yourself. Think of your future, your—your—"

"Good name," she said ironically. "Do you think I haven't thought of all that? There are not many things I haven't thought of this past month."

"I'm sure." He looked at her pityingly. "So you have decided to have the child. And I shall help you." He clamped the cigar in his yellowed teeth. "There's a place I know near Bukuvu. You will go there when the time is near. It's a hospital run by a fine order of Sisters. They have been understanding of many situations worse than your own. They will keep the child. It will be raised Catholic. And you will come back. I shall arrange everything."

"No," she said.

He took the cigar from his teeth and gaped at her. "No?"

"No," she said. "It—" She smiled reflectively. "Isn't it strange how you think of a fetus as 'it' when all the time *it* is developing into *him* or *her*?"

"My God!" Lecomte said and struck a match with an explosive crack and lighted his cigar, looking at her over the flame. Then he chuckled. "Your philosophical asides assuage the grimmest situations, Rachel. So! You say 'No' very forcefully before the aside. What do you propose?"

"To have my child. Our child. To have it in Dibela. *It* will have the best of care. I'm a good midwife and I'll teach Kulu midwifery."

Lecomte rubbed the top of his head violently. "I believe, Rachel, you could deliver it yourself. Go on. You have the child. You raise it. And then? What, as I'm always asking myself in my business here, of head-quarters?"

"I have thought of that." She looked at him steadily. "I wish you would think of it and tell me what comes to your mind."

The clock ticked on. Slowly the sun's old crow's-feet spread about his eyes. He was smiling.

"For a woman of saintly goodness, Rachel, you sometimes display a Du Barry craftiness." He rose and opened a filing cabinet drawer and began fumbling through it.

"Henri," she said suddenly, "just one thing. What have you really been thinking since I told you about this?"

He looked around at her, one eye half closed against the curl of smoke from his cigar. "Thahu," he said calmly. "Old Africa striking back against the white invader."

"I've thought of that. But no." She smiled faintly and looked out a window. "Because, you see, I don't think of what has happened as a curse."

"I know you don't." He shook his head. "That's why you might per-haps be the only person I ever knew who escaped a really serious thahu. But to any old hand like me it's still thahu."

"But what has happened is so unrelated to my climbing the moun-tains."

"To us whites, yes. But any old-fashioned African would see it quite differently. You defied the gods and climbed the mountains and attained knowledge. When the plane crashed, you used your knowledge to save an earthling. You know yourself you'd never have gone such a way to find the crashed plane if you hadn't climbed the mountains first. The ordinary kitchen variety of missionary wouldn't have ventured so far into the bush. He'd have sent the boys and the boys would have given up. By the time I found the plane next day Paul would have been eaten by hyenas. But you changed the ordinary course of events. So, under old Africa's rules, your rescued earthling set about destroying your heart, performing the work for the violated gods."

Her right hand moved to her breast. "My heart is not destroyed," she said in a low voice.

"Good," Lecomte said cheerfully. "If it is not, if you never let it be, the thahu is defeated. You and your God have proved yourself stronger than they and their ancient gods. But your life becomes a battleground of faith. And it's very wearying for one to be the battleground of anything." He stepped away from the filing cabinet. "Rachel, would it not be better if you do as I suggest and—"

"No," she said sharply.

"Very well." He turned again to the open drawer and in a moment he pulled out a long official form. He held it up, smiling faintly. "For such corrupt acts officials are disgraced and retire to a miserable pension in Brussels. But I'm being dramatic again. Actually, since the situation is as it is and we face it without hysteria, I find it rather—exciting." He looked at the paper in his hand. "I believe I'd have made a very successful corrupt official. For I flatter myself that I see to the ends of things so well. At least I see all the steps to the end of this certificate which will state that I married Captain Paul Wilton of the Royal Air Force and you in Dibela on—" He looked at her questioningly.

She named a date ten weeks ago, and his pen scratched. Without looking up, he said, "Captain Wilton is a citizen of the United States, resident in?"

How absurd. It seemed that she and Paul knew everything possible about each other, but where was his home? Where was the street he followed on rainy afternoons and the corner lunch counter that lighted his path on winter nights?

"New York," she said.

"Yes," Lecomte said. "And Miss Rachel Cade is a citizen of the United States, resident of Dibela, Congo Belge, with passport number so-and-so and visa number so-and-so. You'll have to copy those in when you finally receive this precious bit of paper." He looked up. "It would be preferable, I believe, if you rather than I forge the bridegroom's signature. And then, of course, we have the matter of two witnesses."

"Witnesses?" Her tone was startled. "I'll have Kulu and—"

"No." He shook his head. "You forget that Kulu does not exist—legally. Kulu is—" he sighed—"unrecognizable in a white man's court. He has no official identity. On the other hand, François does exist. He is a black man who has willed himself into official cognizance, who has taken the legal steps to evolve himself from the bush. He is an *evolué*, a man with a set of papers proving his existence. François will do. And we need one more. My wife."

"Your wife!" She leaned toward him. "Wouldn't it be better if—if— say, Father Gilo—"

"Not him." Lecomte held up his hands. "Gilo is a priest and so does not exist when it comes to these necessary acts of perjury whereby the rest of us survive. He cannot, he would not commit perjury. To ask him would hurl him into the abyss of despair at being unable to help you. No, Rachel, it must be my wife."

"But—"

"An interesting thing about *her*." Lecomte tipped his fingers together with a sad expression. "In small matters my wife is an incredibly dull and stupid woman. But in large matters like this she is—understanding. It will take very little urging from me for her to perform the necessary perjury. She is fond of—" Lecomte smiled bleakly—"babies. She has had three and none has lived six months. That was a long time ago, of course. But she's still infatuated with babies. Not the making of them, just the having of the—the finished product. So she will sign. And then it will be necessary for her to go to Father Gilo and confess her perjury. So no one will know except Gilo and Marie and myself. François won't know. François will merely sign a piece of paper where I tell him to."

"But it will be recorded in Stanleyville or somewhere?" Rachel asked.

"Definitely not." Lecomte shook his head. "The necessary duplicate will be lost in transmission, lost in the files, if the matter ever comes up. There is only one copy and you will have it. That's what I meant by seeing all the steps. It could be awkward someday to attempt a divorce from a man you never married. It would be awkward when you came to marry him to find your marriage already recorded. This paper is merely for—for the child. And his—or her—birth will be recorded and sent off promptly to Stan so that when and if you and it—the child, I mean—leave this lovely land, there will be no question of who—"

"I see." She touched his knee and smiled. "I see, Henri. You are very kind to—"

"Don't thank me," he said. "Since the situation is and since you choose to face it this way, I find I rather enjoy discovering a means to defeat—or let's say merely stave off—fate." He raised his head and bellowed, "François!"

François opened the door and tiptoed in, smiling politely.

"Sign this thing, François. Here."

François started to unfold the sheet which Lecomte had carefully folded, but Lecomte snapped, "Sign it, you fool. I didn't ask you to read it."

"Yes, Colonel." François signed slowly, his tongue slipping from a corner of his lips, and then he left the room.

"All that's left," Lecomte said, "is to inform your headquarters that you were married a few weeks ago."

Rachel looked at the floor. "I wrote a friend of mine there to that effect three weeks ago."

When she looked up, Lecomte was smiling at her.

As they drove away from the administrative office she told Wanga to go to Father Gilo's mission south of Rugeri. She dreaded seeing him, and yet she felt that she must. She had to tell him, to confess to him, as imperatively as if she were a member of his faith.

Then, trenchantly, she wondered if this were a true desire for confession or simple expediency. He would know in time, from Marie Lecomte or when he visited her and noted the swell of her pregnancy. So it was better if she told him now herself. Expediency? Or confession of error? Oh, these things used to be so clear, so simple. Truth and error, good and evil, right and wrong. Never again would she view them in sharp outline. For she felt no sense of error. If it were all to do over again, she would not change anything. She wanted the child. She, who had never become ecstatic over the mere fact of children, now wanted the child. She was, she thought, like the female animals of the plain and mountains. Like the lioness who certainly never pondered the *fact* of cubs, but, once impregnated, was dedicated to bearing the new life within her.

As the car churned and skidded over the muddy road cut straight through the towering bush, it began to rain again. Rachel fingered the letters in her lap. Mail came infrequently from the States now. There was nothing from Phyllis Haricort. What would Phyllis Haricort say if she knew this had happened? Dedicated as she was to the causes and committees of organized religion, would she possibly understand what had happened to the human soul and body? Oddly, she probably would, Rachel believed. But whether she would or not, the lie about marriage must be written to her too.

Here was a letter from Dr. Spencer. As she tore open the envelope, she thought that she could not lie to him. It was better to wait until he returned to Africa and tell him what had happened whenever she saw him. She did not want to be simply a woman who got away with a lot of lies. The fewer she told, the less it would be necessary for her conscience to live down.

It was a fine, encouraging letter, complimenting her on the work in Dibela, telling her that they there in the States would make sure the Dibela post remained open. And then, her heart sinking, she read a couple of closing lines:

It doesn't appear, Rachel, that they're going to let me return—at least for a long time. It's the most ridiculous of reasons—my liver, which doesn't worry me but troubles the physicians who have studied it. . . .

One more friend removed when she so badly needed every friend possible. She closed her eyes as she folded the letter.

There was the usual letter of credit from headquarters which would contain the usual curt note from Ralph. There was one from Edith Barney. She opened it.

"Congratulations, congratulations!" Yes, Edith had received her letter and accepted her lie.

Not only a doctor for you in Dibela, but a husband too! How wonderful, Rachel. . . . It's a shame you won't be able to stay together long and continue working together, but the time will pass quickly, as you say, until he's released from service and can return. . . .

The lines seemed to leap up at her. She frowned and read again slowly.

Just to let you know, so that you may be forewarned. I think it's a shame, but this is Ralph for you with his insane jealousy, and I honestly think that's what it is, Rachel, now that he hears you're married and your husband's going back to the war. He's talked Rev. Prosser into sending a minister out to work with you in Dibela. As if you need a preacher! (Though I wouldn't want Rev. Prosser to know how I feel about this.) Anyway they're sending out this preacher named Caleb Aldrich in a few weeks. Really, Rachel, it's terribly unjust of Ralph—both to you and to Caleb himself—to send him out there. Caleb has been out here two years, down in the swamps near Letardi, and he has had a really bad case of malaria that's worn him down. They sent him up here to the hospital for a rest. Personally I think they ought to send the poor man home, but he's very cheerful and doesn't want to go home. Then Ralph gave Rev. Prosser the sales talk on sending him up to Dibela. And the Rev. Sam, who admits from the records of patients you've sent back to Ralph recently that you're certainly doing a great *medical* work there, was impressed. But you know how the Rev. Sam is always thinking less of us in the medical department than of starting schools and saving souls. So now he wants to push religion in Dibela too and thus you're getting Caleb when I know the only man you'd like to see there now is your dear husband. They could send you someone *worse* than Caleb, but they could send you someone so much *better*—like a doctor. . . .

[203]

Not this, Rachel thought. Not now. A preacher in Dibela! She wanted to laugh hysterically. You could plan and be quiescent and try to avoid the error of sorrow for self and take everything as it was handed out because you'd asked for all of it. You only asked that if they could not send a *doctor* to Dibela let them not send anyone. All you asked was, like the lioness, to lie under your chosen thorn tree and bear your young. But they were sending a preacher, a *cheerful malarial* preacher to Dibela.

She opened Ralph's letter, which curtly informed her that the Reverend Caleb Aldrich was coming to Dibela. Then she opened a letter from the Reverend Sam Prosser, who wrote warmly and at length, expressing pleasure at learning of her "marriage to Dr. Paul Wilton who must so regrettably be torn from you to return to the arduous tasks of war." Then he informed her that he was sending Caleb Aldrich to Dibela "to minister spiritually as you are so ably ministering physically to the folk there and to exercise his great talents in the field of teaching." Oh, he glowed over the Reverend Caleb. And he concluded, "Yours in Christ, Sam Prosser." Well, she knew the Reverend Sam was a kind, gentle, good man who, with his wife, had endured great privations and dangers during forty years in Africa. But for the first time she wondered exactly what he meant when he always concluded his letters, "Yours in Christ."

You must take care, she thought suddenly. The mountains you have now started to climb are infinitely more dangerous than the Mountains of the Moon. Bitterness can destroy you. Somehow you must cling to faith.

"Madami?" Wanga was looking at her. The car had stopped. They were, she saw, halted before a tin-roofed building surmounted by a cross. Father Gilo hurried toward the car, a large umbrella raised against the rain.

She tried to speak pleasantly to him as he covered her with the umbrella and led her into his small bare cottage. A cot, two chairs, a crucifix upon the wall and rain beating on the roof. She sat down and the priest went into a farther room. He was making them some tea, he called, making it himself because no one here could make it properly. He drifted out on the stream of his own conversation which lapped, unheeded, about her own preoccupation. Quite soon she found herself holding a cup of tea and facing him in silence.

She sipped the tea and smiled. "I'm a strange woman, Father Gilo. I came to tell you of something which you'll consider a mortal sin. But on the way I learned by mail of something—something sounding very fine that annoys me to distraction. It makes the mortal sin seem quite unimportant."

[204]

Father Gilo raised his brows. "So? Perhaps the two things are related."

"Oh, they are," Rachel said. And she told him what had happened.

He listened impassively. When she had finished, he set his cup upon the floor and leaned forward, elbows on knees, hands clasped tightly.

"If it were in my power to forgive you," he said, "I would forgive you. For everything. I can see how it all began and how one step led to another. From the moment you came to Dibela your intentions have only been good."

"With only bad results," she said. "Do you believe in thahu?"

"Thahu!" he said scornfully. "Of course I don't believe in thahu. I believe in God."

Then what, she wondered, is God up to now?

"Thahu is for a romantic mind like Henri Lecomte's," the priest said. "I choose God. And so do you, Miss Cade." He looked at his hands. "You recognize, I suppose, how detached you are about this—situation. I suppose that's why you give me a sense of detachment, and I'm sure you gave it to Henri when you—you made your arrangements. You make it very difficult for one to feel that anything—wrong has really happened."

"But that's just it." Rachel leaned toward him. "I don't feel that anything wrong has happened. I don't feel like a bad woman, Father Gilo. I only feel like a bad woman when I think of that preacher coming to Dibela."

Father Gilo smiled faintly. "Poor man," he murmured. Suddenly he sighed. "I must think and pray," he said, as if to himself. "I am—confused. I know what sin is, but sometimes, here in Africa, I— It's true that you desperately needed a doctor in Dibela. And when *he* came, when Dr. Wilton came, you naturally wanted him to stay because you knew your people needed him. But he, I presume, wanted to leave there as quickly as he could. And you wanted him to stay. And he, being a—a—"

"No, Father Gilo," she said quietly, "you are trying to make me a martyr to the work in Dibela. I did what I did knowingly and willingly. I am not a martyr."

XXI

SHE DID NOT FEEL WELL that morning. Long after sunlight had flooded the room she lay listlessly in bed, staring down at the swell of her belly under the sheet, raising her slender hands and gazing at them as if they were a stranger's. Waves of nausea broke over her and she felt feverish.

Morning sickness, she told herself. Or perhaps it was a recurrence of that old malaria, absent for so many years now. If only it weren't hepatitis. But it couldn't be; she personally boiled the goat's milk which she had begun drinking now, holding her breath as she swallowed the awful stuff. There was a time when she never feared illness. And so never was ill. But now she lived with fear of illness. She must conquer that fear. She raised herself on her elbows and then sank back dizzily.

After a while Kulu said softly in the outer room, "Madami?"

"Yes, Kulu. Come in."

He stood beside her bed, politely pretending not to see her. "Ah, Madami feels the mtoto?"

"Yes, Kulu, I guess I feel the mtoto."

Kulu seemed to live now for the mtoto, the little one within her. All day long he talked about mtoto, son of the Bwana Doctor who might come before his father returned from war. How long today? Over two moons since the father went away. Over six moons before the son appeared. She had suggested that the Bwana Doctor might have a daughter, but Kulu adamantly maintained he would have only sons.

"Madami," Kulu said now, "what was it that the Bwana said?"

She looked up at him dully. The Bwana had said nothing. There had been only one letter from him in Stan. Of course, mail was slow or not at all now. Of course, there was a war on. Of course, of course. But better that she should never rise from this bed again than to dream as she had two nights ago: Paul, the shape of his head, the way he laughed, standing at a bar with soldiers, laughing, saying something that came to her as she awakened, sweating, from the dream. She saying it then, as she lighted a candle and paced the floor, saying it for him as she'd known it in the dream, something like, "A real soft touch in sunny Africa, chum." She'd struck sharply at her forehead. But only with the coming of daylight had she been able to rationalize it. It sounded like him. But he could not possibly have said it. Not after what had happened between them. Then why doesn't he write me?

"Madami? The Bwana said?"

Why must she continue to treat Kulu like a child? Why couldn't she plainly say it? The Bwana's gone away, probably forever, Kulu, so forget him. And so destroy Kulu's faith that began with a vision of God? No, she'd continue playing the game to the end. Playing the game. That stupid slogan, as if life were a big athletic event and all the living, muscular athletes. Yes, playing the elaborate game with Kulu and the other men of finding one letter from the Bwana in each mail. So she'd pretended to read something from him, last time from a circular mailed in New York urging her to give to British War Relief. British War Relief indeed! She was a hundred and eighteen pound package (at the last weighing) of British War Relief herself. Well, what had she read to Kulu from the Bwana, meaning the circular?

"Yes," she said vaguely. "The Bwana said he was depending on Kulu. Kulu will deliver the child, the Bwana said. Kulu is wise and knows the old superstitions are false."

Kulu nodded, his expression rapt.

"Kulu knows that a good strong child may present itself by the feet or the breech. Such children no longer are destroyed, as in the old bad days." She took a deep breath. "The Bwana said that Madami will show Kulu what to do."

"Yes, Madami." Kulu smiled at her. "You have showed me twice now, in two births of Dibela babies. Are you not glad?"

So he was really trying to encourage her. He needed no encouragement himself.

His smile vanished. "Madami, there has been no further word of the Assistant Bwana who is coming here and yet knows no medicine?"

"No, Kulu." She had gone over this a dozen times with him and the others since she'd received the word. She'd explained that the Assistant Bwana was a great teacher, though not a doctor, and would be most useful. They tried to believe her, she knew. But belief came hard to them when they remembered the great Bwana Doctor. And it came as hard to her.

"Madami," he said, "I came to tell you that Chief Buderga is at the hospital with his youngest wife. He is as excited as a sugarbird at a sweet flower. He thinks his wife is going to have a son. He says they will not leave the hospital until you look at her."

Rachel smiled. And, smiling, she thought that she felt slightly better. So Buderga might have a child about the time that she had a child. Which child would lead the happier life, if either survived?

She raised herself on an elbow. "I'll come to the hospital as soon as I can, Kulu." He gave her a fleeting look of concern and left the room as she struggled to sit up. After a while she tried standing. And then she walked a few steps. Fighting nausea, she finally dressed herself.

If she had to go through this every morning she could not possibly bear it, she thought. This was only one morning. And there were two hundred mornings left. She'd better not think of them. Think only of one morning at a time, and this was—this morning.

She walked to the hospital slowly. Her head began to throb. She could almost hear it, she thought dimly, and then she realized she heard a signal drum across the plain.

It seemed that the entire village had gathered around the hospital, peering inside and discussing the possibility that Buderga's youngest wife was pregnant. They called out to Rachel as she approached, making a path for her: "Make it true, Madami. . . . Ah, Madami, it will be great magic if she is. . . ."

Inside the hospital she sank onto the chair before her desk table and wiped sweat from her forehead. Buderga and four male relatives pressed close to her, talking at once. Bina, Buderga's fat, broad-faced wife, sat on a cot; she giggled suddenly and the men stopped chattering and stared at her. Bina giggled very loudly and covered her eyes with her hands.

"Kulu," Rachel called, "fetch me two aspirin and water, please." He brought them, watching her worriedly as she swallowed them. At last she said, "Bina, come to the inner room, please."

She ordered everyone out of the room while she examined and questioned Bina. Yes, Bina believed she was pregnant. Rachel believed so too. But Buderga, when she let him enter the room, wanted to *know*. He paced and slapped his hands together. He wanted to *know*. Patience and time, she told him. He held his head and scowled at her. She wanted to hold her head and scowl at him. But she stood there, regarding him calmly and even sympathetically, while she wondered just what was happening to herself.

There was a tap at the door and Kulu said urgently, "Madami, there's a message. May I bring in the drum-talker?"

A message, she thought wildly. Maybe it was from Paul! She flung open the door, her eyes wide and strange, so strange that Kulu fell back a step. The drum-talker spoke:

"A strange bwana, coming to work for Madami, has halted near Kalina and he comes no farther."

She stared at the drum-talker. Not Paul. Still no word from Paul. Tears welled in her eyes. She sank onto a chair and the tears spilled down her cheeks. She didn't care. She knew they were gazing at her in astonishment. But she didn't care.

"Madami," Kulu's face was troubled.

This would be the preacher. This would be Caleb Aldrich, now near Kalina, twenty kilometers down the road to Rugeri. And he comes no farther. The language of the drum did not explain whether he refused to come farther or could not come. She must be careful not to laugh hysterically now. When her whole being cried out to hide away with the child within her, all these children clamored for attention. Even Caleb Aldrich, a great white child who had come as far as Kalina and now came no farther. What was she supposed to do about him?

"Madami," Kulu said, "I shall ride to Kalina and tell the Assistant Bwana to go back, he is not needed here."

Suddenly, remembering Dr. Bickel, she wondered if he had felt somewhat as she did now when he'd heard of her coming. There must be something wrong with life here that one's isolation became so valued.

She got to her feet. "No," she said to Kulu, "we shall go together. Fetch Wanga and the car."

As they left Dibela, Kulu turned in the front seat and asked, "Madami, does the Bwana Doctor know the Assistant Bwana?"

"No, Kulu."

"Then they cannot be circumcision brothers."

"No, Kulu. Of course not."

She closed her eyes. He was asking, of course, whether it would be proper for the Assistant Bwana to lie with Madami. He was thinking in the tribal terms: it was quite moral for a man to lie with the wife of a circumcision brother. She had told him and the others repeatedly that it was wrong. They had listened and nodded. But now even Kulu, most advanced of all, reverted to his tribal thinking when it pleased him. She had failed as teacher. She was weary, weary with trying.

She dozed, her head nodding to the jouncing of the car, until she was awakened by Wanga saying, "Look, Madami."

They were passing the score of huts that composed Kalina. Far ahead there were many people on the road and the glint of sun on the glass or metal of a car. A man wearing breechcloth and carrying a spear waved to them and Rachel told Wanga to stop.

"Jambo," she said to the man. "What's happened here?"

"Jambo, Madami." The man's teeth flashed in a grin. "A bwana coming to see you is there." He waved down the road. "He will not leave his iron thing. It stopped with him last sundown as it grew dark. My brothers and I found him as we returned from hunting. We asked him to the village, but he would not get out of the iron thing. He stayed in it all night." The man grinned again. "In the night two from the village crept near and made the sound of a lion. The man cried out in fear from the iron thing. He has fear-sickness, Madami."

The fool, she thought. The stupid fool. She said severely to the man, "That was very wrong to treat the Bwana so."

"Yes, Madami." The man looked at the ground, then up. "But we asked him to come to our village and eat with us and he understood our language, for he answered us from inside the iron thing."

"Drive on," she said to Wanga.

As they approached his Chevrolet sedan, she saw his head rise slowly in the back seat. The people of Kalina sat and stood about, staring and grinning and discussing him. Here it was broad daylight and still he was afraid to come out. What a hopeless, cowardly fool. She strode to the Chevrolet and pulled open the door.

Caleb Aldrich was sprawled in the back seat, his rumpled khaki shirt and pants dark with sweat. He was very tall and very thin. His face was long and unhandsome and his lank black hair had fallen over his high forehead. His eyes were surprisingly blue in his darkly unshaven and malarially yellowed face.

He stared at her strangely. "You must be Rachel." Then, "Miss Cade, I mean. But they speak of you as Rachel back there. Sorry I can't remember your married name. Mrs. Wilton, that's it?"

Mrs. Wilton! She would not be reminded every time he spoke to her. "I'd prefer you call me Rachel," she said stiffly. Her anger suddenly boiled up. "I must tell you that you're certainly off to a great start with the people of this country by staying in your car all night."

"Oh?" He looked out vaguely at the people. "Somebody offered me shelter. In the night I wished I'd gone with them. An animal of some sort came around. A lion, I thought, though I've never seen one outside a circus or zoo. It scared me half to death. I yelled blue murder. Half to give myself courage and half to try to scare away the lion."

"I know," Rachel said.

He looked baffled. "You know?"

"Yes. What you heard was a couple of practical jokers from Kalina."

He stared around, troubled. "Then all these grave-faced people here are laughing at me. Shaken by internal mirth." He shook his head. "What an interesting people."

"Why did you stop here anyway?" she cried. "Did your car break down? Are you going to sit there all day?"

"No, I'm not." His big hands gripped the front seat and he pulled himself forward. "The car didn't break down. I did."

She stared at him. "What do you mean, Reverend Aldrich?"

He smiled faintly. "Wish you wouldn't call me Reverend. The way you say it caricatures me, and weak as I am in some ways I'm not that bad." He pulled himself to the open doorway. "What I mean is—" His feet touched the ground and then his knees buckled under him and he would have fallen if she had not caught him.

"Sorry," he muttered.

"You're *sick!*" she cried. "Why didn't you say so?"

"I didn't know this malaria would return. Sorry. Awful sorry."

She closed her eyes, thinking, He's sick and I'm sick and I can't care for myself, let alone him. Then she opened her eyes, still holding him strongly, and said, "We'll lift you to my car and—"

"I don't want to be carried," he said distinctly. "It's an awful thing to be carried around like a baby."

"We'll wrap you in a blanket," she said. "Kulu will drive us. Wanga will drive your car." She looked about at the people and called, "The Bwana does not have fear-sickness. He is a brave man. He has a sudden sickness of the body, but it is not fear-sickness."

The people murmured and looked skeptical. Even Kulu was skeptical, she saw.

"This is Kulu," she said to Caleb. "My best friend, my stanchest help."

"I'm very glad to meet you, Kulu," he said in flawless Swahili. No hasty "Jambo," Rachel observed. He grasped the hand Kulu reluctantly extended. "I've heard fine things of you, Kulu, from Madami's friend at headquarters, Miss Barney, and from the Administrator, Monsieur Lecomte." Kulu backed from him, doubtless recalling that tribal proverb about the bee sting of honeyed words. Caleb turned to Rachel. "Edith Barney sends her best to you. So does Monsieur Lecomte. He's a fine man, isn't he?"

She looked at him, thinking that if she weren't careful she'd come to like him when it was somehow simpler to detest him. "He certainly is," she said.

"We had a good talk. I remarked about a book I noticed on his desk and he took me to his house and showed me all his books and loaned me three. In fact—" He swayed and she gripped his arm.

"Come," she said.

When they'd driven a little way he was shaken by a chill again. He held himself in a corner of the back seat, the blanket drawn about him, his eyes closed, his lips tightly compressed.

Watching him, she thought, Oh, why doesn't he go home? This life was not for him. Yet it wasn't for her either. Her head throbbed and she felt dull and heavy. She could go now, within a week, back to headquarters, and then, when transportation was available, back to the States. She had earned it. Mrs. Paul Wilton sailing home to have her child. And then, looking at Caleb, she thought, But what about him? He was ill and she could not leave him alone. Leave? What was the matter with her? She never would leave.

"Look," he said suddenly. His eyes were open. "The mountains."

She looked ahead. Through a rift in the clouds the sun glinted on snow and there was a bold outline of summit against blue sky. Perhaps the chimney she and Kulu had climbed.

"Beautiful," Caleb muttered, "beautiful." He looked at her, his teeth chattering. "Monsieur Lecomte told me you climbed them. They don't know that back at headquarters."

"I hope you won't tell them."

He made a futile effort to control his shivering. "Of course not. Very fine thing to climb them." He closed his eyes and opened them quickly, staring at the mountains. After a while, when his chill had subsided, he said, "I'm not much of a Bible quoter. But I'm cursed with a good memory. One night at a guest house while driving out here I read in Isaiah— Well, never mind."

"You read in Isaiah?" she asked.

"Yes. I forget the chapter and verse. But it goes, 'For it is a day of trouble, and of treading down, and of perplexity by the Lord God of hosts in the valley of vision, breaking down the walls, and of crying to the mountains.' Very good, I think."

A day of trouble, she thought dully, and of crying to the mountains. She looked at him again, but his eyes were closed, his chin sunken on his chest.

When they came up the slant into Dibela and turned into the compound a great crowd had gathered. Caleb Aldrich looked out at the people and Rachel knew he saw them dimly through his malarial haze. She told Kulu to drive to the door of the hospital where the crowd closed on them, pressing and peering into the car at the new strange bwana.

"Don't carry me," Caleb muttered. "Pride, you know." She gathered he was trying to make a joke. "Suffer terribly from the deadly sin of pride." His long hands gripped the back of the front seat as he pulled himself forward. Kulu got out and opened the door, staring at him impassively, as he slowly stepped to the ground, clutching the blanket about him.

A murmur grew as the people saw his great height, a head taller than the tallest man. Aieee, what a strange-looking bwana. With Rachel holding his right arm tightly, he tottered into the hospital. Some of the sick raised themselves to stare at him as he shuffled blindly beside Rachel to a cot in a corner and collapsed there.

He covered his eyes with trembling hands and muttered, "Sorry. Awful sorry to be this way."

Rachel looked perplexedly at his big feet hanging over the end of the cot. "Just don't be sorry," she said. "Everything will be all right as long as you don't apologize."

Late in the afternoon, when Caleb had fallen into a deep sleep, Rachel went slowly home and flung herself on the bed. She gripped her forehead with both hands and stared at the ceiling. *He* would be all right, but what about *her*? She had taken her temperature and studied her pulse, but both were normal. She was not in sharp pain, but a bone-deep ache like dengue gripped her. Bemusedly, without panic, she thought, This could be thahu. *I shall live long and as long as I live I shall suffer.* After a while she slept.

Guta awakened her as it grew dark, but she told him she didn't want dinner. She turned over and slept again, troubled by dreams. Someone came toward her in darkness with a flaming spear. She cried out. Her eyes were open. Kulu stood beside the bed, a lamp raised above his head, staring down at her worriedly. In the semidarkness she saw Kosongo and Musinga peering at her from the doorway.

"Madami." Never had she heard Kulu sound so worried. "Are you ill?"

"No, Kulu," she said calmly, "I'm resting."

"Madami, the new Bwana is very ill. His body is on fire and he cries out constantly in a strange tongue."

She did not think she possibly could rise and go to him. But she must. Getting up slowly, forcing each muscular movement, she swayed to her

[213]

feet and began to walk. Musinga backed from her, his eyes glittering strangely in the lamplight. Suddenly he turned and ran into the night.

Now she was walking across the compound, Kulu carrying a flashlight beside her, and as she walked the ache began to leave her. She looked up wonderingly at the limbali and thought, When I try I feel better. But I won't think about feeling better, I'll only continue to try.

As she entered the hospital Caleb cried, "Sam! Sam! Give me a hand with the stoneboat. . . ." The patients stirred in the darkness, listening to the strange cries of the strange bwana who lay behind a screen in the corner. "Mrs. Ridgely bakes the best cherry pie," Caleb said in a conversational tone as Rachel stepped around the screen. His thin face shone with sweat in the candlelight. "There are fields of buttercups beyond the Corners," he said distinctly. "The fruit blossoms are beautiful."

Rachel rested a hand on his hot forehead and he started. "Nancy!" he cried. "Nancy! I love you. I *love* you, Nancy." Tears streamed from his closed eyes. "I love you so much, Nancy. Don't ever leave me."

Rachel saw him dimly through her own sudden tears and she removed her hand and sank to the stool beside his cot. He groaned and turned and was silent.

There was nothing she could do. She had no medicine to give him except quinine and she dared not give him more now. She dipped a cloth in the basin of cool water on the crate and bathed his face.

"Sorry," he muttered. "Awful sorry about this, Nancy."

She sat down and watched him again. Kulu squatted on the floor beside her. After a while he murmured, "I'll stay, Madami. You go back and rest."

"But I'm not tired," she said. And she realized she was not tired now. It was strange; everything seemed so strange, as if the world, not she, breathed under light anesthesia. She could do nothing for him, as so often she could do nothing for others. She could only sit and wait, hoping that at some random moment her mere presence might be of aid.

She ordered Kulu to go and sleep and she stayed. Eventually she dozed, for she awakened with a start, hearing nothing but sensing something. Caleb was looking at her. He smiled faintly.

"I'll be all right," he said indistinctly. "Please get some sleep, Rachel."

She nodded and smiled and went away quietly. But she did not go home. She lay down on the cot in the operating room, leaving the door open, listening to the night sounds of the hospital and the country.

Awakening in gray dawn, she thought that she never would rise again.

She simply could not. The ache extended from her scalp to the soles of her feet. This definitely is thahu, she thought. And then she thought, I must get up.

First the right leg and then the left, thinking of gray mucous-plaited muscle, thinking of bone and the socket of bone. She was sitting on the cot. She was thinking of the outline of foot bones under X-ray. And she was standing on numb feet. She walked stiffly to the door and through the doorway and across the corridor and through the outer doorway. She paused, gazing at the vast shadowy limbali rising in the dawn. A cock crowed and suddenly she heard the sweet clamorous morning music of birds. They must have been singing for some time and she had not heard them. Yet now she heard them and she was walking, the water pail in her right hand. Under the limbali and around the bungalow to the wooden-roofed spring that bubbled eternally from the rocks.

She filled the pail and returned to the hospital, walking slowly, her shoulders slumped. The ache persisted. But so, she thought, do I.

He was awake and smiling at her as she silently poured a dipper of cold water into a cup and held it out to him. He drank thirstily and his eyes asked for more. She refilled the cup and he drained it again.

"Thanks," he said then. "You must be tired. You look it."

"And you must be better." She forced a smile. "You look it."

"Thanks to you."

"I had nothing to do with it. I found the quinine formula they gave you at headquarters in your shirt pocket. I don't think it's a very effective formula."

He fell back, rubbing his unshaven jaw. "I guess I was—delirious."

Her smile, she knew, was small and tight. "That's usual with a bad fever."

"I seem to recollect," he said slowly, "that I called you Nancy."

"You may have. People say many things in delirium."

"I wish you'd call me Caleb—Rachel."

She nodded indifferently. "All right—Caleb."

"Can you sit down for a minute?"

She sat down, looking away from him.

"One thing I know," he said, "and nobody told me. It must be a big disappointment to you to need a doctor so badly here and then to field a —a minister."

She turned her head quickly and looked at him.

"I wish I were a doctor, Rachel. I know that's what's needed here. But I'm too old—I'm thirty-seven—to go back home and try to become a doctor.

So you and I are stuck with the fact I'm a preacher. May I have another drink of water?"

He drank again and fell back and said, "Did you ever read or see the play called 'Rain'?"

"Yes," she said quickly, "yes, I read the Maugham story the play is taken from."

"I never forgot the preacher in that, I can't remember his name—"

"Davidson," Rachel said. "Reverend Davidson."

"Yes, Davidson," he said. "That story really scared me the first time I read it. I live in constant horror of being a missionary like him."

Her eyes darted from him again as she thought of Paul and her, of what by Caleb's standards constituted temptation, yielding—and the retribution of the child within her.

Caleb sighed. "Well, I'm not a doctor. So I'll do my best to be a good teacher here and help you about the hospital any way I can. One thing." His eyes commanded her attention, which he sensed was wavering. "I'm in charge here in name only. I never could really be in charge. You always will be. But I want you to know something else. I don't *want* to be in charge. You must go on living as you have and doing things as you see fit. Dibela is yours." He smiled faintly. "In a way you are Dibela."

She didn't know what to say. Was it possible, she wondered, if much of her love of Dibela was love of her power in Dibela? What had Paul said once about her being treated like a queen here and there not being many places left in the world where one was treated like a queen? A queen? Did the bones of a queen ever bear such a mortal ache?

"I understand—Caleb." She stared at the floor. "I—appreciate. I—you and I can work out any problems, I believe." She looked up at him suddenly. "You were raised in the country, weren't you?"

"Yes." He looked surprised. Then he smiled. "It must show, I don't know how. I was raised on a farm in New York State and when I was fourteen my father moved to a small village and took over a store. It meant a lot to me, that village. I don't know why—well, never mind."

"You don't know what?"

"I don't know why American writers are always complaining about the villages. My life in one was wonderful. So wonderful I never got to like a city."

"Are you—" She hesitated.

"Am I what?"

"Literary? Interested in writing, I mean."

He grimaced. "Heavens, no. I like to read, but I wouldn't think of writing a book. I'm a fairly good appreciator, I guess, but not so much of a doer." He stirred. "Could I have some bread and coffee? I'm sort of hungry."

She rose quickly. "Indeed you can. An appetite is a good sign." She hurried away. She had gone some distance before she realized that she did not ache now. It was interesting, she thought detachedly. Then, detachment leaving her, she wondered who Nancy was.

XXII

IT WAS THAHU, Musinga thought. It had begun its dark rushing, as clouds rush darkly before inevitable rain. Soon the full storm would strike Madami, destroying her with its magic lightning.

Once he would have gone running to the palaver house with his likembe to sing one of his great songs such as he used to sing in the days of Dr. Bickel. Ah, how the people had applauded his endless death song on the night that Dr. Bickel died. Those days were past, but they would return when Madami died. He would wait patiently, as the gray spider waits for the green fly. It would be unwise to sing against Madami in the palaver house now. There were many who would strike him down and some who would slash him with panga and spear. And there was Kulu, who assuredly would track him anywhere and run a spear through his bowels.

Aieee! The thought of Kulu's spear in his bowels made him sweat. For Kulu did not understand. Kulu thought he was against Madami. He was not. He simply knew, as Kulu should know if he paused and thought, that thahu was stronger than Madami. It was as inevitable as that night must follow day, so why believe that night would not fall? Yes, thahu had at last begun on Madami, and he and Kosongo and Kulu saw its signs, but each was afraid to speak of it to another.

It was evident the day the new Bwana arrived. It lay on the bed with her and made it difficult for her to rise. Its shadow followed her, as inseparably as a man's shadow follows him on a bright afternoon. He had watched her the next morning going to the spring, thahu pressing on her shoulders. On the second night the new Bwana had been sick again and Madami had sat with him again, afraid to lie down with her thahu. But it had found her as she sat by the Bwana's bedside, for he had watched and seen the pain on her face when she tried to rise. On the third, fourth and fifth nights the Bwana had been better and Madami had slept in her house. But she had cried out often in her sleep. Last night he had crept near to listen when a hand gripped his throat so tightly that his heart stopped for a long time. The hand belonged to Kulu, who sat on the steps in the darkness, watching over Madami and listening to her cries.

"You jackal!" Kulu whispered when he'd finally let go his throat. "I'm going to kill you, Musinga, if harm comes to Madami."

After gasping for breath, Musinga croaked, "Your God the Father wouldn't like that—"

Kulu had grasped his throat again until his sight had gone blacker than the night and he was certain he was dead. Then Kulu had shaken him to life again and he had hopped away to safety.

Aye, Kulu knew too. But he dared not mention it to others. It did not matter. Others would soon see and know.

The curse was that Madami should live long and suffer long. Ah, but she would not live long here. Perhaps she would live and suffer long in some other place. But not in Dibela.

Musinga strolled along the fringe of Dibela that sixth evening after the new Bwana arrived. He pressed his likembe softly to his cheek, humming softly, touching the likembe so and so and so. Nobody understood. It was sad that Madami must perish. But sadder still was the fact that no one could listen to the song in his heart.

"The shadow of thahu, the shadow of thahu," he murmured, "lies over Madami, lies over Madami." Tears gathered in his eyes and he snuffled. It was such a beautiful song and there was no one who could hear it. Why was there no place in the world for a singer?

"Our hearts will wither and dry." There was one haunting note. He halted and played it again and again until his tears rushed hotly. What would happen to him when Madami died or went away? He stopped crying and thought about it again.

He saw himself in his white smock and shining spectacles. Doctor Musinga. The new Bwana was not a doctor, they said. And Madami would be gone. And with her would go Kulu, on whom there was just as bad a curse. That left the new Bwana—and Doctor Musinga.

He hurried purposefully to the hospital.

His smock, with the spectacles in the pocket, hung on the rack. His shoes were on the floor. Kosongo, dozing in a chair, looked up at him as he forced his feet into his shoes and pulled on his smock.

Kosongo yawned and said, "Whose wife are you going to surprise tonight, stupid one?"

"I'm reporting for duty, noisy one," Musinga said. "Go bury your head in pombe."

Kosongo got to his feet and stretched and strolled outside.

Adjusting his spectacles low on his nose, Musinga walked through the darkened hospital with a great slapping of shoes, thinking of the approaching time when he would cure those he liked and kill those he disliked. Doctor Musinga, head of the hospital.

The new Bwana looked at him as he came around the screen. He lay with his feet resting on a box because the cot was too short for him. He was reading a book thing by the light of the lamp.

"Hello," he said, "who are you?"

Musinga bowed so low that his spectacles fell off, and to his great astonishment he caught them as they fell. "Doctor Musinga, Bwana. I come to serve you."

"Hmmm." The Bwana had very searching eyes that should not be looked into. "I'm very glad to meet you, Doctor Musinga." He extended his hand—certainly a promising sign, Musinga thought as he touched it quickly. "I haven't met you before. What have you been doing?"

"Healing the sick," Musinga said. "I've healed many these past six days."

"You're too late to heal me," the Bwana said. "I'm all better and I'm leaving the hospital tomorrow."

Musinga sat down on the floor and scratched an armpit. He wished the Bwana would pick up the book thing again and not watch him.

"Tell me, Doctor Musinga," the Bwana said, "what do you do best in all the world?"

"Do best?" Musinga scratched his other armpit.

"Yes. What are you best at? Hunting? Running? Eating?"

"Singing," Musinga said quickly. "I'm a great singer, Bwana, and I have the finest likembe in the country." He reached under his smock and took out the likembe.

"Ah," the Bwana said. "Perhaps you would sing me a song."

"Yes," Musinga cried, "I'll sing you a song, Bwana. What would you like to hear?"

"Let me see," the Bwana said slowly. "Of course, I'm not sure what songs you know."

"I make up my own songs," Musinga said proudly. "I carry them in my heart and they burst like birds from cages."

"Like birds from cages," the Bwana said thoughtfully, and Musinga nodded happily. "Is there any new song caged in your heart that you would release?"

Musinga bobbed his head, his spirit soaring on fluttering wings. His song had been contained too long.

He thrummed the likembe softly, striking the true notes again and again before he began to sing. "The shadow of thahu, the shadow of thahu, lies over Madami, lies over Madami, and soon she will go from us. Aye, she is going, going, fading in pain, fading in pain, under the shadow of thahu. . . ." Dimly through his tears Musinga saw that the Bwana had risen on an elbow and was staring at him strangely.

There was a jarring crash, a deep pain in his skull, as the world flew into fragments, his spectacles going one way and his likembe another. He was being lifted into the air by the shocked hair of his head and whirling dizzily through the darkened hospital where the patients yelled. He screamed frantically as he went, around and around, straight toward the screen door, and when he stopped screaming to catch his breath he heard heavy breathing under him and knew it was Kulu. Straight toward the door they rushed and he began screaming again. Dimly he glimpsed Kosongo, standing upside down, fling open the screen at the very moment he went hurtling through it into darkness. He hit the earth and rolled by some weird momentum even though no hands were on him. Somewhere he felt his numbed legs, and he put them under him and ran.

"Kulu!"

The Assistant Bwana (as Kulu thought of him) might be sick, but he had the roar of a lion. He plunged out into the darkness after them and stood now in his pajamas a few yards behind Kulu as he started after Musinga.

"Kulu!"

Kulu stood, panting, as the Assistant Bwana came up behind him and rested an arm on his shoulder. He did not want to chase Musinga now, but for some unfathomable cause, perhaps for the cause of the good Bwana Doctor now gone away, he didn't want this Assistant Bwana to touch him. His anger at Musinga was gone, but there was a sudden strange smoldering anger against this white bwana, or any white bwana, who laid a hand on him, even though the pressure was gentle, as now.

[220]

He started forward and the pressure grew tighter. It was a great wrong, punishable by years of captivity in the jailhouse, but he strained against the pressure of the hand holding him. Then there were two hands on him, the terribly strong hands of the tall and deceptively thin, sick Assistant Bwana. What madness, but he'd show him! He whirled, but the hands caught him. His muscles knotted, and he could feel the muscles of the Assistant Bwana knotting. They stood, straining. He gathered his strength and the sick Assistant Bwana gathered his strength and neither could break the other.

He let go. Now he would go off to the plain or the mountains and die of indignity. But the Assistant Bwana let go.

"Kulu." The Assistant Bwana was breathing heavily. "Let's go inside and talk this thing over."

He followed the Assistant Bwana toward the light, not looking at him, staring at the ground and wishing to be an ant. The Assistant Bwana's pajamas fluttered around his thin legs as he walked. Kosongo, his face slack with amazement, held open the screen door. They walked through the hospital as the patients chattered and cried out.

The Assistant Bwana paused and said firmly into the darkness, "Rest, everyone. There is no trouble. Be still and rest." The patients were still.

He sat down on his cot and looked at his big white feet. "Sit down, Kulu." And Kulu sat down on the stool and gazed at the floor. "Now, Kulu, what is this about a thahu on Madami?"

Aieee, for the good days of the Bwana Doctor when there was no communication of tongue but only one of spirit. Yet, grudgingly, he had to admit that the Assistant Bwana was strong in body and had not tried to break his spirit. He faced Kulu now as a man, in the way that Madami, while a woman, always faced him as a man. Quite suddenly it was imperative that he tell the Assistant Bwana about the thahu.

So he told him, and when he had finished the story, the Assistant Bwana sat for a long time staring at his big white feet. At last he said slowly, "Thank you for telling me, Kulu. I've heard of thahu—but always at a distance. You say you do not believe in it?"

"No, Bwana."

"But you are worried now for Madami. And you say she bears her husband's child. It seems more likely that her—her fatigue is a physical thing caused by the child."

Kulu shook his head boldly, for he saw that another good thing about the Assistant Bwana was that you could disagree with him. In fact, he expected you to disagree, as he demonstrated when they wrestled and he was not angry.

"I'm a man, Bwana, and never a father that I know of. But I know the ways of women and Madami is a woman. She is very strong and the carrying of a child would not affect her so."

"There is only one thing we can do," the Assistant Bwana said slowly. "We don't believe that a man can cast a thahu, and we do believe in God. We can pray to God to give Madami strength and to give us the strength to help her in any way we can."

Pray? Yes, pray to God the Father and Jesus the Christ. He had thought of it, but he had dreaded to bring the matter of thahu to God and trouble Him when He was so busy with the northern wars. Yet now the Assistant Bwana said it was the thing to do.

"When shall we pray, Bwana?"

"When?"

"Shall we pray right now?"

"Why, yes." The Assistant Bwana paused at the sound of approaching footsteps.

Then Madami appeared.

"What are you doing sitting up? Get back under those covers, Caleb." She almost smiled at his alacrity. And why was Kulu in such haste to go?

"I'm better." Caleb's gaze seemed to search her face. "You said I can get out of here tomorrow morning." He raised himself on an elbow. "May I talk to you, Rachel?"

She sank down wearily. She had been to the hut of a woman who certainly would die of tuberculosis, and on the way back she had been thinking, Perhaps I have tuberculosis. Perhaps that's what's wrong with me.

"I've been talking to Kulu," Caleb said. "He told me about—about the thahu cast on you."

Her left hand strayed to her cropped hair and lingered there. So Kulu had seen the thahu on her. Thahu, ha! There was not such a thing as thahu. There was tuberculosis. And yet, and yet, her temperature was normal.

"I suppose," Caleb said, "you now expect me to tell you thahu is impossible."

"It is impossible," she said dully. "There isn't such a thing as thahu. Do you think I believe in it?"

[222]

He smiled. "You may have reason to. And, I suppose, I have no reason either to believe or disbelieve in it. But I can see how it must be in your mind. And I'd remind you that you're working awfully hard. And that you're pregnant."

She looked at him alertly. "Did they tell you that at headquarters?"

He shook his head. "Kulu told me."

This awful lie she was living. Supposing she confessed everything to him now? What would he say? What would he do?

"Are you married, Caleb?"

"No." He looked away. "I was. My wife died three years ago."

And so he had turned to Africa.

"We were married for three years," he said, still not looking at her, "and she died. I had a church in Vermont at the time. Nancy was from my home town in New York State." He tried to smile and failed. "We weren't childhood sweethearts. She was quite a bit younger than I. But she grew up in my town and I went back there one summer to visit my parents and I met Nancy."

He paused, and she knew that he was thinking of the elm shadows of a town and the fields and orchards beyond a town and the way a special woman must have walked beside him. He had loved a northern country and he'd turned his back on it for Africa.

"I didn't come out here because—because Nancy was dead and I—I wanted to escape."

His words startled her, for he almost seemed to read her thoughts. Their sense of communication warmed her before she suddenly knew it would be better if they failed to communicate too closely. For there was Paul and there was the child and the prison of her deceit.

"I'd wanted to come to Africa for a long time," he said, "and Nancy wanted to come with me. I'd been at them in New York to send me."

"Why?" Her involuntary question surprised her.

"Why? I don't think about it much any more. Well, I believe there's important work to be done out here. And there is. I guess there's important work at home, too, but I was always vaguely dissatisfied simply being a preacher and trying to get along with the prejudices of my people." He smiled. "I'm not a great preacher or theologian. It's simply that I—believe. Perhaps I'm really more of a farmer who—believes."

"I envy you," she said.

He frowned. "You mean?"

"Being able to say you believe with such conviction."

"Don't get me wrong," he said quickly. "I have many doubts about

[223]

myself and my ways of doing things. But not in a good many years have I doubted the existence of God or doubted that everyone has an immortal soul."

"And that's why I envy you," Rachel said.

"Do you doubt the existence of God?"

"Sometimes."

He sighed. "It seems that most intelligent people of feeling do at times. Perhaps I do and am not aware of it. Perhaps I'm dishonest with myself. Or perhaps I'm just not very intelligent."

She smiled faintly. "So you aren't going to try to—save me?"

He smiled too. "No one can save another. Only God can. And I believe He saves you every day, Rachel."

"Even from thahu?"

"Even from thahu."

Each morning Kulu prayed for Madami, but he doubted that God heard him. He did not blame God, for he knew that He and His Son were very busy in the northern wars, and he believed that when They could They would return and protect Madami. Meanwhile, was it possible They had sent the strong Assistant Bwana to watch over her? It was a good thought that fortified him.

Still, it was sad to see Madami moving so heavily about the compound. It was true that she walked and ministered to the sick. But it also was true that she walked heavily, almost tottering sometimes, as women totter under great burdens of thatching in hut-building time. He watched her frequently put the temperature thing in her mouth at the hospital when she thought no one was looking, she who never used to bother with the temperature thing for herself. He often saw her feel her pulse and he came upon her once in the operating room moving her arms strangely and studying herself, as if her eyes could penetrate skin to muscles themselves and see what was wrong there.

The Assistant Bwana saw too. He had left the hospital and lived now in the cottage across the compound and he was busy organizing the classes and teaching. He was a great teacher, the Assistant Bwana, even greater than Madami, and the people came eagerly to listen to him. He was very busy, but he always found time to try to help Madami. He found time, too, Kulu knew, to pray for her. He would sit sometimes on the little porch of his little cottage with his eyes closed, and Kulu knew he was praying for Madami.

One morning after Kulu had prayed for Madami, he looked out at the compound and saw her walking slowly toward the hospital, her head bowed. Beyond, he saw the Assistant Bwana come out on his porch and stare at her broodingly. Then Kulu closed his eyes again, but not in prayer. He concentrated on the black-eagle thought, a thing he had not done in many seasons.

In the black-eagle thought, as he had learned long ago, he was an eagle soaring above plains and mountains. His gaze fell piercingly, as the eagle's falls piercingly, on mountain crags and frozen rain, on bush and shimmering plain, on villages and twisting watercourses. The eagle, as ever, would know his quarry when he saw it. And the eagle's quarry would be his. It would point the way to what he must do.

Suddenly he saw his village clearly, its shambas and huts rushing up to meet him as the eagle dived. He opened his eyes. Madami stepped into the hospital.

"Madami?"

"Yes, Kulu." Did she see him?

"Madami, may I go to my village for two or three days?"

Now she saw him. She was going to ask him why, he knew, and he would not know what to answer. But she did not ask. She simply looked at him gravely and said, "Go, Kulu."

So he went, but not as a leading citizen of Dibela. He went as young Kulu, wearing only breechcloth, and carrying spear and bow and panga, hurrying fast along the track, as the warrior grandfathers had strode this way. The land turned under his bare feet and he smelled the old keen scents of country. But his heart did not leap to meet the land as once. It was a stone he bore in his chest all day through sunshine and rain, through flashing clearing and dark winding forest.

When an hour of daylight remained and he was near his village, a leopard's scream shattered the stillness. Ah, it was a good sign. He laughed silently. Then, around a curve in the track, he saw a man running ahead of him, a man who must have been frightened by the leopard's cry.

"Stop!" he shouted, and the man leaped nervously and looked back fearfully. "It's I, Kulu of Dibela, the son of Kulu, returning to my village."

He strode toward the man, not thinking, as the eagle does not think in its dive.

"What do you want in our village, Kulu?" asked the man.

Kulu said, "I have returned to see Kalanumu die."

[225]

The man's eyes widened. The spear trembled in his hand. Turning, he ran toward the village.

Now, as he strode on, his heart no longer was a stone. Ah, distance-eating feet and the sound of many brooks upon the mountains. Soon there came the barking of dogs and the babble of voices. He was out of the forest and passing through the shambas. The voices were still and then the dogs were still as he came on. The people moved off the track to let him pass. Hello, hello, hello. They merely muttered in reply, but after he had passed, they came padding silently after him. The word went ahead of him and the people streamed behind him through the old village smells of wood smoke and palm oil. When he came to Kalanumu's shamba, the eyes of Kalanumu's wives glittered whitely at him above the cooking fires.

"Where is Kalanumu?" he demanded.

They bowed their heads and did not answer.

"Show me Kalanumu."

Then Kalanumu's son, Duru, his own circumcision brother, came slowly from the old man's hut with lowered head. Though he knew that Kulu came as an enemy, he could not forget their circumcision brotherhood, and he gave Kulu the old grip of thumbs.

"My father cannot talk to you, Kulu. He cannot talk to anyone."

This, thought Kulu, was not black-eagle magic. It was the power of God the Father. For the black-eagle thought was only a clearing of the mind, a purge available to all men everywhere at any time. Into a man's clearing of his mind God the Father placed the true, the powerful thought.

"He lives?" Kulu asked Duru.

"He lives."

"He sees?"

"He sees."

"He hears?"

"He hears. But he cannot talk."

"Aye." Kulu nodded. "Carry him out here to me."

Duru hesitated.

"Have him carried out to me."

Duru, feeling a power greater than his father's magic, spoke to the wives and they went reluctantly into the hut. The people of the village gathered in a dense throng, watching silently. Kulu glimpsed his father and Giza and many friends and cousins. Momentarily his heart warmed to all of them, and then he thought sadly that they were neither of his place nor time now.

The people murmured as from the hut came the three wives of Kalanumu bearing him on a mat. Could this old wasted creature be the great Kalanumu? His right arm and leg flopped uselessly, his head was drawn to one side, and from a corner of his open mouth poured a tiny stream of saliva. But his eyes, when he tried to raise his head, were the same hard shining eyes. For a moment Kulu dreaded to do what he knew he must. Old Kalanumu, friend of his youth and now his bitter enemy.

The wives lowered Kalanumu to the ground with his back against the hut wall. Kulu sat down facing him, his legs crossed. Kalanumu's eyes burned at him and saliva trickled from his slack lips.

"Old Kalanumu, I've come back to see you die." Kulu reached in his quiver and drew out an arrow and tossed it lightly next Kalanumu's gnarled left hand on the ground.

"If you hear me, Kalanumu, pick up the arrow and tap it once on the ground."

For fully a minute Kalanumu did not move. Then, slowly, his fingers fumbled around the arrow. He raised it and let it fall. The people murmured and many sighed.

"If you wish to say no to me, Kalanumu, tap the arrow twice. If yes, tap it once."

It was a cruelty, Kulu thought, yet necessary, even though there was no hatred in his heart now for Kalanumu. God the Father was not cruel, but His great spirit had directed him here, as the eagle dives. So he plunged with no plan except his free instincts. Instinctively he knew that some power of evil had been directed at Madami, and against its cruelty must be pressed the cruelty of good. The evil must be sought out and found and crushed, even if it lay in the heart of a helpless old man. For God the Father knew there was evil in the world and He pressed strongly against it.

So he was not thinking or planning, he was simply feeling and saying and acting, as the strong spear comes between the good hunter and the springing leopard.

"I come here, Kalanumu, in the name of God the Father, to watch you die. And you think you have summoned me here to see my death. So I shall sit here and you shall sit there until one of us falls dead. If your people try to move you, you shall die. We may sit here many days and nights, but only one of us will rise alive. Is that right?"

Slowly Kalanumu raised the arrow in his tremulous hand and let it fall.

"Is there any change in your heart, Kalanumu, toward me and Madami and the God we serve?"

Kalanumu lifted the arrow and let it fall, lifted it again and let it fall.

"Very well. Then I tell you that I am strong and of good heart. And Madami is strong and of good heart."

Kalanumu raised and dropped the arrow twice, denying what Kulu said.

So Kulu knew that the old man had made great medicine against her since they came down from the mountains, working all his magic in an effort to destroy her so that he could die discrediting God the Father and giving all credit to the old gods. Ah, he had failed. For Madami had loved and taken a husband and conceived a child and worshiped God the Father and done much good and saved many lives. Her magic was too great for Kalanumu's. Then why did she walk with a burden now?

It was dark then and the fires were built up. The people came and went, some eating and some simply sitting and staring at Kulu and Kalanumu. A leopard cried on the mountain and the night insects talked. There was the smell of roasting meat and Kulu hungered for it, but he did not eat. Kalanumu must hunger too, he knew, but his people would not feed him. To feed or move him would be a sign of lack of faith in his medicine. This was the medicine he had taught them to respect and they dared not show disrespect now, even if he starved. Many of them expected, Kulu knew, that he, and not Kalanumu, would fall dead.

There was a night shower, and they sat motionlessly through it. The moon came out and the night grew cold, but they did not stir. The moon waned, and in its waning Kalanumu nodded. His eyes closed and opened, closed and opened, blinking slowly while the people watched. Just before dawn he urinated on a withered leg and fell over in sleep.

Kulu spoke for the first time in many hours. "Let him sleep. It is his last sleep."

Kalanumu snored and his snoring grew softer in deep sleep. Kulu watched him, forcing his eyes to stay open.

The dawn was slow. Nearly everyone slept now, snoring loudly, their bodies twisted grotesquely in the gradually growing morning light. Cocks crowed and birds sang. People rose, stretching stiffly, hacking and spitting in the cold morning air.

Duru went slowly to his father and knelt beside him, careful not to

[228]

touch him. He placed an ear close to Kalanumu's mouth. Slowly he got to his feet and gazed stolidly at Kulu.

"Kulu, my father is dead."

Kulu ate cold topi meat and drank deeply at the stream and lay down under a tree and slept. He awakened at noon, the sun shining in his eyes and the mourning wails of Kalanumu's wives ringing in his ears. Duru and a half-dozen other young men were seated around him in a semicircle.

Duru said, "We would hear more about the new God, Kulu."

"He is a kind God," Kulu said, "and He does not strike down in vengeance. He moves only to protect the innocent when they are oppressed by the cruel, moving between them like a strong shield."

"As you moved last night between the curse and the accursed," one young man said.

"I did not move," Kulu said. "God the Father moved me. For it came to me that Kalanumu had worked all his power against Madami."

"That is true," Duru said. "After you and the white Madami left the mountains long ago my father worked great medicine against both of you."

Perhaps my own time will come, Kulu thought. And then, As God the Father sees fit.

"Does a thahu go on forever?" he asked suddenly. "What happens after its maker is dead?"

"Every thahu seems different," Duru said. "But you and the white Madami should not be afraid, for you seem to have found a strong God. I would like to learn more of Him."

Kulu got slowly to his feet. "You will in time. You should come down to Dibela and listen and see." He looked about him, thinking, Here in my own village by my own effort I might someday do much good. But he could not stay now. He must return quickly to Madami.

He said good-by to the young men and strode along the track. When he entered the forest, he began to run. Tiring at last, he drifted, and then he ran again, his heart singing like the brooks that poured from the mountains.

He returned in darkness to Dibela. Putting away his bow and spear and panga, he pulled on pants and padded from the sleeping hut where Guta and Kosongo and Musinga snored. The lamp burned in Madami's living room, he saw. And suddenly he heard her laugh, as he had not heard her since the Bwana Doctor went away.

[229]

Walking quietly up the porch steps, he saw her and the Assistant Bwana seated at the table under the lamp. They were playing at the little game thing that had pegs and a board and cards. The Assistant Bwana was puffing on his pipe and talking. Madami was leaning forward, smiling, and her shoulders were not slumped.

"Madami," he called softly, "I have returned."

"Come in, Kulu," she called. "Come in. How are things in your village?"

He looked at the floor and shrugged elaborately in the way he had learned from the Bwana Administrator.

His eyes darted up to hers. "You look well, Madami."

"I feel fine. I woke this morning feeling fine. I think I've had a cold or a touch of rheumatism."

"I'm glad you feel better, Madami." His heart swelled with happiness, and he looked up, smiling, at the Assistant Bwana.

The Assistant Bwana stared at him with a strange and inscrutable expression.

XXIII

MADAMI CARRIED the little one, the mtoto, within her very well. She was not ill, either in body or in spirit, and though the mtoto grew large in her, she continued to work in the hospital. Sometimes, it was true, Kulu would come upon her staring far off and his heart was filled with sadness, for he knew she was thinking of the Bwana Doctor. Then he would remind her of what the Bwana had said in his latest letter to cheer her. Two letters had been especially good, he remembered. For both times she had torn them open with trembling hands, once standing bareheaded in the hot sun, and tears had come to her eyes, and he had seen her reading them again and again by the lamp at evening. So when he found her sad, he reminded her of the letters, especially the two good letters, and he knew he cheered her.

Kulu knew there were many things in Dibela now that pleased and cheered Madami. One good thing was that Chief Buderga's youngest wife also was with child, and Buderga was a changed man. He came under the influence not only of Madami, but of the Assistant Bwana as well. He came five days a week to the Assistant Bwana's school, where he was much taken up with learning to read and write. On the seventh day he came to worship God the Father, and while Kulu doubted that Buderga actually had seen Him and so believed, he had to admit that Buderga did the things which the Assistant Bwana said God approved. God, for instance, approved of a man having only one wife, and so Buderga divorced his two older wives. That is, he moved them to a more distant part of his shamba and did not lie with them, though still seeing that they and his children were well fed. Since he had not lain with them for some time it was puzzling to see how any real change had been worked. Also, Buderga lay often with a girl named Tika as his wife grew big with the child, and while he had not actually married Tika and so broken God's commandment about having more than one wife, it was truly puzzling to see just what had been accomplished if God's commandment meant that a man should lie with only one woman as long as both lived.

The Assistant Bwana did not know about Tika, of course, and Kulu felt it wiser not to mention her lest the Assistant Bwana demand that Buderga give her up too. That probably would be more than Buderga could do, and he probably would stop coming to worship God. If he did that, there doubtless would be goatlike men and women of Dibela who would follow him away. Many would remain, it was true, but not as many as there were now. And numbers were important, for the Assistant Bwana wanted everybody to attend school and to worship God, the women as well as the men.

He said and did strange things, the Assistant Bwana. He said it was especially important that the women learn God's ways, for it was the women who raised the children and instilled in them that strange thing which could be said only in the French tongue: *la conscience*. Kulu learned to say the word in both the French tongue and even the English tongue, mystified for a time because it was spoken differently but looked the same when written on the blackboard: *conscience*. It was, the Assistant Bwana said, what Kulu had when he wished to take good care of Madami. Aye, he understood that. He understood it here in Dibela. But he was puzzled when the Assistant Bwana told him in personal conversation that women more than men must create this conscience for all of Africa. What was *all* of Africa—and why? The Assistant Bwana asked him if he understood, and he answered no, for he had long since learned

[231]

it was no good if you pretended to know, like Musinga, when you actually didn't.

Africans were brothers, said the Assistant Bwana. They were easily guided by powerful men of either black or white skin who had their own selfish interests. Here in Congo the Belgians were good leaders for the most part, trying to help Africans grow slowly. But it was not thus everywhere. There were white leaders in some places who oppressed Africans and there were black leaders in other places who oppressed their fellow Africans even more cruelly. The only thing that could guide people through the long times of trouble that stretched ahead was *conscience,* the Assistant Bwana said. It would take a long time. It must begin now in Dibela with the parents, especially the mothers, and go on to the children and be reinstilled in *their* children years hence. On and on. It must happen in Dibela and a hundred thousand other places. That, said the Assistant Bwana, was why he was here.

Kulu thought much about these things and came to understand them. As his understanding grew, his liking for the Assistant Bwana grew. And that troubled him. The more he liked the Assistant Bwana, the more he felt he was disloyal to the absent Bwana Doctor. The Bwana Doctor and he had never conversed because they lacked the tongue, but he had understood him instinctively. He had always known what the Bwana Doctor wanted, and he always had known the Bwana Doctor would take what he wanted. But the Assistant Bwana seemed to want nothing for himself. He ate little, for one thing. He did not drink the white man's transparent wine. He did not look at Madami with a white man's desire for a white woman as had the Bwana Doctor and the Bwana Administrator and the Bwana planter from near Rugeri. He did not want to go hunting. His respect for life was vast, so vast that he would avoid descending his cottage steps in the morning when spiders spun dew-jeweled webs there. He'd leap off the porch and look back at the web, smiling delightedly, moving around until he caught its full dewy shining in the morning sun. Then he'd go off, smiling and shaking his head. What did you do about a man like that?

He was truly, as Madami had said, a great teacher. He knew ways of making everyone learn. Reading and writing and Bible and the new thing he had introduced, figuring, and that even more dazzling thing, the French tongue, came easily to those he taught. Although he always was just, he favored the intelligent. Tiza, the young man who had been the first to come to the hospital with an ulcerated leg many months ago, was one of his favorites, for Tiza was quick to learn and of good heart.

Kulu also was a favorite (secretly pleased at the same time he was greatly troubled for fear he showed disloyalty to the Bwana Doctor by being pleased). Tiza, in fact, became to the Assistant Bwana in the teaching what Kulu was to Madami in the hospital: a salaried assistant. Kulu and Tiza became good friends and sat much together, discussing such matters as what the Assistant Bwana had said about *conscience*. Tiza understood and, most important, made his young wife, Yuki, understand. Yuki attended school, with their mtoto slung on her back, and it developed that she, too, was quick to learn. When Tiza invited Kulu to his shamba to eat, Yuki ate with them and talked freely with them, as if she were a man. It was a new and delightful experience to Kulu, this talking and enjoying a woman without wanting to lie with her. Indeed the thought of lying with Yuki was horrifying to him, not because she was uncomely, but because of his great friendship with Tiza.

One day when Tiza and he were eating together in the compound, during the noontime break, he told Tiza how he felt about this and Tiza was greatly pleased. It would be good, Tiza said, if Kulu had a wife like Yuki. And Kulu agreed.

"Kulu, your eyes are poor," Tiza said to him one day as they sat under the limbali with their bowls of manioc. "You do not see well. During the morning you don't come and look at the classes."

"I'm very busy mornings, Tiza," Kulu said with a touch of self-importance. "I'm very busy with Madami in the hospital."

"Some morning," Tiza said, "you must go out for a drink of water and look at the new class and test your blindness. Some morning, perhaps tomorrow."

"I'm very busy," Kulu said gravely.

But the next morning he found his feet carrying him out of the hospital, even though patients waited, and taking him toward the spring in a wide circle that led to the farther end of the compound. There, in the thatch-roofed, open-sided schoolhouse they had built only last month at the Assistant Bwana's direction, Tiza was teaching reading to a class of men and women and children. Kulu walked along the side of the schoolhouse, as if on an important errand. Tiza saw him and nodded and then interrupted a man who was reading.

"Now let us hear Vudi read," he said.

A girl rose slowly and began to read. She was indeed comely, being tall and finely proportioned, with neat hair and white teeth and good eyes and fine taut breasts. She read well in a clear, firm voice. Aye, how blind could a man be?

[233]

He stood there, staring in at her, while people grinned at him, and when the girl had finished reading she sat down and glanced at him, and then away.

"Is there anything I can do for you, Kulu?" Tiza asked pleasantly.

"It will wait," Kulu said calmly. "I shall not interrupt the class now."

He walked straight back to the hospital, dazed, having forgotten to go to the spring. When Kosongo asked where he'd been, he merely stared at him stupidly. He felt very good and soon he felt very bad, with the uncertain hope of feeling good again eventually.

When he went out at noon he found Tiza under the limbali listening to Musinga play his likembe. Musinga's music was mournful to Kulu and he had no appetite. He sat down beside Tiza and closed his eyes.

"Your eyes are closed," Tiza said to him, "but you see better now than you did yesterday with them open."

"Aye." Kulu sighed.

"Come tonight for supper," Tiza said.

That evening he did something he never had done before. He rolled up his white smock carefully and left the compound. When he was out of sight of the compound, he put it on. As he came to Tiza's shamba he saw Vudi bending over the cooking fire, her face burnished by its glow, and he had a mad impulse to turn and flee. But he went on, his heart knocking. Tiza and Yuki greeted him and then Yuki introduced Vudi, her cousin. Vudi smiled at him and looked away.

"Your cousin?" Kulu said stupidly to Yuki and couldn't think of anything to say to Vudi. He said little all evening, in fact, not even when Vudi talked shyly.

When he left, Tiza walked a way with him along the road. "Your eyesight has improved, Kulu," he said, "but now it's your voice that has failed. Let's hope you can still hear. For listen to me. Vudi is much sought after and can bring her father a fine price whenever she wishes."

"Aieee!" Kulu wailed suddenly.

"Then you can hear," Tiza said. "Are you poor?"

"I am rich," Kulu said, grinding his teeth.

"How rich?"

"I don't know. I give most of my earnings to Madami and she keeps them for me. She tells me from time to time how much it is, but I never remember."

"Then you are rich enough to—"

"I suddenly do not like this buying of women," Kulu said.

[234]

"Neither do I," said Tiza. "But it's the custom. And some customs cannot be changed between sunset and dawn, as the Bwana says."

"As the Assistant Bwana says, you mean."

"All right," Tiza said genially. "But to me he is the Bwana. So do you not wish to speak to Vudi?"

"Yes, I wish to speak to Vudi," Kulu cried. "But I have great responsibilities. I have Madami and the mtoto that's coming. I have no time for wives and shambas."

"Vudi will not take up your time like a country girl. Vudi is like Yuki. She knows you're the most important person in Dibela next to Madami and the Bwana. She is interested in God. Next seventh day she plans to come and begin learning how to worship Him. Vudi is interested in you, Kulu."

"Aieee!" he wailed again. "Tell her to wait until after the mtoto comes."

"Now you're being sensible," Tiza said and turned back home.

They needed the Bwana Doctor as badly as ever, but it was good to see that the people finally understood the things Madami could do and the things she could not do. It was good to see the school raised and the people attending classes. It was good to go there on the seventh day to worship God.

He remembered with nostalgia the days when he had thought he'd seen God the Father and Jesus the Christ under the limbali. He never saw Them now. He believed in Them as much as ever, he knew They were here. But he knew he could not see Them or others would have seen Them too and mentioned it to him. For he was like others, he knew. If he tried very hard he might pretend he saw Them again, but it was foolish to pretend. He didn't mean to have pretended in the past, and if it had been merely pretending it was still a good thing to remember, even as it was good to remember the summits of the mountains where he knew he never would climb again.

The Assistant Bwana brought a meaning to the seventh day that had not existed before he came. The Assistant Bwana believed in ceremony as a way to talk to God and live close to Him. And Kulu admitted to himself that ceremony was better than the old wild, chance talking to God. There was prayer, both silent and spoken, in which your spirit sought His. There was preaching, in which you learned how to live like Him. There was song, in which you praised Him joyfully. There was the church itself, the Church of Dibela, a society powerful though in no sense secret. You became a member by choice and acceptance and entered it with ceremony. It would have been easy for the Assistant Bwana to let in many, like a stampeding herd of zebra, Kulu knew. But he was not in a hurry. He started with a dozen, of whom Kulu was one, and he invited others as they showed genuine interest. This again was wise, Kulu admitted to himself, as it was wise of antelope leaders not to let their herds despoil a watering place. And within the church were the fine ceremonies of the three important events of a man's life: birth and marriage and death, those times when God's presence was so essential.

Yes, it was all good. But sometimes he wished he could find the Assistant Bwana wrong so that he could scorn him, as he had scorned him on the day of his arrival after he had fear-sickness on the way. The memory of that had faded from people's minds as the changes came. It was true, of course, that he had been ill with fever. But it also was true, as everyone in Kalina knew, that he had cried out in fear when he imagined he heard a lion. It was difficult to scorn him just for that, Kulu knew. Yet if he could scorn him it would be easier to remember the Bwana Doctor. Sometimes it seemed the Bwana Doctor never would return.

Kulu thought constantly of the mtoto. He waited and Madami waited and all Dibela waited for the coming of the child. The people came often to see Madami now: Father Gilo; and the Bwana Administrator, accompanied always by the Madami Administrator, who brought many packages and was much excited by the advent of the mtoto; and even the white planter and his big white wife, also bringing gifts. Sometimes the tension was almost more than the Assistant Bwana could bear, for he was everywhere now, in and out of the hospital and pacing up and down, urging Madami to lie down and rest until she laughed at him. It must have been like this, Kulu thought, when Christ was born, with the wise people coming from afar by elephant and zebra, and the goatherds inquiring, as the people of Dibela inquired, and Father Joseph pacing nervously, like the Assistant Bwana, while Mother Mary was as calm and sure that all would be well as was Madami herself.

Late one afternoon, when it was raining hard, Madami walked slowly to the hospital carrying a small bag. She hung up her raincoat on the customary peg, and when she turned to Kulu, her face was pale and drawn. She tried to smile.

"Now, Madami?" Kulu asked.

"I think so, Kulu."

He could scarcely hear her, for she spoke in a low voice and the rain was loud.

She lay down in the operating room, as planned. And, as planned, everyone took his place. Mzimba stood at the door to keep out the curious. Guta began heating unnecessarily large amounts of water. Kosongo joined Kulu. Musinga, as everyone had expected, ran off through the rain toward the palaver house, shouting, "The mtoto is coming to Madami!"

They had not reckoned with the Assistant Bwana, however. He came squish-squishing in, having forgotten his raincoat, and stood there, dripping rain, his eyes large, crying, "Where is she?" Then he lunged into the operating room and knelt beside Madami's cot and took her hand in both of his. His face was wet with rain, of course, but Kulu, standing nearby, saw that there were tears in his eyes too, and he wished he could scorn him for his tears. But he could not. Madami saw his tears too, and she looked at him strangely. Then they spoke in their own English tongue until Madami's face twitched with pain and she told him to go.

The people streamed to the hospital. They made a path for Chief Buderga, who strode up in his great goatskin cape, and demanded entrance. Mzimba quailed before him, but Kulu went to the door and told the Chief that Madami said he must go home and sit by his wife. Then the drum-talker appeared. The Bwana Administrator had told him he was to send the word when the child was near, but Madami had told him he was not to send any word until she personally ordered it. What should he do? Come inside and wait, Kulu told him.

The Assistant Bwana came back, wearing his raincoat this time, and smoking his pipe. It was forbidden to smoke in the hospital, as the Assistant Bwana well knew, but he sat down at Madami's desk and smoked his pipe and no one dared forbid it. For he looked very angry now, as he never had looked before, and every time there was any sound, he started and then sank back.

So darkness fell and the rain continued its incessant drumming. No one spoke and the alarm clock on Madami's desk ticked. No one ate or even thought of eating. They simply waited. Kulu stood by Madami's cot, mindful of everything and unafraid because he was mindful. The rain fell and the drum-talker dozed on the floor and the clock ticked its hands around until a new day was beginning.

The spasms of Madami's pain were more frequent now and falling at regular intervals by the clock. This was as it was supposed to be. Her face was white, her eyes closed, and sweat poured from her. Suddenly she cried out. She cried out again and gasped something to Kulu in her own tongue. It did not matter, for he knew the birth had begun and he knew what he was doing.

[237]

It was over quite suddenly. He held the mtoto by the heels and the mtoto began to cry.

Madami's eyes were wide open now and she said something in her own tongue again and Kulu smiled and nodded to her. He handed the mtoto to Kosongo and opened the door and said to the drum-talker, who was wide awake and standing now:

"A son is born to Madami in Dibela."

XXIV

ONE DAY, shortly after he came to Dibela, Caleb saw a lean pariah dog attack a small wobbly pup. The pup was too small to run or fight and it simply stood cowering before the big dog's unprovoked attack. Caleb picked up a stone and hurled it at the attacking dog. He missed and picked up another stone and rushed at the dog, kicking at it. The dog ran off and the pup looked at Caleb. He spoke kindly to it and walked on. Looking back, he saw the pup was wobbling after him. He paused and asked people in the huts nearby whose pup this was. No one knew the answer to this surprising question. So Caleb picked up the pup and tucked it under his arm and carried it back to the compound.

The pup was a male. Caleb named him Job because he was a patient pup. Job grew into a dog, his dog, in a country where most dogs seemed to belong to no one. He had no breed. He was simply a brownish, wiry, tough, intelligent, dignified dog who loved Caleb and only tolerated others. Wanga, who trained Job to hunt, reported that he was a good hunter. Except when Wanga borrowed him, Job was almost constantly with Caleb.

A dog's life in Dibela, Caleb sometimes thought as he looked down at Job. For his own life here had the same cycles as Job's—except for hunting and mating. He read a great deal when he was not engaged in the work of the mission. That is, he reread once he had exhausted the books that were available. And, interestingly, he read the Bible. For he knew that most clergymen do not really read the Bible; they use it as a student uses a library, as a source to support theories they hope are true. Yet he read it as people in lonely places always have read it, as demonstrable truth itself.

In the evening he'd sit on the small porch of his cottage, puffing at his pipe, a book in his lap, Job at his feet. He was still a young man, but he lived now as an old man. He tried not to let it trouble him. For what could he do about it? This was the life he had chosen. He saw signs of progress in the people, which was, after all, the most he could hope for in his work; he could not seize the staggeringly great problems of all Africa and shake them into shape; he could only try to bring some enlightenment to this microcosm, Dibela.

Yet sometimes he longed for—what, he wondered, would you call it? A personal life. He came of a certain culture, he believed in a certain creed. Much as he admired Father Gilo, he was not Father Gilo. He did not want to be. He was Caleb Aldrich, and Aldrich men always had married and had children and lived close to the land and fought in wars. Now his nation was involved in a great war, but he was not in it; he was thrust away off here without, it sometimes seemed, either a personal or a national identity. He had loved Nancy, and Nancy was dead. Occasionally this image of himself was unbearably clear.

It was so this evening. The air was pellucid, the light was blue. It was as if the world were under a bell jar, with figures as immobile as the waxen figurines used to be under the domed glass in his grandmother's musty sacrosanct parlor. Here he sat, and over there in her bungalow sat Rachel, and forming the third point of an equilateral triangle towered the limbali. Landscape with figures. The world under glass.

He glanced from Job, the dog at his feet, to Job, the sufferer, in the Bible open on his lap. "How should a man be just with God? . . . If I say I will forget my complaint, I will leave off my heaviness, and comfort myself: I am afraid of all my sorrow, I know that thou wilt not hold me innocent. If I be wicked, why then labor I in vain?"

The baby suddenly yelled. Paul Wilton, Jr., yelled for nourishment. Caleb stirred. That was what he meant by a personal life. He wanted to be over there. He'd be over there all the time if he followed his instinct. And then he was thinking of Wilton, Senior, again. When he thought too much about Wilton, Senior, he found it hard to believe in the fellow's existence. Which was, Caleb knew, ridiculous and a sign that he wished Wilton did not exist.

She was married, wasn't she, and the mother of the fellow's child? The evidence was plainly here. Henri Lecomte, whom he'd questioned with casual care, had been guarded; he didn't seem to care much for the fellow.

But Lecomte had married them. Once, many months ago, Rachel had asked him to get something from her desk in the bungalow and there, left carelessly on the desk, had been her wedding certificate. He had not meant to spy. The fact he had looked at it troubled him. When he returned to the hospital with the thing Rachel wanted, he'd remarked to her that she'd left the wedding certificate on the desk and gently chided her for carelessness with an important document. She hadn't answered him. She'd merely stared at him strangely and then walked out of the hospital. She was gone for some time, doubtless putting the paper in a safe place.

Paul Wilton, Jr., yelled again in the bungalow over there. Caleb stood up suddenly and knocked out his pipe. He went down the steps and strode across the compound, Job trotting beside him. He did not know his purpose in going. He simply wanted to see her.

She did not see or hear him at once. She was nursing the child, her dark head inclined as she looked down at the small face nuzzling her full breast. She was smiling and humming tunelessly.

I shouldn't be here, he thought dimly. He started to back away, when she looked up. She smiled at him. "Hel-*lo*," she said, meaning, What are you doing here? She was not self-conscious. That was one of the wonderful things about her. But he was.

"Good evening, Rachel." He dropped into a chair.

Slowly, as she looked at him, her face flushed. She sensed his self-consciousness. He never had been present when she nursed the child. She turned and glanced over a shoulder at him. There was surprise and something else—confusion—on her face. The impersonal breast of motherhood, so natural to her here in Africa, was not impersonal now.

"I just dropped by," he said lamely.

She still looked over her shoulder at him as the baby sucked noisily.

"I suddenly got sick and tired of sitting over there reading," he said. He groped in his pocket for his pipe and took it out and looked at it with a surprised expression, as if a pipe were a new invention.

She smiled faintly, and the baby was quiet again in her arms.

"I've read everything once and I've read everything twice." He began exploring another pocket for his tobacco pouch. He forced a smile. "I'm like a child with nothing to do."

"So you've come to me to learn what you should do." Her tone was so dry that he felt relieved. Dryness was a quality that always made him feel at ease.

[240]

"To you, the earth-mother." The ease with which he said it, his first really personal remark to her, surprised him.

She caught it. She looked around at him quickly and smiled. "The earth-mother," she said. "I like that. I guess that's what I'd like to be—now."

He began filling his pipe. "What needs doing in Dibela now, Rachel?"

She didn't answer him. She laid the baby in her lap and buttoned her blouse and turned to him. Lifting the baby, she carried him over a shoulder to the net-covered crib which Mzimba had built.

Paul Wilton, Jr., fixing Caleb with his large blue eyes, laughed and waved both arms over his mother's shoulder at him. "Bara dara gyuk," he called. Approximately.

Caleb waved and replied in similar language. The baby yelled gleefully and began squirming.

"Here," Rachel said to Caleb, "Hold him, will you, while I fix this thing."

He rose and took Paulie from her. They chatted vigorously in the baby's special language while Rachel rearranged the crib.

"I think it's Arabic you're teaching him," Caleb said while the baby fingered his chin. "Why don't you teach him Swahili?"

Rachel turned, looking up at him seriously. "It's time he spoke some English."

"He's only six months," Caleb said.

"Six months and thirteen days," she said, "and all he talks is this gibberish." She looked critically at Paulie's beautifully proportioned head. "I hope he's all right. Well, I know he is. But I mean I wish he'd learn to say just one intelligible word. The men spoil him. Every time I come in, one of them is down on all fours with him, chattering Swahili and howling with laughter. They think he's speaking English or French, I do believe. The poor child must be utterly confused." She took Paulie and he began to wail.

"Let me hold him," Caleb said. "Just for a little while."

She looked at him steadily. "All right," she said at last. "Just for a little while."

He sat down and took off his steel-banded wristwatch and dangled its brightness into Paulie's clutching hands. "What's he going to be when he grows up?" he asked, looking down at him.

"I don't know." Her voice was strained; she looked away. "Be a friend to Buderga's son, who's two months younger. Be a friend to the child of Kulu and Vudi who's on the way. That's what I hope."

"You want him to be a citizen of Africa, then?" he asked.

"A citizen of the world, I hope," she replied. She smiled wryly. "That sounds just idealistic enough, doesn't it, to come from a mother and a—a missionary?"

"Yes. But you want him to grow up here?"

She nodded. "I do."

"Not a very solid background," Caleb said, "for one who may end up wanting to run the best automobile agency in—say—Trenton, New Jersey."

"I hope he never wants that." She sounded worried. "But if he does, I think Africa will have been the best place for him to grow up."

"So you plan to stay here?" He looked at her.

"I certainly do."

"And you expect Dr. Wilton will join you out here?"

She looked down and her fingers plucked at her skirt. "I don't know what he wants to do after the war," she said in a low voice. "But I know what I want to do." Rising suddenly, she took the baby from Caleb and placed him in his crib, drawing the netting tightly about it. She seemed to take a long time to light the lamp. "You asked me a question a while ago."

He lighted his pipe, watching her above the flaming match. "Yes. I asked you, Rachel, what needs doing in Dibela now?"

"Let me fence with you, Caleb. What do you think?"

"Well," he said slowly, "not just more religion. We obviously need a doctor. Eventually we've got to get a doctor here. But it may take years, depending on how long this war lasts. Could I somehow be of more help in the hospital?"

She shook her head. "You've been a great help there, taking a lot off me. But you have the school. And that's very important. And you have the church. And that's very important."

"We can extend the school and the church eventually if we can raise the money to pay the teachers," he said. "There are at least a half-dozen coming along brilliantly who can be sent out to other villages in a year or so. If we can get the money to pay them. But what interests me is where we're heading. I can visualize having a really first-rate school for teachers here in a couple of years. So they will go out and teach the people to read and write and be hygienic and learn some simple carpentry. In short, discover the wheel and believe in God and live sanitary lives. But when the people can read, what are they going to read? And when they can write, to whom will they write and how will it be communicated? And when they can build a wooden house, will it really be a better house than a hut of mud and straw?"

She looked at him oddly. At last she said, "I never thought of it."

"You never thought of what?"

"The—" she raised her hands and gestured outward—"the distant future. When I came here there was nothing and it was so long before I could get anything going. Now it really is going, even though we still lack a doctor. But it's going and I—I never think of the ending." She leaned toward him. "You—you interest me, Caleb. For a year now I've had you marked as a—a man of strong faith who never questions certain basic things. I thought, for instance, that you felt it was enough if people were—converted to Christianity. But now you say, in a way, what does it profit one to believe in God if—if—" She gestured helplessly.

"I'm not saying that a man and his family must have a bicycle and a sewing machine and a phonograph and a cottage—those things the *evolués* down country first strive for—in order to make a belief in God pay off. I don't mean there's an economic pay-off in religious belief. I detest that idea so much that it's one reason I wanted to leave America. But here in Africa we see the same patterns taking shape as we come in *civilizing* and—and sowing all those complex seeds that may be reaped some day when this becomes known as the bloody instead of the dark continent. Africa no longer is the dark continent of the imagination. We're seeing to that. But aren't we in danger of making it the *frustrated* continent and so, eventually, the bloody continent? Well, my question is rhetorical, because that's just what we're in danger of doing. And how can we prevent it? Certainly we aren't just going to pull out. We've come this far and if we pulled out tomorrow—every last one of us whites—it would be a mess here with the technological vestiges we left behind. Wars and disease and famine again. So we're staying. But what are we staying *for*?"

He realized he was leaning forward intensely, his voice raised sharply. He sank back in his chair. "I didn't mean to rant."

"You're not." Her eyes were fixed brightly on his. "It does me good to listen. I've never heard you— Well, it does me good because—maybe because I'm a woman and women don't usually study the ends of civilization. You make me think about things I haven't in a long time and never did think about very clearly. You must have thought a lot about it."

"Not enough," he said. "I've been sitting over there on that porch too long. I'm getting lazy. So what needs doing here? Just here in Dibela and this country hereabouts, I mean, which is the small bit of Africa's

[243]

future over which you and I have any control. Let's forget for a moment the formal worship of God and the practice of medicine and education. As I see it, we've got to think about economics. Being whites, we have to think in terms of economic *progress,* because that's all we know, and you can't offer something you know nothing about yourself. Here's what I mean. The men complain that game is increasingly scarce in the land. The women complained last season of poorer crops."

So he began to talk about the land, drawn quite out of himself. He must have been thinking about it more than he'd realized, but he never would have expressed it (or, heaven knew, ever tried to do anything about it, he often thought later) if it had not been for Rachel. She inspired him that evening. Her eyes, her parted lips, her nursing of the child—all these (he thought later) were what he meant by a *personal* life again. And without a personal life no one ever gave much thought to the land.

He had questions and theories, but he lacked the answer to anything—yet. The land was changing. So-called civilization was nibbling at the fringes of the country and so-called savagery at its heart. With the cessation of tribal wars and the introduction of medicine, more and more people were trying to live on less and less land. He had been raised on a farm and now he'd plunge his hands in the earth again. Why, for instance, weren't there cattle here when cattle could do more than anything else to raise the standard of living? Did anybody positively know that the tsetse fly existed around Dibela, since it was obvious there was no sleeping sickness? Well, he was personally going to find out. Yes, standards of living was what they had to think about, for only standards of living could determine the eventual value of all their medicine and education. Certainly other problems would be raised. But at least they wouldn't be the old problems of savagery that Rachel found when she first came here.

"Does any of this make any sense to you?" he finally asked her.

"More sense than you realize, Caleb." She was looking at him with an expression he never had seen on her face before.

After Caleb left that evening, she rolled Paulie's crib into her bedroom and snuffed the candle and undressed in the dark. She started to pull on her nightgown and then she paused. Reaching to the bedside table, she relighted the candle and slowly faced the small imperfect mirror on the wall. She saw a part of a woman, an imperfect reflection in the dim light. Looking down at her naked body, whole and perfect, she slowly ran her hands over her hips. Turning quickly, she blew out the candle and pulled her nightgown over her head and swung into bed. She did not fall asleep. She lay there thinking of the lie.

In the months that followed she thought of it every day. Caleb constantly reminded her of it. He would come toward her, smiling, saying, "Rachel . . ." and there would be something in the way he looked at her or a slight inflection in his voice that reminded her she was caught in the prison of her own lie.

Sometimes she felt that he loved her. And she knew he would not tell her as long as he believed she was married; he clung tenaciously to probity. As some men sought physical danger, he sought virtue; it was his Everest, his Mountains of the Moon. His very presence in Africa proved that he sought the dangerous life of a true morality: he wished to be dedicated to a disinterest in himself. And if she confessed she was not married? It would violate his moral sensibilities and shatter his respect for her. How could she continue to work daily with one whose respect she had lost? Possibly he would understand and pity her. That would be worse. And why should she confess? She did not love him.

As the months crept into years, she learned the meaning of impersonality. She tried to learn that one had only one day to live, today, and not to think of the future. She devoted herself to Paulie as he learned to walk and talk and effortlessly molded a child's personality from his shapeless infancy. And she never ceased thinking of Paul, writing regularly no matter how infrequent his letters. He was in France now, a lieutenant colonel in the United States Army after his transfer from the R.A.F. She forced herself not to remember him as he was in Dibela or to imagine what he would be like when the long war was over. Rather, she always tried to think of him today: What is he doing today? Where is he? How is he? Is he thinking of me? His letters were the most valued events in her life, she believed.

But sometimes, on the very day she'd received one of his letters, she would forget about him for hours when the activities of the hospital and the mission pressed on her. Paul was personal and Caleb impersonal. But Paul was far away and Caleb was here in Dibela, and Caleb's activities always interested her and sometimes excited her.

He had turned to the land. He borrowed books and government pamphlets on tropical agriculture from Henri Lecomte and he interrogated Ducasse, who actually knew something about the tropic land, and he drove to the north and the south gathering information from other white farmers. He obtained the seeds of a rare clover from a government agricultural station and set about proving to the people of Dibela that the soil was not inexhaustible. In the past, when a patch of soil was exhausted, they had simply turned over a new field with stone mattocks, quarreling and finally arbitrarily settling to whom this and that patch belonged. Now he demonstrated, with his precious clover, that soil could be replenished. He struggled against the prejudices of centuries when he insisted that rotation of crops was necessary.

It was slow work. It would not be completed in their lifetimes, he and Rachel agreed. "But there are signs," he said occasionally, "of that thing called progress." As the seasons passed he was aided by the fact that game was growing scarcer. It troubled the men. They were a meat-eating people, and each season there was less meat and less hunting. Yet the land remained, the Assistant Bwana kept telling them, and they gradually listened to him.

There had been a time, not long ago, when it was beneath a man's dignity to work in the fields. Yet the Assistant Bwana—a man of great dignity, everyone agreed—worked in the fields. It was as if the whole country were one great shamba to him, for he went everywhere, talking to everyone, clearing brush and wielding mattock and sowing seeds. He seemed to spring across the earth, pausing often to break its richness in his fingers.

He was taken up by many things besides the school and the church. He was taken up by coffee trees and that strange tree brought from the far places, the eucalyptus. He planted some on the mission shamba, which lay beyond the compound, adjoining the new cottage where Kulu and Vudi lived with their new son, Vanga. He planted both the unshaded variety of coffee tree and the variety which required shade. Among the shaded variety of bushes he set out eucalyptus trees. The men watched with interest and began to work with him, for he told them that if the trees prospered every shamba in the countryside should eventually have some coffee trees. The coffee berries and the oil of eucalyptus could be bartered in Rugeri, he explained, thereby arousing much speculation over the possibility of bartering for bicycles such as the one Wanga had obtained. But the days of barter in coffee berries and eucalyptus oil lay far ahead, if they ever would be realized, for trees grew slowly and trees might die.

No single effort contained him long. He was forever bursting out of one limitation into another without losing interest in his original efforts. From crop rotation to trees to cattle. He told Rachel that he was frankly dubious whether coffee trees would thrive. But he never lost his enthusiasm about cattle. Especially after the results of his great tsetse-fly hunt. Somehow, to Rachel's surprise, he aroused the enthusiasm of the people by offering the prize of a goat to the first person who brought him one of the two specimens of the brownish insect banded or mottled with darker marking which are called *Glossina palpalis* and *Glossina morsitans*. Hundreds of men, women and children wandered through the bush catching thousands of insects which they brought to the hospital. With a French book of etymology before him he studied the insects night after night by lamplight. After nearly a month he announced to Rachel he was convinced the country was free of any species of tsetse fly that could transmit sleeping sickness among humans or nagana disease among domestic animals.

But how, he asked rhetorically, could they be sure until they obtained some cattle? He began a correspondence with government agriculturalists in various parts of the Congo, learning much about cattle without ever seeing a cow, he ruefully told Rachel. Finally he declared he was going to buy a couple of cows and a bull from a white farmer up near Irumu. But no truck was available to transport the cattle. So, with the aid of Mzimba and Wanga and Kulu, he fashioned a two-wheeled trailer after removing the rear wheels from his Chevrolet. Then he and Wanga and Kulu drove off toward Irumu. They were not seen again for three days, while Rachel worried. And then Wanga appeared alone in the car and reported that the Bwana (everybody had stopped calling him the Assistant Bwana by this time) and Kulu were twenty kilometers down the road leading one cow. It turned out that the white farmer had changed his mind about selling any cattle, but after Caleb had pestered him for a full day the farmer had consented to sell one, apparently just to get rid of this mad American missionary. On the road from Rugeri, despite Caleb's cautious driving, the trailer had slithered off the road and collapsed, pitching the terrified cow into the brush. At first they'd thought she'd broken a leg, but when she got to her feet she scampered off agilely enough. They finally caught her and saw the hopelessness of repairing the trailer. So Wanga put the precious Chevrolet wheels in the back seat of the Ford and Caleb and Kulu started walking home to Dibela. The next afternoon, a bright day with the sun warming the compound, they trudged in surrounded by at least two hundred chattering Africans who were excited by this lean, brown, tough animal they never had seen before.

"Nothing comes easy in this country," Caleb said cheerfully to Rachel. "But it comes." And he went off to admire his cow.

She watched him go. Paulie trotted behind him calling, "Bwana, Bwana, wait, wait, I comey, I comey," until Caleb paused and picked him up and set him astraddle his neck, while Job, the dog, danced around them excitedly. Above the heads of the milling people Paulie saw the cow standing at the end of the tether which Kulu held. "Bwana, Bwana," yelled Paulie, pulling at Caleb's hair, and then, "Kulu, Kulu," crying to him in Swahili while Kulu and a score of others grinned and called to the Mtoto Bwana on the shoulders of the Bwana.

Watching them from the porch, she felt close to tears. Such an incident as the arrival of the cow should bring a sense of completion. The man was back, his goal achieved after some trouble, and the child rode gleefully on his shoulders while she stood here. If only the man were Paul. But Paul never would have bothered with any of the things that Caleb did; Paul didn't understand these things as she and Caleb understood them.

She raised her eyes to the clouds feathering the upper flanks of the mountains. It seemed so long ago that she had climbed there. And the day would come when it would seem so long ago that Caleb brought home the cow. Time worked great changes here, but it could not work the great completion. This, she thought despairingly, is thahu. This is the mystery and the curse: time and change, but never completion.

"Hey, Rachel!" Caleb shouted. "Come look at the cow."

She went slowly, the people making a way for her. There was the cow, poor baffled creature. There was Paulie, clinging to Caleb's leg and the scruff of Job's neck while he stared at the cow. And there was Caleb, not handsome, as she had come to remember Paul as handsome. But strong, in a way Paul was not. Earth and weather had worked on him. He loved the earth, and earth reciprocated with strength.

"Here she is," he said to Rachel. "The new cow. I think we'd better not give her a name. If we ever decided to butcher her I couldn't eat a bite if she had a name. . . ."

He came for dinner that evening, Job padding behind him. She was not as intensely aware of him as she always had been aware of Paul's presence. No, she thought, there was not an intensity in his presence any more than the shades of dawn or nightfall were marked by intensity. But if being with him was like being in dawn or nightfall, it was much lighter—or much darker—now.

She fussed with Paulie's food until her maternalism irritated her and she ceased. It seemed that she was looking down on all three of them, viewing the domesticity of the scene: man, woman and child at table. Its falsity suddenly choked her. Yet she had willed it thus. Could this be thahu? Thahu! She had long since dropped it from her thoughts, she told herself, and yet here today it returned hauntingly.

She was looking at Caleb's strong hands, his tanned face. She did not want to look at him. Rising suddenly and finding herself standing with no errand, she began fumbling with the lamp. He looked at her in surprise. It was not dark enough to light the lamp. She lighted it anyway.

"More cheerful," she said sharply.

He knew that something was troubling her. But he could not remotely realize what it was. He had trained himself not to realize. Yet now it suddenly seemed she had not been able to train herself. That was the curse.

She scarcely listened to him, and after a while he stopped talking. They finished dinner in silence and she put Paulie to bed. It was dark then. He was lighting his pipe when they heard the drum. He raised his head, listening, the match flaming unheeded until it burned his fingers and he dropped it with an exclamation.

They went to the porch. Kulu came out of his cottage, followed by Vudi carrying Vanga. "I'll find out what the message is, Bwana," he called.

Now the Dibela drum-talker was answering the distant drum. They listened silently, uncomprehending. Soon they heard shouting.

"I'm going down to the palaver house and see what it is," Caleb said.

"I'll go with you." She called to Guta to stay with Paulie and went down the steps after Caleb. In the darkness she took his arm.

They had gone only a few steps, with Job following at their heels, when they heard the sound of running and Kulu called, "Bwana! Madami! The big war is ended. We have won the big war and it's ended!"

She clutched Caleb's arm convulsively. So it was over. They had lived to the end of something. There was, after all, a completion. Now Paul would—what? Why didn't she laugh or cry? In all the cities and towns of the Western world people must be laughing and crying for joy. But she stood here in the insect-ringing darkness without any sense of completion, neither laughing nor crying.

"Is it not good news, Madami?" She could not see Kulu's face in the darkness, but she heard his tone. A doubtful tone actually. The ideologies of this war were vague to him. But he remembered that the end of the war meant the Bwana Doctor would return. Once that had been the good toward which he lived. It still was. Wasn't it?

[249]

When she did not answer him, Caleb said, "Of course it's good news, Kulu. It's great news."

But Kulu said, "Madami?"

It was nearly two months since she'd heard from Paul in France. And it was much longer since Kulu had asked about the Bwana Doctor.

"It's very good news, Kulu," she said.

Of course it was good news for the world. It was the completion of something for the world. But was it the completion of anything for her?

"Yes, Madami, it's very good news."

But Kulu's tone was troubled. He was thinking of the Bwana Doctor and his allegiance to the new Bwana. He didn't ask now about Paul because he was waiting for her to say that the Bwana Doctor would return soon. And Caleb waited too.

She merely needed to say, "The Bwana Doctor will be back soon now." Yet she couldn't bring herself to say the words. It would be one more lie, and she was tired of lies.

Caleb said suddenly, "Let's tell the people that we'll gather at the church, Kulu. We'll light torches and sing songs and give thanks to God."

XXV

THE ROAD to Dibela seemed a little longer to Henri Lecomte on each journey. It was a much improved road, too, since the day when Rachel first went there. It was more traveled and carefully tended by the road menders, for Rachel and Caleb Aldrich had brought Dibela into the world. The trouble, Lecomte ruefully told himself, was not with the road; it was with him. He was getting old.

On that day just one month after the war ended in the Pacific, as Lecomte rode toward Dibela, his bones ached. It was a general rather than a specific ache. It would go. But it would return. Eventually, when it no longer left him, he would be a very old man.

But take heart, old bush-happy fool, he thought. There are a good many years left in you yet. And you won't spend them in the dank mists and freezing rains of Brussels; you won't creep miserably along the sands of Cannes in the annual two weeks of winter sun your miserable pension would afford you. They were going to depose him by retirement in a few months, but they could not eject him from Africa like a spent cartridge. Even Marie, who for so many years had pretended to detest Africa, had agreed at last. They would stay. They had selected their land south of Rugeri. If not Lecomte, District Administrator, then Lecomte, farmer, savant, philosopher.

He smiled as the car rattled across the bridge and sped toward Dibela. He had a mission in going on this beautiful day. Also, he wanted to tell them the good news: though deposed in Rugeri, he would continue to reign nearby.

He glimpsed the mountains far ahead, and then he closed his eyes and thought of Rachel and Caleb. What a tragic pair! To be always together and yet never joined. To be always in each other's presence and yet never intimate. What an unnatural state for a naturally good, strong, passionate man and woman. What an unholy mess holy Christians could make of their lives.

Oh, he saw their awareness of each other. But to him their awareness was a martyrdom. To be assigned to Dibela with Rachel, as Caleb had been assigned, to look on her beauty and strength daily, as Caleb looked each day, and then to believe the beauty and strength untouchable would be a bittersweet misery inconceivable to the designers of hell themselves. For Rachel did not age and weaken and wilt; she grew more beautiful, like some strange and everlasting plant of the deep forests. Caleb, if aware of his martyrdom, never mentioned it. Apparently there were dimensions to the American character that De Tocqueville himself had failed to assess.

And what of her? Somehow she had refused to assess Caleb's strength. No, she'd assessed it all right, but somehow she had managed to refuse to make his strength hers. How she had refused and still retained her serenity was incredible. But she had gone on, at least with outward serenity, apparently believing that everything somehow eventually would end happily for Paul and her. Ah, these Americans. Such strength and beauty and vast dimensions of character; veritable lions, but lions sometimes frightened by the smallest, most harmless mice. Whence came their mouselike ideas?

Given a European woman in Rachel's circumstances— But then no European woman would so quixotically bear a child; she would have nailed the man. Only a Puritan woman would have done as Rachel did. And apparently the Puritans, by some obverse process, were the most

[251]

romantic of souls. For Rachel had been acting romantically for some years now in ignoring the reality of Caleb and clinging to the myth of Paul. A European woman, in Rachel's circumstances, would not have indulged in such nonsense. She'd have taken Caleb. And the lie about her marriage?

Lecomte, jouncing along the road to Dibela, raised a hand and snapped his fingers. Pouf! All men were understanding, especially Caleb. It must be the lie that troubled her more than the fact of the bastard son. Yes, it was the lie and the sense that she had sinned and so must be punished for her sin; if no one else would punish her, she would punish herself. Oh, the terrible tragedy of these Puritans, so easily resolved by a small frank conversation. He had been tempted many times to try to bring it about. But he never had dared, he never would try it now. They were too moral; and a small frank conversation seemed almost impossible between moralists.

So, dozing, thinking, muttering to himself, pulling at his scraggly mustache and snapping his fingers in the air, Henri Lecomte came to Dibela that day.

Rachel, looking out from the hospital, saw him climbing stiffly from his car. She hurried out to greet him as Paulie raced from the house, shouting the first French phrase she had taught him, "Monsieur Lecomte, comment ça va? Comment ça va, Monsieur Lecomte?" He flung himself upon Lecomte and the old man caught him strongly under the arms and swung him into the air as Paulie squealed with delight.

When he set him on the ground again Lecomte's eyes were dim with tears. "You are the one person to whom I speak English, Paulie," he said and handed him the bag of rock candy he'd bought at the Greek trader's.

"Rachel, it's good to see you," he said in French, extending his hand to hers. "As beautiful as always. Marie sends her best. This morning she had one of her rare strokes of genius. She was struck by a divine idea, one that brought me here in a hurry."

Rachel smiled at him. "What is that, Henri?"

"We shall come to it." He looked down at Paulie, who was cramming candy into his mouth. "He looks more like his father every day."

Rachel glanced away at Caleb coming toward them from the schoolhouse.

"Like his father," Lecomte said cheerfully, "I believe he rotates around the world. The world does not rotate around him."

Rachel forced a smile. "He's a wanderer all right. I'm certain he has hairbreadth escapes from snakes and scorpions that I know nothing about. He's stung by wasps and spiders and exposed, I'm sure, to every germ of disease. But he's never ill. He's—durable."

Lecomte sighed. "It is good to be durable— Ah, Caleb." He turned and they shook hands. "I bring mail today."

Involuntarily Rachel extended a hand. Anything from *him?* Lecomte pretended not to notice as he turned to the driver for the mail. There was a letter from Phyllis Haricort. There was none from *him.*

"Come into the house," she said to Lecomte. "Come in, Caleb, and read your mail."

"Thanks," Caleb said, trailing behind them, tearing open an envelope.

She glanced back at Paulie walking beside him. The deep affection that joined them often troubled her. Merely seeing them together reminded her of Paul. Yet she took great care never to come between them. For she knew that even at his young age Paulie needed the companionship of a man of his own race. He needed a father, and Caleb was a father to him. Someday he would ask who his father actually was, and she did not know what she would tell him. But for the present Caleb —"Bwana" as Paulie called him—was the strong, kindly force that joined with Rachel and the men to give Paulie a sense of security.

"I'm being deposed in three months," Lecomte said, sinking into a chair. "Retirement."

"No!" she exclaimed. It would not be the same without him. He would go and someday Father Gilo would go. Eventually all of them would go. It was their country, but they could not stay. The work begun would languish or die or take another direction in different hands.

Lecomte smiled, savoring fully the extent of her regret. "But," he said, "we are only going down the road a little way. I'm going to be a rustic philosopher and complain about my few coffee trees that never bear."

"Oh, good!" She clapped her hands under her chin. "That's wonderful, Henri."

He grinned at Caleb, who stood with a letter open in a hand. "She's glad we aren't leaving, Caleb."

"And so am I." Caleb smiled at him. "I'm awfully glad, Henri."

"Meanwhile," Lecomte continued, "Marie and I at last have three weeks vacation. We're going to drive down through the game park to Goma and look at the beautiful lake and then take a boat down to Bukuvu and sit in a hotel like rich tourists. There's a little business I have in Bukuvu about the new farm and building the house. Then we shall return."

"It sounds like a wonderful trip," Rachel said.

"Would you like to go with us?" asked Lecomte.

She hesitated momentarily, and then she shook her head firmly. She'd love to go, she thought. But soon, almost any day now, surely she would hear something definite from *him*. "Thanks, Henri, no. I can't."

He sighed. "Then would you let us take Paulie with us? That is Marie's stroke of genius. That's why I'm here." He looked at Paulie, who leaned against Lecomte's knee, noisily sucking on candy and staring fixedly at him.

No, she thought. He must never be separated from me. Simply being with him always restored a sense of completion. If she had loved and could not love again, she at least had the child who brought not only the memory but the very attenuation of her love. And yet, she thought, even at his early age I may be setting out to destroy him and so to destroy myself by keeping him constantly with me.

"He never has been farther than Rugeri," Lecomte said gently. "It would be good for him to see something of the—outer world." He smiled sadly. "To say nothing of how good it would be for Marie and me. It would be, you see, as if we had a grandchild. Marie could tuck him in nights and fuss about his food. I could be a knowing god, telling him all kinds of fantastic things, some of them partially true. Old people alone make only passable travelers. But with a young child they become the best of travelers."

Paulie ground at his hard candy shatteringly, surely bent on breaking every tooth. "Ask him," Rachel said indistinctly to Lecomte.

"Paulie," Lecomte said in English, "would you like to go on a trip with Madame Lecomte and me?"

"Are you going to see any lions?" asked Paulie.

"If we don't see any in the park I'll have the King of Urundi send us one."

"Yes," Paulie cried. "I'll go. I'll get my gun and go."

"Paulie." Rachel leaned toward him. "You'll be gone many days."

His eyes widened. "For a moon?"

"Almost a moon."

"Are you going, Mama?"

"No."

He looked at Caleb. "You going, Bwana?"

"No, Paulie, I'm not going," Caleb said.

[254]

He chewed thoughtfully. "What else'll we see?" he asked Lecomte.

"We'll see elephants, hippos, zebra and all kinds of antelope. We'll cross the equator at seven thousand feet where the mountains are all shaped like giant cones."

"Yes, yes!" Paulie shouted, spitting out his candy in his excitement. "What else?"

"We'll see the land of smoking mountains, the volcanoes flaming in the night. And we'll swim in beautiful Lake Edward where there are no crocodiles to eat you. And then we'll ride on the lake, down through the beautiful green islands to the white city on the hills. And I'll send word to my old friend, the King of Urundi, and we'll drive out into his country, where the land turns purple at three o'clock in the afternoon and many of the people are giants seven feet tall and all the cows are sacred. And the King of Urundi will have his giant warriors perform a great dance for us and—"

"Yes," cried Paulie, "I'm going."

And much too quickly, to Rachel, he actually was going. His packed bag was beside the driver and he was sitting straight in the back seat beside Lecomte. He had kissed Rachel and the Bwana and said, " 'Bye." He shed no tears. He was looking for lions.

Lecomte rolled down the window and winked at them. "These old bones no longer ache," he said.

The car started away and the old man looked back and waved. But the boy stared ahead, intent on exploring Africa.

Finally Rachel could not see the car through her tears. "Sorry," she murmured, "sorry." She blinked and looked up at Caleb and cried, almost passionately, "But he does it so easily! He simply goes away and it doesn't seem to matter to him."

"I know," Caleb said. "I know." He touched her shoulder gently. She did not remember his doing that before. It was a gesture of sympathy and understanding, she knew. But somehow it troubled her, and she almost shrank from him.

She started toward the house and turned. He was looking at her with —yes, compassion was the word. And suddenly she didn't want his compassion. She just wanted—what?

"Oh, come sit on the porch with me," she said and walked on.

They sat in silence, looking toward the mountains. Doves murmured in the limbali and there was the heavy scent of lilies. He was a wise man. He did not probe. He gave her heart without seeming to propose to, as he sat there relaxedly, fingering his pipe.

"Rachel," he said suddenly, "will you teach me how to shoot a rifle?" She sat up alertly. "Why?"

"It's rather a long story, but I'll begin at the beginning and get to the point eventually. It begins with cows—our cow. She's doing fine, as you know. Thanks to your laboratory experience, she even gives Paulie tuberculin-tested milk. She's fat and prosperous and there are no tsetse flies on her. And, as you well know, the food supply, the economic situation, isn't getting any better here in Dibela. So I've decided it's time the economy had a shot in the arm. Underwent a real revolution, in fact. Well, I decided that a long time ago. But at last I've found the way. I'm bringing twenty head of cattle in here."

"But where are you getting them?" she exclaimed.

"From the agricultural station at Bilak."

"But that's a hundred and fifty miles north of here. How are you going to transport them?"

"I don't know," he said slowly. "Probably we'll have to walk them in. I'm not sure. All I know is that I've been pestering a fellow up there for over two years now, and just today a letter came from him saying it was now possible for the government to sell us twenty head. I've convinced them we're free of tsetse and they agree on what cattle can do here economically. Henri's been a tremendous help writing letters and throwing his administrative weight around. Well, we're getting the cattle, a mixed herd—"

"But twenty head of cattle," she said. "How are we ever going to pay for them?"

"Oh, that's taken care of."

"But how? The church would never—"

"Well, I'm paying for them. They're sort of my cattle, I guess, except that I'm not going to keep 'em. I've got a kind of New Harmony scheme of ownership for a while until we can increase the herd and move from socialism into private capitalism."

"You're paying for them! Are you that rich?"

He smiled. "Only temporarily. I've saved my salary. There's nothing to spend it on anyway. I told Henri about it while you were getting Paulie ready to go."

She looked at him wonderingly. "So you're going to—"

"Yes. I'm going to take Kulu and Kosongo, if you can spare them.

Wanga can drive us to Bilak. I know he hurt his leg when that jack broke last week. He can't walk any distance, but can he drive?"

"Certainly."

"We may have to drive the cattle home on foot. There may be some unpleasant country and I think I'd better take the rifle. So I'd better learn to use it in the next couple of days before we leave."

To teach him how to use the rifle, she thought. Kita had demanded that, and Kita had died. She must be thinking superstitiously. Yet it was not just the rifle that troubled her. There was something else vaguely disturbing in his proposal. He was a wise and gentle man who now wanted to do something that was, basically, alien to his experience. Just as Kita had wanted to do something alien to his experience.

"Well?" He looked at her questioningly.

She did not answer him.

"You don't approve the idea," he said.

She stirred. "I don't know," she said vaguely. "I understand the principle. Of bringing cattle here, I mean. But will it really work? Can twenty cattle be multiplied to a hundred? And what—"

"They can," he said firmly. "And we'll never know whether it will work until we try. And if we don't try, what do we have? We're left with hymn singing and treatment of the yaws."

"And what's wrong with that?" Her voice rose. "The missionary effort is not designed to revolutionize social order. It—"

"The missionary effort never was designed at all," he said. "It simply grew. It plays by ear and instinct. But one thing I'm sure of. We aren't here just to add one more group of people to the world's long relief rolls. And we aren't here just for the aggrandizement of our own souls, sending back reports on two hundred more converted to Christianity in Dibela and receiving barrels of cast-off clothing in return."

"I know," she said. "I said I understand the principle and I never can win an argument with you on principles. I'm simply saying that I feel you—you're doing something—alien to your experience when you undertake this. It troubles me somehow."

"Rachel," he said gently, "when you set out to climb the mountains—"

Her gaze fell and she plucked at her dress.

"We have to try and try to do the impossible," he said. "Why should it have been right for you to climb the mountains and wrong for me to bring cattle here? Each of us, in his own way—"

"It was not right for me to climb the mountains." She looked up at

[257]

him, trying to phrase the words that would explain exactly what she meant.

"Not right for you?" He stared at her. "What do you mean? Surely you don't mean you believe in that superstition about thahu."

"I think I rather half believe in it," she said measuredly. "I know that I'm a different person now than I was before I climbed the mountains."

"We're all different than we were a couple of years ago. We've lived and worked in Africa and—"

"And Africa has lived and worked on us because we're trying to change it." Instinctively she stretched a hand toward him. "Oh, Caleb, don't— don't—"

"Don't what?"

She buried her face in her hands and shook her head. "I don't know how to tell you. I can't tell you." At last she looked up at him and tried to smile. "I'll try to teach you what I know about the rifle."

That night she dreamed that she was chained in a cage under the limbali while around the cage paced Caleb, dressed in black sackcloth and reading from a small black book. Then she saw a small lion cub following Caleb. And then Caleb seemed to change into a black-maned lion and she into a lioness. Finally she saw and at last became a part of a pride of lions strolling across a yellow plain.

She awakened, startled, thinking she'd heard Paulie call to her. It was a long time before she slept again, and when she awakened next it was dawn. She rose and drew her robe around her and walked out to the porch. Red streamers flared westward in advance of the invisible sun, as if the mountains were on fire. To the north and west the plain rolled in amber light.

Caleb was right. They had to try and try to do the impossible. *I'm going with him,* she thought. *He needs me with him.*

He came out of his cottage at that moment, wearing a robe, and walked toward the shower.

" 'Morning," he called.

"Good morning, Caleb." She took a deep breath. "I'm riding to Bilak with you."

He paused and gaped at her in surprise. "But—"

"I'm going," she replied and went inside before he could say anything more.

XXVI

THE WESTLEY-RICHARDS .425 express rifle was a heavy gun, but it was the only rifle available. Doubtless Caleb would not have to use it, Rachel thought, yet he was wise to carry it. She tried to forget that to her the rifle was a symbol of something so vague she could not explain it. It had to do with violence in a gentle man, with action not altogether necessary. He had a vision of change, as she had had such a vision when she set out to climb the mountains. There was challenge and passion and love in such vision, but God save him the end of a sense of despair that had sometimes assailed her.

He took naturally to anything that he believed served a good purpose. As a boy raised in the country he had used a shotgun in hunting rabbits and pheasants, and he showed a surprising accuracy with the Westley-Richards when he fired it on target. Together they stripped and cleaned it. His fascination with it was surprising, since he never had showed the slightest interest in shooting during all his time in Dibela. So he practiced loading until he could do it with his eyes closed, hands familiar with the forwarding hinge and locking lever of the protruding box magazine.

Only once in the two days of preparation did he try to dissuade her from going to Bilak with him. He stopped when she told him it would be a change for her. For it would be a little change. A ride to Bilak through the fringes of the Ituri Forest. A pause overnight there. And then she would be certain that his bargain was consummated and he was under way. Perhaps, in some way, she might be able to help him. Then she would return in the car with Wanga.

Since they did not know what their sleeping accommodations would be in Bilak, she decided to take her bedroll and knapsack. Of course he took his own. Since she was taking a knapsack, she found herself packing it with more things than were necessary for an overnight trip. In loving memory of the mountains, she thought wryly, as she put in extra socks and shirt and soap and matches and flashlight batteries and several tins of food and a first-aid kit. Looking at her heavy knapsack, she thought,

You'd believe I was going to walk back with him. But she wouldn't. It would not be—proper. She would simply take this pack, and when they reached Bilak he would inevitably find he'd forgotten many essential things. And she would have them for him. The thought pleased her inordinately.

He looked at her bulging knapsack dubiously, but he said nothing. They were, in fact, so laden that it was necessary to hook to the car the new trailer which Mzimba had built. On that clear morning they loaded the trailer with bedrolls and knapsacks and ponchos while Kulu and Kosongo put in their spears and bows and blankets.

A large crowd had gathered to see them off. They pressed close, chattering and laughing. Vudi held Vanga above the heads of the crowd so that Kulu could chirp and ogle at his son. Job ran about barking and finally leaped into the back seat of the car between Rachel and Caleb. Kulu and Kosongo crowded into the front seat beside Wanga.

Wanga started the car and the people called, "Kwaheri. . . . Kwaheri. . . ." She wished they wouldn't say good-by.

Kulu, leaning far out the window, shouted back, "Kwaheri!"

The road to Rugeri wound through many memories now. Beyond nearly every turning waited a familiar scene: a hut where someone had been gravely ill; the place a leopard had sprung across the road; the place where a great tree had fallen in flood and the men had labored strenuously to get the car past. The land of grim faces on her first passage here had now become a land of smiling faces. "Jambo, Madami . . . Jambo, Bwana," called the road menders and the rare hunters and the numerous women laden with faggots and grass and babies.

There was the place where Caleb had stopped his car on his way to Dibela. He glanced at her, smiling faintly, remembering that first day they met. It had been more than a year since he'd suffered a mild malarial attack. Now he seemed about to speak of it. But he didn't. He was such a quiet man, always shunning the obvious remark, but always somehow conveying his thoughts to her.

As they entered Rugeri, Caleb told Wanga to stop at the administrative office. "We'll see if there's any mail," he said to Rachel.

Oddly, she hoped there wouldn't be any unless it might be from the Lecomtes with news of how Paulie was faring on their trip. But they had been gone only a couple of days and so . . .

Caleb walked from the office. François, standing in the doorway behind him, exchanged mild insults with Kulu and Kosongo. "Couple for me. One for you." Expressionlessly he handed the letter to her as he climbed into the car.

It was from Paul. She tore it open as the car moved on. He was in Washington. At least he'd been there five weeks ago. *Dearest Rachel* . . . "Dearest" for the past few months after so many years of being only "Dear."

Dearest Rachel . . . She closed her eyes, then opened them quickly.

Tomorrow is a day I've often thought would never come. I'm being discharged from the army. Knowing me, I guess you'd expect me to be out on the town. But here I sit in the rec room of the B.O.Q. at Ft. Myer with ping-pong balls whizzing around my ears and the jukebox playing "Paper Doll" . . .

Rec room, she thought. B.O.Q. Jukebox. "Paper Doll." His letters always sounded like a foreign language.

Tomorrow I'm leaving for New York. I've had enough horsing around in the army. I'm going to work. A real opportunity is coming my way and I'm grabbing it. At the base hospital in France I worked with a very able guy named Ed Jennifer. He's a whale of a good surgeon who had a terrific practice in New York before he got patriotic. He beat me out of the army by a couple of months and now he's back in the East Seventies removing gold-plated gall bladders. Apparently there are more gall bladders and stuff than he can handle himself. At any rate, he's asked me to join him in his practice and I've accepted. This is it, baby, the chance of a lifetime. . . .

Yes, she thought, that must be it for him. He had said he wanted to be rich and this was the chance of his lifetime.

Now I know what you're thinking, Rachel. As you read this you think there went Paul disappearing into the New York gold coast. You think—well, it doesn't matter, because I want you to know what I think. As the years go by I think more and more of you. I remember so many things, leaving Dibela that morning in the rain and you standing back there in the road at Rugeri when I daren't look at you, and so many things like the day by the creek that I can't put on paper. . . .

The page trembled as she turned it.

What I want to ask you, Rachel, is to come back to New York and marry me. . . ."

Tears filled her eyes. Unbelieving, she read the line again and again.

"Let's have our own life together here. Let me show you what it can be and let you show me the things I didn't understand before I knew you. I say this badly, but you know I never could say things well. So I'll stop. I'll only say that I'm waiting for you in New York and hurry back.

She looked blindly out a window. Then she read, *All my love always*. There was a postscript.

Write me at the Warwick Hotel, Sixth Avenue and Fifty-fourth Street. I'll be staying there. If I move they'll forward your letter. If there's any delay because of money let me know and I'll cable what you want.

She read the letter again, her eyes fixing avidly on each word against the jouncing of the car. "All my love always," he said.

Stop the car, she thought. Stop the car! Let me out, for I must leave now. I must leave and go back to *him*. Must? Of course. This was the incredible moment she had been waiting and hoping for and finally almost had abandoned thinking about in these long years. Wasn't it? Of course it was. Of course, of course. Then why did she look out at the bush through tears now as they rode north toward Bilak? Tears of happiness, that's what they must be.

She looked at Caleb and his gaze fell.

"A letter from Paul." Her voice was tremulous. "He wants me to leave for home as soon as possible."

Caleb moved suddenly, bracing his feet, as if against some greater shock than the jouncing of the car. At last he said, "Oh." And then he said, stating a fact rather than asking a question, "And you will go."

"Yes," she said indistinctly. "I must."

"Must?" He looked at her. Then, "Yes, I understand." Impulsively he reached out and touched her hands tightly folded in her lap, consciously touching her hands thus for the first time. "We'll miss you, Rachel. It won't be the same without you."

"Oh, don't make it harder for me!" she cried and turned her head quickly and tried to blink away her tears.

She sensed Kulu glancing back at her. He did not need to understand English to sense that something had happened, that Madami was at one of those forks in the track. How would she ever tell him? How would she ever say good-by to him and all of them?

Caleb said, "Perhaps you'd rather not go on to Bilak now. We could—"

"Of course I'm going on to Bilak," she replied, keeping her gaze averted out the window from him. "Paulie will be gone for three weeks. There's much to do. I can't just—just pack up and go in a day."

They fell silent as they rode on north, dipping down from the Rugeri highlands into the fringes of the Ituri Forest. Staring out at the trackless bush, Rachel thought she had missed a whole exciting era of the world while living out her life far back here. Sounds and flashes of the world had come to her in letters and old magazines and the disjointed fragments of official messages that Lecomte pieced together at the end of the telegraph line. But she knew that she lacked much insight into the world as it was now and that her opinions could be naïve.

Take such a simple thing as the songs. "Paper Doll," which Paul had mentioned, must be a popular song. Here you made up your own songs and you never learned what the world was singing. The last of the world's songs she remembered was "The Easter Parade." And that always reminded her of the world's clothing. Were skirts long or short now? In the advertisements of the rare magazines she had watched them grow long and then short. But what would they be at the exact moment when she stepped off the ship and he was waiting there? That critical moment when an inexact hem length, an odd neckline, an absurd hat (a *hat!*) could wither the love of a sophisticated man for his jungle princess.

In imagination she made the awesome journey. The long ride to Stanleyville by auto. The river boat down the Congo to Leopoldville. The curious little railroad that ran around the Falls to Matadi where she'd wait restlessly in the high-ceilinged Spanish hotel on the hill for the ship that would lie like a child's toy boat in the river far below. And then the voyage out of Africa, past Banana dozing at the Congo estuary where a million Africans had last glimpsed their land as the Yankee slavers made sail for the hell they were digging in America. There would be many farewells for her before that last farewell to the green shores of Africa.

But she would do it. She was not afraid, as once she had been afraid to go back for the last time to die in some village of the western plains where even the crickets of the endless nights would forever remind her of Congo. For she was not going back to die. She was going back—she was going home (she must learn to think of it as home) to live. She'd learn the songs and hem lengths and politics. She'd apply whatever intelligence she had to discovering what people talked about and thought. She, Mrs. Paul Wilton, wife of that prospering young surgeon. . . .

"Mrs. Brown [or Smith or Jones], may I present my wife?"

The quick penetrating glance of Mrs. Brown. Wilton's wife, someone he'd met in Africa during the war, a nurse, they said.

"You must be glad to be home, Mrs. Wilton."

"Indeed I am." A warm, convincing smile.

"Let me offer you a cocktail, Mrs. Wilton."

"Thank you, Mrs. Brown."

(Was that the way it was done?)

"Paul tells me you were way out in the wilds, Mrs. Wilton."

"Well—yes."

"Just where were you?"

But explanation brings a look of distraction to Mrs. Brown. That was one thing you must remember about—what would you call it?—the world, society. You must never explain anything. Never, never, never explain. No one had to tell you. You knew it instinctively.

So you simply smile and say, "Off near the Mountains of the Moon."

"The Mountains of the Moon! How exciting!" Turning to her husband: "George, just listen to this. Mrs. Wilton lived near the Mountains of the Moon. Isn't that romantic?"

George, a realist, looks at you speculatively. He wonders how you are in bed.

"Tell us about the Mountains of the Moon," says Mrs. Brown.

What would you say? That they are austere and dangerous and wrapped in mist and mystery and myth? That they are your brooding neighbor, always there but always unattainable?

"Did you ever climb them?" asks Mrs. Brown.

"Yes. Once."

"How wonderful. Why?"

Supposing you should try to explain the legend of thahu. Supposing you told the story very well, even to the incredibilities of that time so long ago when you *had* to climb the mountains or leave Dibela. What would you have? Not Africa, even as a child could not hold sunlight in a brown hand. You would merely have Mrs. Paul Wilton, a minor celebrity at a cocktail party. The raconteur could not impart the mystery of experience; the raconteur could only corrupt its truth.

And I shall stand there with a cocktail glass in jeweled fingers and be a mockery of all I once had meant to be. The sun of Africa in my diamonds, the icy mountains in a glass, the rolling plains upon my palm. Bigger than the continent, I'll stand there in a crowded room. And I had wished to stay so small and enchanted within the vast mysteries of God's creation.

Oh, Paul, rescue me! Would he be the sort of husband who caught her pleading glance across a crowded room and took her away? Or would he take her away only when she acted a fool?

Well, now, this fantasying must stop.

There was much work to be done: articles and arrangements, passage and planning. For she was going. He had asked her and she was returning after all the years of doubt that this ever could be. Why he asked her did not matter. It was obvious, of course. He loved her. He signed his letter "All my love always," didn't he? These many thousands of miles away she could chart his course with intuitive accuracy. After he first left her he decided he was in love with her. He was faithful to her. It was there in his letters. And then, in London or Kent or Surrey or Oxfordshire, he met a girl and he was unfaithful. It was there in his absence of letters. And at some time, in pub or bar, as she had dreamed, he had talked of her. It was there in one forced letter, guilt as discernible as ink. And then forgetfulness and many girls, or no girls. Next France and, girls or not, the slow erosion of war that eventually bared memory. He wanted something good to remember and perhaps, after all, the only good to him had been those chance days in Africa with her. Oh, it must have worked on him. Not enough, of course, to lead him back on a sentimental journey. Of course not. He was a realist, and to him that meant he liked the *real*, and it was the way of his world that the real should be money and respect. What had been so real to him in Dibela could not really be. But it had preyed on him. There was so much a part of him back in Dibela that she *knew* he sometimes wondered if she bore a child. So that was it. He wanted to dispel the whole mystery of the unreal and set it in perspective with the reality of the America he knew. He wished it even to the extent of asking her to come back and marry him.

It was courageous of him. Foolhardy, even. But perhaps, she thought trenchantly, he was only one of many men who fanned the sparks struck by women they had met in war. When they returned home they found America alien and, courageously or foolishly, they wished to see it now through the eyes of women who found it as strange as they. "Let me show you what it can be and let you show me the things I didn't understand before I knew you," he'd written. Yes, America was not quite real to him yet and he knew it would not be quite real to her. But America would become real again to him quickly enough. He not only wouldn't wait forever for her; he'd wait only a measured time. So she would go. Quickly.

Yet in the midst of trying to concentrate on plans she found herself thinking of that terrifyingly special moment when the ship throbbed slowly up the Hudson. It would be an early morning with the towers of Manhattan piercing mist. He would be waiting. And she would take that irrevocable step down the gangway. But she would not step alone. Paulie would be walking with her. When he saw Paulie, that image of himself, he'd be overcome. His dim intuition would be vindicated. Like most men who prided themselves on being "Realists," he liked to have his intuition vindicated. Like most such men he was incurably romantic. The only truly realistic man she'd ever known was Caleb. Not Paul. The incurably romantic Paul would never quite recover from the shock of Paulie's and her revelation; it would sustain their proper marriage after he'd hastily made an honest woman of her, after he'd discovered the touch of gray in her left temple and the weather-roughened skin of her hands and the small blue vein that had appeared inside her left knee.

So there it was, complete. Not the recapture of an old affair. But the tentatively slow beginnings of a solid marriage. It was life, it was time, it was the way of the world when romantics such as she and Paul involved themselves in love and war.

I must go, she thought.

XXVII

GAME DOES NOT LEAVE a country overnight. Yet it seemed to the people west and north of the mountains that they awakened one morning and the game was gone. They remembered its scarcity during many seasons, but there came a time in village after village when men realized that nearly all had returned from hunting empty-handed for many days now.

It was a mystery. The rain fell and the sun shone hotly on the plain and the grass grew with its old ripe luxuriance. There was no drought and no great grass fires spread ominous dark smudge along the horizons and the sky never darkened with the whirring of a grasshopper plague such as had consumed the land once in the memory of the oldest inhabitants. The game did not gather in herds and march away, but it faded and the land was empty.

In the emptiness a pride of lions wandered from the north across the plain, impelled by hunger, the force that makes wanderers of both beasts and men. They were observed first near a tiny clan village on the northern mountain spurs where lions had not been seen in many seasons. A man who had climbed a screw pine to scout the plain for game saw them pacing slowly, a male and his females and cubs. The man held his breath, hugging the tree tightly until the sweet resin gummed his sweating chest, as the lions passed from view.

They were not seen at a village farther south where a goat belonging to the headman wandered afield one day. The following morning the headman's son found skull and bones and hoofs and torn hide. Gazing down incredulously, he saw the spoor of lions, and he ran, yelling, to his village. The thorn boma that once had surrounded the village had fallen in disrepair, but it was built up in a day, and that night huge fires burned within the boma and the people listened fearfully inside their huts. They were too distant to hear the sounds from the shamba of an independent man who had moved from the village and built his own grass hut where he lived with six goats. The lions killed the goats and ate their fill while the man crouched, quaking with terror, in his hut. The next morning, when the lions had wandered off to sleep in shade, the man ran to the village.

Then the signal drums sounded along the mountain wall: There are lions in the land. In many villages, from the mountains to the river and beyond into the fringes of the forests, men sharpened their spears and talked of hunting lions. But none went forth, not even from the clan village surrounded by the new strong thorn boma which the lions circled for another day and night, sniffing the strong smell of tightly tethered goats that had become desirable meat to them.

The lions prowled on, south and east, seeking a rich land. But the land was lean and they could not find even the new meat of goat in it.

It is said that no one goes unknown in Africa. When a man travels alone he makes his destination as well as his presence known. He may disappear, and none may try to learn what has happened to him, but eventually his fate will be learned. Always, if he stays with the land and away from the teeming cities, his fate will be learned.

Thus, much later, it was learned what had happened to a young man from the village of Dika. The story was told by the ground on which he died. He had gone east and north from Dika toward a village where he sought to bargain for a wife. He carried a spear; its broken shaft lay there. The hyenas had gotten to him, but only to his remnants. Hyenas do not kill men, they only finish their remnants. Only lions would kill a man in a shallow draw while the hot sun blazed.

North of Rugeri the narrow road runs between the fringes of the Ituri Forest and the savannahs that roll toward the mountains. It's a moderately good road now, but in those days it was a bad road, winding serpentinely in and out of the Forest, fording the smaller streams and crossing the larger streams on narrow trembling bridges. The pygmies who live in that country watch the infrequent traffic of the road from the shelter of the bush with somber expressions and are not inclined to aid the traveler in distress.

About a hundred and thirty kilometers north of Rugeri the road forks. The left fork leads the weary traveler far on west through the bush to Stanleyville. The right winds up into high treeless plains where the Bilak Agricultural Station is situated.

Early on the morning after they arrived at Bilak they started the journey home. They were in luck, Caleb thought. Douvalle, the Station Director who had entertained them royally at his home, had provided two big trailer trucks to transport the cattle. He had seemed somewhat reluctant at first to loan the trucks and drivers, even though Caleb had pointed out to him on the Director's own tsetse-fly chart that the precious cattle unquestionably would be infected by tsetse if he had to drive them on foot through the Ituri country to Rugeri. But Rachel, as always, had helped. She somehow had appealed to the Director's sense of chivalry; she had made him feel he would loan the trucks for *her* sake instead of for the sake of either cattle or Caleb. *Mais, oui!* The Director had refilled the wine glasses; the Director was a gallant man.

They rolled out of Bilak in rain. Rachel, riding with Wanga, went ahead. She had wanted to follow the trucks, but Caleb insisted that she lead, for if the car developed trouble she would be left far behind. Riding in the cab of the first truck, with Job between him and the African driver, he noted that she, in turn, was concerned that the trucks might be left behind. Wanga drove fast in his delight at traveling new roads. But every few miles Rachel would make him pull up and they would wait until the lumbering trucks came into sight.

He did not think much about the cattle as they roared across the plains and past the Stanleyville fork into the Ituri. He was thinking of Rachel. Or perhaps, he admitted to himself, he was merely thinking about himself. *For I don't know what I'll do with myself when she goes.*

It was difficult now to remember a time when he had not loved her.

Was it somehow necessary that he be in love? Love, said some, was merely a symptom of emotional instability. Love? The world had tilted and spilled him down its rough incline toward Rachel. But he had reached out and seized a root, a stone, a tree to halt his downward pitching. He had clung on. It had become important that she never see his precarious hold. So, when all else failed in human relationship, an elaborate courtesy was the best protection of the self—and the other. But why?

Because, you fool, she's married and the mother of Wilton's child. She has loved him all these years, she loves him now, and she's taking Paulie and returning to him. It would have been so much more difficult working together in Dibela if he'd ever told her he loved her. It would have become impossible. As it was, each had meant everything to the other. Well, not exactly everything. Sometimes he had thought of adultery; he was a man, not a saint. But he resisted it, both for the sake of his immortal soul and for his mortal life.

Now they roared through the insect-ticking silence of the Ituri. A pygmy, bow in hand, stood motionlessly in mottled sunlight. Caleb waved. The pygmy did not stir. In a few minutes Caleb heard the barking of baboons.

A hundred and seventy-eight kilometers to Dibela now, he saw by the speedometer. "Poli poli!" he said sharply to the driver. The man grinned and nodded and did not release his foot from the accelerator. He was a bad driver. He slammed too quickly from first to second gear. He lacked any sense of the power of the heavy truck and any consideration for the cattle that jounced behind them.

"I told you to slow down!" Caleb shouted as the truck thundered into a gulley and splashed through a stream and choked up the other side. The driver looked away contemptuously, but he slowed down. Caleb glanced through the rear window at the ten cattle jammed together, heads lowered in the rain.

Opening the door while the truck moved, he stepped onto the running board and looked back as the second truck topped a rise with Kulu and Kosongo jouncing in the cab beside the driver. When he signaled the driver to slow down, Kulu waved in reply.

A hundred and seventy-six kilometers to Dibela. He spread out the excellent map which Douvalle had given him at Bilak. It covered the territory from the mountains to the Ituri Forest. On it Douvalle had carefully sketched-in the known areas of the tsetse fly. The savannah was free of the fly. But it existed in the Forest fringe and along all of the Rugeri highland.

They could not have crossed the savannah on foot. Except at one place. Douvalle had been specific about this, and Caleb had listened to him carefully. About fifty kilometers north of Rugeri at a village called Nuli a bad road branched toward a village called Dika. There was, Caleb had heard, a poor track from Dika to Dibela. If it had been necessary to drive the cattle on foot, he would have turned off the Rugeri road and somehow forced the cattle to swim the river and pass on through Dika to Dibela. From Nuli to Dibela was one side of a triangle, while the roads between Nuli and Rugeri and Rugeri and Dibela formed the other two legs. The road between Rugeri and Dibela was blessed by a bridge across the river, of course. But he would have taken a chance on swimming the cattle across near Dika rather than to expose them to the tsetse flies of the Forest road. Well, it was all hypothetical now. They were traveling by truck, and traveling fast—too fast.

He gripped the door and braced his feet as the truck slued in slick mud. The driver spun the wheel and the truck lurched. Caleb winced as the cattle slammed against the tail gate. But they were still on the road and still going ahead. He looked back at the cattle. His personal gift to the economy of Africa. A great and noble experiment, Douvalle had declared with Gallic sententiousness while not lowering the price by one franc in the name of nobility. An experiment, said Douvalle, of which the Belgian Government heartily approved in its benign desire to improve the living standards of its African people; otherwise it would not thus sell surplus heads from its fat herds. So here rode the twenty head, a stolid crossbreeding of Swiss and Guernsey. A bull with a ring in his nose and two bull calves; thirteen milk cows and four heifers. Aldrich's noble experiment. Milk for the babies of Dibela, but no meat yet for the men. The herd must increase until each family had its own cow. That would do more to end polygamy than all the missionaries and moral tracts let loose on a hapless people. Eventually there would be meat as the land was depleted of game. Eventually there would be economic stability, even as the cow had been the stability of Israel and of Elizabethan England. A people always needed cattle to lead them from dark ages. So this could be the beginning of something in Dibela. And if it were not, he would at least have tried.

Rachel and Wanga had stopped at a wide place in the road. She stood under a mango, dark hair curling under her peaked bush cap, a hand on the tree trunk, her other hand resting on her slim waist. She smiled at him abstractedly through light rain as he climbed from the truck cab and walked to her.

"I wish I had a camera," he said.

"What?"

"I wish I had a camera. You look the way I'll always remember you, Rachel."

She glanced at him oddly and slowly lowered both hands and thrust them in her slacks pockets. Gazing beyond him, she said, "How are the cattle riding?"

"All right, I guess." He turned away, despairing of talking with her. He climbed the side of each truck and studied the cattle.

After a while they went on, wheels churning in thick mud which almost but never quite halted them.

The road improved briefly and Caleb dozed. He had not meant to sleep. He awakened with a start in bright sunlight. They were rushing down a slope toward a narrow bridge. Beyond this stream was Nuli, he remembered. And then, with certainty, he knew the frail bridge would not support the weight of the heavily laden trucks. They'd have to unload the cattle and walk them across.

"Stop!" he told the driver. Then, in panic, he saw the man was dozing. He seized the wheel and the driver started wide awake. "Stop the truck!" he shouted, his foot lunging for the brake.

The driver slammed the brake and they began to skid. Together they swung the wheel frantically against the skidding. The truck straightened and they eased to a halt. Caleb groaned and wiped his forehead. The driver grinned at him and then slipped into low gear and started onto the bridge while Caleb shouted at him and flung himself at the emergency brake.

There was a splintering crash. The world tilted. The nose of the truck sank into the brown waters of the stream. Uttering a whimpering sound, the driver reached to the rack behind him and seized a mango and began eating it.

Caleb opened the door and lowered himself cautiously into the stream. The murky water came to his waist. As he waded to the bank, Job leaped recklessly and swam behind him. At least the trailer had not followed the cab into the stream. The cattle were safe. The second truck halted and the driver, Kulu and Kosongo leaped out, chattering excitedly.

"We'll unload the cattle," Caleb said calmly.

They lowered the ramp and Caleb slipped a halter through the bull's ring and led him down and tethered him to a tree. Kosongo herded the rest of the cattle along the road where they began grazing. Kulu dived under the motor and reported that the front axle was broken. So, Caleb thought dully, there was no point in trying to tow out the truck and repair the bridge. They would have to go on afoot.

People were streaming down the road from Nuli, shouting. Staring across the stream at them, Caleb lighted his pipe. At the moment the only pleasant fact in life was that he'd kept his matches dry.

"We'll unload the other truck," he said to Kulu.

They led the cattle down the ramp from the second truck. He told Kulu and Kosongo to gather their belongings together and he took his rifle from the truck cab, where the driver still sat with a dazed expression. Then he untethered the bull and told Kulu and Kosongo to bring the cattle. The bull floundered unprotestingly across the stream after him. When they emerged on the other side, the people of Nuli yelled in astonishment.

Kulu and Kosongo handled the cattle ably, Caleb saw. But the greatest help was Job, who had enjoyed herding the one cow in Dibela and now was deliriously happy at herding twenty. You'd believe he was pure collie, Caleb thought. The cattle came across in good order and the people of Nuli, who believed they were some strange species of buffalo, scattered before them.

"Bwana!" the driver of the second truck called across the stream. "What shall we do now?"

"Turn your truck around and go back to Bilak for help," Caleb replied. "We're going on."

They went slowly up the road toward Nuli, driving the cattle before them, looking ahead for Rachel and Wanga. As they entered Nuli, Caleb called up to a man who had climbed a mango tree to escape the strange buffalo and asked him the road to Dika. The man pointed wordlessly.

"Where is your chief?" he asked the man. "I want to hire some men to go with us."

"To go where, Bwana?" asked the man in the mango tree.

"To Dibela by way of Dika," Caleb said.

The man stared at him, his eyes wide. "No one will go that way with you, Bwana. Lions have come to that country again and the people are afraid."

Rachel rode beside Wanga, unaware of the country. When they reached Dibela tonight she would tell Caleb everything. In imagination she often had gone through the process of confessing her lie. But she had always concluded she should not tell him. Now, however, she wanted him to know the truth. For some reason unfathomable to her he must know it before she left Africa.

For a long time she had been certain he would understand. But sometimes, too, she'd thought that he loved her. So it seemed better to continue living the lie. The lie created a necessary orderliness in their lives. For there had been times when she'd thought there was completion only in love, in passionate love. And that, she told herself, meant Paul. That was why she had waited for him, hoping all these years. Faithfulness was essential to her. The lie had helped her to remain faithful to Paul —and to herself. Now she would confess to Caleb without divulging her inchoate reasons for having lived this lie. She did not seek forgiveness. There was nothing in his power, or that of any mortal, to forgive. Only God could forgive.

They were riding in bright sunlight. She dimly recalled passing through a village some time ago. Looking back and seeing no sign of the trucks, she told Wanga to stop. She got out of the car and restlessly watched the road behind. When fifteen minutes had passed, she told Wanga to turn the car around and drive back. The trailer became stuck in mud as Wanga turned and it was almost half an hour before they were on the way back.

As they entered Nuli, her eyes widened at the sight of the milling cattle. Caleb stood under a mango tree, the rifle slung on his shoulder, the haltered bull standing patiently beside him. He had pushed his old hat far back on his head, as he always did when perplexed, and he seemed to be talking up at the tree. Then, as she leaped from the car, she saw the man in the tree.

"What happened?" she cried.

Caleb told her patiently.

"Then we'll wait until they repair the bridge and get the truck going," she said.

He shook his head slowly. "That's too long to wait, Rachel. With Lecomte away heaven knows when that bridge will be repaired. Furthermore, the truck's front axle is broken. Douvalle will be furious, to put it mildly. If and when his truck is repaired we won't have the use of it. Meanwhile, all these—" he stabbed his pipestem around at the cattle— "will be infected with the tsetse."

"Oh, Caleb." She suddenly wanted to cry. Not for herself. For him. He'd spent the savings of years on these accursed cattle. And here he stood in a mud village with them. Not he, she thought suddenly. Here *we* stand with them.

[273]

"We're lucky it happened where it did," he said. "This is Nuli, and you remember what Douvalle said about the way from Nuli to Dibela. By going that way we can still avoid the tsetse."

"Yes," she said thoughtfully, gazing across the shimmering plain toward the distant dim bulwarks of the mountain. "We'll take them that way."

"*I'm* going that way, Rachel," he said firmly. "You and Wanga will go back to Dibela. With his injured leg he can't go with us."

"I'm going with you."

"No. We'll come across country with the cattle." He hesitated. "At least that's what *I* want to do. But Kulu and Kosongo are going to have a voice in this too. The cattle will belong to Dibela and they're Dibela men, so—"

"But what is there to *decide?*" she asked impatiently. "If that's the way you think it's wise to go, shouldn't you *lead?*"

"We'll see." He turned to the trailer and lifted out his bedroll and knapsack.

She stared at her own sleeping bag and laden knapsack in the trailer, thinking how odd that she should have prepared so carefully. Uneasily she remembered her dim forebodings about his venture. Silly, she thought, do you believe you're Cassandra? But still—

"I'm going with you," she said.

"No, Rachel—"

"I *am*. You'll need more than three to herd those cattle." She tried to smile. "Don't forget I'm from Kansas. I'm an old cow hand."

He attempted a smile too. Then, authoritatively, "I don't want you to come, Rachel."

His tone hurt her. Not until he and Kulu and Kosongo had shouldered their belongings and said good-by to her and started driving the cattle out of the village along the faint track to Dika did she think that he had purposely intended to hurt her. He had done it, she knew, because he wanted to make sure she did not go with them. But why?

She stood rooted in the road, staring after him. The cattle moved slowly. Despite the recent rain they raised a yellow dust, and in the dust the figures of the men grew indistinct as they walked with lowered heads. Around their necks Kulu and Kosongo carried great lengths of the rope Caleb had purchased from Douvalle. Far ahead, leading the bull, Caleb walked at his shambling gait. Unaccountably her eyes dimmed with tears. She could scarcely see them now as they moved in

[274]

the cloud of dust that crept across the infinitely stretching treeless plain toward the mountains.

"Madami?" Wanga looked from her to the car questioningly.

"I don't know," she said aloud in English. The people of Nuli had come out of their huts now and stood gazing after the herd of cattle. They were shaking their heads and talking dubiously.

"What is it?" Rachel asked a man. "Why are the people concerned?"

"They go toward danger," the man replied. "There are lions in that country now. We warned the Bwana."

Lions! Now she understood. That was why he had forbidden her to go with them. That way lay danger and he did not want to expose her to it. He did not even want her to know of the danger. He was going alone, as she had gone alone to the mountains. There he went, winding into Africa, as soon she would leave, winding out of Africa. Every road had many forks, and this was a fork in a mud village.

She got in the car and Wanga climbed in beside her and started the motor. "Turn off the motor," she said. He did, looking at her questioningly.

She sat in the late afternoon shadows of the village, staring at the yellow land that stretched to the mountains. In its vastness the settling cloud of dust grew smaller. And in the small cloud the figures of men and cattle were lost. Caleb, Kulu, Kosongo. They moved slowly, purposefully out of her life. Perhaps she was thinking hysterically. Driving those cattle across country to Dibela was man's work. Yet climbing the mountains had been man's work too. They needed her out there. Vanity? Perhaps. Perhaps the truth was that she needed them. Perhaps, as Henri Lecomte had once hinted, she was simply an adventurer. The country out there called to her and she needed to go into it one last time before she left it forever.

About two miles out on the plain from Nuli, where the track forded a shallow stream and the luxuriant grass rustled in a rising wind, Caleb halted. Nowhere was there a gray thorn tree, that haunt of the tsetse fly.

"We'll stop here for the night," he called to Kulu and Kosongo.

He and Kosongo tethered the bull and began cutting the rope into shorter lengths and hobbling the cattle while Kulu took his bow and Job and went upwind. He returned with a half-dozen francolin by the time they had finished hobbling the cattle and started a small fire. In the dropping of the equatorial sun their figures suddenly looked blue; eastward toward the mountains a few faint stars trembled into sight.

"The wind is strong off the mountains tonight," Kulu said.

"And that's good," Kosongo said. "We're downwind of—" he looked at Caleb—"whatever is out there."

The wind bore the *yooo-eee-yooo* howls of hyenas. Job bristled.

"There's something we must discuss before we milk the cows and eat," Caleb said. "We must decide which way we'll return to Dibela."

Kulu looked at him in surprise. "But have you not decided, Bwana?"

"No." Caleb shook his head. "I brought us out this way for tonight because I want to get away from the forest area. You understand why, don't you?"

"Yes," Kulu said, and Kosongo nodded. "The fly that poisons the cattle lives there. But he doesn't live here on the plain."

"But the lion who doesn't live in the trees now lives again on the plain," Caleb said dryly. "This is where we are." He took a stick and drew on the hard earth.

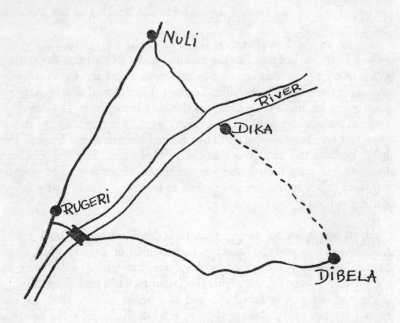

"We are here outside Nuli on the track to Dika and Dibela. You see that it's shorter than if we went on along the main road to Rugeri and then out the road to Dibela. So we have the advantage of it being shorter and it being a land free of the tsetse fly. But we have the disadvantage of carrying heavy loads, and we have to get the cattle across the river on this route. By the other way there's the bridge on the Rugeri–Dibela road. And we have the disadvantage of this being a wild country with—we hear—lions at large in it now."

"The people of Nuli are timid," Kulu said. "They live on a main highway."

"Such as it is, Kulu." Caleb smiled at him. "Do you doubt that there are lions?"

Kulu shrugged. "There are often lions in the country, Bwana. But they don't chase men."

"True. But if they smell cattle it will be a different story, I think. They would love to feast on our cattle."

"That's true, Bwana," Kosongo said. "I have heard what lions do to goats and cattle and so has Kulu. They go upwind and let them get the lion smell. The cattle panic and then the lions come downwind and kill as they choose. If the cattle do not panic, a lion will urinate on the ground and the cattle go mad with fear at the lion urine smell."

"Kosongo speaks the truth," Kulu said.

"Then we all know what we're up against," Caleb said. "Now listen to me. These cattle are not mine. They belong to the people of Dibela. You are men of Dibela. So we shall decide what we'll do by a *vote,* as we decide many things in my country."

"A *vote?*" Kulu looked at him, not comprehending the English word.

When Caleb explained, Kosongo said, "But your word is the law, Bwana."

"No. *Our* word is the law." He looked at Kulu. "What would you do?"

Kulu stared at the fire for a time. At last he said, "I would go on through Dika even though it's a bad country between Dika and Dibela."

"Kosongo?"

His eyes darted to Caleb and away. "It's a very bad and hilly country between Dika and Dibela, Bwana. It's a long time since I've heard of men traveling there. I would go along the highway through Rugeri."

So it was up to him after all. Moving so slowly through the tsetse country the herd unquestionably would be infected—and so destroyed. For the infection of even one cow meant the rapid infection of all. And moving this way there was a good chance the herd would be depleted. Yet they'd win through somehow, and a depleted herd was better than no herd.

"We shall continue to Dibela this way," he said slowly.

[277]

Kulu grinned at him across the fire. Kosongo stared at the ground and finally said, "Bwana, when I chose I did not know how you would choose. I did not mean to go against your will. I follow you loyally."

Caleb touched his shoulder. "I understand, Kosongo. Think of this, and you think of it too, Kulu: if you both had chosen one route and I the other, I would have gone your way."

"That is *vote*," Kulu said to Kosongo.

"Aye," Kosongo said, "that is *vote*."

Job barked suddenly and raced away. Caleb strained his eyes into the gathering darkness after him. Someone was coming along the track.

"Jambo!"

She came out of the darkness into the firelight, her bedroll and knapsack on her back, Job prancing beside her. She was alone. She was smiling.

"Rachel!" He sprang to his feet. "You fool!"

Her smile would have faded, but Kulu cried, "Madami! Now we'll have good luck."

XXVIII

"So you THINK I'm a fool, Caleb." She rested an elbow on her sleeping bag and gazed at him in the flickering firelight.

She had helped them milk the cows. They had drunk their fill of the warm milk, and they'd roasted and eaten the francolin. Kulu and Kosongo had wrapped themselves in their blankets and fallen instantly asleep. The cattle, restless, moved closer to the fire, ringing it with tossing, liquid-eyed faces. Job whimpered softly in a dream.

Caleb took his pipe from his mouth. He smiled, revealing that he was glad to have her across the fire from him. As she was glad to have him across the fire from her.

"Not a fool," he said. "Perhaps—impetuous."

"Not impetuous," she said. "I spent nearly an hour back there in Nuli thinking as I watched you come out across the plain. And then I had a little trouble with Wanga when I decided to follow. He wanted to come with me. I had to *order* him back to Dibela with the car."

"What did you think about for nearly an hour, Rachel?"

"About—everything, I guess. Dibela and you and Paulie and—and Paul. I guess especially about me. I thought how strange it was that I should have prepared for this, the knapsack and sleeping bag and all. As if I knew something like this would happen. And I thought how vain of me, as if I had profound insight. You know the cardinal sin. One's self the center of the universe instead of—God the center."

"The cardinal sin." He smiled again. "Yes. So the theologians have figured it. And so, it seems, it's true. Yet we all keep on trying to be the center of our universe, calling on God only in the pinches."

"Paul—" She paused, thinking how difficult it was even to speak his name now. "Once Paul said to me that there aren't many places left in the world where a woman can be treated like a queen. He thought that was what I liked about Dibela."

"Your husband—" he hesitated—"can't have fully appreciated what you've done in this country."

My husband! Let it pass now.

"But he had a point," she said. "There can be a great selfishness in appearing selfless. As when I followed you out here. I may have seemed to want to—help you. But I also had a selfish wish to—just to come along and be with you—and Kulu—and Kosongo. I *can* be of help, Caleb."

"Of course you can. And I'm glad you're here, Rachel." He hooked his hands around a knee, frowning at the fire. "You don't want to leave the country, do you?"

Oh, he knew. She did not answer him.

"I understand," he said. "It will be the same with me. Someday. When I have to leave. Because the land has possessed us. But we never can possess it. It isn't ours. It belongs to them." He nodded toward the still, sleeping figures of Kulu and Kosongo. "And we will go. We have to—to find something in ourselves that can sustain us after we leave this land, this people."

She did not know what to say to him.

"You have something to—sustain you away from here." He gazed at the fire. "Paulie. Your husband."

"My husband!"

Her exclamation surprised her, and it must have surprised him, for he looked up at her and said mildly, "Of course. You're going and—"

"Do you want me to go?" She hadn't meant to ask that, but suddenly she realized she was sitting up, a hand extended questioningly.

[279]

"*Want* you to go?" He sounded amazed. "Of course I don't *want* you to go. But you've said you're going and—"

"And I *am* going," she cried. "I *have* to go back because—"

"I know you do, Rachel. Your husband is there and—"

"My husband!" Her voice rose and now she could not look at him. "There was something I was going to tell you when we got back to Dibela tonight. And now I'll tell you here. Maybe it's why I followed you—I don't know. Paul is not my husband."

As at a distance she heard his voice. "I beg your pardon?"

She forced herself to look at him as he leaned closer to the fire, frowning.

"I said I'm not married to Paul." No emotion in her tone now. "I never was. I had an affair with Paul. Paulie is an illegitimate child."

He swung to his feet and stood above the fire, his big hands hanging loosely. He looked stunned, and then it seemed he suddenly looked old.

"Sit down, Caleb."

He sat down slowly.

"So it shocks you."

His gaze circled the ring of darkness, hunting something, until it found and held her direct gaze. "Yes." His voice sounded muffled. "Of course it shocks me."

"So you see I'm not a very good woman after all," she said levelly.

"That's not what I was thinking."

"What were you thinking?"

"It doesn't matter," he said. "I wish you had told me before."

"Before what?"

"Before now." His voice rose, almost harshly. "Years before now."

"I couldn't tell you before." She lifted her hands to her face. "I had to live this horrible lie or they'd have made me leave Dibela and then leave Africa. They'd have driven me out. I knew I'd done wrong, what *they* consider wrong, but it didn't seem wrong to me. Not really wrong. I didn't want to be driven out. I had no place to go back to. I wanted to stay, I *had* to stay. And the only way I could stay was to lie."

"Rachel."

"Yes."

"I'm one of *they*—of them. I'm a—a preacher and I understand. I—"

"You're different." She lowered her hands and looked at him calmly. "You know the church. You know how it would have been. And I'm not blaming *them*. I just blame myself for having had to lie. I—I don't want sympathy. Because I haven't really suffered. Much. I—I don't even want to have to give reasons why I lied. I don't want to be just a woman who got away with a lot of lies and is to be let off—easily. But I want *you* to know why I lied, Caleb."

He cleared his throat. "Your husband— I'm sorry. Paul, does he know—"

"About Paulie?" She shook her head. "No."

"My God," Caleb whispered. "You must have known, but you didn't—" His eyes widened. "You didn't— You loved him."

"Of course I loved him," she said. "Otherwise—" She looked away.

"And you love him now?" he asked gently.

This, she thought, was the question she'd avoided since receiving Paul's letter yesterday. She had loved him and surely she never had stopped loving him. So she must love him now. Then why was it so difficult to tell Caleb that she did? Why did it seem that she might only be compounding the enormous lie by proclaiming love for Paul now?

"I'm thinking of Paulie," she said indistinctly. "Right now I'm thinking of Paulie. Of his future. His name, his—his self-respect."

"Isn't it possible," asked Caleb, "that you're thinking now the way *they* do?"

"And *they* don't think so wrongly," she replied quickly. "I certainly am not in favor of—doing what I did. None of it can hurt me any more. Just in telling you I feel removed from it a little more. But what can it do to Paulie someday?"

"Nothing, I dare say. As long as it does nothing to you."

She frowned. "How would you have me feel? Just pretend that nothing ever happened and go on, a woman who got away with a lot of lies, with—with bearing a child out of wedlock?"

He sighed and Job awakened and cocked an eye at him. "There's one danger with people like you and me, Rachel. We're too certain we know what sin is. And we're too certain that punishment must follow it. If God fails to punish us we'll punish ourselves—which makes us pretty presumptuous toward the Almighty."

She never had thought of *that*. But was he merely trying to comfort her? And then, Just what is wrong in being comforted?

"The older I grow," he continued slowly, "the less I'm certain about what constitutes *sin*. I only become more certain of what you might call the general human condition. And it's in our condition to love and hate and sorrow and fear. Whatever incomprehensible rules God applies to our emotions are better than any rules we make ourselves." He stared into the fire. "I don't mean to preach, Rachel, but why not stop *pushing* against yourself. Leave yourself with God, who understands everything and gives you many choices. You have plenty of time to—decide. But your important decisions can only be for yourself—never for others."

He got to his feet and took a step around the fire toward her and paused, gazing down at her. She sat, arms hugging her knees, looking up at him. He was a good man, she thought. He did not play God, as some of *them* did. He did not probe at her immortal soul.

The muscles of his jaw strained, as if there were something he hesitated to say. They had said enough tonight, she thought. She looked away, passing a moment that might somehow have been crucial if she'd kept her eyes on his.

She rose. "I'm sleepy. Thank you for talking to me, Caleb."

Hyenas circled nearer and the cattle stirred. He turned and walked among them, murmuring confidently and patting their flanks. In a few moments she crawled into her sleeping bag and turned her back to the fire. She felt its warmth as he built up the fire and then she heard him lie down quietly on the other side of the flames.

"Good night," she said.

Good night, Rachel.

Be impersonal, he told himself. Don't think of her there so close. If you were that star up there looking down at the people by this tiny fire, what would you see? Pathos? No. Tragedy? In part, yes. For tragedy combines nobility with guilt. And she is noble and suffers from guilt. Tragedy is consciously choosing evil for the sake of good. And she must have felt she *had* to do what her training told her was evil for the sake of what she instinctively knew was good. Dibela had needed a doctor and one had dropped from the skies and she had detained him by the only means that could detain the man. Oh, that Paul Wilton! She did not need to explain. He saw it clearly.

But what had followed? Keeping your mind detached from her lying there across the fire, what else did the white star up there see far down here on the dark plain? Irony. While tragedy involves a conscious resolution, irony involves an unconscious weakness. When wisdom fails to recognize its limitations it stoops to folly; when strength is tainted by vanity it becomes weakness. So is irony made. This is the human condition. Irony for her. And irony for me these long years. Be impersonal. But it has been irony. For she is passionate and the conception of the child could not have been some quickly painful and rigid act for her. It was part of the life flow too long dammed up in her. And too long dammed in me. If I had known, what would I have done? Told her I loved her, of course, and asked her to marry me. Now it's too late. Wilton has summoned her and she is bemused at the idea of his making an honest woman of her. She, who is so wholly honest now and can only be corrupted by his good intentions. . . .

Turning and twisting in the cramped sleeping bag, he watched clouds extinguish stars across the sky. Three times he climbed out and built up the fire, each time looking at her over there, so still in soundless sleep.

At last he sank into troubled sleep. Rain on his face awakened him. In a cold gray world Kulu coaxed a flickering fire. Rachel sat beside the fire in her poncho, smiling at him cheerfully.

"Good morning. Are you going to sleep all day?"

"'Morning." He sat up, groping about for his boots.

She laughed suddenly.

"What's the matter?"

"You look so—baffled." She laughed again, and her laughter released a coiled spring in him. He laughed too. At nothing. Except that it was so good to see her sitting there.

"Coffee." She handed him a steaming cup. "We've even milked the cows. Your ration is in that gourd. Milk and coffee. That's breakfast. You see you *did* need me along."

"Yes, Rachel, we *did* need you."

"Sleep well?"

"Oh—fair."

"I thought you spent most of the night making fire."

So she had been awake when he'd thought her so deep in sleep. What had she been thinking?

They unhobbled the cattle and looped each length of rope high and secure on each cow's neck. Caleb led the way, tugging at the bull with one hand while his other carefully held his poncho over the heavy rifle slung on a shoulder. The cattle streamed behind. Kulu and Kosongo, with spears aslant their shoulders, moved on the flanks, prodding the reluctant. Rachel brought up the rear, slightly bowed under the pack which she would share with no one, gaily swinging a staff which Kulu had cut from a mimosa. Job raced everywhere. A ghostly procession trailing through the misty rain.

The rain stopped and a pale sun shone on the silent land which undulated into haze. Only occasional clumps of palmyra and mimosa placed any perspective on the country and their slow snaking across it. Once

[283]

a wart hog galloped before them, but there was no other sign of life. In the afternoon Kulu took Job and went ahead, searching for game. They found him waiting for them an hour later.

"I've lost my skill, Bwana." He looked crestfallenly at his bow. "I crept close to a topi and missed him. He fled, and my second arrow went wide too. I must be getting old." He frowned. "There are no birds in this country either. Job couldn't raise one."

Caleb asked him to lead the bull and he fell back to Rachel, who was having trouble keeping a calf with the herd.

"Job will take care of that calf," he said. "Here he comes now. Are you tired?"

"Of course not." She was glad to be of help with the herd, he knew. And, surprisingly, she did not look tired.

"Do you want to come ahead and try hunting with me?"

"Sure."

They ranged ahead, the rifle cradled on his arm.

"I'm sure you'd be more likely to bring us down meat than I'll be," he said. "But I have to learn." He did not mention the gossip about lions in the land; no one had mentioned it since they'd taken the vote last night.

"I'm no expert," she said, "and you'll learn."

The wind was in their favor as they strode silently, eyes searching the country alertly. When he had almost abandoned hope of seeing any game today, she touched his arm and pointed. They paused. He caught a movement against the yellow haze ahead. A solitary bongo grazed out there.

Rachel sank to the ground and he moved forward cautiously. About a hundred yards from the antelope he knelt and rested his left elbow on his left knee. The leaf sights seemed to shine brightly in the yellow light and his hands were not steady. He closed his eyes for a moment. When he opened them, the bongo had raised his head. He held his breath and squeezed off the shot. As the rifle crashed, the bongo bounded away and disappeared.

She watched him return with lowered head. Poor man. He knew it had been an easy shot.

"Pretty bad," he said ruefully. "I should have spent more time shooting all these years and less time condemning hunting."

"Your luck will change." She looked at a giant goliath beetle waddling in the grass.

"I don't suppose there's much point in going farther," he said. "That cannon must have scared everything for miles."

Would he let her take the rifle? But that was vanity again, she thought. Suddenly she knew that she didn't want to use the rifle on this trek. He must be the one who used it. Even if he missed everything he fired at, even if they grew very hungry for want of meat; this was his journey, his Mountains of the Moon. She went with him only as—a friend and good companion. This was her farewell to plains and mountains. For she was going and he was staying and he must learn to be able in the country.

Sitting silently in the grass, staring at the golden haze that shimmered everywhere, she felt depressed. There was a golden joy in Africa, and she was leaving it. They sat, not speaking, drawn quite out of themselves into the haze itself, she felt, until they heard the muffled thud of the approaching herd.

They traveled about ten miles that day, they estimated. They drank milk and ate canned meat. Curled beside the fire that evening, Rachel told herself she would not think as much as a day ahead until she stood once more under the limbali in Dibela. Then she would write Paul and headquarters; as soon as Paulie returned with the Lecomtes she'd perform the last rites on her life in Dibela—and go. But she would try not to suffer the pain of leaving until that final day of parting.

That night hyenas panicked the cattle. She held the flashlight and Caleb shot two of the creatures in its beam. Job, too wise to approach the snarling pack, helped them hold the cattle in check near the fire.

When morning came, they went on tiredly. Toward noon they filed past a couple of deserted shambas. Presently the land dipped and before them curled the river, dark and shining as oil under the lemon sun. One of the cows bawled and somewhere along the river a hippo rumbled. A boy hallooed on the opposite shore a hundred yards distant and a man emerged from a hut and stood on his right leg, like a stork, staring at the strange cattle streaming to the bank. The cattle drank and then bunched together while Kulu and Caleb shouted to the man to come over. Women and children and other men came to the opposite shore and finally two men stepped into a dugout and paddled across with short, vigorous jabs. But they did not land. Working their paddles cautiously, they stood the dugout off and stared suspiciously.

One spoke in a dialect neither Rachel nor Caleb understood, but Kulu answered him. Then the other addressed them in Swahili.

"We've heard of you, Bwana and Madami of Dibela. Why do you come this way with the cattle?"

"We're returning to Dibela," Caleb said.

"You'd better go back the way you came, Bwana of Dibela. The land between your village and ours is dangerous with lions now. The game is very scarce and the lions have taken some goats. It's very bad when a lion gets a taste for goat. He turns next to men. The people are afraid."

"That's why I came this way," Caleb said, "with this." He raised his rifle. "I've heard that the men of Dika are great hunters but now they lie in their huts all day because there are lions in the land. So I came to drive these cattle through and kill lions. Send me your chief."

The men talked to each other and then swung the dugout about and paddled away.

"They're impressed, Bwana." Kulu smiled at him. "I see your plan now. It's a good one."

"It's not much of a plan," Caleb said. "I just thought of it."

After a while a throng of people gathered on the opposite shore and three dugouts put out. A fat African wearing a pair of Belgian Army general-issue pants too small for him rode in the first canoe. He stepped ashore, holding up his pants and smiling, and introduced himself as Chief Kava of Dika.

There was indeed a great problem, he explained. He had sent word to the Bwana Administrator at Rugeri and nothing had come of it. A great pride of lions had wandered from the north and boldly taken to eating goats since game was so scarce. It was forbidden to kill lions and the people were angry, but the Bwana Administrator had sent no one to kill the lions legally.

"That's why I'm here," Caleb replied. "I have permission to drive these cattle through and to kill as many lions as I can find. I need twenty of your best men, Chief Kava."

It would be costly, the Chief said dubiously. The profit would be to the people of Dika, Caleb replied. But there were personal considerations, the Chief said. How many francs would take care of those personal considerations? Money, said the Chief, was not a consideration between friends, but personally he fancied a milk cow.

This bargaining! Rachel thought, remembering her bargaining with Kita on the mountain. This greed and boastfulness in men. She wanted to touch Caleb's arm consolingly as he stood, hands in his hip pockets, hat far back on his head, gazing perplexedly down at Chief Kava. One of his precious cows. She moved nearer, looking up at him sympathetically as he parleyed.

The Chief would not budge from his fixed idea of acquiring a cow. In return he promised nineteen men, one to a cow, to go to Dibela with them.

"There's no other way," Caleb said to her at last.

"Oh, Caleb." She touched his arm, and then quickly withdrew her hand.

Holding the bull's halter, he stepped into a dugout handled by two paddlers and tried to lead the bull into the river. The bull bellowed with rage at the painful ring in his nose, but he would not step into the water. Caleb roared and the bull bellowed while Kulu and Kosongo pushed at his unyielding hindquarters.

At last Caleb cried, "Rachel, how do you make a bull understand there are no crocodiles in this river?"

She laughed suddenly, and then he laughed and came ashore.

"So," he said, "we'll build a ferryboat."

He really was magnificent, she thought. She wanted to tell him so. But she dared not say, "You're a magnificent man, Caleb," because then he might . . . Oh, the whole proper structure of their lives all these years had been so tenuously supported. She had confessed her lie, but that most precious thing, candor, still was not hers. Apparently she never could be candid with him now.

"I'm going to cross over to Dika and collect dugouts for this shipbuilding project," he said. "Do you want to come?"

"Yes. I'll try to buy some food."

She went up the track from the river into the dusty, sun-baked village. It was a squalid village in barren country. She was shocked by the prevalence of yaws and rickets among the children and adults who trailed after her or sat listlessly in the shadows of their huts. She stepped carefully among tiny snakes that slithered in the dust and she brushed at swarming flies as she made her way along a filth-strewn lane to Chief Kava's shamba. There she bargained with one of his wives for four chickens and a grass basket of yams. At her direction the woman chopped off the chickens' heads and bled and picked them.

She carried the chickens and yams back to the river and crossed to the other side where the men had begun to build a raft. She hunted and found a spring upstream. After filling the cooking pots with water, she collected wood and started a fire under a small kapok tree, the only shade against the blazing sun. Gnats and mosquitoes swarmed about her as she rigged a pot stanchion and cut up the chickens and dropped the parts into the boiling water. Wearily she wished for a place to sit comfortably as she leaned against the kapok, patiently fanning away the gnats with dry banana leaves and watching Caleb and Kulu and Kosongo lash a log platform onto five borrowed dugouts.

The sun was setting when they finished the job and Caleb climbed tiredly up the bank to the kapok tree. He was wet with sweat and his unshaven face was swollen by mosquito bites and gnat stings.

"You've worked a long time in the heat, Caleb." Her voice rose in concern.

He forced a smile and gestured to the cooking pots. "You've been working hard too."

"I found a spring." She led the way and he followed, carrying a cake of soap. Watchful for snakes, they went up the muddy river bank and through tall ferns, until they came to the spring which poured into a basin of black rock.

He sighed gratefully and knelt beside it and then looked up at her. "Ladies first."

"I had a bath a while ago, such as it was. But I'll have another drink." She knelt across the rock basin from him and lowered her face into the cool water, drinking deeply.

When she raised her wet face, smiling at him, his expression was troubled.

"Rachel, I—"

"I've got to get back to the cooking." She rose quickly and fled.

She must not let him say it, she thought. If he managed never to say it, the parting would be so much easier for both of them.

Except to praise the food, he was not inclined to talk that evening. They ate standing in smudge smoke which gave little protection against the swarms of insects. Afterwards they crawled into their sleeping bags and tried to cover their faces. The grumble of a hippo nearby awakened her in the night. She lay awake for a long time, thinking that he was right. She was a fool to have come on this trek.

In the morning six paddlers crossed from Dika and boarded the raft. Caleb coaxed the bull onto it and held his head firmly while the men paddled across the river. Late in the morning he completed the last trip with a heifer. A crowd gathered on the bank shouted appreciatively.

"Now," he said to Rachel, "the lions."

XXIX

THE EARTH HEAVED into barren ridges and settled in deep draws south and east of Dika. Into the draws and over the ridges wandered the faint traces of the old track which men seldom followed now.

The strange procession that left the campsite outside Dika at daybreak reached the edge of this country at nightfall in a heavy rain. It was led by Kulu. Behind him walked the Dibela Bwana and Madami, accompanied by the Bwana's small fierce dog. After them filed nineteen Dika men with spears, each leading "a cattle" on a rope, and behind the nineteenth man walked that other Dibela man, Kosongo, so that to the men of Dika it was like being in a jailhouse file. There was no dignity in it, they grumbled. They were hunters and the grandsons of warriors, yet here they walked like prisoners or, worse yet, women led by cattle. They had come out for lions and there were no lions. There was only rain and cattle. And when they stopped for the night there was no meat and only poor fire. Each was to watch his own cattle during the night. It was a bad life. Just before dawn eleven men slipped away and hurried back to Dika.

"We'll drive the cattle," Caleb said after praising the shivering eight who had stayed.

Kulu went ahead of Caleb, up a slope where the rank wet grass grew shoulder high. Rachel followed Caleb.

"And now there is no track," he called to Kulu.

"No, Bwana. The grass has eaten it up. But we'll find it on the ridge again."

They found its faint trace, winding eastward along the ridge where the grass was short. From the slope below rose the unmelodious cries of the Dika men and the barking of Job as they herded the cattle up the hill through the tall grass.

Caleb looked back at Rachel. "Painfully slow progress."

"But progress," she replied.

The sun burst through clouds. The dew glittered briefly on the plain and then was gone. The land was harsh and dry.

Like a harsh dryness in himself, Caleb thought. She knew what he wanted to say to her and she would not let him say it. Her mind was sealed. She dreaded to hurt him, but she could not hurt him more than she had by closing her mind to him. She walked behind him, but he wandered alone in a harsh dry country. One's self the center of the universe. How could he help it?

The land glared hotly in yellow light and his head began to ache. It would pass, he thought. But the pain increased, throbbing with each step. At last he turned and asked Rachel for an aspirin. She took one from her first-aid kit and handed it to him. He unhooked his canteen and paused, the aspirin in his mouth. It was dry country. He swallowed the aspirin and replaced the canteen without opening it. They would manage somehow, but how long could cattle survive without water?

"Are you ill, Caleb?" She looked at him searchingly.

"No," he muttered. "Little headache in this glare." Suddenly he swung the rifle off his shoulder and passed it to her. "I want you and Kulu to go ahead as far as you think we can travel by nightfall. We can use game all right. But water is more important. Mind your compass. You know the direction. We'll follow."

"But I don't want the rifle. I—"

"Take it," he said harshly, "and keep alert for water—and game."

She hesitated, then went ahead after Kulu as Caleb sank to the ground and waited for the cattle to come up.

Even the insects were silent in this land. There was no sound but the rustle of grass in the hot dry wind. The brown ridges rolled infinitely toward a dimness that might be mirage or might be the bulwarks of the mountains. The dimness took form. There were the mountains, rising whitely, a blue lake at their foot near a forest of palms. It was mirage, she knew.

"Do you see the mountains, Kulu?"

"No, Madami."

"Do you think you see the mountains, Kulu?"

He grinned back at her. "I think I do, Madami, but I do not." In a moment he looked back again and said, "It is good to travel with you again in a strange country, Madami."

"Yes, Kulu." She lowered her head, squinting at the ground as they trudged on.

They had experienced so much together. And now . . . She tried to concentrate on her feet. . . . Both of them had been cursed and yet they lived in strength. To suffer as long as she should live. To live long and suffer long. Yet she did not suffer. Oh, don't I? She almost said the words aloud. Of course she suffered now. She would suffer if she went and suffer if she did not go. She could not escape it. But what could it possibly have to do with thahu?

"Kulu."

"Yes, Madami?" He looked back as he walked.

"Do you believe in thahu?"

He paused and faced her, his expression troubled. "You have not mentioned that in a long time, Madami."

"I know. But do you believe in it?"

He looked away vaguely. "There may be such a thing."

"Do you remember a time before Paulie was born when I seemed ill and I couldn't tell what was my illness? Well, I wondered then if it was thahu. And you went back to your village and when you returned I was feeling better. I haven't felt that way since. What did you do in your village, Kulu?"

"You have never asked me, Madami."

"But I ask you now."

He squinted far back along the ridge where the cattle and herdsmen trailed slowly. "I found Kalanumu very sick, Madami, and we faced each other and I told him only one of us would live. And before morning he died."

She frowned at him. "I don't understand, Kulu."

"Neither do I, Madami," he said gravely. "I just did what God the Father told my heart to do. I did not lay a finger on old Kalanumu. I just watched him die. That's all I understand, Madami."

Her neck chilled suddenly in the blazing heat. She knew it was all he understood and she knew it was something she never would understand. Perhaps it had been thahu. If so, it was gone. Now there was no thahu. There was only herself and her own decision.

"Let's go on, Kulu," she said wearily. "The Bwana hopes we'll find water."

"I fear the Bwana will be disappointed, Madami." He turned and they went on.

The figures of Rachel and Kulu seemed to dance upon the ridges in the waves of heat. Through heavy-lidded eyes Caleb watched them returning toward the slowly moving herd in late afternoon. They had not found water, he knew. Kulu carried no game. It would be a bad night and a worse tomorrow. If tomorrow came at all.

[291]

Snap out of it, he told himself. But he knew it was an inane thought; the malaria was on him again after this long respite. His bones ached and he had a fever. He had taken two quinine pills, trying to hold it in check, trying to walk a tight steel wire that seemed strung within himself.

Rachel stared at him worriedly when they met, but she said nothing.

"It will be a dry camp, Bwana," Kulu said.

"Here's what we must do." It was an effort for Caleb to speak. "The wind has been from the east all day and the smell of the cattle is over all the country behind us." He took the rifle from Rachel awkwardly. "Stay with Kosongo and the herd, Rachel. Ahead there where the ridge widens is a flat, clear spot. We'll camp there. Kulu and I are going back a way."

"Going back? Caleb, won't you let me—" She paused, staring up at him. "You— All right." She turned away.

As he and Kulu strode past the herd one of the Dika men called, "Where is the meat, Bwana?"

"We go for meat now," Caleb replied.

But the Dika men knew he lied, for he and Kulu were going downwind, sending their smells before them.

At a narrow place on the ridge, Kulu nodded to him and dropped on his belly and rested his chin on a fist. Caleb unslung his rifle and knapsack and bedroll. He checked the rifle and lay prone beside Kulu and placed a flat yellow package of ammunition near his right hand.

Lying there, feeling his heart beat, he gazed from the draw on the left to the draw on the right of the ridge. There was nothing. The silent country stretched into the haze of heat. His eyes blinked tiredly. He closed them, then opened them quickly. The second hand of the watch on his left wrist turned slowly. He knew he should keep his eyes on the draws, but he wanted to study the second hand of his watch. He kept his eyes on the draws. There was nothing. They were not being followed. There was absolutely nothing back there.

Kulu's left hand moved slowly and touched Caleb's right hand upon the ground; he raised a finger and pointed down the right draw. There was nothing. A breeze rolled the tall grass in waves as restful as the sea. But that was all.

Caleb frowned at him. But Kulu lay frozen, pointing down the draw. Caleb squinted into the western yellow glare. Then he saw a counter-movement to the waves in the grass, a darker yellowness. The shape was suddenly distinct. A lioness paced slowly, her form rising as she emerged from the sea of grass. She paused, motionless, her head raised alertly.

His confounded hammering heart! Did she smell cattle or man? She was perhaps four hundred yards distant; he was uncertain in this glare. She tossed her head suddenly, rocking it from side to side. "Aieee," whispered Kulu.

Then Caleb saw a smaller lion emerge from the grass behind her, followed by a second. Her cubs, growing into yearlings. She moved on slowly. The cubs filed behind her, pausing when she paused, raising their heads to sniff the wind as she raised hers, moving on as she moved. He was so absorbed in watching them that he started nervously when he saw a second lioness pacing with lowered head a hundred yards behind the cubs. Beyond the second the tall grass shook counter to the wind and a lion emerged. He stood, tawny mane stirring in the wind, broad nose raised, as a third lioness emerged. The lion slowly sank on his haunches until he was invisible in the grass, watching the females and cubs ahead of him.

Six lions. At least four mature and skilled enough to attack the herd. His confounded heart! He slipped the safety off the rifle and pivoted cautiously on his belly. If the leading lioness continued on her present path she would pass within a hundred yards of them down in the draw. What did the books say? A lion charged, kill or be killed, at forty miles an hour from his initial spring. And the books said that no one ever knew when a hungry lion would charge.

He let his arms and hands relax until that last moment when he would rest his weight on his elbows and fire. The leading lioness strolled slowly ahead of the imitative cubs. She halted and raised her head, scanning the ridge. It seemed to Caleb that she was staring directly at him. He did not stir. She moved on along the lower contour of the ridge, momentarily invisible in tall grass and then slinking into sight again, until he could make out the ripple of plaited muscles beneath the tawny skin. Now.

Slowly he raised himself on his elbows and the stock rested snugly in his shoulder. His hands were steady. He held his breath. Her head was lined in the leaf sights. But she would come nearer. He would hold one instant longer while he tracked. Suddenly she was lost in the grass. Furious with himself, he swung the barrel toward the second lioness. She was distant. But he had her. He was certain. Now. He pressed the trigger and the rifle crashed. The lioness sank from sight in the grass.

He started to rise exultantly and, in that moment when the rifle was out of position, the lioness sprang up and bounded from sight into the grass. He gazed wildly up and down the draw. The grass bowed to the wind in waves and there was no sign of lion.

"Did I hit her?" he cried to Kulu in English.

Kulu, his hands still clapped to his ears against the deafening crash of the rifle, looked up at him sadly.

"I missed her," Caleb said in Swahili.

"You missed her, Bwana," Kulu said and got slowly to his feet.

God give him strength, she kept thinking, for I cannot. There's nothing I can do. She was simply here, as they were here, suffering thirst, chained to cattle, prisoners of the ominous darkness. He was ill and she could not cure him. He was ill, but through some miraculous reserve of strength he did not succumb. He moved exhaustedly on the periphery of firelight, almost tottering sometimes, but still moving.

She followed him and he called harshly, "Go back, Rachel. Stay by the fire."

She paused, looking about helplessly.

Somewhere in the darkness Kulu said bitterly, "The Dika men are not lion hunters. They're not even men. Except that one. His name is Lebo."

Lebo, a short thickset man, pounded the bull's stake deeper into the ground with a rock. The other eight Dika men pressed together close to the huge fire. Kulu and Kosongo and Caleb and Lebo had hobbled the cattle so tightly that they could not graze far. They stood now in a ragged circle, heads tossing nervously, as Job and the men paced watchfully around them. There were a few stars overhead, but no moon.

"Bwana!" Kosongo shouted suddenly from the other side of the herd. "There's something over here!" His tone was shrill with fear.

Job began snarling and a cow blatted as Caleb and Kulu trotted around the herd. Caleb carried his rifle at ready and Kulu carried the flashlight. Rachel followed them, gripping her staff in both hands.

"There." Kosongo pointed his spear into the darkness.

They could see nothing. There was no sound. They stood together, eyes straining into the darkness. Then, distantly, they heard the snuffling grumble of a lion.

The bull raised his head and bellowed. The cattle milled, blaring in terror. A heifer, her legs too tightly hobbled, fell squealing, and another stumbled over her. The men spread quickly, with Job rushing back and forth, snapping and barking. But the terrified cattle were uncontrollable. The fallen heifer staggered to her feet, freed of the hobbling rope, and galloped away into the darkness. She paid no attention to Job as he leaped and snarled at her side, trying to turn her. She plunged straight on.

Caleb shrilly whistled Job back as the heifer disappeared in the darkness. In a moment they heard a scream, more human than bovine. The herd was suddenly stilled, falling back toward the fire, gathering compactly in a circle again while the Dika men cowered by the fire. In the sudden silence Rachel smelled the sweat of the men and the ammoniac stench of the cattle.

Out there a few hundred yards away the lions were feasting on the heifer. Only eighteen cattle bound for Dibela now, she thought numbly as she walked beside Caleb to the fire.

His eyes looked black in his drawn, dirty, unshaven face. "You should not have followed me out there," he said hoarsely. "I told you to stay by the fire."

She had followed him instinctively. But she did not tell him so.

"Remember," he said, "Paulie. And . . ." He could not bring himself to speak Paul's name.

Paulie, she thought. Paul. She must remember she had responsibilities; she had a responsibility to remain—safe. But she did not want to be simply safe now. She wanted— Never mind.

"I'll remember," she said quietly. "Lie down for a while, Caleb."

He dropped down on his sleeping bag and she told him to cover himself against the night chill. Slowly he crawled into the bag. He muttered something, but when she leaned near him she saw he was asleep.

She sat beside him and laid the rifle across her knees. She heard distant lions and jackals, and at last she dozed.

Toward midnight she was awakened by the cattle panicking. She sprang to her feet as Caleb staggered up. With Job and Kulu and Kosongo they calmed the cattle in a few minutes. They could see nothing in the darkness.

They slept by turns until dawn when Caleb awakened her. He smiled down at her wanly. "I feel better," he said. "We'll make it. I feel better."

They unhobbled the cattle and found that all but one of the cows was dry. There was about a half cup of milk for each. They drank it, and then one of the Dika men walked hesitantly to Caleb.

They were returning to Dika, he said with his eyes fixed on the ground. They were fools, Caleb said, because the lions would destroy them. The man merely smiled at the ground. They were not fools, Rachel thought in despair, for they knew the lions had eaten their fill last night and would be sleeping somewhere off the track now. They would slip safely back to Dika in daylight while they still had a chance. From here on it could only grow worse.

Should they turn back too? One day's march would bring them to water. They might never find water ahead. Yet they lacked the strength to go all the way back and around by the roads. They could only go on. Then, looking at Caleb, she wondered how long he could endure.

The Dika men filed away. But Lebo did not join them.

"You're going on with us, Lebo?" asked Caleb.

"Yes, Bwana. I've heard of Dibela and the things that happen there. I'd like to see it."

"You're a good man."

"Yes, Bwana, I am."

The thought of water obsessed her as the hot morning wore on. Her tongue seemed to swell and she scarcely could bear the effort of speaking. The men plodded on stoically, with heads bowed to the blazing sun. Job padded with lolling tongue behind the last exhausted cow. Douvalle wouldn't have recognized the fine herd now, Rachel thought grimly. They were gaunt and mud-plastered and stuck with briers. Each hour their heads sank lower and they walked more slowly, indifferent to the jabs of spears and Job's croaking bark.

Kulu was out of sight far ahead, more concerned now with finding water than following the track. Kosongo and Lebo took turns leading the bull at the head of the crawling column. Rachel brought up the rear with Job. Caleb ranged from the rear of the herd, sometimes falling far back and scanning the rolling brown country for a sight of the pride of lions that stalked them and would strike again. Rachel watched him constantly, amazed at the determination that forced him on, fearful that at any moment he might fall in malarial attack. She tried to plan what she would do then. They would have to make a stretcher and carry him, letting his precious cattle follow as best they could, leaving them to the lions.

In early afternoon Kulu returned. Caleb walked past the herd toward him and Rachel followed.

"There's no water ahead that we can reach by nightfall, Bwana." Kulu was panting, but his face was impassive. Suddenly he dropped to the ground and lay there, his arms shielding his face.

Kosongo, who was leading the bull, let the halter fall and lay down. The bull sank to his knees. Behind him the cattle lay down, one after another. Far back on the track Lebo and Job lay down. Caleb looked at them dazedly. Slipping off his knapsack and bedroll, he slowly sank down and covered his face with crossed arms. And then Rachel found herself lying on the ground, hands pressed over her sunburned face and cracked lips. There was no sound but wind in grass.

After a while Caleb said, "There's only one thing to do, Kulu. You must go on to Dibela alone. Get many men and have them carry water out to us."

Kulu was silent for a long time. Finally he said, "It's better that I not leave, Bwana."

"Why?" Caleb demanded harshly. "If I tell you to go, you will not?"

"I'll do as you say, Bwana," Kulu said, "but it's better that you not command me to go. I do not think it wise. I don't think it's the way God wants it."

"It was not God's will that a herd be brought to Dibela." Caleb's voice sounded remote. "It was my will."

"Have you prayed to God, Bwana?"

Painfully Caleb raised himself on an elbow and stared at Kulu. Rachel knew he hadn't prayed, nor had she herself. You didn't pray for the deliverance of your cattle. You tried to deliver them to Dibela yourself. God was not a magician.

"I've been praying," Kulu said when Caleb did not reply. "I prayed when I walked as far as we can go today and found no water. I've been praying again." He removed his arms from his eyes and smiled at Caleb. "I pretended I saw God the Father, as I used to see Him long ago." He sat up. "It made me feel better. God said to me, 'Stay with the Bwana, Kulu,' and I promised Him I'd stay."

Caleb's fingers dug at the earth. "Then I'll send Kosongo ahead."

Kulu sighed. "If you must send someone, Bwana, it's better that I go. Kosongo doesn't like to travel by himself in the country."

"Someone must go, Kulu." Caleb meant his tone to be gentle, Rachel knew, but his parched throat ground out the words roughly.

"Madami?" He appealed to her.

It did not seem wise to her to send away Kulu, the strongest. But Caleb was the leader. He believed this was the only means of saving the cattle. She did not answer Kulu.

Caleb and Kulu rose slowly, staring at each other. Caleb said, "We'll need thirty or forty men carrying water and—"

"Bwana, men cannot carry enough water that distance. They can't save the cattle. Only God can save the cattle now."

"But we have to try!" Caleb cried angrily. "Go!"

As Kulu started away slowly, Caleb called urgently to Kosongo, "Ja! Ja! Pese!"

Kosongo staggered to his feet, tugging at the bull, who moaned as he lumbered up heavily. Caleb moved toward the cattle, shouting hoarsely at them. He halted, gaping, and Rachel sprang up in amazement as the cattle began bawling and rising. They milled for a moment, and then the bull bellowed and yanked himself from Kosongo's grasp and ran down the draw. The cattle stampeded after him. A cow caught a leg in a hole and somersaulted on the steep incline. She tried to get up and fell back as the others scattered.

There was a sudden movement in the tall grass of the draw. A lioness leaped, her rear claws clutching the haunches of a cow. Her right fore-paw seized the cow's nostrils and tore. The cow's neck broke with a sound of a whipcrack.

Caleb ran down the draw as the lioness turned, a paw on her kill, glaring at him. Her tail lashed. He stopped and raised the rifle quickly and fired. The lioness fell back.

From Caleb's left another lioness suddenly bounded toward him, her tail straight as a staff. He did not see her. Rachel screamed piercingly and raced toward him, her heart hammering in terror for him. He whirled, working the bolt, and fired. He missed. Job, seeming to materialize from Caleb's feet, leaped toward the charging lioness. There was a sound like a loud handclap and Job was flung through the air. Caleb fired again. The lioness rolled twice and lay still a half-dozen yards from him.

In the sudden silence both cattle and humans seemed rooted. Only she was running on toward Caleb, sobbing hysterically. He stared at her dazedly as she clutched his arm.

"Job," he muttered. "Job."

"Bwana!" Kulu dashed down the slope. "Two! You killed two! But load the rifle again, Bwana. There must be another up there—" he pointed to the ridge—"the one that frightened the cattle."

Caleb did not seem to hear him as he knelt beside Job's smashed body. Tears welled in his eyes. Gazing at him through her own tears, Rachel pressed his shoulder understandingly.

"We must bury him," he muttered.

"No, Bwana, there is not time," Kulu said.

"We can't just—"

A cow cried in pain and they looked up and saw her on the slope, a foreleg bent grotesquely. Kosongo and Lebo were rounding up the remaining cattle.

"The killing isn't done yet," Kulu said.

[298]

Reloading the rifle fumblingly, Caleb walked to the cow and shot her in the head. Kulu slashed the throat with his panga and held his cooking pot to the spout of blood as Kosongo and Lebo ran up with their cooking pots.

"Drink, Madami." Kulu held out the cooking pot to her.

She shook her head.

"Drink, Bwana."

"No," Caleb said thickly.

"You need strength, Bwana and Madami. This will give it to you."

Rachel shook her head again, but Caleb slowly took the pot from Kulu and raised it to his lips. He gagged and spat and handed it back.

"A great victory, Bwana of Dibela," Lebo said solemnly.

Rachel and Caleb looked at each other. Killing the lions gave neither of them any sense of triumph, she knew. They were blooded, but they could not drink blood. They wished to survive, but their bellies knotted against survival. They were in Africa, but they could not be Africans.

XXX

KULU AND KOSONGO AND LEBO clambered out of the draw, talking excitedly, revived by danger and fresh blood. They carried great chunks of meat wrapped in their blankets.

"At least we'll eat tonight, Bwana," Kosongo said. "You're a great hunter. Two lions! Wait till this is heard in Dibela."

"It's as God said, Bwana." Kulu looked at him gravely. "When I started just a little way toward Dibela danger fell. These are hungry lions to attack in daylight. They'll have food tonight. But tomorrow—" He shrugged.

"If the cattle last till tomorrow," Caleb said dully.

"May we be as strong as they," Rachel said. "Look at them. They're going on."

The bull, trailing his halter, had started along the track, and the herd followed. Kulu moved ahead of them and Kosongo and Lebo fell in behind. Rachel and Caleb followed silently, watching the sixteen head of cattle and the three men with spears aslant their shoulders winding into the golden glare. Looking back, they saw vultures dropping from the sky.

"Probably Job saved my life," Caleb said hoarsely. "Certainly you did, Rachel, when you screamed."

She shook her head. She did not wish to think so. "It was—" she hesitated—"hysterical. I might only have distracted you."

"No. You cried, 'Left, Caleb, left!' "

She looked at him in surprise. "But I thought I only screamed. I didn't know I said anything."

"You did, I heard you." His eyes fixed on hers were feverishly bright. He tried, without much success, to smile. "You've saved many lives, Rachel."

He was thinking of Paul, she knew. She must change the subject. "Sometimes Kulu almost troubles me," she said.

"You mean his assurance that God speaks to him?"

"Yes."

"It's wonderful," Caleb said, "but sometimes a little terrifying." Again he tried to smile. "It almost makes me want to consult him, as if he were an oracle, and find out whether we'll win through with these cattle."

"He wouldn't pretend to know that," Rachel said. "He'd simply say that only God knew. And that, of course, is true."

"Yes, it is true. But the chances look slim." He swayed slightly as he walked, looking down at her. "Do you think you can stand this thirst yourself? If it gets much worse we'll have to abandon the cattle."

If she had not come with them, he never would have entertained such an idea, she knew. He would die with his cattle. Call it obsessive, if you would, but then call obsessive everyone who accomplished any good against difficult odds. Her tongue touched her dry cracked lips and she tried to shut from her mind a sudden vivid image of cold brooks on the mountains.

"We won't abandon the cattle," she said. "I'm all right. But how are you? How's the fever?"

"All gone," he lied. "I'm doing all right."

But occasionally he almost staggered as they walked. Never mind the cattle, she thought. *He* is the one.

They descended from the ridge into a shallow valley, and when they slowly climbed a farther ridge late in the afternoon they saw before them a white-pillared cloud in the east. Lightning flashed among its cones.

"A raincloud!" Rachel exclaimed.

Caleb gazed at it. "Yes," he said vaguely. "You see it too. I thought it might be mirage." He blinked and went ahead toward Kulu with an odd wavering step.

She gazed worriedly from him to the distant cloud. The cloud might evaporate or move away from them. Just as he might evaporate or move away from her, she thought lightheadedly. He had some plan, she saw, as he talked to Kulu and the two hurried on. Despite his fever he was ingenious. There was the cloud and here were they, and what could a tiny mortal crawling across this vast and desolate yellow land do about a distant cloud?

She began counting her steps and then lost count and was relieved to be free of the effort. Far ahead Kulu waved to Kosongo. Kosongo dropped the bull's halter and hurried toward him. The bull paced on with rolling head. Lebo croaked at the cattle and jabbed at a cow with his spear, but they could not be hurried. They crept on as the great cloud crept. Caleb and Kulu and Kosongo had disappeared now, as if the earth had swallowed them. But the cattle moved on and the cloud moved imperceptibly. Lightning forked among the cloud heads and thunder muttered. But what good would it do them, Rachel wondered dimly, if rain came?

At last, she saw. Unbidden, the bull left the faint track and the cattle filed after him into a deep draw where, at the conflux of old watercourses, Caleb and Kulu and Kosongo hacked frantically at the hard earth with pangas and spears. They were forming a shallow basin. The exhausted cattle sank to earth around the working men, as if they understood their purpose. Lebo joined the others, wielding his panga. But when Rachel began scooping out loose earth with her hands, Caleb told her to collect brush and start a fire.

She looked frequently at the blue sky as she cut brush. The men, too, threw quick, almost fearful glances over their shoulders as they dug. The ridge above them jutted against the eastern sky, shutting off view of the cloud. She set the brushwood but did not light it, straining meanwhile to hear thunder. She did not hear it; the sky was blue. She put the rifle in her sleeping bag and spread her poncho and Caleb's with centers depressed to catch the rain. But the sky remained blue and there was no sound of thunder.

She fell back on the ground and closed her eyes, thinking that this was the end, they could not go on, they would die here. She opened her eyes and saw the men, their work finished, lying on the ground, staring at the ridgeline. They were still and the cattle were still and the earth seemed hushed in waiting.

At last Caleb got stiffly to his feet and stumbled to her. He stood over

[301]

her, swaying slightly, trying to smile, and she knew he saw her dimly.

"Any water in your canteen, Rachel?"

She shook her head.

"Here." He took off his canteen. "Drink this."

"No," she said thickly.

"Drink it," he said fiercely. "We're going to leave these accursed cattle and go on."

"No."

Thunder crashed suddenly. Caleb turned quickly and gazed up at the ridge. The blue skyline was growing gray. The men murmured and got to their feet, staring upward. The high white cloud head, crimsoned by the western sun, crept into view and then was lost in the churning gray mass of pendulous lower clouds. A hot wind fanned the earth. A few drops of rain fell.

Rising to her knees, Rachel lighted the fire. As the flames rose, the rain began to fall heavily.

Somewhere Caleb said distinctly, "Thank you, God."

Yes, thank you, God, she thought.

"It's God's will, Madami," Kulu cried.

Yes, it was God's will. But it was also theirs in making use of His will.

Soon the watercourses sang. They knelt beside them, splashing their faces with the cool muddy water, laughing like children as they flipped aside small green lizards that slithered in the mud. They turned to the ponchos and filled cups and drank thirstily. They pushed exultantly among the cattle that crowded around the basin and watched them drink greedily. They lifted their faces to the sky and stood, transfixed with joy as the rain beat down.

Somehow Kulu and Kosongo managed to keep the smoking fire going. They cut strips of beef and ate them, half cooked, with their fingers. And the rain continued to fall and they lifted their faces to it.

"I feel pretty good," Caleb said as he stood beside the fire, licking his fingers. "I can't forget Job, but I feel pretty good." He shivered suddenly. "It's turning cold, isn't it? But I even feel pretty good about killing those lions." He shivered again. Suddenly he laid a hand on his flat belly and sat down and looked up at Rachel oddly, his body shaking convulsively.

"Get in your sleeping bag," Rachel said.

"I'll be all right in a minute." His teeth chattered. "Just a little chill."

"Lie down, Caleb."

He seemed unable to rise. She caught him under one arm as he half crawled to his bag. She unlaced and pulled off his boots and he crept into the blankets.

It was dark then. In the faint glow of the smoking fire his lips looked blue. She laid a hand on his forehead. It was like ice. His body shook uncontrollably.

He's going to die, she thought in panic. Oh, God, he's going to die.

"Sorry," he muttered. "Sorry."

Must he say that, as he had the first time she saw him? Must he leave her life as he had entered it? She told herself to be calm.

"Kulu," she called into the darkness, "we must build up the fire."

He ran to them.

"The Bwana is ill with a bad chill. See what you can do with the fire and we'll move him close to it."

The fire would not build up with all their coaxing. It would die soon, she knew. And she tried to shake off the conviction that he would die too.

"Never mind, Kulu. You and the others must be responsible for the cattle tonight. I'll care for the Bwana."

She did not hear what Kulu said. She knelt beside Caleb, listening to his teeth chatter. She had come all this way with him, doing nothing to help him. And now he was ill and suffering and she still could not help him.

There was only one thing to do. She did not hesitate. She tugged off her boots and placed them under the poncho with his. Pushing him over almost roughly, she crawled in beside him.

"Rachel?" he muttered. "Rachel?"

"Yes. Be still and sleep."

If animal warmth was all she could give, she gave it to him gladly. If death were ice, she'd face it with fire. If pressing here against him and covering his cold body with her warmth were somehow immoral, then immorality was necessary. For he must live. In him were wrapped all the hopes of Dibela. And yes, she knew at last, all her hopes too. He was the best that God could send to this awakening continent.

"Rachel."

His arms drew her closer to him and his hands trembled in her hair.

This is good, she thought. If God will let him live, he won't live alone again.

"Be still and sleep," she said.

Now the fire was only a smoldering glow. The rain fell steadily and in the darkness the cattle cropped grass. His terrible shaking subsided slowly in the warmth of her body. His rigid trembling arms relaxed and his breath fell steadily on her hands. She could feel his heart. He slept.

Heart and rain and cattle cropping grass. She dozed and wakened and knew that she must go. Wide awake, she thought, I'll leave him now, but I'll never go away from him and Dibela and Africa.

A sense of peace such as she never had known suffused her and she slept. When she awakened again, the rain had stopped and a few stars shone in the east. Cautiously, with great effort, she forced herself to move out into the cold. Bending down, she gently kissed his lips. Then she groped her way through the dark to her own cold bed.

The smell of wood smoke and then the whole dazzling world shone in on her. She sat up quickly, blinking in the glare of sunlight on dew-jeweled grass. He rested on a knee, smiling down at her.

"Good morning, Rachel."

She was sure she dreamed. Her right hand groped out. His strong hand was real enough.

"I didn't mean to sleep so long," she said. "You're—"

"Better," he said. "All better. You—" He smiled broadly. "I'm a case for the medical books." His hand gripped hers more tightly. "Thank you, Rachel."

She looked away and tried to disengage her hand, but he would not let it go.

"I love you, Rachel. I want to marry you."

It was such a bright morning in such a beautiful world that the sudden hotness of tears was incredible.

"All right," she murmured.

"All right?" His voice caught. "Not just 'all right.' I want to marry you only if—"

"I *love* you, Caleb." Her voice rose.

His hand reached to the back of her head and he kissed her lips. Her hand rested on his neck and she held him tenderly. She opened her eyes and let him go.

"I—" he swayed to his feet, gazing down at her dazedly—"I can't believe it."

Neither could she. But she did love him. Not relatively, she thought dimly. Not more than Paul, but as if she had not loved Paul, as if Paul never had existed.

As she pulled on her boots she smiled up at him. "It is—unexpected," she said. "I didn't know. I planned—" He was about to kneel beside her again. Beyond him she glimpsed Kulu staring at them in surprise. "Are you going to tell Kulu or shall I?"

Caleb turned. "Kulu, Madami has said she will become my wife."

"Aieee!" He grinned widely. "This is great news. This is the greatest news of all time in our country. You and Madami will stay forever and the land will be big with love. Kosongo! Kosongo!"

"The land will be big with love," Caleb said meditatively. "I like that."

"And I like it," she said, rising. "I like it because you say it in Swahili. I can talk to you in Swahili, as now, and you understand. I like it because this is our country and we don't have to leave it."

"Not now," he said, still speaking Swahili, "not yet. But in time we shall have to go. And we'll go together when the time comes."

He drew her to him and kissed her. "I love you, Caleb," she said in English.

They filed out of the draw, Kulu leading the bull, and Kosongo and Lebo driving the cattle behind. Rachel and Caleb followed slowly. When they reached the ridge, they saw the mountains, so near now in the pellucid morning air that it seemed they could touch them.

Do I love him or the country more, she wondered. Then, There is no difference. And then, There is no "relatively" with him and me. There are only we and the place where we happen to find ourselves.

It did not seem strange that she had lived so close to him and failed to realize she loved him. It was only strange that she had failed to realize she did not love Paul. What had she been thinking? Of her living a lie, her "sin" which did not seem a sin now. Of Paulie and the importance of Paul and her giving him—what? She and Caleb could give him as much and more. Life and hope. They gave him Africa.

"You're smiling." He looked down at her. "What are you thinking?"

"I'm thinking of a certain party I'll never have to attend in New York."

"A party?"

"An imagined party. But I dare say it would have become real enough. Caleb, what am I going to tell Paul?"

"The truth."

"You mean—"

"Yes. As soon as Henri gets back, he'll marry us. And you'll write Paul."

"About Paulie?"

"Yes."

She nodded. "The truth."

"He can come out and see for himself if he wants," Caleb said. "We'll be married and I'd like to adopt Paulie legally."

"You wouldn't mind if he came here?"

"Of course not. Would you?"

There had been a time when she would have minded terribly. She would not have trusted herself to see Paul again. But not now.

She told Caleb so, and she said, "You make everything seem so simple. Not just seem. It is simple now. I'll tell Paul the truth and then—" she hesitated—"I'll write Phyllis Haricort and tell her. If you think I should. If it isn't going to make you embarrassed and ashamed of me to have others know and—and possibly make them withdraw us from Dibela."

He rested a hand gently on her shoulder as they walked. "I never could be ashamed of you, Rachel. And I'm quite sure they'll never make us leave Dibela unless we want to. But whether they would or wouldn't, let's get it off our minds and forget it. Let's—well, throw ourselves on the mercy of the court. Most of life is rather like that, isn't it? And nearly all the courts of public judgment are mercifully lenient."

She seized his hand on her shoulder and gripped it tightly.

The sharp ridges began to flatten as the country swelled toward the mountains. Distant stubs of green rose like wishful mirage and became actual mimosa and kapok trees. The desolate land ebbed slowly behind them and they recognized the contours of their own country.

"One more day, Bwana, and we'll march into Dibela," Kulu said.

Shortly after noon Caleb sent him ahead to find a campsite. They caught up with him late in the afternoon. He had killed a topi and picked an excellent site in the bend of a small deep stream which almost joined itself in a great loop. Across the neck of land, measuring about thirty yards at its narrowest, he had begun raising a brush boma.

They drove the cattle onto the neck and finished building the boma while Rachel bathed luxuriously in the cool stream. Then Caleb and the men bathed, shouting and laughing, while she tended the roasting topi. They ate heartily around the fire behind the boma. Afterwards Caleb said the four men would take turns on guard tonight. They drew lots with bits of grass which Rachel held, the drawer of the longest piece to stand the first watch and the drawer of the shortest to stand the last. Lebo drew the longest piece of grass.

"Be watchful," Kulu told him. "The lions may not be hungry tonight. But they've tasted new meat."

The clamor of the cattle awakened Rachel. She saw Caleb and Kulu leaping up as she snapped on her flashlight. The fire had burned low and Lebo slept soundly. Caleb fumbled with the rifle as she climbed from her bedroll and flashed the light in a wide arc.

The beam struck a maned lion, frozen in the act of dragging a dead bull calf toward the boma. The lion let the calf fall from his jaws. His tail lashed.

"Quick!" Rachel cried to Caleb.

He fired. The lion slumped sideways and he fired again.

"Bwana!"

Rachel whirled at Kulu's cry, her light flashing along the boma. She saw the lioness spring and she knew Caleb could not fire accurately in time. Her scream died in her throat as Kulu seemed to leap in front of Caleb as swiftly as the lioness leaped, his spear raised.

There was a smash and tear of flesh, but Kulu did not cry as he went down. Caleb sprang back, aiming at the head of the lioness, and pressed the trigger. The rifle crashed. The lioness moaned and rolled away.

Sobbing, Rachel dropped to her knees beside Kulu. His left arm and shoulder were mangled and bleeding, his left leg torn horribly.

"I wish I could die now, Madami," he whispered.

XXXI

It was Musinga's greatest song. The people listened, enchanted, as he sang in the palaver house. By day and night he struck inspired notes on his likembe while the people passed him pombe. It was an endless song.

Madami and the Bwana and Kulu and Kosongo had come across the wild northern country with twenty marvelous cattle. And the sun had struck them and the land had risen against them and the lions had attacked them. But they had fought back. The Bwana had lost five cattle, but he had slain four lions. He was the greatest hunter in the land. Yet one lion had sunk his claws in Kulu. Then Kosongo had run on to Dibela. . . .

Head dizzy with so much pombe, Musinga always rose at this moment in the endless song, feet scratching the hard earth of the palaver house, thin legs moving rhythmically, so that the people again saw Kosongo as he had run into Dibela that noonday, gasping for breath, to fetch Madami's magic bag and forty men with spears. Off toward the wild northern country they'd trotted, men with spears and resurrected shields, as the warrior grandfathers had trotted forth to war. Oh, Musinga's two thin legs could seem like eighty warrior legs in the palaver house where the pombe flowed. . . .

Mournfully now, as the dove is mournful in the sundown shadows, the trotting Dibela men had come at last on a strange sight. There was a swell of land, and on the swell a strange procession marched. There came first a stranger from barbarous Dika, bearing the head of a stretcher, and then the stretcher, and then the Bwana himself bearing the foot of the stretcher. And on the stretcher lay Kulu. And behind the Bwana walked Madami herself, leading an enormous bull who followed docilely, his great white-faced head rolling, rolling. . . .

Aye, the people had marveled at the bull. They had gathered to watch him since he came to Dibela, staring at the wondrous rolling of his head, and they agreed that Musinga imitated him perfectly. But how would Musinga's song end? It was endless because it had not yet come to an ending.

Now Kulu lay dying in the hospital, sang Musinga. But he had not yet died. Madami and the Bwana sat by him constantly, waiting for him to die. And Musinga's song could not end until he died.

There were new verses as time passed. How Chief Buderga had thrown in his personal influence with God the Father by praying under the limbali. How old Muwango had decided to forget the gloomy past and personally prepared a magic owl broth and taken it to the hospital. How Vudi, carrying Vanga, never left Kulu's side. But there was not yet an ending. There would not be until Kulu died.

In the forest were many shadows, and somewhere in the shadows raged his pain, a thing he carefully kept from him with arm and shoulder and leg, as the old warriors once held pain beyond their shields. If he could crawl within the darkest shadow of the forest he would fight and slay his pain.

Slowly, as slowly as the sun creeps across the sky, he knew this was the hospital and the shadows were those who came and went, came and went. But some stayed. On the left was Madami and on the right the Bwana, and somewhere Vudi, the warm shadows that never went. Coming and going were Kosongo and Kalanumu and Musinga and Kalanumu and Buderga and Kalanumu. His old friend Kalanumu, who had taught him much. An arrow gleamed in the forest shadows. But Kalanumu was dead. Kalanumu had cursed him and Kalanumu was dead and now he lay dying.

He opened his eyes wide to look death in the face and he saw the Bwana.

"Kulu," the Bwana said.

He tried to rise, but the pain crashed through his shield and he sank back.

"Rest, Kulu," said the Bwana.

"Madami," he said.

"Here, Kulu." He felt her cool hand on his hot forehead.

Now it was better.

"Kalanumu?"

"Kalanumu is dead, Kulu," said Madami. "He's been dead a long time."

So now the living were separated from the dead and he was still among the living before he joined the dead. He saw the living clearly, Madami and the Bwana, their faces troubled by the sight of death. Turning his head slightly, he saw Vudi holding the mtoto, both staring at him gravely with faces untroubled. Aieee, they knew death better than the others, for they were Africans. He smiled at them. Vudi knew it was better that a man should die than to live a useless cripple. This was the way of the country. To be crippled was worse than to die.

He closed his eyes and hunted God the Father, but he could not see Him. Troubled, he opened his eyes.

"Madami, I can't find God the Father. I only find Kalanumu and I remember the thahu."

Her hand held his. "There is no thahu, Kulu. You are better. You're going to be all right."

"I won't be the same," he said. "I'm not sure that I'll stay with you. I'm not sure I want to stay with you now. If I stay I must creep instead of run. I cannot climb the mountains again or cross the northern plain. I'll be like an old man. I think it better that I go."

"No, Kulu." Her voice was insistent. "It's better that you stay. There are many people who need you. Vudi and the mtoto need you. The Bwana and I need you."

"You and the Bwana will go away, Madami."

The Bwana spoke. "No, Kulu. We are not going away."

"Not now perhaps. But in time you will go and I shall have to stay."

The pain crashed through his shield again and he closed his eyes.

"So you think he'll live," Caleb said.

She wanted to say, "He's *got* to live." But she said, "I'm positive he will. He's lain there five days now and he's passed what I'd call the crisis." She shook her head. "Those filthy lion claws. If we hadn't received that sulfa last month he'd surely have died from the generalized infection."

"I wish," Caleb said, "that he seemed to *want* to live."

They were passing under the limbali then, on their way to breakfast. She looked up at him, thinking, Yes, Kulu must *want* to live. If I'd been maimed I'd *want* to live now. But there have been times in the past when I'd have wanted to die.

"We'll have to—to help him, Caleb. We've *got* to."

"Yes. It's not just saving his life because he saved mine. It's—" His tone grew bitter. "I tried to develop a white man's theory about cattle and because of it a black man must suffer and be crippled. Oh, I know that's oversimplifying it. But basically I feel—" He gestured outward.

"Guilty?"

"Guilty," he said.

"I know. I've felt it many times since coming here. I've felt guilty at trying to change the things that were. Did you ever feel that we whites here are like that pride of lions? We come prowling on an innocent country."

"And we can't bear to leave," Caleb said.

As they climbed the steps to Rachel's bungalow they heard the signal drum. She told Mzimba to go to the drum-talker's post and learn the message. Then she paced the porch uneasily, thinking of Paulie, until Mzimba trotted back.

"Good news, Madami. The Bwana Administrator and mtoto Paulie have returned to Rugeri."

"Good!" She turned to Caleb, smiling. "He'll be home today. Henri will bring him."

Caleb looked at her thoughtfully. "Has it occurred to you we might go for him?"

"Why—yes. Kulu will be all right with Kosongo taking care of him until we get back."

"And since we're going to Rugeri . . ." Caleb's voice trailed off.

"Yes." Her eyes, she knew, were bright. Today, she thought. Her heart beat faster, and then she regarded herself with tolerant, ironic amusement.

"You're smiling," he said. He was smiling too.

[310]

"Not at what you think," she said. "I'm smiling because my heart is beating faster."

He started toward her slowly and she deliberately walked around the table, leaving him standing, baffled. Then she laughed aloud.

"What is it?" he asked.

Middle-aged woman so young, she thought. But she said, "Explanations are tiresome. Let's eat breakfast."

She sent Mzimba back to the drum-talker's post with the message that the Bwana and Madami would go to Rugeri today. After breakfast she went to the hospital and took Kulu's temperature and instructed Kosongo to stay with him until they returned from Rugeri.

Then she bathed and dressed leisurely, carefully setting the room in order before she left it. Caleb was waiting on the porch for her.

"You're beautiful," he said.

She wasn't beautiful. But she was glad he thought she was.

He held the car door for her and then climbed behind the wheel. "It's a wonderful day," he said.

"It's the most beautiful day I ever rode to Rugeri," Rachel said.

As they passed the palaver house, they did not notice Musinga rise and wave to them.

It's sad to be popular and lose your popularity, Musinga thought. The people were growing tired of his song. He needed a new one. Even some of the men who had made the warriors' march to rescue Kulu and enjoyed being extolled in song had stopped listening to him. Yes, he needed a new song.

The inspiration struck him when he saw Madami and the Bwana driving away fast. He sipped some of the thick beer and thrummed a few notes on his likembe. After a while he began to sing.

"Madami, Madami, the Bwana, the Bwana, have left Dibela, Dibela. . . . Yes, they are gone forever and our hearts are sad. . . ."

The men stopped talking and listened and one said, "That's a good song, Musinga." But another said, "It's not a true song."

Musinga struck two more notes and looked at the men and said, "It's a true song. I know. Listen . . . Our hearts are sad that Madami, Madami, the Bwana, the Bwana, have gone without farewell. They have gone forever, gone forever. . . ."

He sang and drank beer until early afternoon. The crowd liked it and he was happy to be popular again. There was some discussion as to where the Madami and Bwana had gone. Some doubted they'd gone anywhere, but one went up to the compound and returned with the news that they had indeed gone away.

When Musinga heard this he was pleased that his song was vindicated. But after drinking some more beer, he began to be sad that they had left so hurriedly without saying farewell. Tears came to his eyes as he sang.

Finally he decided to go and see if they actually had gone away. He wandered up the road to the compound. Aieee, the house was deserted. He wandered to the sleeping hut and called, "Guta!"

Guta's snores answered him.

"Guta!" he shouted.

Guta groaned and told him to go away.

"Have Madami and the Bwana gone away, Guta?"

"They've gone away, you fool," Guta mumbled. "Get out of here and let me sleep."

He walked away, sniffling, and passed under the limbali to the hospital. Kosongo nodded in a chair beside Kulu's cot. When Musinga called to him, Kosongo started wide awake and said, "Keep your voice low, you fool. Kulu sleeps."

"Aieee, it's sad that Madami and the Bwana have gone away."

"There's nothing sad about it," Kosongo muttered. "You're full of pombe."

"Everybody in this whole accursed village is sleepy," Musinga said. "Except me."

"Then sit here by Kulu for a time," Kosongo said, getting stiffly to his feet. "Be quiet and don't awaken him. I've given him medicine, as Madami ordered. I'm going to lie down over there." He pointed to an empty cot. "If Kulu wakes, awaken me."

Musinga sat down beside Kulu and looked at him. "Poor Kulu," he whispered and closed his eyes.

He would have sworn he was not sleepy, yet he must have slept, for when he opened his eyes again Kosongo was snoring and Kulu was looking at him.

Kulu smiled faintly and murmured, "Hello, Musinga, old singer."

"Aieee," said Musinga, "it is sad."

"What's sad?" asked Kulu.

"Listen." Musinga took his likembe from a pocket, struck a few notes and began to sing, "Madami, Madami, the Bwana, the Bwana, have

[312]

left Dibela, Dibela. . . . Yes, they are gone forever and our hearts are sad—"

"That's not a true song," Kulu said.

"It is a true song," Musinga replied. "They have gone. I saw them go. The house is empty."

Kulu tried to struggle up, but he fell back with a groan. "Where's Kosongo?" he muttered.

"He sleeps over there."

"Kosongo!" Kulu called, but his voice was weak and Kosongo snored.

"You must lie still," Musinga said. "Lie still and listen to my song. . . ." He sang in a low voice so he would not awaken Kosongo. The sadness of it overwhelmed him as he sang and tears rolled down his cheeks.

Kulu begged him to stop the song, but he did not wish to stop it. Since he was sad, let Kulu be sad too.

"Aieee, Madami, Madami, the Bwana, the Bwana, have gone forever. . . . Madami was cursed and now lives with her curse. . . . Kulu was cursed and the curse has come to him. For Madami and Bwana, Madami and Bwana, have left him to die. . . ."

If they had gone, Kulu thought wearily, he would die. But they had not gone. This fool, Musinga, was drunk again and trying to torture him. When he recovered, he would—ah, but he wouldn't. Never again would he have the strength to hurl him from the hospital.

But if they had gone away, they would not want him to die. They would want him to live. And if he lived, what would he be? There was a glimmer of light there, like a shaft of sunlight in thick forest. A clearing there in the darkness. If they had left, they would want him to continue their work for them. But what would he do? A clearing in the forest. His own village. The old black-eagle thought, too tiring now. He would return to his village someday, hobbling on a staff, and he would try to be in his village as they had been in Dibela.

Musinga was singing, but he did not hear him now. Smiling faintly, he drifted toward that clearing in the forest. As at a great distance he saw Vudi, carrying Vanga, enter the hospital and come toward them quietly. Then she heard Musinga's song and she cried out wrathfully. She set down Vanga and struck at Musinga. Kosongo awakened and leaped to his feet and seized Musinga by the throat and dragged him, screeching, to the door.

There was much excitement among the other patients, much tiring excitement. Vudi leaned over him, her eyes filled with tears. Dear Vudi. Kosongo stood there. Good Kosongo.

"Carry me out under the limbali," Kulu said to them.

They hesitated.

"Please take me under the limbali," Kulu said.

Soon he sailed across a forest clearing and the limbali rose above him. He closed his eyes and saw clearly God the Father and Jesus the Christ.

"God the Father," he said, "I'm glad You had time to come and bring Your Son with You."

God started to answer, but suddenly Madami stood there and interrupted Him most impolitely. They were both speaking at once so that he could hear neither until God smiled and shrugged at him, saying in effect that He understood the loquaciousness of women, having created them, but if He had it to do over again He would not make them so prone to talk. Then Madami was silent and God spoke.

"Kulu, My Son and I have come to take you with Us provided you understand one thing. You're dying because it's Our will and not the will of Kalanumu with his curse as you've been thinking."

"I understand, God the Father," Kulu said.

"No," Madami said suddenly. "Kulu must not die."

God the Father and Jesus looked at each other in surprise. They sat down slowly and traced a pattern on the ground with their sticks, the sun gleaming on their muscular black arms.

"There is so much for him to do yet," Madami said.

"So much to do," God said thoughtfully. He looked at Madami. "He has cared for the sick and climbed the mountains and taken a wife and had a son and fought the lions. He has hunted and worked and slept and walked and run and loved and been loved. What more is there for him to do?"

"There is more of everything," Madami said. "And there are many new things he has not done."

"But he will not be the same if he does not go with Us now," said God. "He will walk with a limp if he walks at all and his arm never again will have its strength."

"Is that a curse?" asked Madami.

God frowned and the light grew dim. "I do not curse my people. You know that better than anyone."

"I know that," Madami answered boldly. "But I want Kulu to know it too."

[314]

"Kulu knows that," said God.

"But does Kulu know that You give choices as well as having a will?" asked Madami. "You and Your Son come now and tell him You would take him away. Is it Your will to do that if he does not want to go?"

"Let Me speak," said Jesus to His Father. "I believe that Kulu should have a choice. He may go with Us now or he may stay on earth for a time yet. But he must know that never again will he climb the mountains or range across the plains. He will walk slowly instead of running quickly. He will sit alone much with his thoughts like an old man while he is still young."

"It's a difficult thing for a young man to do," said God.

"But We love Kulu because he has done difficult things," said Jesus.

"True." God looked thoughtfully at Kulu. "We shall let him decide."

They smiled and nodded to him and then They were gone. There was no trace of them except the markings of their sticks upon the ground.

Opening his eyes wide, Kulu saw that the markings had been made by Vanga when he was playing with a stick under the limbali. He heard the murmur of doves. For an instant, before he closed his eyes again, he saw the flash of snow upon the mountains.

Perhaps he slept, for when he opened his eyes again it was almost sundown and he felt refreshed. Vudi, holding the mtoto, sat beside him. She rose to her knees, gazing at him.

"Has Madami been here?" he asked.

"She has not yet returned from Rugeri," Vudi said. "You seem stronger, Kulu. I feared we brought you out here to die."

Kulu smiled. "I came out here so that I might live."

When the motor sputtered and finally died, Caleb groaned. "Where are we?" he asked.

"Near Kalina," Rachel said. "We can almost see its fires."

"Kalina! That's where I—"

"That's right." She laughed delightedly. "Along here is where you spent a night in this car."

He climbed out with the flashlight and raised the hood. She glanced at the back seat where Paulie, wrapped in a blanket, slept. The night was cold. There was a bright moon in the east and a great sluice of stars poured down the western sky. Contentedly she pulled a blanket more tightly about her. She didn't care if they stayed here all night. For she was happy as she did not remember being ever. She smelled the earth and heard the incessant clamor of insects and saw the moon and stars. Mrs. Caleb Aldrich was at home.

Leaning out, she said to Caleb, "Can you get drunk on one glass of champagne?"

"I don't know," he muttered.

She laughed again. "You're never going to fix that thing, whatever it is."

"I know it," he said, his head thrust somewhere in the motor.

"Then why don't you give it up?"

"Well—" He slammed down the hood. "I guess I'd better walk on to Kalina and ask them to put a message on the drum to Dibela and have Wanga—"

"You mean you don't want to stay here in the car all night?"

"Well, no." He sounded worried. "I mean—well—"

"You did once, you know."

"Yes," he said, "I did once."

She opened the door. "Then I'll carry Paulie and walk with you."

"I'll carry him." He lifted him onto his shoulder.

"Where are the giraffes?" muttered Paulie. He slept again, his arms hanging loosely over Caleb's shoulders, as they walked along the road to Kalina.

"These high heels," she said. "If I'd known I was going to walk on my honeymoon I'd have worn boots." She squeezed his arm. "Aren't you happy, darling?"

"Of course I'm happy," he said. "I'm just sorry about this car breakdown and—"

"I'm not." She breathed deeply. "I think it's fun. Smell the earth. Hear the insects. Isn't it wonderful?"

"It's wonderful, but—"

"Oh, stop fussing. Be as happy as I am. Really it wasn't that glass of champagne. But it was nice of Henri to open that rare old bottle. I felt so sad when Marie cried while he read the ceremony, and for a moment I thought Father Gilo was going to cry too. But let's only have happy thoughts now. Let's not even think about Dibela. Let's just walk along in darkness and feel Africa under our feet."

Caleb stumbled and said, "Maybe you *can* get drunk on one glass of champagne."

"Darling, I'd so hoped you were a gay person."

"I'm a very gay person." He stopped and kissed her and over his shoulder she saw a flickering fire in Kalina.

[316]

The dogs ran out barking, there were voices in the darkness, and then exclamations of great surprise. The Bwana and Madami and mtoto of Dibela walking in the darkness! There was pandemonium in the palaver house. Those asleep were awakened and fires were built up.

An elder wise man proposed that they slay and roast a goat. Caleb thanked him and said they wished only to send a message to Dibela on the drum. Indeed the message would be sent, replied the old man as he stood on his left foot with his right foot tucked comfortably behind his left knee. Would they spend the night? The people of Kalina would be honored. This very day one of his wives had completed a new hut, with fresh mats which no one had slept on. If the Bwana and Madami and mtoto would share a hut, they were welcome.

"Let's," Rachel said.

He looked at her. "The ground is hard."

"We have a blanket." She looked at him levelly. "We've slept on the ground before. I think it would be—" She shrugged.

He smiled. "Appropriate?"

"Appropriate."

"And so do I." He turned to the old man. "We gladly accept the hospitality of your hut, my friend."

"But first we must send a message to Dibela inquiring about Kulu," Rachel said.

"Yes. And if he's not all right, we'll have Wanga come for us in the other car."

The old man summoned the drum-talker. In a few minutes the Dibela drum muttered in reply. Rachel, seated by the fire with Paulie asleep in her arms, looked up expectantly as the drum-talker approached.

"The man who climbed the mountains and was torn by lions sleeps well, Madami. That is the mighty one, Kulu."

"Thank God," Rachel said. "Send word that we stay tonight in Kalina."

The old man smiled thoughtfully from her to Caleb. Then he told the people to disperse and gestured to the hut.

"It is a good hut," he said to them as they entered it. "It has good fresh earth. Sleep happily."

He put more wood on the fire and sank on his heels. He smoked his pipe and stared at the leaping flames.

Later, as the moon waned westward, the drum-talker came and sat beside him. "You do not sleep tonight?" he asked.

[317]

The old man shook his head. "There is much to think about." He pointed his pipe toward the hut. "They would not lie down until they knew that one of our people slept in health. It's a sign of a better time in our land."